NECROW

QUERUS ABUTTU

Scary Dairy Press LLC

Contents

9. JUDITH

Breathe

10. THOMAS

Crash

11. JUDITH

Closer

12. JAGGER

Rites

13. JAGGER

Warning

14. BOBBY

Tap Tap Tapping

15. CHRISTOPHER

Passage

16. LU

Semper Verus

17. THOMAS

Medallion

18. CHRISTOPHER

Holy Hell

19. CHRISTOPHER

Precious Moment

20. LU

Quarter Moon

21. THOMAS

34. RENNY

Believe

35. JUDITH

Chase

36. LU

Honesty

37. SEPHANIE

Snap

38. LU

Awakening

39. HATTON

Potion

40. JUDITH

Don't Tell Me

41. LU

Pieces

42. JUDITH

Founder's Day 1

43. LU

Founder's Day 2

44. MASON

Founder's Day 3

45. THOMAS

Founder's Day 4

46. MASON

59. THOMAS

Voice

60. JUDITH

Road Trip

61. CHRISTOPHER

Climb

62. JOB

Fast

63. LU

Revival

64. JAGGER

Retribution

65. RACHEL

Crow Moon

66. THOMAS

Apeiron

67. LU

Bloody Monday

68. LILITH

Beware

69. MASON

Charisma

70. JOB

Gone

71. CHRISTOPHER

Solo

72. RENNY

Traitor

73. THOMAS

Bonus

74. JUDITH

Race

75. HATTON

Doggies

76. MELODY

Falling

77. JUDITH

White Wolf

78. RACHEL

Alternate

79. CHRISTOPHER

Life

80. JUDITH

Electric

81. LU

Transfer

82. JAGGAR

Replaceable

83. JUDITH

Red

Dedication

True friends in my life have crossed my path in various forms.

They presented to me as a husband, my children, an adopted mother, a karate pal, a fellow writer, an editor, a recluse with dysautonomia and a touch of Aspergers, a nun, a forensic nurse, a scuba diver, a former boyfriend, a karate instructor, and a neighbor or several neighbors. Many four-legged friends and two-legged friends (some who left this world) have shared my life as well and just might meet me on the rainbow bridge later.

While I might have been able to do the things I've done in life without the friendships (doubtful), my life would have been far bleaker, less colorful, less warm, and depleted of joy without all of the wonderful individuals who have helped me along the way. I am extremely grateful for each and every person I've encountered. For every friend, I only wish I was as good a friend as they have been to me. I know that it is a goal I set for myself every day.

And so—to my dear friends—I will work to earn all that you've given me. I dedicate this book to you. It's a book that took many years before finally getting its wings. Thank you—those who encouraged me—for believing in me and knowing that I could finally get this creature into the sky. You've known me as Mom, Wife, Cin, Cynthia, Tara, Querus, Dr. Q., Sempai, Kohai, and most of all, friend. I love you all.

~Q.

18 July 2018

CROWS SOMETIMES HAVE SEX WITH THEIR DEAD

"In the most dramatic examples, a crow would approach the dead crow while alarm calling, copulate with it, be joined in the sexual frenzy by its presumed mate, and then rip it into absolute shreds."

Ed Yong
The Atlantic

PROLOGUE

JUNE 1864

Colonel Pickett Profitt gasped for air as he lunged through the brambles. Thorns tore at his gray jacket and trousers, ripping his face and hands. With his next steps, he tumbled downhill full force, a scream and then curses flying from his mouth until his spine smacked against a jagged rock in the stream below.

He shook his head, forcing himself back into clarity—and when he turned his head toward the bank of the stream, a wide black hole in the earth stared back at him. A pair of ancient oak trees screened it from casual view, a few feet from the water. It looked deep enough to hide in.

Pickett struggled to move. Couldn't. He tried again and barely managed to roll away from the rocks. He fell face-first into the water, sputtered, and pulled himself slowly to shore.

Jesus, I don't want to die. Don't let me die.

Union soldiers were not merciful. "Hard War" Union policies had seen to that.

After a few more moments, Pickett found he could move, and he was grateful. He stared up at the clouds in the sky.

"Thank you, Jesus," he croaked.

Pickett always took time to give thanks to Jesus, even though the Son of God hadn't done much for him lately. A month ago, his wife and three sons burned to death in their home. Pickett had asked Jesus to get them sum-bitches who done it. But not a Union soldier died because of it—not that he knew of.

Then, someone shot his best friend, Wendell, as his unit retreated after losing a skirmish. Pickett asked Jesus to save Wendell's life. Later that day, Wendell died in Pickett's arms.

Well, it seemed Jesus was finally helping him now. As he slid through the mouth of that hole in the Earth, the space opened into a much larger room. In the gloom, he counted six tunnels going off in different directions.

The sunlight was fading. He pulled a Lucifer out of the tin in his pocket and struck it. The bedrock looked as if it had been dug out by hand. A natural cave turned into a mine of some sort. Timber braced the mouths of tunnels for support. It was difficult for him to see much more.

He moved further inside and spied something odd on one wall. It was a large, white marble shelf set into the rock wall. A black statue perched on the center of the shelf—a bird—maybe a raven or a crow? The statue's wings looked spread as if it were ready for flight. And its eyes were strange. They glowed a bright blue; the color shifting from dark to light and dark again. He had seen nothing like it.

The light in his hand died. He snapped another match into a sputtering flame and reached out to touch the strange bird. The tips of his fingers tingled, and the statue's eyes glowed brighter. Pickett dropped his match and lurched away, trembling as an odd tingling sensation crawled up his arm.

He lit another match and glanced around once more. Shock gripped him, and his body went cold. From the surrounding tunnels, grotesque figures glided toward him. They were tall as he was— maybe taller.

Black capes of feathers covered their backs. And what was protruding from their faces? Large pointy beaks. Masks? No, that was their actual face! And above their beaks, brilliant blue crystal eyes. They glowed hard and cold—just like the statue.

Pickett backed away. Outside the cave was safer than this place. He could find someplace else to hide. And if the Yanks found him when he popped out, well, it was better to face the enemies he knew than these hell creatures.

He threw a frantic look over his shoulder toward the mouth of the cave. It was close enough. He could make it. But then he tripped and fell. His match flailed, the flame struggled, and then the world went dark except for the eerie blue glow of several eyes surrounding him.

A strange noise rose in the air. Its origin puzzled him until he realized it was coming from his own lips. It was a horrific yowling sound, like that of a terrified dog. He fumbled for his matches, but they spilled from his hands.

Far beneath the forest floor, the earth swallowed his screams.

JUDITH

NEW MOON

*M*arch 11, Monday, 2024

7:45 AM

Chilly high winds whipped around the two-story farmhouse where Judith Ware had lived most of her life. The scent of the coming rain swirled in the air.

The town's coffee spot, Bia Cup, already had its rich morning coffee brewing and the appetizing aroma of quiches baking in the oven.

Judith sniffed. *Spinach mushroom.*

"Lilith!" Judith stuck her head out from the bedroom doorway and called to the girls as she put on her uniform. "Rachel! You guys, come get breakfast! Hurry, please! I need to be on time and so do you!"

Judith had served the town of Iron Shores as police chief for nearly three years now. There wasn't a day that she wasn't excited to get to work. The town was small, but her office was understaffed and there was always something of interest going on.

Little Lola, a compact bundle of white and brown fur, raced around her legs, yipping as if pleading for her not to go. Judith bent down and ruffled the dog's head, grabbed a stuffed toy, and threw it down the hallway. Lola dashed after it.

Judith smiled as she grabbed her Motorola and her Sig 9mm, made sure her magazines were full, and then strode toward the kitchen. The two plates she'd prepared earlier—an omelet on each—sat on the oak table in the breakfast nook untouched, as were the glasses of orange juice. She'd set out two lunch bags, making sure all was ready to go. The girls were so predictable, but Judith lived in a world where she hoped her girls might one day value time as much as she did.

"Lilith! Rachel!" The thud of young feet drumming down the steps at the pace of a funeral dirge caused her eyes to slide toward the clock. It was a quarter to eight. Thankfully, it took only fifteen minutes to get to the station. "You guys—I put breakfast on the table and packed lunches for you," she pointed to two lunch sacks, one red and one blue as she caught sight of their sleepy faces. "I've gotta run. Umbrellas are by the door. Don't be late. Wear your rain jackets and be safe out there!"

Both girls rolled their eyes. Rachel meaning it—with the "Oh my God, how many times are you going to tell me?" and "I'll wear a jacket if I need one," look and Lilith copying her older sister's mannerisms to say the same thing.

Judith knew that Rachel felt she didn't need to be reminded of these things, but a mom had to do what a mom had to do.

One day, she'll understand.

Lola yipped, and Judith wanted to play with her a little more, but she was the Chief and had to be an example to her crew. They never left her waiting. Well, almost never.

"Okay—this is the *last* time now." Judith threw the squeaky toy as far down the hall as she could, and Lola dashed away. In seconds, there were squeaks and growls as Lola vigorously shook the plaything side to side as if it were the enemy, and she was ready to destroy it. It was like a signal from Lola that she understood there was no more time for play. She'd take her frustrations out on the squeak machine and vanquish it until it was time to fight again.

Judith pressed her lips together in a sad but resigned smile. She hated this time of day. Leaving the girls and Lola—never knowing what was waiting out there until they all returned home safe. Iron Shores wasn't a hotbed of crime or violence, but it had its quirks.

"I love you both so much." She reached out to hug the girls. "Let me know if you have any problems getting to school, okay? I know you're tired. You're missing that lost hour of sleep from Daylight

Saving Time the other night. Good 'ol spring forward! It shouldn't be too bad though, right? That's assuming neither of you was streaming Demon Slayer or something like that on your phone late last night."

The girls both nodded, and Judith grinned, knowing better. Her daughters were usually pretty good about sleep, but an episode of their favorite show or a favorite game could tempt them into the wee hours.

When Judith peered outside and saw how hard the rain was coming down, wondered if she should drive them. Their high school was less than a half-mile away. She opened her mouth to ask, then shut it. No, they were tough. If they wanted a ride, they'd say so. Judith knew she had to practice letting them do things on their own. It was important for them to learn to navigate the world as growing women—as much as they could be at their age.

Lilith was fourteen, a freshman finishing her first year in high school. She'd been ahead of the others her age. Rachel was sixteen, a sophomore and a bit of a rebel but still extremely bright. Lilith was more of a loner, and Rachel was more social. But despite their differences, they looked after and cared for each other. And Judith was thankful both of them stayed out of trouble for the most part. They'd held up well since their father's death four years ago.

When the 2020 COVID pandemic happened, home schooling became a thing, and there were more adjustments they had to deal with, but they'd done well. Judith thought she probably struggled more than the girls because her law enforcement position required her to respond in person to cases when they couldn't be handled on the phone or on Zoom. But, as with everything in the town of Iron

Shores, families pitched in, and teachers as well as helpful neighbors discovered alternative methods to teach groups of kids their lessons, whether on Zoom, or in small groups while wearing masks. It was a blessing, though when the kids finally returned to school. They saw their friends in person again and dashed outdoors to play. Gradually, life returned to a semblance of normal.

Normal for Iron Shores, anyway, Judith mused. *As normal as it was ever going to get.* And the girls, no matter what came their way, they got through it.

Judith pulled behind the station and parked her Ford Interceptor in her designated spot a couple of minutes before eight. When she opened the door and sniffed the air, it only took an instant to know something wasn't right. The powerful odor of blood, mud, and tea tree oil hit her like a runaway coal train.

As she entered the back room for morning report, she found her team standing in a circle around Aaron Mann, one of the younger officers. He sat hunched over in a swivel chair, his pants leg covered with red clay, and the fabric split up to his knee. Someone had propped his leg up on a fold-out chair, and put compresses over his shin. They'd also tightly wrapped another bandage around his calf.

Aaron grinned at her sheepishly. "Well, Chief," he sighed. "Guess you oughta know that the Rogs are awake. Hungry, too."

Great, Judith thought. Moving closer, she knelt down and surveyed his wounds. Definitely Mudrog bites. As far as she knew, the creatures were unique to Iron Shores. They made their homes deep in the red clay earth, and it just so happened that there was a lot of red clay in the area, especially near the river.

Typically in the winter, Mudrogs were inactive. But as soon as the spring rains started in March, they rose closer to the surface, and they were ravenous. If a living thing crossed where the Mudrogs lived at that time, the creatures rose up from the soft, red clay, and they sank their teeth into their prey. Most often, they caught shoes, and that sucking mud sound alerted a person to lift their feet run. But for those who didn't know about the Mudrogs, and for those who were careless, the creatures grabbed their victims and dragged them down into the depths of their lair, never to be seen again.

Adult Mudrogs grew to be about the size of a full-grown hog. Now and then, some got much bigger.

"You just had to test that red dirt, huh, Aaron?" Judith couldn't help but tease the man a little. Everyone in Iron Shores knew not to walk across red clay in spring.

"Spring thaw and all—yeah. But my grandkids go to the river this time of year, though. They fish. Whatever. They tend to cut across Carson's field sometimes. I had to be sure it was safe. We were on our way back for roll call and report when it was just gettin' light outside." His face flushed a little, which was a telltale sign he felt embarrassed that he hadn't been more careful.

"Obviously, it is *not* safe," Judith replied. She eyed Aaron's leg as blood seeped through the cloth covering his shin. "You don't do anything halfway, do you?" Judith eyed him. "Must have been a big one."

Officer Harvey Luck, a man with curly short hair the color of a copper penny, flecked with gray at his sideburns, sidled over to her. "It was likely a nest. See? He's got quite a few bites, and different sizes. They said it happened maybe thirty—forty minutes ago."

"Guess you'll be off duty at least for tonight," Judith pressed her lips together and looked around. "Okay. Who wants to pick up Aaron's shift? Anyone?"

No one piped up right away, but then Officer Luck volunteered, "I got it alright, Chief. Won't be the first time I've flown solo." He eyed Judith as if trying to decide whether he wanted to say more, then said, "If we'd watched for the Rogs coming back, we might have seen the mud stir. But we weren't watching the ground at the time because the sky—well, it was filled with . . ."

24

"Crows," Aaron interjected. "Truckloads of 'em! They looked like black clouds darkening the sky; there were so many. And the noise they made—well, we forgot about Rogs and . . ."

"Bam!" added Harvey. "They jumped on him faster than young Bobby tells a lie."

"Harvey pulled me out quick though," said Aaron. "Rogs got him too, on his arms."

Judith gently gripped Harvey's arm to assess the damage. Mixed deep and shallow punctures oozed blood at the top and bottom of his thick forearms. She shook her head, and grabbed a roll of gauze from a table and started wrapping his injuries. "Why didn't you guys tell me about that? You okay?"

"I'm fine, Chief, really. Just a few Rog scratches. Nuthin' Renny can't patch up with some of her magic lotion or whatever she's got," Harvey nodded.

The men could have continued their war story about the Mudrog fight, but she called the group for roll call and report. While her insides twisted as she thought about the work that needed to be done to increase Mudrog awareness, at least all the officers knew to steer clear of Carson's field and any area near the river where the red clay was soft. She'd make sure all the first responders knew to keep tourists away from those areas as well. It was an inevitable fact that a tourist or two found scenic places within the borders of the I.S. and it was up to their patrol teams to herd the "less aware" away from the more dangerous spots.

As a rule, Iron Shores—sometimes called the I.S.— was a town that kept to itself. Many of its inhabitants, which included several generations, had lived here for years. Some residents had ancestors who called this place home long before the town was even founded. There was one common thread that connected all the townsfolk who stayed. Each of them knew Iron Shores was a unique place to live. The town had idiosyncrasies that were best hidden from the rest of the world because if the world knew its secrets, it would probably stomp this place out of existence. The world outside the I.S. borders just wouldn't understand that while there were dangerous creatures and a vile ugliness that hid in this place, there were also benevolent spirits and an unfathomable beauty in the hills and rivers as well. In the end, they balanced out just fine.

Usually balanced out, a small voice added in the back of Judith's mind. And that was the truth too. Sometimes the scales of justice, and circumstances of good and evil, seemed a little heavier on one side than the other. But that's where she and her team came in, and other guardians in the I.S. too. It took careful eyes to be stewards of this place, but every moment was worth it.

Judith handpicked every member of her team not just to fight crime, but to help keep the balance of strange oddities in this place they called home.

"Crows," Judith muttered. Then she realized her officers were staring at her, their faces suddenly full of questions. She breathed in the surrounding air, not failing to notice who wore Old Spice aftershave, who hadn't bathed in about 24 hours, and who had eaten a can of sardines with saltine crackers for breakfast.

"Okay," she called out with a strong upbeat voice. "Morning team, you're up!" When she left Harvey to look after Aaron, she made sure that they'd both call on Renny together. Renny was the town's local healer of sorts. She also owned the Tattered Page, the one and only used bookstore. Her shop opened up around eight.

She'd give them some Mudrog poultice, then Judith hoped Aaron would go right home to his wife and rest through the night. She needed him ready to rumble with Harvey the next night shift.

Judith's teams were on ten-hour shifts, and they took turns each week in terms of who did late nights. It was always best when officers partnered up, but depending on local events, weather, and other factors, some of them did a solo patrol while Judith stayed on call, and often, they paired off in the afternoons and evenings.

In Iron Shores, it was also important to pay attention to the moon's phases. Tonight, there was a new moon, and with the storm clouds in the sky, it was likely to be darker than dark. And in the black of night, they all needed to be on guard.

CHRISTOPHER

EMERGENCE

*M*arch 11, *Monday*

5:00 PM

It wasn't raining yet, but one glance toward the heavens and Christopher Miles instinctively knew a torrential rain was going to pound his body any moment. If he had the capability, he would kick his own backside, harder than his mom ever beat him, for being so stupid.

His usual thirty-minute hike had taken an hour before he reached the scenic view of Moon's Overlook. Yes, rain had thundered on his roof this morning, and while on his hike, he'd seen the surrounding creeks and riverbeds swell a bit, but he hadn't looked at his weather app to see if more rain was coming before his walk. He'd been thinking about the repairs he needed to make on the church and what he had left in his budget. And there were the funds he needed for helping some families in town too.

At least he'd worn a rain jacket. The black clouds overhead seemed to chastise him as they gathered closer together, and the low rumble of thunder made him press his lips together and shake his head.

Then, he noticed a strange sound separate from the thunder. Something like a crow cawing. No—more than one crow.

The noise came from somewhere ahead and down below. The flapping of wings and a sudden cacophony of harsh voices erupted into the air near him, but Christopher couldn't see where the sounds were coming from.

In moments, he emerged from the forest, along the rocky path of Moon's Overlook, where a short cliff allowed for a view of a lovely meadow. Moon's was a common spot for hikers, lovers, climbers and anyone else who wanted to get away.

Curious, he made his way to the edge of the cliff and peered down.

It took a few moments for Christopher's brain to translate what his eyes were seeing. At the bottom of the drop, an ebony carpet of undulating beaks and feathers roiled on the earth. There had to be more than a hundred crows gathered there.

A murder of crows.

The birds flapped their wings vigorously and hopped around, their harsh voices echoing beneath the blanket of black in the sky. He swallowed hard when he caught a glimpse of something pale lying beneath the birds. He squinted to see more clearly.

Is that an arm? No. Can't be. That's insane.

If not for the question in his head and that minuscule moment of what he was sure looked like an arm, he'd have done a 180 and headed back home. But the birds behaved so strangely, tightly clustered and fighting to be on top of whatever lay beneath them, that he stayed a little longer to watch. The crows undulated oddly— as if participating in a bizarre mating ritual.

The more Christopher studied what was beneath the mass of feathers, the more certain he was that he was staring at a human arm. He spied a softball-sized rock, plucked it off the ground, and threw it toward the crows, careful not to hit what was under them. He yelled, "Get out of here! Go!"

A multitude of wings flapped, and the ebony creatures lifted into the sky—a dark cloud of feathers beating against the rising wind.

Christopher's gaze riveted on the body they'd uncovered. The corpse was female. She was sprawled across the long grass, face up, completely naked.

Her arms and legs were contorted at odd angles as if she were participating in a macabre death dance. He wondered if it was due to rigor mortis. Something he knew very little about except for the descriptions he heard when he watched CSI and information he gleaned from time to time from Marty at Hatcher's Funeral Home.

Caught between shock and morbid curiosity, he found it difficult to think of what to do first. He should call someone. The police. What would he say? What would *they* say? No matter. He had to call. He reached into his pocket to pull out his cell phone, then stopped.

A movement between the woman's legs pressed the pause button in his brain. He squinted, trying to determine what it was he was seeing. Then he recoiled, feeling a strange sense of horror, fascination, and disgust all at the same time.

Something black, pointed, and shiny poked out from the hairless lips of the woman's private region. Then it *moved*. More of it pushed further out.

Christopher's heart quickened.

Is it . . . ?

Cell phone forgotten, he stood staring at the woman's genitalia as the lips of her sex parted wider and something twisted and pushed forward in the throes of an unfathomable birth. Finally, it emerged. Black wings flapped. An eerie caw issued from its throat and the other birds, perched in various trees around him, answered with harsh cawing responses.

How . . . what the . . . ?

Then the woman's hand twitched ever so slightly. But that couldn't be. She was dead. Wasn't she?

You're seeing things, Christopher.

The newly emerged but full-grown crow hopped onto the woman's abdomen, shook itself much like a dog shaking water from its coat, and with a jump it spread its wings and launched into the air. Christopher's eyes followed it as it banked into the trees to join the others.

A jerky motion teased at his peripheral vision. He lowered his gaze and sucked in his breath. It wasn't his imagination. The woman's entire arm moved now, jerkily, as if she suffered from spasms of pain.

Christopher's hand was still in his pocket. He jerked out his cell and dialed 911.

A woman answered his call. "What's your emergency?" Her voice was young and very Southern, so it came out more like, *"Wats yur emurgencee?"*

"That you, Darla?" There was only one 9-1-1 center near Iron Shores, and he knew the four people who worked there.

"Yeah. That you, Reverend?"

"Yes," he responded, feeling more grounded after hearing her voice. Hey, I found a woman at the bottom of Moon's. She's semi-conscious. There is no obvious injury, but her lips are blue, and she has no clothes."

He heard Darla clear her throat, trying her best to stick to protocol.

She confirmed his information. "Sending a team your way," she said.

Done with the call, Christopher clenched his teeth and assessed the height of the cliff. Four stories maybe five? Not too bad.

There were several promising lips and handholds. He'd done a good bit of face-climbing in his youth, and although he hadn't climbed much this winter, he decided to down-climb anyway.

His fingers grabbed onto an edge, and his foot searched for a solid purchase. Putting more weight on his toes, he found a small lip for his other foot and then reached down to grab a lower piece of rock.

Earth crumbled beneath his supporting foot, and he started to fall. He yelled out and crimped hard, hanging by one hand, grunting, feeling tendons strain in his fingers as he supported most of his weight with the other hand and a toe. Swinging his free foot along the wall, he found another purchase. This one was more stable, and he continued to descend. It took a few minutes to get to the bottom.

Huffing from the exertion and covered with mud, Christopher ran over to the woman. He dared not move her. What if she had a broken neck or spine? She moaned, her chest heaving. Her eyes remained closed. Long blonde hair sprawled over the ground. He saw her naked breasts, puckered nipples rising, falling. He kneeled next to her and used his rain jacket to cover her torso. Next, he removed his tennis shoes, pulled off his tube socks and put them on her feet. Anything he could do to provide some warmth had to be good.

When he'd done all he could, he took a hard look at the woman's face. He knew her. Back in high school, she'd been a bit thinner.

Womanhood had filled her out over the past fifteen years. More generous curves, a more mature face, but she was still stunning. Her blue-tinged lips trembled, worrying him. Still, the pillows of her mouth were not much different from the day he'd first kissed her.

Hellen Profitt.

The last time he'd seen her was also the last day he'd been seventeen. The next day was just one of many birthdays that made him wish he'd never been born.

I should talk to her. Tell her it's going to be okay.

Instead, his mind cycled through the memories of Hellen—her swimming naked in the river their junior year, the rosebuds of her nipples hard from the chill of the early spring waters. In the handful of circumstances that had thrown them together, she'd been evasive when he'd asked her about her family. Instead, she'd laugh. Dared him to do something, or—

Hellen gasped and her eyes opened wide. Her lips turned a darker shade of blue, and her breathing was rapid. The low hum of engines caught Christopher's attention.

The paramedic team—Nick Moon and Sammi Ware, whom he knew from the River Rage brewery in Iron Shores—arrived on red ATVs with their equipment strapped on back.

Nick, a tall, thin, athletic man with ebony skin in his mid-twenties, hopped off his ATV and brought over a backboard and neck collar. "Hey, Reverend. How long have you been here?"

"About fifteen minutes. I take this hike most every day," he said. "Found her when I looked out over the top."

"Chopper's on the way." Sammi was a stark contrast to Nick. Pale skin, ice blue eyes that were almost white, stockier than Nick, huge shoulders, muscular midsection, and thick, powerful thighs. "Move back. We got her."

"Hellen Profitt," Christopher said. "That's her name. Spelled with two L's." Feeling inadequate and insignificant, he watched the two paramedics as they stabilized Hellen, took her vital signs, slid a backboard under her and prepared her for transport. He wished there was something, anything, he could do to help.

A few minutes later, the chopper arrived. It swung dangerously back and forth in the wind like some macabre pendulum, but it finally managed to land. In minutes the medics loaded her onto a transport stretcher and into the chopper.

Christopher approached them as they prepared to airlift her.

"Headed to UVA?" he yelled over the sound of the rotor blades. The University of Virginia Hospital in Charlottesville had a major trauma unit.

One of the medics, a young woman with a long black ponytail, sticking out from beneath her helmet, shook her head and yelled back. "James River General. UVA's got major incoming trauma! MVA on I-64. Semi and two buses!"

James River General was the town's only hospital. It was not a major trauma center, but at least it was close.

The chopper lifted off, a sudden gust of wind fishtailing the back rotor. As the echo of the rotor blades faded over the trees, Christopher turned toward home.

Sammi drove by him along with Nick, and they stopped. Sammi's blonde hair was pulled back in a ponytail. Nick wore a beanie, which kept his ears warm. Sammi looked up at the sky. "Rev! Want a ride home? I can put you back here. No problem at all."

Christopher shook his head. He wasn't going to keep these two. What if they were needed when they were carting him around? "I'll be fine, guys. Thanks for coming. Take care of yourselves."

They nodded; Nick sent him a peace sign, and they headed back the way they'd come, looking reluctant but not going to argue.

After just a few minutes, the heavens opened up, and a massive downpour pummeled Christopher's head and shoulders. Without his coat and socks, the walk back home would surely be miserable.

God, protect me, he prayed, although he wasn't sure he believed in God. Still, another prayer couldn't hurt. *And please help Hellen.*

But he found he couldn't focus long on prayers. Despite the freezing rain, his mind drifted back to the memory of her warm lips, that succulent kiss, and the cold, hard nipples of her breasts bobbing in the water.

THOMAS

HEARTLESS

*M*arch 12, Tuesday

7:30 AM

Thomas Craig had tried to save a man with no heart. Last night the patient presented to the ER with no respirations and no pulse, and Thomas and his team had tried to resuscitate him.

Obviously, they'd failed. The ER attending, Dr. Maria Maxwell, just stared at the X-ray in disbelief. Thomas stood alongside her—

both of them silent. Maria managed a grim smile when her gaze rolled over to Thomas.

"Well, no doubting it." She shook her head. "We'll wait for the autopsy, of course. One thing is for sure, you'll have a hell of a case study to present."

"Right." Thomas ran his fingers through his thick black curls. Black courtesy of his Japanese mother and curly thanks to his Anglo-Saxon father. "Except I can't present this case. There's no way to explain it. Dude is missing a *heart,* Maria! How the hell would I present this case?"

The computer screen on the wall, showing the bizarre image in front of them, was the only light in the room. The digital X-ray showed ribs and lungs. Every structure that was supposed to be there. Except one. No heart.

And the man didn't have a mark on him. No lacerations on the chest cavity. Not even a scar.

"Yes . . . well . . ." Maria flicked off the image.

In that instant of darkness, Thomas had a strange sense of something even darker closing in, moving around him—he heard a muffled flapping of wings—and a shadowy figure lurched toward him. Then he was in a dark room underground—a room that smelled of wet rock. A drip-drip sound of water and he turned toward it to see a giant stone in the center of a lake. It glowed an icy blue and lit the water around it, but its light could not penetrate the darkness of the room. The shadowy figure was in front of him once more, leaning toward him, smelling of death and decay. It opened its mouth and said a word—something he didn't understand. "Ap . . ." He arched backwards, trying to get away, and nearly fell.

" . . . there's that," Maria continued. "A case study needs a resolution. We don't even have this man's name." She flipped the overhead light on and cocked her head—her dark eyes staring at him—clearly waiting for a response.

Thomas shook his head quickly and focused on Maria.

"Are you okay?" Maria studied him head to toe, as if to ensure that he was physically fine.

Thomas took a deep breath. "Yeah. I just thought I saw . . ."

"Saw what?"

Thomas managed a weak smile. "It's been one of those nights. You know how it is. No sleep. Sometimes it gets to you?"

Maria nodded slowly. "Who brought him in?"

Thomas only half heard her question. He was still pondering over the thing he'd seen—or—had he felt it? Was it a giant bird? A strange vision of a hunched figure—an old man with long hair or maybe an old woman?

Man, these long hours are messing with my brain.

"The EMT's," he shook his head once as he answered. "Nick and Sammi."

Maria arched an eyebrow as if expecting him to say more, but Thomas didn't have a shred to offer. This was the second bizarre case to come through the doors during his shift.

First, the Profitt woman yesterday evening, found naked at the bottom of a cliff with extreme blood loss. She had some broken bones, but there was no determination as to which part of her body was bleeding. No one could find a wound or blood pooling inside her anywhere.

39

And then the man with no heart early this morning. No fucking heart. What do you say to that? What do you do wit that?

He rubbed his eyelids. There would be no answers tonight. And he could barely focus on anything. Major fatigue had settled into his bones.

"I got to get home," he said.

He inhaled through his nose and wished he hadn't. The stench of blood, urine and sour puke rose up and smacked him from his dirty scrubs. Hell, he needed a shower and some shuteye.

Maria continued to study him, her eyebrows knitting together. "Fine. I can see you're exhausted. Catch you back here in twelve hours." She rubbed her lids as well, one of them making a wet smacking sound against her sclera. He noted the dark circles under her eyes when she removed her hand. "Try to get some rest," she said.

For Thomas, stepping out of James River General was akin to shedding a serpent's skin. The morning sun had just crested the horizon, turning the expanse of the sky and the clouds that lined it into a deep scarlet panorama.

Red sky in morning, sailors take warning . . .

It was something his grandmother used to say. A common phrase that was used when she was in the Navy. Red sky or not, he loved the scent of early spring on the morning breeze. At least it wasn't raining right now.

A slight chill in the air made him shiver. Not an unpleasant feeling, if he hadn't suddenly felt that something was watching him, that something invisible was pressing in on him. The birds, normally active at first light, remained silent, and Thomas quickly unlocked his Subaru Forrester and climbed in.

Shutting the door and locking it right away made him feel instantly better, though a little stupid. As if a mere lock could be true protection in a vehicle with glass windows. His experience with MVA victims told him otherwise.

Time for home and bed.

NPR news rattled on the radio as he curved along roads flanked by forest on either side. He accidentally dropped his phone on the floorboard between his feet and bent to pick it up only to narrowly avoid hitting a green Volkswagen Beetle that was stopped in the road. He screeched to a halt beside it and peered over at the driver's side.

A young woman hugged the steering wheel. She turned her head toward him, and he noticed she was crying. The light of the new day caught her tears and made them shine like little diamonds.

He rolled his window down, and she rolled hers down in response. "Hey, there! Are you all right?" he asked.

Then his heart drummed against his chest as his eyes took her in. She had dark hair and dusky eyes. Her soft pink lips were full—perfect—on a face unadorned by layers of makeup. She was a natural beauty all the way.

She shook her head. "No. Not all right. The engine's stopped." She cast her eyes down and then looked up once more through long black lashes. "Okay, I feel stupid," she continued. "But the truth is, I ran it out of gas. I don't have a cell phone and I can't push the car to the side by myself. I don't have a gas can and the closest station is maybe five miles away."

More like ten, Thomas thought. Jesus, he was tired, but the woman was in distress. He'd be a dick if he didn't offer an assist.

"I can help you out if you like," he said. "I know you probably don't accept rides from strangers, but you can use my cell to call roadside assistance if you like. Whatever I can do to help. Right now, to be safe—put your hazard lights on—your blinkers."

She eyed him warily at first, but then he saw her flip her blinkers on and heard the characteristic ticking they make when engaged. The corners of her lips tipped up just a little.

Thomas guessed she'd noticed his lab coat and scrubs. People trusted doctors.

"I *would* appreciate a ride," she confessed as she opened her door. Bending to talk through the window of his passenger door she asked, "May I use your phone on the way?"

Thomas handed her his cell through the passenger window. "There's no PIN or password. And, of course, you don't even need them if you want to dial 911." He smiled knowing his smile could be disarming.

Her shoulders dropped, and her face eased. After all, what kind of serial killer would give a stranger their cellphone?

"Station is about ten miles up the road," he said. "It's on my way. That okay? If they don't have someone there to give you a ride back, I'd be happy to take you. Just don't mind me napping while you get gas. It was a really long night." He tried to give her his most, *I'm a trustworthy guy* look to put her at ease, and then felt a little guilty about it.

She beamed at him and stuck out her hand. "I'm Hatton."

Her hand was cold. How long had she been stranded out here?

"Like the ferry?" he asked. "Hatton ferry?"

She flashed her teeth. "The very one. Last pole ferry in the U.S.A. Yes, I'm a local, born and bred. And yes, my parents were very strange to name me after a ferry." Her nervous giggle had an endearing quality. She added, "Or more like after an 1800s postmaster general."

"I'm Thomas. I'm a resident at the hospital. Originally from C'ville. This was a place close to home, and I needed a residency. It's worked out well so far."

She laughed, the sound reminding him of wind-chimes, and her perfume was earthy but exotic. Sandalwood. And cinnamon, maybe?

On their way to the gas station, Hatton filled him in on a couple of local legends and lore of Iron Shores. Before he knew it, a little convenience store with a gas station was right there in front of them and he suddenly realized he was going to be sad to lose her company. It had been quite a while since he'd done any real socializing. Residency was a social-life killer.

"I'll buy a gas can and check to see if anyone can run me back to my car," she said. She sauntered away and he couldn't help but admire how nicely her glutes filled out her tight blue jeans.

CHRISTOPHER

PROFESSIONAL

*M*arch 12, *Tuesday*

9:22 AM

Christopher sighed, closing the dining room curtain after inspecting his front yard. The deluge pounded the roof and rattled the windows, and he knew that today the weather would punish anyone who dared venture outside. He consulted his phone for weather info.

The town website warned of flooding, telling people not to cross any roads covered by rushing water. Christopher had just finished reading the updates when a knock came at his door.

He opened it to find Judith Ware, drenched.

"Reverend." She removed her uniform hat, the Smokey Bear saying "business" even when it wasn't business. "I've got questions about last Wednesday. Not many." Her manner was terse and matter-of-fact, even though he'd known her well over the past few years. So, today was all business.

"Come in, come in." He motioned her to the rustic dining table. His granddad had built the oak table before he was born, and as a boy, he'd eaten most of his meals there. When his parents died in a car accident a couple of years ago, it was one of the few things he kept.

When she had taken a seat in one of the matching oak chairs, she rubbed herself dry with the checkered towel he offered her and then pulled a notepad out of her jacket.

"You knew her well, right? Back in the day?" Like Christopher, Judith had gone to school with Hellen. "Memory serves, you two even dated."

"I knew her some—high school, like you and me. I haven't seen her since I left—from back then, you know." There was an awkward pause. "We never really dated. I don't guess you've seen her either?"

Judith shook her head. "Maybe from time to time. At the Dollar Store or passing by the pharmacy. But we didn't run in the same circles in high school." Another tense pause filled the space between them. Judith sniffed. "She was a free spirit; I was the daughter of a farmer. There were a lot of people I didn't keep up with during school, much less after."

"How is she now? Have you heard?"

"Critical condition. Looks like she either fell or someone pushed her over that cliff. When we searched, there were no clothes to be found anywhere."

Judith's cell phone rang. Her ringtone was a song about a girl's father wiped away by a twister. There weren't many tornadoes in the state of Virginia, but he understood the reason for the tune on her phone. Judith and he shared a common upbringing. Common in a way no kid wants to share. Sure, it wasn't her biological father who abused her, but . . .

He watched as her thumb swiped the Accept call button. "Chief Ware," she answered. Christopher got up from his chair and filled two glasses of water.

"I see," she said. "Yeah. Thanks for telling me." She ended the call and looked at him as he set the water down in front of her.

"Hellen Profitt is dead," she whispered as her eyes met his. Judity cleared her throat and went on. "Seems she had internal injuries from the fall. Blood loss. Broken bones. Not unexpected, but I know you hoped she'd make it. I'm so sorry, Reverend." When he didn't respond, she said,"I've gotta go and notify her family. No one has been able to reach them yet."

Christopher barely heard the words that followed the first four she'd just spoken. *Hellen Profitt is dead.* No. It wasn't right. He'd just helped Hellen yesterday. Made sure she got to the hospital. He'd tried to keep her warm, and her lips—he remembered kissing those chilled lips.

"Reverend?"

Christopher's gaze swiveled toward her. Concern was obvious on her face—the way she tilted her head, the way her blue-gray eyes opened wider, just a little, as if questioning, her mouth softening. He always thought the color of her eyes looked like the ocean—or the color of storm clouds, depending on her mood. And her brunette hair shimmered around her face as if it were wild and free—like golden oak—a living thing unto itself. She was just beautiful.

He'd never met Hellen's father and didn't really know the rest of her family except for when he'd seen her brothers and sister at school many years ago. Later, when he'd moved back to town, he'd caught glimpses of her siblings here and there but never had the opportunity to speak with them.

His next words sounded foreign to his own ears—dry and cracking.

"You know where the Profitts live?" Christopher asked.

And just like that, in the time it took for a finger-snap, the concern in Judith's voice was gone. She became a police chief again. She placed the hat back on her head. Back to business. As often as the Profitt boys had been in trouble, he thought she would have visited them at least once.

Judith pursed her lips. "You've never been there?" she asked.

The fingers on her right hand twisted a strange ring on her left ring finger. It was a mixed-metal band engraved with several symbols. He'd always supposed it was her wedding ring, but he'd never asked her about it.

He hadn't realized she'd been wearing it all this time after her husband's death. Had she recently taken to wearing it again? If so, he wondered why.

Judith cleared her throat, her eyes studying him. He hadn't answered her question. And she hadn't answered his.

"No, I never went there," he admitted. "We always met at school and sometimes in town or at the river."

"Huh." Judith drank down her glass of water and stood up. "Well, I'm sorry about Hellen. Really, I am. But duty calls." She brushed a strand of her golden-oak-colored hair away from her face. "Take care of yourself, Reverend."

"After all these years, you still can't call me by my name, Judith? At least when we're alone?" Christopher examined her face—the determined set of her jaw, the steady gaze of her blue-gray eyes.

She pressed her lips into one of those polite smiles that don't crinkle the eyes. Not that he blamed her. The next job she had to do was one no sane person wanted. Telling a parent that their child was dead—that had to be one of the hardest things in the world to do.

"Not meaning to be rude, Reverend. It's just . . ." Her eyes lingered on his face. "It's professional." When she opened the door and strode through it, she didn't look back.

When he closed the door behind her, he still smelled the lingering scent of Dove soap in the air. And there was another scent, too—just under that. It was not a perfume. Maybe her shampoo.

Apples, he thought. *She smells like apples.*

And not for the first time, he wondered why he, a single minister, would stay in such a small town. The prospects of finding a companion were slim here, and his childhood had not left him with many fond memories of the place. Still, once he'd come back and set foot on the river town's soil, he felt like he could never leave again.

He strode to the window to watch Judith leave, her Ford practically leaping onto the road. His fingers reached out and touched the glass in a reflexive gesture that said he wished she hadn't had to leave.

One day, he thought. *When the time is right, maybe we'll get beyond "professional."*

Judith was a remarkable woman. *If she weren't widowed and still so in love with her dead husband,*" he thought. *Or if she had never married, what kind of future could we have had?* He pictured them laughing together, holding hands and—he shook his head. He remembered the ring on her finger. Maybe it was still too soon. His thoughts sped like a racecar blasting circles around a track, and he knew he'd be better off taking some time to pray or meditate. Clear his mind, that's what he needed. And maybe he'd even ask the God he didn't really believe in to take Hellen's soul into his arms and hold her close.

When he went into his bedroom, he lay down on his bed instead of going to his knees, and he closed his eyes. The vision of Hellen's plump lips and the tight pucker of her nipples invaded his thoughts, and though he tried to think of something else—something like planning eulogies and burials in the rain—his mind wouldn't let her slip away. In moments, his genitals tingled, and his penis grew hard.

I should pray, he mentally admonished himself, but as if possessed of their own will, his fingers reached down and unzipped his pants—the shaft of his penis growing firmer—then stiff. He got to his feed and pulled a sock out of his dresser drawer. Hellen's beautiful face still burned in his brain. And when he thought of the last time he'd seen her, with those blue lips, and cold pale skin, guilt flooded his mind as he found himself wondering how those lips would have felt wrapped tightly around him.

Then, he imagined Judith's face coming close to him, kissing him. In moments, he found his release and ejaculated into the fabric. Shame burned inside him. He would never deserve her. He withdrew his softening flesh and rolled over onto his side, tears in his eyes.

Frustration, loneliness, and a strange sense of dread washed over him until he fell into slumber with the cawing sound of crows echoing in his ears.

CHRISTOPHER

BROKEN

*M*arch 12, Tuesday

10:00 AM

A swirling mass of black birds covered Christopher's body, and he tried to beat them back with his hands. He bellowed in anger and fear, but the birds just kept coming at him, dragging him down with the weight of their numbers until they pinned him to the earth, and he was unable to move. As terror engulfed him, he tried to call out once more, to scream for help, but the word was stuck in his throat and wouldn't pass his lips. "He-el-e-e ——!"

The word was jammed there, choking him. The ground shook, and something primal in the center of Christopher's soul, a dread that twisted his stomach and pricked his skin, caused him to tremble. *It* was coming for him.

He didn't know what "It" was, but it was coming—and still the birds pinned him. Their wings flapped against his face. Their claws scratched his cheeks, and their beaks pecked at his body. He smelled his own blood. And then, his pants felt wet. Had he just pissed himself?

After this unspoken question, the pressure of the birds lessened, and the crows cawed loudly with an air of triumph. The ground shook harder, and although the birds still pinned him down, they parted from his face, allowing him to see what was coming for him. The grotesque feature above him pushed his dread beyond the cliff of sanity.

The creature had a long black beak for a mouth—a beak with small, razor-sharp teeth—and eyes of piercing, crystalline blue with a dark mist swirling in their centers. The creature's features were surrounded by lumps of black feathers and covered in shadows. The hunched dark figure loomed over him, and its breath was a wave of noxious fumes threatening to drown him. The stench reminded him of rotten eggs and maggoty animals, sulfurous and sickeningly sweet—mixed with the scent of muddy hair.

He stared, still trying to scream for help—immobile—as this thing—this—this monster, opened its beak and clamped down on his neck —squeezing. Squeezing hard. Now cutting with knife-like teeth . . .

Christopher's eyes flew open. He was in his bedroom. The white ceiling was a welcome view until he tried to sit up and found he still couldn't move. He breathed in deep through his nose and counted in his mind. *One. Two. Three. Four.*

Next, he tried opening his mouth and managed it. The pounding in his chest subsided, and he tried wriggling a finger—success. Finally, he was able to sit up.

The clock in his room read five minutes after ten. It hadn't been a long nap, but apparently long enough for him to sink into one hell of a nightmare. How long had it been since he'd had such a dream? Maybe when he was at UVA, sometime before he'd finished his degree in religious studies. He'd suffered from the night terrors frequently as a teen, the first one occurring the morning of his thirteenth birthday.

There was no memory of the dream, but he'd wakened with fear drenching his body, trying to scream, only to lie there for minutes while shadows seemed to flit around him. When he was finally able to move, he'd yelled so loudly from the horror of it that his mother had thundered up the stairs and burst through his door, snarling, "I told you, no noise in the house! Shut the fuck up, Christopher!"

When he started to cry, she took care of him. Oh yes. Good old mom had dashed over to his bed and caressed him with multiple hard slaps to his face. She'd beaten him even harder when she noticed he'd wet the bed.

"Get up, you lazy no-good use of a son! You get that bed clean, you hear me? Strip it now. Wash those sheets! And if this ever—" she'd eyed him with disgust on her face, " . . . EVER happens again—you can sleep in your pissy sheets for a week, then I'll hang them out the window for the whole world to see! You got that?" She'd stormed out and slammed the door, making his entire room shake in the process.

And for the most part, even though the dreams and the morning paralysis happened weekly, and sometimes more than that, he'd made sure his mother never heard a squeak from him about it. And every single time, he woke up in a puddle of urine. He stripped his own bed and washed his own sheets.

His senior year of high school, on his eighteenth birthday, it was the worst dream of all. And when he could move, the fear inside him was explosive, and he *did* scream. He screamed like Satan was taking him to hell.

His mother burst through the door with a cast iron frying pan in her hand, whaling on him so hard that some of the bones in his face were fractured.

His father, a man who had never raised a finger to help him, a man who silently watched as his mother beat him and verbally attacked him over the years, had driven him to the hospital.

"You tell them you fell," he'd said. "Down the stairs to the basement. Hit your chin on a step and the concrete block at the bottom."

And that's what Christopher had done, even though the nurse who checked him in and cleaned the blood from his face had asked if he was okay at home.

What was he going to say? He was eighteen now. Grown.

Christopher had offered no information other than to say he'd tripped and fallen down the basement stairs. He'd endured his internal pain and embarrassment as they'd cleaned him up, X-rayed him, and then admitted him overnight. The doctor told his father that Christopher had a broken nose and fractures to his lower jaw. He had injuries to the scalp, too, but only needed stitches there.

The next morning, they'd taken him to surgery, pinned the broken bones together in his face, and wired his jaw shut. When he finally made it home, his bedsheets were hanging out of his bedroom window, which faced the road. A large yellowish stain announced to everyone what he, Christopher, an eighteen-year-old, had done.

His mother had looked at his jaw with an air of satisfaction and then told him that over the summer, he needed to work his ass off to pay for the hospital bill. He'd gone to his room, taken down the sheet, and packed a bundle of clothes and personal items into the two pillowcases in his room.

Emptying his backpack, he stuffed more items into it—he'd never need his pack for schoolbooks again. Then he went to one of his pictures on the wall and took it down. He had been hiding money from his mother inside an envelope there on the back.

Over the years, he exchanged coins for bills, and when he counted the paper notes, he had two hundred and five dollars. It wasn't much, but it would be enough to start.

Late that night, he crept down the stairs, afraid his mother would hear him, and slipped out of the front door. By starlight he walked along the country roads, not considering he'd just gone through surgery, not knowing what to do except to head for the city. Charlottesville was maybe forty miles away.

And in the wee hours, as if some celestial being had finally taken pity on him, the Reverend Loma Lamb gave him a lift. A woman sent by some higher power to help usher him out of his hell. She gave him a place to stay. Helped him apply to the University of Virginia, where he majored in theology, and she helped him find scholarships to pay for it.

Christopher shook his head. All of that seemed so long ago. Sixteen years since the night he'd left Iron Shores and sworn he'd never come back. One of his greatest regrets was leaving Hellen.

And even though he knew that she was dead now, she still haunted the crevices of his mind. She had been in many of his dreams over the years, and now the thought of her image, her smile, and her coy laughter hooked him harder than a perfect day of sport climbing in Thailand.

He picked up his phone and called Hatcher Mortuary to see if they'd received her body yet.

Marty Hatcher's boy, Justin, answered. "No, sir. Not yet. They're still waiting to take her to the medical examiner's office."

The boy assured him that he'd give a call back when Hellen's body went to Richmond and when to expect her body to come back into town.

Why did the medical examiner see her? Surely, they knew what caused her death. She'd died of internal injuries, falling off a cliff.

Of course. They'd need to know she wasn't drunk, drugged, murdered, but the thought of someone, anyone, cutting up her perfect body . . .

He realized he was still on the phone. "Sorry. Uh, give me a call when she gets there, will you Justin? Let me know if any of her family comes. If not, I'll handle the burial." He surprised himself by saying that. He hadn't planned it. The words just happened.

And I will handle it, he affirmed. *Hellen Profitt's body will have a place to rest.*

JUDITH

DELIVERY

*M*arch 12, Tuesday

10:20 AM

Chief Judith Ware drove her Ford Interceptor along the far side of the state forest. She'd never been to the Profitt place, and she didn't know them very well. They weren't on welfare. She knew that much.

They owned a hundred, and forty acres, and they paid their land tax. They allowed certain hunters to hunt on their land and took payment for that, or so she'd heard.

Otherwise, she didn't know how they earned money. Town whispers hinted at weed, shrooms, and maybe even moonshine, but she could never find enough proof to begin an investigation.

Despite the chill in the air, Judith rolled down the window to get some fresh air. Christopher's scent still surrounded her. He was everywhere, a constant presence that permeated her very essence, as if he occupied every single pore.

He was such a sweet man that she hated herself and the way she kept him at a safe personal distance. Still, she could not afford to be weak, to put him in danger and possibly lose him like she had her dear husband, David. Her world had shattered into millions of bleeding pieces the day David died. In the blink of an eye , she'd become a widow and a single mother—a professional woman with responsibilities to her town as well as her family.

And despite her role, she had to think of her girls first. They were her priority. Her youngest was about to enter one of the most significant phases of her life, and Judith knew she needed to be watchful and ready for when that happened.

The road up the mountain narrowed, and the holes in the dirt made her vehicle bump like an angry stallion. The only way she knew she was on the right path was the tire tracks that remained visible despite the rain that washed across the road.

The road finally emerged into a small meadow, the scent of wild autumn grasses filling the air. A primitive log home stood against a line of tall cedars, its rough-hewn logs hinting at a long history.

Despite the pouring rain, the battered green pickup sat in the driveway, its sides still caked in red mud. From behind the house, the baying of hounds filled the air. As the wet hair, excrement, and mud's combined stench hit her, she shivered, the sensation prickling at her neck.

Judith sighed as got out of her vehicle and marched up to the door. She knocked. No answer. She knew someone was inside.

More than one person inside, actually, and their individual scents were strong. Her nose picked up three men, one woman—and a child. When she turned, prepared to go around the back to investigate further, the front door opened wide.

The man who pushed forward into the doorway was lean and muscular. Her keen eye noted how he carried those muscles in a threatening way, not an athletic one. His white T-shirt was dotted with yellow stains, and his black faded jeans, torn in places hipsters wouldn't consider cool, bore splotches of the red mud she suspected he shared with his truck. Dark blue and wary eyes met her gaze, and then she caught a sudden glint in his eye that reminded her of a coyote before it took its prey.

"Afternoon, officer," he drawled, his voice lengthening the word 'officer' into a prolonged four syllable word. His frame blocked the cabin's entrance, and despite the icy waterfall of rain pummeling her, Jagger's posture only punctuated his intention to deny her entrance. There'd be no invitation to come in and get warm, because obviously the genuine warmth of Southern hospitality didn't exist here.

Judith cleared her throat before she spoke, hoping to project her voice with a measure of strength. "Mr. Jaggar Profitt? Hellen's father?"

The man gave her a curt nod and ran his scarred fist along the line of his jaw where an untrimmed scraggle-beard framed his missing front tooth.

The unappetizing odor of greasy, overripe meat cooking over a wood fire overwhelmed Judith's senses, and she suppressed a coughing retch. "I need to talk to you, Mr. Profitt." Judith placed a foot forward. "Mind if I come in?" Jagger shot the palm of his hand out almost as quickly as squeezing the trigger on a rifle.

"Matter of fact, I do," Jagger replied. He tilted his chin down as he leveled his stormy eyes at her and leaned casually against one side of the doorway. It took every ounce of Judith's will not to press her lips together when he glanced down and picked at a ragged, dirty fingernail, and then tore the top of it off with his teeth, spitting it at her feet. "What's this about?"

Judith heard voices inside the cabin but saw no one else. She drew in a breath, and said, "Mr. Profitt, it's about your daughter, Hellen."

Jagger's eyes turned to steel as he clenched his jaw. "Go on."

Not like this. She didn't want to tell him like this. "If you'd let me in," Judith started.

Jagger's face burst into an angry web of twisted, sun-baked wrinkles with his next words. "No *fucking* way. You can say what you gotta say right there, Chief. Tell me 'bout Hellen right now, goddammit! What 'bout my girl?"

Before she even opened her mouth, Judith mentally kicked herself, but her rising anger sparked the fire of her words, and they launched from her tongue before she could reel them in. Her tone was anything but kind.

"Hellen's dead, Mr. Profitt. Reverend found her at the bottom of Moon's Overlook. The town hospital has her remains right now. We tried to notify you earlier to let you know she was there, but no one had your contact information. That's why I'm here. Your daughter's body is being transported to the Richmond Medical Examiner's Office. When they bring her back, I'm guessing you want Hellen to go to Hatcher's Funeral Home." It wasn't really a question. Iron Shores had only one funeral home. Judith waited for the man to react, but Jagger Profitt only stared at her, and when he didn't respond, Judith finished up with what she'd come to say. "I need you to come to town tomorrow—to my office. You and your wife need to answer some questions."

The man before her made no response.

Shame washed over her at her lack of control and her unprofessionally delivered rapid-fire words, but before she could begin to make an apology, Jagger took a step back and slammed the door in her face.

Judith stood there dumbfounded as the rain cascaded over her. *What the actual hell?* she thought. Then the raucous barking of the hounds, their horrid stink, the rain pummeling against her cheeks, and the rising wind sent chills through her bones and finally brought her back to the present moment.

Berating herself, she trudged back to the Interceptor, her body shivering from the freezing rain. That could have gone better—or could it? It puzzled her that Jagger had barely reacted to the news of his daughter's death. He'd shown anger and irritation, but no shock or tears. He hadn't even wanted to know what happened to her. Judith ran her top teeth over her bottom lip as she slid into her vehicle, buckled her seatbelt and glanced at herself in her rearview mirror.

It troubled her that she'd reacted to Jagger's behavior the way she did. Still, something about the man had lit a sudden rage inside her, igniting a visceral emotion that she couldn't explain. Perhaps it was his scent. Something about it raised the small hairs on her neck. But maybe she was reading more into the situation than it was. After all, everyone reacted to grief differently. She'd seen her fair share of families devastated by the loss of a loved one. She'd also witnessed the faces of seasoned killers.

Although Judith wanted to give Jagger and his wife some time to deal with the family tragedy, the odd circumstances of this case told her she couldn't wait. *If he doesn't come in tomorrow, I'll come back, probably with reinforcements, and talk to him and his wife at least.* It was important that she figure out how Hellen had died, and something told her she needed to do it quickly.

After Judith started up her Ford, she pulled out her phone and checked the weather. What she saw when she pulled up the screen surprised her. The screen showed no tropical storms or hurricanes. Instead of rain, the forecast showed it was partly cloudy with only a twenty percent chance of rain.

And yet, the water continued to fall from the gray clouds in the sky. If this kept up, the creeks would swell even further, washing more water across the roads and making dirt roads nearly impassable, maybe even taking out some of the weaker areas of the paved ones. When she got back to the office, she'd have to do an in-depth check into this strange weather pattern. Try to determine whether they needed to plan for major flooding in the town.

There were three main roads leading into and out of Iron Shores, and all three crossed over substantial waterways that effectively cut them off when consecutive days of rain caused them to swell. Maybe the rain would finally stop, and she wouldn't have to worry about calling the mayor and requesting emergency teams.

The fire department was always on standby, but she didn't want to call them if she didn't have to. Roy Basset's wife had a brand-new baby at home, and he was on leave spending time with his spouse and infant girl. Janice Lee had a sick grandmother and was seeing her through her remaining days.

As she drove down the mountain, Judith rolled down her window and tried to wash away the memory of the repulsive stench of the place she'd just visited. Sticking her hand out, she caught rainwater in her hand and rubbed it across her face.

Maybe this is nothing. Maybe it will all be just fine, she mused.

The rain battered against her vehicle with even more force now, and she struggled to see the road as she bumped and slid back down the hills toward town.

A voice seemed to hiss inside her brain. *Then again, maybe it won't.*

THOMAS

YONDER

March 12, Tuesday

11:30 AM

When Thomas opened his eyes, his scrub shirt was drenched with perspiration and it clung to his chest. He turned off the heat and opened a window. Water splattered in. The sun would be high in the sky if not for the rain—he was sure. It had to be close to noon.

His fingers stretched to pull his phone from his pocket. Gone. Then he remembered. He'd given it to the girl. To Hatton.

Dammit!

How was he supposed to find her? She hadn't told him her last name. His best guess was to go into the convenience store and see if anyone there knew her.

The name of the place, plastered on a giant white sign on the outside wall, was Ked's Store. The building looked like a little one-story house, probably converted into a business operation once the family decided to open a gas station. When he walked through the door, it reminded him of one of the small stores near the campsites at Lake Anna, where his family used to take him sometimes on summer weekends.

There were essentials like bread, peanut butter, grape jelly, milk, orange juice, hot dogs, Vienna sausages, sardines, bug spray, pickled eggs and fried potato wedges. No one was at the register. He walked around, waiting for someone to return, and decided to check the back. There was another room back there, and he caught a glimpse of large glass jars filled with different herbs and barks. Snake skins, plain fabric dolls, buttons, and red thread.

Thomas started to walk further in, thinking maybe there was someone back there who could help him, when he heard a voice behind him.

"Private quarters back there, sir."

He spun around. An older man, maybe somewhere near his seventies, reached around him and pulled the door shut. "I'll take care of you up front." It was said more like, *"I'll tack car o yu up frunt."* More than once, Thomas had found it interesting that just a few miles outside of Charlottesville, sometimes local dialects and accents changed drastically. Still, he knew what the man meant.

On the way to the register, he plucked a Coke out of the refrigerated section. He put the Coke on the counter.

"That be all for you, sir?"

Thomas nodded. "Yes, sir. But, if you could help me . . . "

The old man squinted at him, his bottom chin pushing his bottom lip up into the top lip. He remained quiet.

Not receiving any encouragement from the old man, Thomas plowed on. "You see, there was this girl, a young lady I brought here a couple of hours ago? Her car was out of gas? Name was Hatton?" He realized every sentence he spoke sounded like a question—something some of the folks did with their speech around here. Evidently, either his manner of speaking or Hatton's name brightened him. It sure wasn't his medical scrubs.

"Well, now." The man brought out a pair of spectacles from his pocket and put them on. "You the young man here, helped our little Hatton?"

Little Hatton? Thomas supposed an old man might see her that way, especially if he knew her when she was a child. That thought was encouraging. He'd probably know where to find her.

"Yessir," Thomas replied, adding a trace of accent. "She borrowed my cell phone. Probably forgot all about it, but I need it back. You know where she lives?"

"Roundabouts," he replied. "Just over yonder." His index finger pointed in the direction of the door.

Thomas had some experience with 'yonder' and 'a ways.' Technically 'yonder' could be anywhere in the direction of a point though sometimes it could mean anywhere in the known universe. But usually, it meant five hundred feet to about ten miles. After ten miles, that's when 'yonder' turned into 'a ways.' As in, *'Boy—you got a ways to go . . . .'* which he'd been told before when asking directions.

"Any idea how I can reach her? Phone number? Directions to her house?"

The man was starting to look annoyed. "Maybe call your own phone number—thought about that? I'll let you borrow my phone. Maybe she'll pick up. Local call, right?"

Thomas wished he'd thought of that sooner. "Yes, local call," and he hoped the old man wouldn't end up with a charge for it. He'd have to check back with him later and pay any charges.

The man brought up a vintage phone from under his desk. Rotary, not touch button. Hard line attached.

Thomas dialed in the numbers, and then there was ringing. It rang long enough for his own voice mail message to answer. He tried once more under the watchful eye of the old man. A voice answered.

"Hello?" It was that sweet voice from yesterday.

"Hatton? It's Thomas Craig. Sorry to bother you, but you still have my cell."

A musical laugh. "Thomas! Yes! I'm *so* sorry. Got caught up in getting gas for my car. Was so worried with it sitting there. My cousin, Bunny, well he gave me a ride, and when I got home I realized I still had your phone. I was gonna go to the hospital. Try to find you later."

He breathed a heavy sigh of relief. "Great. Can I come get it?"

Momentary silence. He wondered if the line had gone dead.

"I need it in case they call me back to the hospital, Hatton. It's important."

Another moment of silence. Thomas was about ready to start talking again when she spoke in a hushed tone.

"It's kind of easy to miss if you're not looking for it. Remember where you saw my car? There's a little gravel road to the right, just down the road, on the same side where the car was. Take that and pull in. You'll see the family graveyard in a field on the left. I'll meet you there." She hung up before he could say anything else.

At least she' hadn't said it was 'a ways.'

The old man gave him a Popeye stare, squinting with one eye while opening the other one wide.

"Thank you kindly," Thomas said.

"Don't mention it," the old man said and stuck out his wavering hand. "Name's Ked, case you didn't guess." He slipped something into Thomas's hand, a little burlap bag, the size of his palm. Red and blue threads sewed it shut. "Don't ask and don't open it—keep it in your car. Glove compartment or under the seat."

"Th-thank you," Thomas stammered, taking the item, not wanting to be rude. "I'm Thomas. Thomas Craig."

"I heard ya on the phone," Ked grunted. "That's an old family name 'round these parts—Craig. Craigs are alright." With that, he left the counter and headed to the back of his shop again.

And Thomas gripped his little burlap bag with red and blue threads and turned toward his car in search of Hatton out yonder.

THOMAS

RUN

*M*arch 12, *Tuesday*

12:45 PM

It was still raining when Thomas pulled onto a muddy road.

The road was about the right distance from where Hatton had said he would find it. *Yonder.*

Tree branches stretched over the narrow lane, their stark boughs hinting at the coming spring with their tiny buds still waiting to burst out into green.

The road sported a smattering of granite stones here and there, but it was more red mud than gravel. Still his tires traveled it okay, and he was thankful for that. The last thing he needed was to get stuck on a muddy road before his next shift.

He'd gone a few yards and was beginning to wonder if he had the right road when he broke through the trees. The graveyard Hatton had mentioned was in a clearing to his left. Old wrought iron surrounded the space where maybe two dozen worn headstones, pale white, some cockeyed and one broken, sat beneath the shelter of an old oak.

And Thomas breathed a sigh of relief. There was Hatton, sitting in her VW. The winds picked up as he pulled over to her. He was about to get out when his SUV passenger door opened, and she hopped in his vehicle instead, wet from the brief transfer from her car to his. Even with the rain on her, he caught that scent again: sandalwood and cinnamon. Something inside him stirred.

She was wearing a different set of jeans, a red-checked flannel shirt, and a large denim jacket hanging open to show a faux woolen sheep lining inside. Her dark hair was loose and wavy, and Thomas couldn't decide if it was dark brown or black.

"Hey, there!" she said, tilting her chin toward him. She lifted her buttocks off the seat and pulled out his phone from her back pocket. "Sorry again. I didn't mean to keep it." Her lips curled into a half-smile, and her eyebrows hitched up a bit as she handed it to him.

Her fingertips touched his as he reached out to clasp the phone. His gaze flicked to her fingers. No wedding ring on her hand. He should have noticed that yesterdayor paid attention to it. God, he was feeling like such a kid.

"No worries," he heard himself respond. "It's all good. Glad you got home okay."

"I still feel bad about leaving you without saying goodbye. It's just that Bunny was there, and—"

"I said, no worries. I'm glad you're okay." Thomas glanced down at his phone. It was after two in the afternoon. He had five hours before he had to be back at work, but he didn't want to be rude, and she was very attractive.

She smiled again. "Let me make it up to you. Dinner at the Tavern later?"

The food at Temper's Tavern was good, and so was the atmosphere, but he shook his head. "I'd love to, but I start my next shift at seven. It's another all-nighter."

"They ever let you guys have a day off or what?"

For a second, he thought she might just be flirting with him. "Yeah—" he started, but his words stuck in his mouth when he spied a battered green pickup barreling their way.

Hatton turned to see what he was staring at and then spun her head back toward him. "You gotta go, Thomas. Get out of here!" Her voice held a tremor. She was clearly afraid, but of what? The person in the truck?

"NOW!" She slid out of the SUV and slammed the door, rain pounding against the window. "Go!"

Thomas hesitated, wondering if he should stay. She might need help. But the terror gripping her face told him he needed to leave and fast. Then he heard gunshots pierce the air.

Survival instinct took over. Hatton clearly knew the man. Could be her father, brother, or someone else, but he was *not* going to stick around and see. Virginia law allowed someone to shoot someone in the defense of others, and all the man had to do was claim he was defending his daughter or whoever she was to him.

He pushed the pedal to the floor and threw the Subaru into a 180-degree spin, nearly crashing into the cemetery fence. Then he was on the muddy red road, spewing what little gravel kept it together, and headed toward home. He glanced back in the rear-view mirror at Hatton standing in the rain, the battered truck pulling beside her, and the tall, lanky male in a sleeveless wife-beater getting out, grabbing her by the arm. It looked as if he were yelling in her face.

Thomas found himself wondering if he was even going to be able to grab some sleep. The strange but alluring Hatton, her peculiar behavior, and the man in the green pickup barreling down toward them in fury would certainly keep his brain running full speed by the time he went to bed. All he could think about was seeing her again. He pulled out onto the main road, still picturing her face when an oncoming car plowed into his SUV.

JUDITH

BREATHE

*M*arch 12, Tuesday

1:10 PM

Judith had just slid into the seat at her desk at the station. Pulling out a cloth lunch tote, she was happy to finally be able to eat her peanut butter and jelly sandwich and dill-flavored Kettle chips, when a radio call came from I.S. E-Comms. That's what they called their 911 Emergency Call station. And theirs operated differently—because I.S. was a different ballgame. The voice was Darla's.

"MVA up on Route 6, Chief. Four or five miles from Ked's Store near Hazard Creek. Ambulance en route."

"Ten-four." Determined not to miss another meal, Judith scooped up her sandwich and chips, grabbed her water bottle, and headed for her Ford. Her hopes of getting off work in time to see the girls before they went to bed were dashed to pieces, but she'd be damned if this kind of thing would keep her up all night.

Tomorrow was Harvey's turn for a twenty-four-hour shift. For the hundredth time—and probably more than that— she swore she wasn't going to answer her phone on her day off.

When she stepped out the door, Judith felt her heart deflate like a flattening tire. Water pooled in the road and in the yard across from the station. As she hopped into her Interceptor, she checked to make sure she had a rain poncho on board.

She headed toward Route 6, hoping to holy hell the crash wasn't someone she knew, though likely it was. It was mid-afternoon, so it probably wasn't someone out driving drunk. It was a Monday in March, during a damned purgatory of a rainstorm.

If it were any other day of the week but Monday, it would be something like texting while driving. Judith flipped on her police bar and headed in the direction of the crash.

Jesus, don't let it be one of the teens from town, she thought as she raced along the rain-drenched highway. *Don't let it be any of the family, or . . .*

She slowed a bit, seeing a cloudy darkness ahead of her, momentarily figuring it was related to the heavy rains. But the closer she got, the more a strange feeling crept over her—almost as if something were tickling the top of her head. Testing. Probing.

Her normally calm breath quickened. She slowed her breathing, forcing it to be steady and even, and studied the darkness ahead.

It's just a thick fog bank, nothing else.

Squinting, Judith became convinced she wasn't seeing ahead properly. And yet, her mind couldn't conjure any reasonable explanation as to why the cloud in front of her was so dark. So densely black. And she couldn't turn around. She had to go through it to get to the crash. Still, she halted in front of it, watching it hang there above the pavement. Yet her mind couldn't explain why the cloud in front of her was so dark and threatening—like a predator waiting for prey. Her throat constricted.

And there was that testing, a sense of something probing at the top of her head again, almost a questioning tapping—like one of those bobble-birds—its beak coming down on the crown of her head, planting sinister kisses with every dip of its bill. A chill ran up her spine and she felt the fine hairs on her neck stand up.

A Mack truck burst through the cloud, its horn blaring so loud that she yelled in surprise. It blasted past her, the black mist swirling in curls as if inviting her in.

It's nothing, her brain insisted. *People are waiting on you to investigate and then write up the report on the crash.* Her brain fought, trying not to give in to a rising fear that seemed to crawl up from her belly and grip her throat from the inside.

Nothing to be worried about.

That was a phrase her father would say when the thunder roared and lightning threw jagged bolts across the sky. He'd hold her, stroke her hair, and point at Mother Nature's fireworks, as he called it, teaching her to mark time between the flashes of lightning and the crashes of thunder so she'd know when the storm was moving away.

Nothing to be worried about. He'd said the same thing as they sat beside the bed in the hospice, both of them holding her mother's hands until aggressive cancer seized her airway and stopped her lungs from breathing.

And he'd said the same thing as he held and rocked her, trying to find a way to make his six-year-old daughter understand that Mommy's spirit had gone to a better place and that the body that once fixed her scrambled eggs and orange juice for breakfast was now nothing more than an empty shell. But she didn't understand because there'd be no better place her mommy could be than with her and Daddy.

Mommy would find out. She'd want to come back. Mommy had to come back.

A month after her mother's death, her father had been unable to return to work, unable to eat, unable to do those things a father should do for a daughter without a mother. One day, while she was sitting on the floor watching cartoons, she'd caught him staring at her with those sad, thoughtful eyes. She'd started to cry because the look on his face was so, so sad, as if his heart was broken to pieces and would never mend. As if she wasn't enough to make him happy.

He'd scooped her up. "I love you," he said. "Don't you ever forget that." And he'd carted her to her room.

Nothing to be worried about.

Those were the last words Daddy had said as he made a strange game of fixing her a bed on the floor of her closet. He'd decorated a pile of blankets with pillows and her childhood quilt. Brought her Droopy, her stuffed dog, and her Raggedy Ann. There was a grilled cheese on a red plate for an in-bed picnic. He'd even let her use his favorite water bottle, the one he always carried with him when he was out on patrol.

"You go to sleep now," he'd said tickling her into giggling fits. Then, he'd hugged her tight and kissed her goodnight. He'd smelled of English Leather and whiskey.

Later, when she'd wakened after sleeping, she'd tried to leave the closet. She turned the knob and pushed only to find out the door wouldn't open. She'd kicked it and yelled for Daddy to come get her.

When he didn't come, she yelled even more, then she screamed. After some long hours, with her grilled cheese eaten and water bottle empty, she'd had to pee in a corner of the closet, trying unsuccessfully not to get it on her covers. Her hands had grown sore from beating the door with her fists, and with every moment that passed, the walls of the closet seemed to press up against her—closer, tighter.

She was asleep when Officer Dennis Murdock, his father's partner, finally opened the door. He had come to look for her daddy. She didn't find out until she was maybe eleven that her father had hanged himself in the shower. He'd twisted the noose around his neck over and over, then let his body weight cause him to pass out so he'd asphyxiate.

He'd been naked, supposedly to make it easier for whoever found him to clean up the mess. He'd left two farewell notes on Murdock's desk. One for him, and one for Judith to receive when she was grown.

Her uncle and his wife raised her in the very house that was her father's. They were grateful for the bigger house and the extra land they received with her father's death. It was actually Judith's house, which was kept in trust until the day she turned eighteen, but her uncle and his wife moved in and managed it after agreeing to raise her.

They were farmers and they used her father's land to raise a few cows and grow soybeans, corn and grains. They were strict and not exactly loving even though they had no kids of their own. If she got out of line, her uncle applied a homemade paddle to her bottom and his wife would strike her with switches that Judith had to go out to the willow tree and pick herself.

Luckily, Judith was rarely out of line. In the morning and after school, she helped with the farm, feeding and milking cows, helping with harvests, and whatever needed doing. There was no time for friends, no time for boys.

When she graduated from high school, she applied and entered the police academy. She passed with flying colors, winning the Director's Award for Academic Excellence and the Physical Fitness Award. She did very well in firearms but came closest to winning another award in Emergency Vehicle Operations (EVOC), which included precision driving.

After graduation, she examined her options and decided she'd prefer to work with the county police. It was there that she fell in love for the first time. And probably the last.

It wasn't until Judith had finished her police academy training and Dennis Murdock had pinned her badge on her that he told her the truth about her father's death.

And that truth—something she'd always known somehow, like a dirty little secret locked in the back of her brain—did something to her. Broke her on the inside and made her stronger at the same time. But she'd never overcome her fear of tight spaces, of feeling closed in—of not being able to escape.

If only he'd told me the truth.

Over the radio, dispatch called. "Chief Ware—what's your twenty?" It brought her back to the present and to that black cloud still sitting in front of her.

"Nearly there, Darla." She'd forgotten all protocol. *Dammit. This is Iron Shores. I'm the Chief of Police. I'm needed, and this black cloud cannot stand in my way. Go through, over, under, or around— but I'm getting by!*

Judith set her jaw and edged slowly toward the cloud, her foot barely on the gas. She inhaled a deep breath and drove her Interceptor in.

THOMAS

CRASH

*M*arch 12, Tuesday

1:10 PM

What the hell?

Thomas's body felt as if he'd been four-point staked to the center of Santo Domingo street during the Running of the Bulls in Spain, and every single bull had trampled him. He was still in the driver's seat, but something warm was leaking into his eyes. He wiped his forehead and smelled the iron scent of blood.

My blood?

A voice seemed to laugh in the back of his head. *Who else, genius?*

A car horn to his right was blaring, not stopping. He could barely move his head, but when he did, he couldn't make out what he was seeing. It looked like the entire passenger side of his Forrester crumpled in toward him.

He tried to clear his vision, wiping his eyes once more. Something protruded through his shattered passenger window. It wasn't until bright lights flashed in the air that he realized the thing in the window was a head. Maybe with those long-beaded braids and thin neck, a woman's head. He couldn't see the face because the head slumped forward, but the neck looked slim.

He knew he should stay still and let the paramedics do their job, but the ER physician in him wanted to get out and check her pulse, to see if she was breathing, and if so, to get her to the ground and stabilize her quickly—treat her for shock. He could move his head a little and wiggle his fingers and toes, but he was stuck. A Mack truck hadn't struck him, but it sure felt like it.

He'd grown up in Ventura, California, and he surfed every chance he got when he was young. He didn't live near a truck stop or know anyone with a semi, but he loved all things "truck." Next to his surfboards in his room, he'd had tons of model trucks and various styles of the Mack Truck.

Now, the part of his brain that knew he needed to sit still until the paramedics pulled him out started running through all the facts he knew about Mack trucks. That would keep him mentally occupied for a moment. He figured he was one of a handful of people who knew that Mack Trucks were created in 1900 by the Mack brothers, Jack and Gus.

The brothers started out with a carriage company, Fallesen and Berry, but their first motorized vehicle was produced in 1900. That was when they moved their business from Brooklyn, New York, to Allentown, Pennsylvania. *And now they were in Greensboro . . .*

Someone was prying open his door. He slowly turned his head, and for a moment, just a brief moment, he felt pressure on the top of his skull. He likely had a contrecoup injury from his head smacking his side window and bouncing back, but that didn't explain the strange sensation at the crown of his head.

Then, hands were on him, checking his pulse. Two of the town paramedics, Sammi and—what was the other guy's name? He searched inside his head for it. He knew the guy's name. In just a moment . . .

"Pulse is rapid but steady at one thirty," Sammi yelled out. "BP is one-fifty over ninety-five. A bit up there, but stable."

I never have a BP that high, Thomas wanted to say. *And what was the other guy's name?* He tried to turn his head to look at them, to see the other guy's face, but it hurt too much to do that—then he remembered. *Nick. His name is Nick.*

Time seemed to move in slow motion. Someone slipped a neck collar around his cervical vertebrae to stabilize his neck before they moved him to the ground onto a stiff backboard.

"I'm alright," he tried to tell them, but the words were garbled. "Check on the other . . ." but his words just did not come out right.

Thomas needed to tell them, had to tell them, to check on the person hanging through his passenger window. Then he heard Nick emit a sound somewhere between a yell and a scream.

"No! Oh God, no, no! Sammi, quick! We gotta get her out! Marlie! Marlie!"

Sammi darted out of Thomas's line of vision.

"Dear sweet Jesus," Thomas heard him say.

Nick yelled, "Save her, Sammi! Bro, do something!"

Then Sammi's heart-wrenching voice sounded so faint he could barely hear it. "Man, I'm so sorry. She's gone, Bro. I checked her. Her injury—it had to be instant. I love you, man, but we gotta help this dude. The doc's here is still with us.

Just like that. Thomas mused, his eyes feeling so heavy now. "Lives are gone, just like that," he mumbled out loud. What he really needed now was some sleep. He hoped he wasn't bleeding to death while the two EMTs mourned over the dead woman. Then Sammi was at his side again, touching his shoulder.

"Stay with us, Doc. No dozing after a wreck like this, right? Concussion, ya know."

Thomas groaned, half in pain and half with the realization that Maria would be waiting for him to come in for his shift, and instead of being a helpful pair of hands, he was about to be the reason she'd have her hands full tonight. After they loaded him into the ambulance, he heard the other guy—*Nick. That's right*—calling in the CRASH report.

"Glasgow Coma Scale, ten," Nick radioed through his sobs. "Respirations, twenty. Pulse rapid at one-thirty. Wearing a seatbelt—" Then Nick broke down.

Sammi took over. "Lacerations to the victim's left ear and forehead. Maybe a cervical or thoracic injury. We got a collar on him, and he's on a board. Possible left dislocated shoulder. Probably fractures of the humerus, radius, and ulna. We've extracted and immobilized him." Sammi paused. "Additional victim on scene. Female, mid-twenties. DOA."

Nick continued to sob, and as is often the case in their rural settings, the voice over the radio became less formal. "Who was it, Sammi?"

"Nick's sister," Sammi radioed tightly, careful not to state her name, not that it would make a difference to anyone in the area. Everyone knew who Nick's sister was. "Ejected from the car, through the windshield, and into the other car's passenger window. No seatbelt." He took a breath, steadying himself. "ETA fifteen minutes. Nick couldn't leave her. We have both souls on board."

Both souls. Isn't that a weird phrase for an EMT to say? And technically, the other passenger wasn't a "soul" anymore. Her spirit was gone. Pain radiated up Thomas's left arm. *Hope it's still the golden hour,* he thought. *People always do best when they get treatment* within the *first sixty minutes after a serious injury.*

Nick sat in the back next to his sister and watched him while Sammi drove. Thomas could barely see anything else around him. His vision was blurry, and everything started to fade into a misty cloud of oblivion. He felt Nick touch him and heard his voice tell him he needed to stay awake, but Thomas was so tired. He wondered how much experience the shock trauma surgeon on duty today had with car accidents.

And what was that noise growing louder in his ears? Some kind of ringing. The nerve network disruption was giving him full-fledged tinnitus.

Then he realized the sound wasn't a ringing at all. It had started off softly at first, but now it was more guttural. Now he could identify the noise—it was the harsh caw of crows, a multitude of them.

His head hurt now and ached badly, but all he could hear, aside from the ambulance siren, was a constant cawing—as if hundreds of the black-feathered birds were trying to force themselves into his head.

JUDITH

CLOSER

*M*arch 12, Tuesday

1:25 PM

Judith was still picking her way through the dark mist when the harsh cawing of crows filled her ears. Accompanying them was the telltale sound of an ambulance siren. She cursed at herself.

If she hadn't let this black mist slow her down, she could have taken photos with each driver still in position. As it was, she'd have to work the scene and do what she could to get the best shots possible.

Maybe the paramedics took some shots. She hoped so. If Sammi was there and he had time, she knew she could rely on him. But paramedics didn't always think about things like that in the heat of the moment. Saving lives was, of course, more important.

Judith pushed her vehicle forward a bit faster, seeing the red and blue flashes of the ambulance lights. She was out of the cloud in seconds and headed toward the crash. The sun was still up, hidden in the gray clouds, but it would be dark soon.

She stole a glance at her rearview mirror, and that strange dark cloud was still there, its mist swirling behind her. For a brief second, she thought she saw—but no—that couldn't be right. A figure of a hunched person walking out of the cloud and dark-winged creatures flying in the air over it?

Judith flicked her gaze to the front, making sure the way was clear, and then chanced another look. The figure and the winged creatures were gone. And so was the sound of that cawing—the echo of it half in her ears, half in her head.

"Shake it off, Jude," she said out loud.

Her therapist had often told her that talking to herself was perfectly acceptable and could be very healthy. The woman had reassured her that sometimes people do these things to process terrifying memories or moments of stress.

"Of course," she'd said, half humorously and half with an air of seriousness, "when the voices talk back, *that's* when you've got a problem."

JAGGER

RITES

*M*arch 12, Tuesday

5:00 PM

Jagger Profitt brushed the damp beads of sweat away from his face. He didn't much like outsiders. To tell the truth, he downright hated them.

Outsiders had no earthly business in his town, much less on his hill. And it was his life-sworn duty to guard this place.

Still, outsiders had their uses. And soon it would be time to make sacrifices. Time to make the sweet Deathwing Queen dreams he had, night after night, come true.

He slipped an item from his pocket. Soft braided hair from his daughter. He laid the blonde lock in front of the giant bird statue. Its black wings were spread as if poised for flight, and its icy blue eyes stared through him, cold—freezing.

Jagger knew the same cold madness roiled in his own eyes. He thought of his father and his grandfather. They'd shown him this cave and taught him the rites.

"I will do as you say," he spoke reverently. "And all of the ignorant will soon understand the awesome power you wield. Yes, they will fall down before you once more. You and your kind shall prosper. Through you, we will grow strong!"

Pain suddenly welled up in Jagger's chest and caused him to gasp. It was as if Raum had wrapped her spectral claw around his heart and squeezed. She was warning him. And he knew what she wanted. He whispered the incantation he'd been taught on his seventh birthday.

"Furca na alle laris Raum."

The end of the sentence sounded more like a wheeze, but the pressure gradually released around his heart and could suck the cold sweet air into his lungs once more.

"Furca na alle laris Raum," he continued to chant. He placed a Tarot card onto the altar—one he had drawn himself using his own blood—the Five of Pentacles. Then he lined up five shiny new pennies below the card. The pain receded, and all it left behind was Jagger's increasing resolve.

Soon, the Deathwing Queen would rip life away from the town.

From death, life would rise—and the Harvesters would spring forward and fly. Their terrifying feathers would blanket the sky. Oh, but how wonderful and amazing—and for his service, his reward for growing the Harvesters, the Queen would add years and years to his family's lives—if they were worthy.

And he wanted them all to be worthy. His great-grandfather had lived well beyond a hundred and fifty years. Unfortunately, Jagger's father had died much sooner. An accident had interrupted his plan to live a very long life.

Well, Jagger *called* it an accident, anyway. And Jagger—he planned to outlive them all. Oh yes, *all* the others, those who laughed at him—those who thought he was feeble-minded and strange—well, they would see the real power of Raum, but only when it was too late.

Jagger had already sacrificed one daughter for the cause. He swore he wouldn't sacrifice another child. Not if he could help it.

Death was for those who deserved it—those like the simpering town folk who gathered in their little white churches and sang hymns to a god who never listened and likely never existed. And now it was time for the Deathwing Queen to take over the land. Time for her to turn it into the long-life paradise of Jagger's dreams.

JAGGER

WARNING

*M*arch 12, Tuesday

5:30 PM

Jagger stared at the time on his phone once more and then forced himself to stand still. He felt like pacing, like tapping his boots, but he had to practice discipline.

If the bitch doesn't get here soon, though, there'll be hell to pay. His patience had limits. He hated standing out in the open. The walk to the power lines wasn't far from the cave, but it was further than he liked to go.

As if the Universe understood, he suddenly caught the sound of a dirt bike engine coming toward him and then saw the girl riding up along the trail underneath the powerlines. It took only a couple of minutes for her to pull up alongside him.

"Hey, Uncle!" Hannah's voice was muffled, but he understood.

Jagger didn't say anything at first. Just handed her a fanny pack that jingled when his niece strapped it on. She secured it in place.

He admired the fresh tattoo on her wrist: a flying crow gripping a skull and flying forward toward the onlooker. His own tattoo, like that one, was worn and faded.

Jagger jerked his chin at her pack. "Don't touch 'em, understand? Wear double gloves. Just drop 'em where I told you."

The girl nodded. Her long hair stuck out from the bottom of her helmet. The hair was a lovely golden color. Much like her cousin's had been.

"All right. You can go," Jagger said.

The girl spun her bike wheels in the mud and headed back down the hill toward town. Lucky for Jagger, he'd stepped back a bit, or he'd be wearing clay. He almost got splattered. If he had, he woulda been mighty pissed—but . . . no.

Jagger grinned. His plan was in full motion, and nothing could stop it now.

BOBBY

TAP TAP TAPPING

*M*arch 13, Wednesday

0:45 AM

Bobby Morris was on the night watch at the Richmond Office of the Medical Examiner. He had agreed to do the extra night for the time and a half pay, but tonight, he regretted it. He was more tired now than when COVID had hit the area like a sledgehammer and the bodies just kept rolling in.

What he needed was some time to sit back in his recliner, pop a Bud, and watch *Deadliest Catch*. Instead, he was babysitting bodies.

The morgue carried a shrouded silence within it at night, as if it was buried six feet underground. With only a few lights on, it was a creepy place. Especially in the autopsy bay. Six stainless steel gurneys butted up against sinks that collected and washed body fluids away after the dead were opened and eviscerated.

The best part about it, though, was that he never had to see the stiffs. By the time he got there, usually, everything was neat and pretty. The smell of decay still lingered in the air, particularly after an autopsy on a decomposed body, but it diminished as the staff used disinfectants to clean the tables and sinks.

An odd sound in the hallway near the larger refrigerator room— Bobby called it the *stifferator*—caught his ear. He paused *Bill and Ted's Excellent Adventure* on his phone and listened intently. Was that a tapping? Or some kind of knocking?

With trepidation, he hefted his pudgy frame out of the chair and shuffled toward the sound. The large stainless-steel door in front of him was the only barrier between him and at least thirty corpses. Another tapping. Definitely from behind the door. Bobby shook his head, slow and determined.

Nope. I ain't gonna open it. Long as whatever is in there stays in there, I'm good.

When the door handle suddenly jiggled. Bobby jumped back, staring. He was sure he'd locked the door—that nothing was coming out or getting in. The tapping sound returned, this time more persistent.

Bobby did the most logical thing he could think to do. He did an about-face, marched back into the security office, locked his door, and kept his eyes trained on the cameras for a few seconds. Satisfied that the door was an inpenetrable force-field, he pulled his headphones out of his backpack, wrapped them around his ears, and plugged them into his phone.

By his logic, what he didn't hear couldn't hurt him, and he'd just do his job—glimpsing at the cameras now and then, while watching his movie. There were only a few more hours to go, and then his shift was over. After that, hell, he was taking some days off. Fuck them if they couldn't find someone to take his place.

The tapping continued even though Bobby couldn't hear it anymore. It continued until the sun broke over the horizon, and then it fell silent.

CHRISTOPHER

PASSAGE

*M*arch 13, Wednesday

8:00 AM

Christopher stared out of his kitchen window, sipping his coffee. He enjoyed drinking it —half coffee and half oat milk—laced with a touch of maple syrup for sweetener and a sprinkle of nutmeg and cayenne.

Another freaking day of rain, he sighed. The puddles outside kept growing larger, and he couldn't help but wonder how long it would be before the rain stopped. His weather app called for periods of sun, but not a shred of sunlight had broken through the clouds in almost a week.

And then his thoughts turned to his recent dreams. They were more like nightmares, but when he woke with his mouth open in a silent scream, there were only a few scraps of memory he could string together to help him remember why they were so terrifying.

Black feathers. Icy eyes. A drum beating like the rhythm of a heart. And then something snapped at his arms, tugged at his elbow, and he was trying hard to run but found he was barely moving. Something hard and sharp snapped at his neck—

A sudden pounding at his front door nearly caused Christopher to jump, and he spilt coffee on his lap. His gaze darted over to the digital clock on the microwave. Eight o'clock.

He drained his cup before answering the door. Most people called Christopher on the phone or shot him a text before they dropped in. When he opened the door, Job Graves stood there in front of him. His dark skin, black hat, and black rain slicker made him look like the old comic book character *The Shadow*. All he was missing was a red scarf.

Next to him was Grinch, the friendliest pit bull Christopher had ever known. The canine's mouth stretched wide in a panting grin that was larger than his head, if that were possible.

"Hey, there, Rev! Fine day, ain't it?"

Job makes a perfect Shadow, Christopher thought. Then he realized he'd been rude—just standing in the doorway staring at the man.

"I'm sorry. Come in, come in, Job!" Christopher opened the screen door and eyed the Grinch. "Yes, you too, fella. It's wetter than the river out there!" He smiled back at Job and patted Grinch's brindled head, hoping to convey his pleasure at seeing the man and man's best friend.

Job laughed as he stepped inside. "It's okay, Rev. I know what you're thinking. Red scarf is missin', right?" His voice dropped low, and he said in a forbidding tone, "W*ho knows what evil lurks in the hearts of men?"*

A strange tingle rippled over Christopher's skull, and for a moment, he had an odd sensation of being internally scanned.

Job smiled, the corners of his mouth reaching for his ears as if competing with his dog, displaying almost every one of his Colgate-white teeth. He chuckled, his tone deep and rolling. Everything about Job said *I don't give a damn about the weather. I'm happy to be here and ready to work.*

"Me and Grinch can only stay for a minute though," Job said. "We gots ta get started soon as we can." He hung close to the door and looked out. "This keeps goin' on, me and the Grinch are gonna need pon-*toons* for Persephone!"

Persephone was Job's backhoe. Technically, she was Persephone number 3.

Grinch set about sniffing the kitchen floor, probably hoping to find a scrap or two on the linoleum.

Job was an oddity in Iron Shores, even though he was native to the area. He came from modest means. His father had worked for the Virginia Department of Transportation or VDOT, and his mother once served as the local librarian.

Christopher recalled Renny, at the Tattered Page, telling him she'd gone to school with Job and that, growing up, Job was both class clown and wicked smart. Never made less than an A in any of his classes and graduated top of his class.

Job had gone to UVA on a full scholarship and studied anthropology. Graduated magna cum laude. Then he'd continued on to get his master's and finally, his Ph.D. focusing on the anthropology of religions or something like that.

For some reason, after graduating with his doctorate, Job had come back to Iron Shores. He never used his degrees to procure work despite university and military offers. Instead, he'd bought a backhoe and set up business as the local gravedigger. If anyone met Job for the first time on the street, his manner and the way he dressed and talked would cause them to assume he was a simple man with a basic education.

Christopher shook the man's hand with a double-hand grasp. Handshakes had fallen out of favor due to COVID, but Christopher kept the practice with those he knew well. Those who expected the tradition. And Job was such a man.

The gravedigger was a couple of inches taller than Christopher, and although he had to be in his fifties, he looked much younger. And those dark chocolate eyes of his almost always seemed like they were laughing. Now and then, his irises seemed rimmed in gold. Rarely did their expression change.

Before Christopher could ask Job how he was, the gravedigger jumped right in.

"What plots you want to be dug, Rev? Man, Hatcher's funeral home is really hoppin', and that's saying something for our little I.S.!"

"Plots? Plural? There's more than one?"

"Oh, yes, sir." Job raised an eyebrow. "Hatcher's not call you? You got two more customers. Rack 'em and stack 'em, Rev!"

Christopher was glad they were inside and alone. He figured that whatever words Job needed to say to do his business was okay, so long as the families didn't hear it. Grave digger/mortuary humor, death investigator, police, and medical humor could get quite dark, and the everyday public would never appreciate it at their expense.

"No, Hatcher's did not call." Why hadn't Marty or Justin called him? "You mind telling me about the others?"

Job's grin turned into a half-smile which told Christopher he was thinking whether he should say more. Then a slight angle of his head showed he'd decided.

"You hear about the accident yesterday? Route 6 near Ked's?"

Christopher shook his head. He hadn't talked to Judith since yesterday. He usually got that intel from her.

"Young ER doc was hurt bad in a crash. Marlie Moon T-boned him coming over a hill. Doc's at JRG. By all accounts, he should be dead. Marlie didn't make it." This was one of those rare times Job's eyes didn't laugh. "It's no wonder Nick didn't ring you. Probably assumed you already knew the way word gets 'round here. Hell's bells, you can't step outta your house without folks knowing what underwear threads you got on for the day."

Marlie Moon. Nick's younger sister. She'd just turned twenty on the fourteenth of February. Christopher didn't remember things like birthdays, though he did try, but Marlie often used to say she was born on "Love-Day."

"The other guy," Job cut in on his thoughts, "was someone local, though I never heard his name before—which for me, ya gotta know, is weirdio." Job's eyes widened as if to emphasize *weirdio* to make it extra weird.

It was true what he said, too. In most towns, no one knew their local gravedigger by name, but just about everyone in Iron Shores and the surrounding counties knew Job. He was that kind of guy— funny and fun. He drank beer at the River Rage and sometimes helped with raft tours at the Foam and Rock. Making fun of the "jack of all trades" phrase, he called himself the "Job for all jobs." Local handyman and gravedigger extraordinaire.

"What was his name?" It probably wouldn't matter, except that the burial plot needed a name.

"Vik, something. Yeah. Viktor. Viktor Odol. Someone called it in to Darla on the 911." He chuckled. "I remembered it because the guy's first name is like Vicks VaporRub, and the last name sounds like 'odor.' "

But the name struck a hard chord in Christopher's chest. He knew Viktor Odol. He'd met the man twenty-four years ago and had been lucky to escape with his life.

Job's keen eyes searched Christopher's face and then his eyes widened. "You know who Odol is!" Job said as the expression on his face opened up like a giant blue morning glory. Incredulity dawned in his eyes. He tone made it sound as if he'd suddenly discovered the beginning of a new mystery, and Christopher was the key.

"Well, sort of," Christopher inhaled a deep breath and let it out. "Honestly, my encounter with him literally scared the BeJezzus out of me. I usually prefer not to talk about it." He tugged on his rain boots and grabbed a black umbrella. His house was right next to the church, near the graveyard. There was no need to drive, but when they stepped outside, he discovered the storm winds had picked up, and his umbrella was nearly useless against the side-blowing rain.

Christopher pointed out a plot to Job situated near a stained-glass window by the church. "That one's for Hellen." Job ambled to the spot, kneeled and took note of the number on the plot marker. Their boots made sucking sounds in the mud as they walked, and Christopher couldn't help but wonder, *How in the world is Job going to keep the graves from filling with water before the burial?*

But he also knew that the man was good at what he did. He might spill coffee trying to serve it while helping out at Bia Cup but the man was a genius.

The other two plots Christopher had in mind for the next burials were further out, but he'd never needed graves during such a rainy period. Not even during the pandemic.

"You sure you're going to be able to dig here?" Christopher eyed the waterlogged area. He'd seen Job dig a lot of graves, but this had to be the wettest circumstance they'd ever come across.

"Don't worry, Rev. I got this," said Job, and as they walked back toward his house, Job started whistling the tune "Slip Slidin' Away."

While Christopher almost wanted to watch Job and the Grinch do their magic and create those three graves under what were near-impossible conditions, he had no obligations for this Monday. There were no congregants to call on, and those he considered seeing were at work. Nope. Today, he planned to make his favorite toasted Havarti and Rye cheese sandwich, crack open a bottle of Johnny Walker Blue at 10 AM, and drift away with Dobie Gray while he wrote in his journal.

The JW Blue was a gift from one of his patrons, a Mr. Mel Rose, who loved his sermons and daily blog entries. And the blue label on the bottle seemed to go with the blues casting sorrow over the day. Blues—like burying Hellen's body, and like drowning his feelings about Judith — and—what else?

He paused and shuddered, a sudden picture filling his mind of the monster that chased him in his dream. It had snapped at his neck, and made him scream. And now, memories of Viktor surfaced as well, and he wondered why he had forgotten about Viktor all this time, until Job said his name?

That time with Victor, it was like a hazy dream, but Christopher knew in his heart it wasn't. He knew it was real because he still had something Viktor had given him. He'd just forgotten where it had come from. His fingers reached up to rub the dollar-coin sized medallion that hung around his neck on a silver chain. The design was intricate—molded with interesting runes on each side that were laced with fine gold. Christopher had struggled to recall where the piece came from until now—until the memory of Viktor's rose like tendrils of smoke in his mind, accented with his gentle voice—"This is for you." They were his last words before they parted.

Job must have been pumped to hear about Viktor Odol because he knocked on Christopher's door again an hour later. It generally took him a good forty minutes each to dig a grave. "Got 'em all done," he said. "Waterproofed and everything." He was rocking on his feet in anticipation of a brand-new adventure tale and even Grinch had a little extra happy wag in his tail.

Christopher handed Job a hand-towel to dry his face, and after mopping the water from it, Job ran the cloth over his head, drying his black-gray crop. Someone had carved designs in his hair, Christopher noted, or maybe Job had done it himself but he wasn't going to ask the man what they meant. If he never knew, then that was fine with him. Instead, he used a dry towel to rub Grinch dry and then spoiled him with a Pupperoni treat. While Christopher didn't personally have a pet, he kept dog treats just for these occasions.

"You want a drink?" Christoher held up the bottle of Johnny and a clean glass. Job eyed them both and nodded with a smile.

"Don't mind if I do. Thank ya. Grandpaps always said it's after five somewhere in the world, right? Kinda weird folks have this hang-up about when it's too early to have a drink. Never matters to me."

Job accepted the glass from Christopher and helped himself to a chair at the kitchen table. Christopher poured another two fingers into his glass and sat down opposite Job. Without waiting for Job to start asking questions, he launched into the tale of Viktor Odol.

"Geez, Job," he started," be patient with me, alright? This happened a long time ago, so maybe I don't remember everything right. It was a rough time in my life—and there's something like neurobiology of trauma that they talk about today where a person has trouble with exact memories—but I swear on all faiths and their bibles on the Earth, I believe *this* really happened."

Job leaned in close as if he were ready to hear a secret—which, in a way, it was. Christopher had never told anyone what he was going to tell Job today.

"It was February 2nd, my birthday, and I'd just turned ten. But there was no party for me except the one my parents had for themselves. That evening after school, my ma fed me shots of tequila and told me I was a man. After a while, maybe when she thought I'd be feeling the booze, she started rubbing her hand up against my," Christopher coughed and cleared his throat. "Uh, between my legs if you catch my meaning," he continued, and he felt his cheeks burn with searing heat as he found he couldn't say out loud what she did to him.

Job was silent, and his eyes took on that rare non-laughing quality that was— if anything —embracing. Accepting.

"So, that night, I crept out of my bedroom window and swore I'd get away from that house, away from her—far away. I brought my backpack with me, and had a bottle of water, a pack of Saltines, and an apple inside it." He smiled to himself. "I remember the moon was full, and I thought that maybe between its light and the snacks, I could get pretty far. It was cold too. February's always so cold. But I didn't care, I was so hell-bent on leaving. I headed into the woods on the east side of town—that area along the river, you know where I mean?"

Job nodded slightly, rapt with attention.

"I must have walked at least two miles. I don't know how far, really. But after picking my way along the river, I saw a light.

Several lights, actually." Christopher swallowed. He'd never told a soul this story, and he was amazed he was telling it to Job now. But there was something about Job that seemed to make the telling okay and so he pressed on.

"As I got closer, I heard voices and saw wooden buildings with fresh paint and signs. Except, they were old-timey, in a style that looked more than a hundred years old. I recall stepping out onto a dusty dirt road, and suddenly freezing in my tracks as I stared at two large horses and a carriage about ready to run me over. In a flash, something pushed me hard from the side, and I hit the ground. The carriage passed by, and the boy who had tackled me helped me up from the ground."

That was the easy part of the story. A mystery town along the river set in the 1800s. Surely, any boy could dream such a thing without it being true. But, Christopher knew if he glanced at Job, he wouldn't be able to go on with the tale, so he stared hard at his yellow rubber boots as more words found their way out of his mouth.

"The boy, well, he was maybe ten years old, the same age as me. Wore a cap, a white shirt, and dark pants with suspenders. Old fashioned style, like after the war. But his hair was the whitest hair I'd ever seen, and he had crystal blue eyes so light and bright they almost looked white, too." Christopher paused to rub his eyes and he could picture the boy clear as day. "He spoke to me right away, like saving me by dodging the horses was no big deal. 'I'm Viktor, with a K,' he said. 'Wanna play?' Of course, being so young myself, I told him my name and said that I did. It didn't matter that it was dark or that the hours might be stretching into the early morning. I had no idea what time of day it was and didn't care."

Grinch padded over to Christopher's side, then sat and licked his hand. He patted the dog's head, finding some comfort in the animal's gesture.

"And I don't remember feeling tired at all. We climbed trees, ran around the town, drank water from a hand pump."

"'You wanna see where I live?' Viktor asked me. And I said yes. He took me on a little pathway along the edge of town. His home was not like I imagined—me thinking maybe it was some little clapboard house like many of the others. Instead, his house was made of brick, two stories high. Fairly fancy.

"'You hungry?' he asked me as we went through the front door. I didn't consider it at the time, but the house was a bit strange. The entrance was narrow, and the red brick ran up, creating an arch. The door was made from a heavy wood. Oak, maybe."

Christopher sniffed. The damp cold in the air had caused his nose to run. He grabbed a tissue from the Kleenex box on the table, blew his nose and continued. "The first thing I noticed when I entered the house was the smell. It was peculiar, like the smell you might be used to when cooking a cow or a pig, but different at the same time."

"'Let me go check the kitchen and see if it's clear,' Viktor told me. I remember nodding my head but feeling a really odd sensation on my body, like a hundred spiders were crawling up my back. At the entrance, I noticed a little table with some papers on it, and I wandered over to check it out. The papers were letters. One of them was addressed to a Mr. and Mrs. Asir Odol. The town address was Passage, Virginia. The last name and the town became fixed in my brain when I saw the postmark. Eighteen ninety-seven.

At first, I thought it was strange—that someone had postmarked the date wrong. But the longer I stood there and thought about the date and the name of the town, the more unnerved I got. You might not have heard the name Viktor Odol, but I'm guessing you know the town name Passage, right?"

Job nodded real slow, his face like a glass window showing the multitude of wheels turning in his brain.

"So, just as I was thinking I needed to get out of there, Viktor comes running back with another boy. His brother. Introduces him as Amadeus. For some reason, it's a name I remembered as well, once I heard Viktor's name again. Just then, a large clock in the living room chimed twelve times. I guessed it was in the living room since I could only see a sofa partway from where I stood. Forgetting I'd run away, I remember thinking how late it was and that I had to get home."

"When I told Viktor this, he grinned, and that's when I noticed his teeth. His eye-teeth were long, you know, like Dracula's?"

Job nodded again.

"Amadeus grinned, too, and he had the same teeth. Same white hair. Same pale blue eyes. The only difference was Amadeus had a mark on his left cheek. Some kind of tiny tattoo. I remember my heart pounding so hard and thinking I needed it to stop because these boys could surely hear it.

"'C'mon to the kitchen!' Viktor said. 'If you're hungry, we can make a sandwich.' With the weird smell in the house, the boys with fangs, and the name of the town and its history—never being found except when certain people searched for it, or maybe people finding it by accident and never living to tell the tale—I tell you I was afraid I was going to die."

Christopher paused for a second to sip his whiskey. *Jeez, this is good,* he thought, and he realized that already he was feeling more at ease telling Job what he'd experienced.

"Still, feeling I had no choice, I followed them to the kitchen and was astonished to see it looked rather ordinary—for the 1800s, anyway. Viktor pulled out what looked like homemade bread, and Amadeus opened the wooden icebox and set a plate of meat on the counter. I watched as Viktor carved slices of bread and then sliced meat for us all.

I was genuinely surprised when they sat and ate sandwiches with me, since I figured I might soon be separated from my blood. I mean, I thought that, as impossible as it could be, with those teeth and how fast they moved . . . " Christopher shook his head realizing his voice had trailed off and he picked his tale up again. "Anyway, I began to feel more comfortable as we told stories and laughed. When we almost finished eating, something made the house shake a little, almost like an earth tremor. Then I heard footsteps overhead.

Viktor and Amadeus quickly glanced at each other, and they seemed quite alarmed. They pulled me out of my chair, and instead of heading for the front door, they ushered me toward the back. On the way out, I saw a room with nothing in it but an enormous hole in the floor. The boys gave me no time to inspect it.

"'I'm sorry, we can't play anymore,' Viktor said as he pulled me through the back door. 'Our parents just got home, and it would be dangerous if you met them.'

"He didn't give me time for questions, and I didn't want to ask. Ever since I'd smelled the inside of the house and felt that creepy spiders-on-my-spine sensation, I'd felt the urge to leave. 'There's a path,' Viktor said and pointed through the trees. 'It might be hard to see, but the moon is full. Go quickly, and don't stop for anything.' And then he hugged me. I stiffened as I closed my eyes and I expected to feel a bite on my neck, but his embrace was warm and friendly, not cold like those creatures are supposed to be. I'm sure you guessed that I thought they were, um, vampires." Christopher let go a deep sigh. He'd said it. The V word.

Job's eyes widened a bit as he nodded, but he said nothing.

"Viktor whispered into my ear, 'Thank you for being my friend today, Christopher. It's a rare thing when I get to know someone new.'

When I opened my eyes, the boy was gone. Well, I didn't waste time. I beat feet down the path with all the energy I had. It wasn't long before I saw the town lights and knew where I was. I climbed back into the house, into my room, and curled into bed before the sun came up. My parents never even knew I was gone."

Job burst out in a hearty laugh. "Wow! You actually found the historic missing town of Passage and lived to tell the tale!" Job rubbed his chin. "Now, how do you think old Viktor ended up here at Iron Shores? And if he's really a vampire—why would someone want to take his heart?"

The two men stared at each other, neither able to answer the question. Outside, the rain kept pouring down.

LU

SEMPER VERUS

*M*arch 13, *Wednesday*

9:30 AM

Dr. Luana Crane looked over at her long-time friend, Dr. Kirk Strider, and arched her eyebrows. They stood across from each other in the decomp room with the body of Hellen Profitt between them on a stainless-steel table.

"I know you're on vacation," Kirk leveled a solemn gaze at her, "but, given the circumstances, it just seemed right to call you over."

Lu's lips pressed together as she stared down at a large hole where the woman's uterus was supposed to be. It appeared as if something had used a set of sharp knives to burst out of it.

"And you're absolutely sure she didn't come in this way?" Lu felt like something was trying to crawl out of the pit of her abdomen too. Breakfast rumbled around in her belly. The almond milk latte and vegan bagel with carrot-lox cheese from the Ethical Eats Cafe were dangerously close to exiting the route it went in.

Kirk looked at her expectantly. "We can't explain it. We've got video surveillance set up in a couple of different places. The front office, the front and back loading areas, and the refrigerator. The only thing out of the ordinary we saw was that our night-security went up to the door, stood in front of it for a couple of minutes and then went back to the security office."

"Why'd he do that?" Lu knew he was dying to tell her, so she had to ask.

"Get this. He said he heard something *clawing* at the door." Kirk leaned back, watching her reaction.

Lu nodded. "And he didn't open the door to investigate." It was a statement, not a question. "Did he say *why* he didn't open it?"

"Said it unnerved him. He knew there couldn't be anyone in there."

"So, one of your assistants brought the body out this morning—"

"No, actually, I got in early and decided I'd take this one. It's a good thing, too. Depending on what we find, we may have to be—

creative in our report. I've told everyone here that I've got this one and will let them know if I need help. If she were from any other town . . . well, you'll see what I mean." He massaged his palm with the thumb on his other hand. "Anyway, the funeral home is asking for her body, and law enforcement wants the post done to rule out a crime. She was found at the bottom of a cliff, naked. Still alive at the time. Could have been an accident. She died in the hospital before they could figure out what was wrong. Likely internal injuries but they couldn't find where she was bleeding. No external injuries. Her blood count was low. Hemoglobin was 6. Crit was 28. They tried transfusing her, but her levels only got worse. No strange blood disorders, no abnormal family history that we know of. CT and MRI were negative."

Lu looked around the room. If the woman had been murdered, she'd see her spirit, but she saw nothing. Dread welled up inside her.

"What hospital did she come from?" *Please don't say JRG.*

JRG was James River General. That meant Iron Shores. The memories of that place held more pain than smiles or laughter for Lu. Sure, there were some redeeming qualities there. People she loved. Renny for one.

"James River General."

Lu closed her eyes and Kirk said, "You want to assist with this one? We've still got you listed as part time; you know. It will freshen you up for when you take your next case." His eyes were almost apologetic and yet he'd known she had to be here to handle this. No one else was qualified.

"Sure." Lu didn't smile. Her vacation day was shot. Her next few days were probably down the toilet as well. The upside was she

116

might have a new case for her television show, though she'd have to change the name of the place where it happened.

Kirk cleared his throat. "After we're done, you may want to stay and help me with one more."

"Kirk, really?" Lu sighed. "Don't tell me they're from the same place, Kirk. Don't do it."

Silence filled the room for two heartbeats. Kirk's gaze swiveled to the ceiling and then back to Lu's "You know it's really hard to look you in those amazing eyes of yours—what color are they really—they're like burnt sienna? Dark reddish brown. With some gold . . . "

When Lu shook her head, with the 'Oh, you are going to tell me what I don't want to hear . . . ' shake, and she could feel Kirk just go for it right before he launched. "Okay. Yes. Both bodies are from the same place. Died within hours of each other."

Lu removed her gloves and went over to the sink to wash her hands. Not a necessary action, but she did it anyway.

"Same type of case?" She began scrubbing her hands hard under the hot water, that feeling of dread more pronounced now. He did manage to surprise her.

"No," said Kirk. "This one—he has no heart." She carefully dried her hands. If a person could hold their breath and their heartbeat at the same time—she'd swear Kirk was managing it.

She graced him with her 'amazing' burnt sienna eyes.

6:30 PM

Neither Lu nor Kirk found any sign of foul play outside or inside Hellen Profitt's body. She may have been drunk, high, tweaking, or tripping on a hallucinogen, but her toxicology wasn't back yet, and even that wouldn't show everything. Some drugs metabolized quickly. Some weren't even tested or could be tested.

No car or clothing was found near the scene of what now seemed like an accident. Kirk told Lu that the father had been uncooperative during his interview but being uncooperative wasn't a crime. And,

Hellen did have a reputation of being somewhat of a wild woman, even though she was in her thirties.

The most peculiar mysteries of this case, aside from the hole in her abdomen and ravaged female organs, were the presence of a black feather in the remnants of her uterus and the absence of blood in her body.

The rest of her organs were intact. There was no sign of internal hemorrhaging, and her circulatory system was fine except for her ruined thoracic arteries and veins. There was no way to explain what had happened to her blood unless whatever had been inside her had sucked her dry first.

The John Doe, with no heart, remained unidentified until an anonymous phone call suggested his name, and the informant did not remain on the line for questions. His case was also peculiar. Not counting the surrounding tissue, arteries, and veins that made it look like the man's heart was ripped out of his chest, his ribs were intact.

They found no traces of blood inside him either. Not a drop. They examined him with everything from digital X-rays to an alternate light source and came up empty.

In the end, they collected vitreous fluid from inside his eyes and urine from his bladder. Swabs and tissue samples were collected to help to confirm his identity, and they got digital shots of his teeth. His brain was removed, as was his pituitary, and after samples of tissue were excised for further examination, the rest of the brain was placed in a small bucket of formaldehyde for storage.

Lu looked over at Kirk as he entered the last bit of information for each case. Modern technology made this all so much easier—the reports and the photos were all stored on computers. This reduced complications when reviewing a case, like in the past when they had to try to read really bad handwriting.

"You going to release her?" Lu knew that Kirk would likely let both decedents return to Iron Shores for burial. They'd find no more answers to their manner of death in the autopsy suite. They'd examined the Profitt woman's body carefully, looking for needle marks or something that suggested her death wasn't from a simple accident, but aside from the postmortem hole in her body and her extremely low blood count at the hospital, there wasn't a thing wrong with her. It was a shame she had not been lucid enough to say what had happened to her when she came in.

The only logical cause of death was unexplained exsanguination. Her internal organs were intact and appeared normal, with the exception of her uterus, which was torn into pieces, and her ovaries, which were missing.

"Police seem to think they have set things straight," Kirk said. "Witnesses said she was seen in town the evening before, riding around with her brother Mason and the Moody boys. They picked up some booze and headed in the direction of Moon's overlook, where she was found. The boys were questioned, and each told the same story—that they'd pulled over near the hiking trail and that she'd drunk a good bit and ran off naked, shouting she 'just wanted to run free.' They went out after her and couldn't find her anywhere.

Mason wasn't old enough to drink, but they said they were all very drunk. There were no signs of a struggle at the top of the cliff. No shoe prints—but of course, the rain could have washed them away." Kirk sighed. "While this case is bizarre in terms of her loss of blood and the hole in the abdomen that we can't explain, I've got no reason to keep her."

"That hole in the woman's belly," said Lu. "It wasn't rats, maybe? Your techs pulled all of the decedents out of the refrigerator. Nothing?" She knew it wasn't rats but felt compelled to ask. The slashes inside the Profitt woman were not the result of gnawing rodents.

"Not one abnormality seen on anyone else other than what they came with," Kirk confirmed. "No sign of rats or any other vermin in the room, and to tell you the truth, I need to get this woman's body back to where it came from as soon as possible. The whole situation gives me the heebee jeebees."

"It *is* creepy," she agreed.

Kirk's phone rang. "Sure," he nodded reflexively, "I'll take the call."

Lu watched Kirk thumb the speaker button. A very well-spoken, cultured voice came on the line.

"The man you received—the one with no heart. I know his name," the voice said quietly.

Kirk opened his mouth to ask questions, but the voice on the line continued.

"His name is Viktor Odel. Find Christopher Miles. Tell him."

And most things associated with Iron Shores were the epitome of that very word. One thing she couldn't tell Kirk but that she felt fairly sure of was that Hellen wasn't the victim of any conventional accident or act of violence. Like her unexplained blood loss, what contributed to her demise defied anything that had ever been written on a modern death certificate.

"Okay. You and I both know what would normally be done for this kind of case," Lu said, eyeing him, "but we both know that these cases defy what would ever be called normal."

Kirk gave her a sad smile. They both understood the world of the unexplainable. The "logical" world would never accept what they knew was true. He understood what he'd known the moment he'd asked her to help with this case. Only Lu could figure out what was really going on here. "You leaving today? What about your show?"

Lu was the host of a popular television show, *Paranormal Murder*. While some folks thought her ability to commune with the dead was just an act, it was an unfortunate fact that she could actually commune with the dead. It's why she solved so many cold cases.

Unfortunately, some of those murders were also committed by unseen forces—energies, demons, skahmats and the like—and those were impossible for traditional law enforcement professionals to accept. It put her and other investigators in an awkward position.

"We don't start filming the next season for another four weeks." She removed the two layers of blue nitrile gloves, doused her hands with sanitizer and then put on a pair of stretchy black gloves before she picked up her backpack from the floor by his desk.

Her battered bag looked out of place, slung against her sleek black mock turtleneck, black pants, and red blazer. Around her neck, she wore a pendant with silver wings that had the word *Broken* in cursive across them. Two scarlet stones were set in the wings. A tribute to the mother she'd lost long ago.

"You know, I'd go with you if . . ." Kirk's voice sounded almost as heavy as the look on his face.

"Kirk, it's okay, really. It's my hometown. I'll call when I'm done. Regardless of what is written on the death certificate, at least we'll both know the truth. *Semper* Verus."

The muscles in Kirk's face relaxed a little now, his mouth softening, his eyes widening a little with gratitude and wonder.

"*Semper* Verus," he replied as she walked out the door into the pouring rain. *Stay true.*

THOMAS

MEDALLION

*M*arch 13, Wednesday

10:00 AM

Thomas needed to have a bowel movement, and there was no sign of a nurse or an aide anywhere. Yes, he could push the nurse call button, but nurses worked hard, and there were probably patients worse off than he was on the hospital floor. He knew a few patients from the I-64 semi-vs-2-bus crash were here. God, he could kick the Universe for landing him in JRG. He should be taking care of patients, not adding to the workload.

Overall, he was lucky. Besides a concussion and some whiplash, he had a few broken ribs, a broken collar bone, and fractures of the radius and ulna in his left forearm. His wrist had taken a beating, and his left shoulder had been dislocated. Add to that some major muscle strains and a couple of herniated lumbar disks, and he was a mess, but the other driver had died.

The deputy sheriff, Officer Luck, who'd come to see him yesterday, had filled him in on some of the details. The woman had been texting on her phone and more than likely hadn't seen Thomas as he pulled out from the dirt road. Their investigation was still ongoing, but the county cop didn't think Thomas would be found at fault. It should have been good news, but it didn't make him feel any better. He couldn't remember if he'd looked right to be sure the road was clear. Sure, there was a hill just before the turn, but still, had he been at fault? Had he been the cause of the woman's death? He didn't know.

He had a partial view of the hallway and a corner of the nurse's station through his door. No one was there. He knew he should push his call button or wait until a nurse came to check on him, but his stomach gurgled, and his abdomen got that familiar cramp. If he didn't get to the toilet soon, the staff would be calling a "code brown." He'd never hear the end of that, for sure. He pushed himself up with his right hand, the unhurt one, and swiveled his legs over the side of the bed.

Step one is getting half vertical. Achievement unlocked!

Unfortunately, vertical was sister to vertigo, and he had to steady himself until the room stopped spinning. After a few deep breaths, the sensation faded.

Time for step two.

He was just beginning to shimmy off the bed when he heard a familiar voice.

"Looks like you could use some help there, Doc." And there she was. Dark hair tumbled around her shoulders. Darker eyes, kind and caring, crinkled with her smile.

Of all the worst times. Nothing about him was manly, sexy, or endearing, of that he was sure. He became acutely aware of the stubble covering his face, his greasy hair, the gown that opened in the back, and the fact that he *really* had to get to the toilet.

Despite feeling like a pile of steaming dogshit on a sidewalk, he smiled. "Hey, Hatton."

Hey Hatton. Could you be any more awkward, Mr. Smooth Move? The "smooth move" thought only brought him back to the cramp in his bowels. He decided it was better if he did get help. "Could you call one of the nurses to help me out here?"

She glanced into the hall, looking left and right, and shrugged her shoulders. "I don't see anyone. Let me help you." She walked over to him.

He knew he had to smell like a dead opossum. He hadn't showered since the accident.

"No, really, if you can get—" and just like that, she was under his good arm and helping him shuffle to the bathroom.

Please don't let me fart.

In all his years, Thomas had never farted in front of a woman. He couldn't remember ever having done it in front of his mother or his four sisters. And then, unbidden, the gas squeaked out high and pinched like when the end of a balloon is tugged into a tight slit after it's filled with air.

But she didn't laugh. She didn't even smile. She had nothing but care and concern on her face. They reached the toilet, and he was embarrassed to find the handicap rail was on his left—the side he couldn't use.

Hatton pulled his gown forward gently and respectfully helped him sit on the toilet. She seemed to understand how he felt. "Just pull that call bell when you're ready to get up. I'm sure a nurse will come. I'll be back in fifteen. Promise!" Then she retreated, and Thomas breathed a sigh of relief only to remember he hadn't thanked her.

"I'll be surprised if she does come back," he muttered.

Thankfully, Hatton was gone a bit over fifteen minutes. Time enough for Thomas's nurse, Jerome, to help him fumigate the room and bathroom with some deodorizing spray. "I don't use this apple spice spray for anyone, Doc. You gotta know." Jerome winked, making sure Thomas was sitting up in bed with the covers over him. He handed Thomas a warm, moistened washcloth and a swish of mouthwash for good measure.

"Look at it this way, Doc. If she comes back after seeing you like this, then you got no worries at all, man." He gave Thomas a confident "good luck" smile before he left the room, and Thomas did nothing else but watch the wall clock as it ticked away seconds that seemed like a stint in purgatory.

Just when he thought Hatton wasn't coming back, her cheery face peeked around the door. "Yay! You've been saved!" She bounced over to him, handed him a paper sack, and then sat down next to him on the bed. He opened the bag, and inside were two packages of Oreos and two packages of chocolate almond milk.

"Thank you, Hatton. Really. And thank you very much for earlier." He had no idea why he suddenly felt self-conscious, and his cheeks burned.

"You really got busted up, huh?" she said. "If my father . . ."

He put a finger to his lips. "No. It's not your fault or your father's. The car came over the hill and didn't see me. They said the woman was texting."

"It was Marlie," said Hatton. "Marlie Moon."

"Nick's family?" He thought for a second. "Nick's sister?"

Hatton nodded. "Her funeral is probably Saturday. Same as my sister's."

"What?" Thomas tried to sit up straighter, but a sharp pain shot up his spine. "Your sister died?"

"You might have even seen her here at the hospital or around town. The Reverend Miles found her at the bottom of Moon's Overlook the day we met. I didn't even know . . ." She swallowed, unable to continue.

Thomas's last bizarre ER shift came back to him. The woman they brought in with low blood levels, the one they couldn't transport to UVA because of the accident on I-64. Her name came to him when he pictured her.

"Hellen Profitt," he said. "Your last name is Profitt?"

She nodded.

Hatton hadn't told him her last name before. He felt a little better about that, but man, she'd just lost her sister, and he had taken care of the woman before they transferred her over to the ICU. He hadn't had time to check on her progress. And then, the guy with no heart came in.

Hatton stared at him, her eyes wet and somber, and there was an emotion there he couldn't describe. Something more than grief. The look in her eyes was—tortured, maybe. But why would that be?

"Anyway," she started again, "this weekend will be tough for sure. My sister in the morning—Pa will want it over with. And Marlie . . ." Hatton stopped, her face contorting and then tears once again pouring down her cheeks.

"Hatton, I'm so sorry."

She wiped her eyes and stood up. "Oh, jeez—I didn't want to come in here and cry all over the place. I just wanted to check on you. Make sure you are okay. And to give you this." She pulled something from her pocket. She took a moment to show it to him. "I made it myself, see? It's extra special." It was a ceramic medallion hanging from a knotted cord.

She slipped it over his head. "Wish I'd done this before your crash, but at least now you have it. Do me a favor, Thomas." Her eyes were wide and serious. "I know it will sound silly, but never take it off. Promise me? It will protect you."

Thomas lifted the medallion from his chest. It was made of red clay, he guessed. There were several interesting symbols on one side, like a half-moon with horns, and one that looked like crow talons, colored light blue. Tiny flecks of gold caught the light. On the other side was the head of a crow or raven, sculpted and then painted. The crow looked back at him as if it were something alive.

"Thanks," he said, looking up but was startled to find she'd slipped away.

Part of him wanted to look for her, call her, and find a way to thank her, but sudden fatigue got the best of him. He closed his eyes and drifted off, only partly aware of the cawing of crows in the distance.

CHRISTOPHER

HOLY HELL

*M*arch 14, Thursday

10:30 AM

The phone rang as Christopher stepped out of the shower. His wet feet slapped across cold green tiles and the wooden floor in the bedroom. He picked up his cell on the nightstand, saw it was Hatcher's and thumbed the "Accept" button.

"Reverend Miles," he said, and put the phone on speaker so he could finish toweling off.

"Good morning, Reverend. It's Marty." Marty cleared his throat. "Justin said you'd like to know when the Profitt girl came in. She's here, just so-n's you know."

Marty's accent was very Virginia backwoods. Christopher had worked hard to lose his southern accent after he'd left Iron Shores, but now that he was back it helped to sound native.

"Thank ya much," he said, nodding as he spoke realizing he was nodding at a voice. "Let me know when I can see her."

"You can come over any time today. Officer Ware said we could prep her. Sounds like her family ain't gonna claim her body. Weren't particularly upset as I understand."

Christopher's anger flared, but then he smothered it. *Judge not, lest ye be judged.*

"Okay. Thank you."

Next, Christopher called Judith's number. It rang six times and went to voicemail. He left a message asking her to call him and then decided he wouldn't wait. If he went to Hatcher's, he could organize a viewing for Hellen's body and arrange her burial. He put on khaki slacks and a blue polo shirt. A simple pair of loafers. Nice, but not too nice. Understated.

Justin Hatcher was standing by a white coffin in the viewing room when Christopher entered Hatcher's Mortuary. Marty's son was a stocky kid, almost dwarfish in stature but wide across the shoulders. His hair was pure white, and his skin was just like his father's, an alabaster shade that never tanned but only turned pink almost the moment the sun touched it.

Justin's face lit up and then sobered. "Hey, Reverend. You're here for Hellen, right?"

Christopher nodded. "Your dad told me she was here." He looked at the white coffin on the stand. Fresh calla lilies flanked each end of it. He arched an eyebrow at Justin.

"Marlie Moon. Visitation today." Justin made a small but sad half-smile. "She's yours too, right? Car accident on Route 6. Put a doc in the hospital and put herself in here. Victims of the evil text monster, or so they say."

It was the way of people serving in the "serious business" of other people. Using dark humor to compensate for the soul-sucking sides of their professions—humor as dark as their days. Christopher wondered if Nick had been on call. If he had responded to the crash only to find his own sister was in the wreck.

If he had, then—Holy hell.

Christopher made a slight jut of his chin toward the back of the funeral home where they prepped the bodies. "Any word from the family?"

Justin shook his head. "Not a peep. You want to see her now? There's something—"

"No one will see my daughter excepting me," a deep, booming voice interrupted. "Got that?"

A tall, lanky man in ripped blue jeans, a navy-blue flannel shirt, and muddy work boots stood in the doorway. His weathered face was lined with the years he'd obviously spent outdoors, and his graying hair was dripping wet.

Christopher guessed this was Jagger, Hellen's father. He'd never had the opportunity to meet the man. Next to him was one of the Profitt boys, soaked from the rain as well. Christopher recognized him.

134

Samuel? No. Savral.

Savral was Jagger's eldest and a spitting image of his father. It was odd to think of Savral as one of Jagger's "children" since he looked to be about the same age as Christopher. And he remembered the family typically used odd names for their kids. At least Hellen had just been Hellen but spelled "with two LLs, like hell." He could still hear her saying those words in his head.

"Mr. Profitt," Justin said soothingly, "would you like—"

"Just get her body ready," Jagger told Justin curtly. The man turned his searing gaze toward Christopher. "You're Reverend Miles, right? Heard you'd bury my girl for free at your place. That true?"

Christopher nodded carefully, his eyes flicking over to Savral, whose face was expressionless as a slate stone wall, but whose eyes burned into him like blue flames.

Christopher turned back to gaze at Jagger. "If that's what you'd like, Mr. Profitt, then yes. This Saturday at ten in the morning we can do it, if that works for you. She was my . . ." he didn't know how to describe Hellen at this moment. Jagger's piercing gray eyes reminded him of stainless steel flecked with glacier ice. "She was my friend."

For just a second, Savral's mouth twisted into a cruel half smile, half snarl, and then the look was gone.

Jagger gave him a curt nod that Christopher interpreted as meaning the burial date and time were fine, and then Jagger jerked his chin Justin's way. "You tell your pa—don't need no fancy box for her. Green burial, they call it now, right?" He didn't wait for an answer. "Just a sheet 'round her is fine. Or if you gotta do a box—they still do those pine ones, right?"

Justin nodded.

Christopher said nothing, though the meaning of *green burial* flitted through his brain. Well, if that was what her family wanted, and if Hellen hadn't had a will or described what she wanted after death, then it was up to her family to make those decisions. It didn't matter if he liked it or not.

"Don't preserve her like no pickle, neither," Jagger called out from the door. "Me and the family will come to church tomorrow 'round ten. No need for extra measures. Just a hole in the ground will do." He did an about-face and headed out the door with Savral at his heels.

Justin stared at Christopher, his eyelids blinking rapidly. He tilted his head to the side and said, "Um. What just happened?"

Christopher's job was both his life and his livelihood. Whether on a Sunday with parishioners, or grocery shopping at the Food Lion, he had to maintain the behavior of what the public expected of a Reverend. Calm. Patient. Kind. Neutral. Avoiding all gossip and negative actions.

Justin, an intuitive kid, voiced what Christopher couldn't. "The family didn't come to see her at the hospital. They didn't do a thing when she went to the medical examiner. And now her pa just shows up making demands like he's planning to plant a field of corn and needs hired hands to do it. Not an ounce of grief on him. No gratitude. Not a sad bone in her brother, either."

He took a few steps toward the back of the building and looked back. "You coming or not? There's something you gotta see."

Moral decision, Christopher thought. He should march out of the building right now, honoring Hellen's father's wishes, and get to the work of making sure the burial plot—*dark wet hole in the ground*—was ready for tomorrow. He started to raise his hand in farewell, turning to the door, then spun on his heels.

"Ah hell," he muttered and followed Justin through the double doors to where Hellen waited.

Justin Hatcher stood by the mortuary table. "Dude, you knew her, right? High school?"

Christopher nodded, his throat constricting. She'd been alive when he'd found her. Had she even known it was him who had found her? Likely not. She'd been so out of it, unconscious during part of his time with her.

"Okay," Justin's mouth set into a grim line. "Might be hard, but I thought you should see this." Justin respectfully pulled the sheet down to just below her hips. That was enough.

Christopher had seen bodies as they were being prepared for burial. Autopsied persons had a Y-incision that went from either shoulder to just below their xiphoid process and then down to the top of the genital region. Men's prostate and testes were removed, and a sliver of each testis was sliced for tissue examination, or there was an examination of a woman's uterus and ovaries in a similar manner. But Hellen's lower abdomen was shredded as if something had exploded out of her.

A heavy silence filled the air, punctuated by the drip, drip of the mortician's sink. Certainly, this wasn't done at the autopsy. Incisions were made in a nice straight line, and then the bodies were sewed up with loose but neat stitches.

Christopher didn't know how long he stared. He looked up. "Any word at all what this was?"

"No," Justin said. "I picked her up at the ME's office myself. The guard on duty said that the night guard wigged out—wouldn't leave the security office until his change of shift was complete, and then he ran out of the building."

"Nothing on the paperwork?"

Justin shook his head. "Cause and manner of death aren't ready for release yet, but they'll likely rule it as exsanguination and accidental. Odd thing is, this injury didn't happen until *after* she arrived at the ME's office. Before that, none of the docs could figure out exactly where her blood went. Her levels kept getting lower and lower, and no one could explain it."

"My god."

"And there's one more thing. The guard told me he overheard a couple of the docs talking."

"And?"

"And they said her uterus was busted up, and her ovaries—and her heart—were completely gone."

Justin's face had turned an interesting shade of pink.

"Holy hell," Christopher breathed. He had that feeling of spiders creeping over his spine again.

CHRISTOPHER

PRECIOUS MOMENT

March 16, Saturday, Just Before Quarter Moon

9:05 AM

In the morning, Christopher stepped out into the rain, which continued to pour from the sky in chilly, wet sheets, to check that the protective tents Job had erected over the graves hadn't blown down overnight. Some water had found its way into the graves, but overall, it would be fairly dry for the families of the deceased.

Because he knew Hellen's family wouldn't bother, he'd ordered a grave marker for her. Something feminine yet natural. Butterflies and flowers etched on a bronze plaque fastened to a black granite memorial stone. Until it was ready, he'd purchased a memorial garden stake adorned with butterflies and added her name to it, as well as her birth and death dates.

The Profitts arrived late, and they didn't come into the church. Christopher was waiting in a pew near the altar when Jagger poked his head in and said, "We're ready out here, Rev."

So, there was no final memorial to say inside, then. Christopher walked through the church with a strange sense of dread overcoming him. Something about this whole thing seemed wrong, and he questioned his decision to bury Hellen here. Then he shook his head. *She deserves a decent place to rest.*

Stepping out, he looked over to the graveyard beside the church and was touched by the somber sight. The coffin was already stationed over the grave as directed, and the rain was pummeling the tent so hard that he decided to double back and grab an umbrella.

He made for the gravesite with purposeful strides and thought about Hellen in that box. A plain pine box. As he got closer, he saw something resting on top of it. Someone had placed a small bundle of yellow and white daffodils on the lid. It hurt Christopher's heart to see Hellen placed into the ground this way, but he supposed it didn't really matter. She didn't live in that body anymore.

The family stood on the far side of the coffin. Christopher worked to keep his gaze soft and the line of his lips somber. A person's facial gestures were a physical but often unconscious language to others, and he'd worked hard to learn how not to show his real emotions. Sometimes, he succeeded.

Please let this be one of those times I succeed.

Jagger stood at the head of the coffin, with Savral next to him. Jagger's face was stony. Firm.

The clothes he wore were similar to those he wore yesterday. A red and black checked flannel shirt, baggy faded jeans. His boots were gobbed with red-orange mud. He looked like he was there to do a chore, something to check off a list.

Savral's face, while serious, looked almost as if he were internally laughing at Christopher. Laughing at the whole series of events. Hellen's death, the rain, the burial—all of it.

The woman next to Savral was someone Christopher barely recognized. At first, he thought maybe she was a visiting family member or Savral's girlfriend, but no. He saw something similar to Hellen in the woman. The curve of her face. The shape of her eyes. The similarity stopped there.

Where Hellen had been fair with alabaster skin, this woman was the opposite. She had chestnut hair, dark eyes, and a deeper tinge of natural red on her lips. She wore a long, tan trench coat that looked like it belonged to a secret agent from the 1940s. The front of it was open, revealing her flowing black skirt, peasant blouse, and oddly crafted necklace decorated with a sculptured relief of a crow or raven's head. Her bohemian flair made her appear quite exotic.

Hatton. Hellen's sister.

Geez, she'd been what—eight years old when he and Hellen were in their last year of high school. He wondered why their paths hadn't crossed until now.

Next to Hatton stood Mason Profitt. Christopher knew him since he frequently came to town doing odd jobs for money. With his long dark brown and curly hair, he was more like Hatton than Jagger. He had similar coloring but a stocky build and was a good deal shorter than the rest.

His eyes went back to Hatton, and he saw a much smaller shape standing behind her coat, peering out at him with silver-blue eyes. She was holding Hatton's hand, perhaps nervous or scared. He couldn't entirely make out her features, but her eyes were Hellen's.

All right then. Christopher had memorized what he'd prepared to say, but when he opened his mouth to begin, Jagger barked at him.

"Just put her in the ground and have done with it." His voice was hard but sharp, like a razor's edge.

Christopher surveyed the children, including the little girl behind Hatton. Hatton and Mason had tears brimming in their eyes. He said a silent prayer for patience to the God he didn't believe in and the one who ignored Jagger.

"I am so sorry this day has come and that you all must endure the loss of your dear daughter and sister, Hellen. I imagine it is even harder with this weather and our worries about flooding, but I am glad to see you all. Jagger—" He eyed the man with as much confidence as he could muster. "Savral, Hatton, Mason, and . . ." he paused, hoping someone would offer a name while he looked at the little girl.

Hatton spoke up. "Precious. Our youngest—sister."

Christopher knew it wasn't time for twenty questions, but this girl looked to be maybe four or five. He supposed that would be about right for when her mother died, but he wasn't sure.

"Welcome, Precious," he said, "and . . ."

Jagger's face twisted. "Reverend, we ain't got time for this. We mights not even make it back up the hill to get home with this rain. Lower parts are already getting flooded. Hurry the hell up!"

Jagger had a point—albeit an abrupt one. Christopher made quick work of the eulogy with a brief quote he felt Hellen would have liked.

"Dig into life with wild roving abandon, opening your mind to delicious possibilities that perplex the mind, entice the heart, and excite the spirit." Christopher paused as Jagger stormed away, and Savral followed. "That was by Maximillian Degenerez, and it reminds me of Hellen and how she lived when we were younger," he finished. The others stayed to place some sprigs of juniper on the pine coffin before they left.

Precious turned her head and stared back at him as Hatton led her away, and she called out to him as if she wanted him to know something important, "My sister loves the smell of the juniper smoke when it burns."

LU

QUARTER MOON

*M*arch 17, Sunday

7:02 PM

Eight days of rain and even though some people were moving to higher elevations with family or finding other shelters in town, the River Rage Brewery was determined not to miss celebrating the March quarter moon. Two years ago, during COVID-19, and even the year after, they weren't able to celebrate phases of the moon because everything was closed and while beer sales for curbside pick-up provided some income, the brewery was still far behind in making up lost revenue from the years before.

The bartenders placed a drop of food coloring to everyone's glass to provide "green beer" in celebration of a new batch of their famous Green-Eyed Witch IPA. People laughed and cheered along with the Saint Patrick's Day celebration. Others toasted to the quarter moon although no one could see any trace of moon in the sky.

Dr. Lu Crane nestled herself into the far corner of the bar and sipped on her own Green-Eyed Witch, casually studying the crowd. If someone didn't know better, just peering inside would make them think that no one here had any idea the surrounding areas were flooding. There were concerns in town that the twenty-year-old levy and flood wall wouldn't hold, but inside the River Rage all cares seemed to melt away.

She absentmindedly traced her fingers around her Broken Wings pendant as she tasted the hoppy brew and suddenly realized she hadn't bothered to look at her phone in over an hour.

"You okay?"

The voice startled her, but it was only the bartender, Colin, a freckled Irish redhead with a bellow of a laugh and a body as wide as a linebacker's.

"I'm fine, thanks." Lu smiled as politely as she could. There was a palpable tension in this place despite the ongoing merriment and laughter. It felt to her like a piano wire stretched too tight, ready to snap. Across the room, the Corn Pickers were plucking banjo strings with amazing dexterity, and the crowd clapped along with the tune.

There didn't seem to be a care in the world here—but then suddenly the cares invaded.

"Help!" A woman's voice screamed over the din of the crowd. "Somebody, please come help me! Oh, Lord! Lord have mercy!" She was sobbing uncontrollably.

The banjo music ground to a halt. Women flew to her side, saying, "What's wrong, hun?" and "Tell us what's going on."

The woman, who looked to be in her fifties, near Lu's age she supposed, cried out: "I tried call'n 911 but nobody picked up! I tried the police office. No one picked up there either! My husband . . ." The woman fell to her knees. "My husband has been murdered! He's . . . he's in *pieces*! Torn to bits! Everywhere! S-s-someone please h-help!" She broke down into uncontrollable sobbing and crumpled to the floor.

It looked as if Colin was trying 911 again, but still no one picked up.

"I'll run to the police office!" he yelled, and Lu was surprised how quickly he was out the door. Lu didn't know the woman's name. Hadn't heard anyone use it. People sat in silence looking at the sobbing woman and the women trying to comfort her. Some sipped at their beers for want of anything else to do.

Then, a police vehicle pulled up outside, lights flashing. Lu left her beer on the wooden counter and sprinted out before the officer could make it inside.

The officer was female, and Colin was beside her explaining the situation.

"Hold up," Lu said.

"Excuse me," the officer snapped. "I need to get by."

Lu's gaze flicked to the woman's name tag. The tag read "Chief Ware." She took note of the accompanying silver stars on her collar. In a flash, she recognized the woman although she'd been many years younger the first time they crossed paths.

Lu flashed her credentials. "Medical examiner's office," she said. "I can help, especially if the forensic team can't make it over the river. I've got a camera, so if you want, I can properly collect evidence. If I can examine her residence, your team can secure the scene, and I'll do my best not to disturb anything but to get you as much information as possible."

The Chief looked at her as if calculating exactly what she needed. "Fair enough," she agreed. "Got a car? Good. Wait here and then follow me when I come back out."

Lu hopped into her red Alfa Romeo just as the rain picked up, spattering from the sky in torrents. She pulled around in front of the pub, wondering if anyone around there was planning to build an ark. Chief Ware finally emerged with the crying woman under her arm and set her inside her vehicle, and Lu followed her a short distance up a hill to a two-story Victorian home.

She imagined the house was lovely when the sun was shining, but the gray painted boards with lilac trim looked more like it was crying now. The mailbox had Snoopy sitting on top of it, helmet and goggles in place, and the line of his mouth was set in grim determination as if he were right on the tail of the Red Baron. On the side of the box were metal letters that read Bugg. She parked behind the police SUV and popped her trunk. When Chief Ware and the woman, presumably Mrs. Bugg , emerged from the vehicle, Lu was already standing ready at the walkway with her equipment in hand.

The rain had let up some, and so they walked a little slower, Mrs. Bugg telling the officer what she knew. When they arrived at the porch, Lu lightly touched Chief Ware's arm.

"It may be best if you let me in first, to start." She tried to say it calmly. Politely and respectfully. But Lu still felt the prickle of the Chief's barely disguised emotion. Chief Ware straightened her back and lifted her chin, her eyes appraising Lu and her camera gear. After a moment, she nodded, apparently satisfied.

Lu turned her gaze on the other woman, now. "Mrs. Bugg, is that correct?"

The woman sobbed, "Yes."

"If it's okay with you, I need to go in first, so I can do this right. It's important to collect any evidence and take the proper photos. Do I have your consent?"

Mrs. Bugg nodded, her eyes already red and swollen. "Yes, yes. Oh god, but it's a mess in there. I barely looked, and I was so scared. There was blood everywhere, but I knew it was my man." She started sobbing again, and Lu hated to keep interjecting, but she needed the information.

"What part of the house is your husband in?" *Damn, it was so hard to say the right things, to do the right things.* But she had the forensic skills. She was here, and there'd never be a better chance to collect the evidence than now.

"K-kitchen." Mrs. Bugg pointed as if gesturing toward the back.

"Okay, thank you." She held her camera where Mrs. Bugg could see—hoping she'd gather a sense of importance as to what Lu was about to do. "I'm going to go in first. If all is clear in the front living room—that is the living room, right?" Lu could see sofas and a television through the windows.

Mrs. Bugg nodded again.

"Once I'm sure there's nothing more in the living room to photograph or any more evidence I can collect, I'll call 'Clear,' and you both can come in and sit while I go to the kitchen."

Taking silence as consent, Lu slipped on a pair of gloves and went in. She circled around the front room, noting the T.V., two sofas and a recliner. Nothing seemed disturbed.

She photographed the room, used her alternate light source—something similar to a black light but with different wavelengths—to look for secretions or other evidence that might fluoresce and dusted for fingerprints. No abnormalities noted. The fingerprints she collected would be compared to Mrs. Bugg's and those of her husband. She sprayed Luminol last—Kirk would laugh if he knew she'd brought her entire kit—and she looked for traces of blood. None in this room.

Lu went to the front door. "Clear!" she called out and headed for the kitchen. She heard Mrs. Bugg's sobbing in the living room and Officer Ware on the phone speaking with someone—the hospital morgue, maybe. At least they could hold the body there until they could transport to the M.E.'s office.

Lu dropped her pack, discarded old gloves, and slid on a fresh pair. The lights were still on although they weren't very bright. She examined the light switch just inside the entrance to the kitchen. It needed dusting for prints, she decided, and she pulled out her gear again taking a moment to notice a large smear of blood on the floor.

Once she'd lifted the prints, she took photos, changed gloves again and then moistened some swabs and collected samples from the smears on the floor. She put on orange goggles and turned off the hall and kitchen lights, then switched on her alternate light source. She'd need to spray Luminol to get any blood to fluoresce, but she wanted to see if the front part of the kitchen held other clues that might fluoresce as well.

Bingo. There were what seemed like biological stains all over the walls and even the ceiling. They were translucent, difficult to see with the naked eye. She took several photos of these under the alternate light and collected swab samples before turning on the overhead light again. Then she went around the kitchen island.

And there he was. Mr. Bugg. He had indeed been torn apart. Lu shot several photos from one side of the kitchen island and then the other. Once she'd processed all she could of the room, she knelt near the body, or what was left of Mr. Bugg.

He was lying face down and his pants were ripped clean off his body, leaving part of his buttocks and lower body exposed. But instead of skin and muscles, Mr. Bugg's legs were stripped to the bone and large chunks of muscle had been removed from his buttocks. His arms were similarly stripped bare, with mostly bone showing. And oddly, the man's head was missing.

Lu took as many photos as were necessary of the body from different angles and then turned the man's body over. It was challenging since rigor had already set in, but not as difficult as it would have been if most of his body was still there. She tried not to gasp when she turned him over and wasn't sure she'd succeeded.

The man's chest was split right down the center, as was his abdomen. Every single one of his internal organs was gone except the intestines. Heart, lungs, liver, stomach—in all her years as a medical examiner she'd never seen anything like this. But this was Iron Shores. If something like this were to happen anywhere, it would probably be here.

Her gaze drifted to the dead man's groin. The penis and scrotum along with testes were gone as well—almost as if he'd been dismembered right there with one giant bite from something. Stringy threads of tissue hung loosely around where his genitalia should have been.

She completed her sequence of photos and took more samples, swabbing everything she felt was important. Then she called Chief Ware in.

The woman's face twitched, barely, when she saw the state of the dead man.

"Poor Mavis," Chief Ware said. "I can't imagine her shock at finding Marvin in the kitchen like this."

Lu swallowed. She admired what the woman in front of her had grown up to be. Chief Ware seemed capable. Strong. Determined. This town needed someone like that.

"His body was face down when I entered. I only moved him after collecting all the evidence I could. But you can see, his muscles are stripped from his legs and his arms. His buttocks too. And his internal organs are gone." She paused. "Genitals are gone as well. I haven't found his head yet."

To her credit, the Chief didn't gag or vomit like Lu had seen some officers and investigators do.

Chief Ware cleared her throat. "I've called the hospital morgue to come pick him up. I'm assuming you'll take a closer look at him later?" It was a statement and not really a question, though she made it sound that way.

Lu realized that because of the rain, they wouldn't be able to transport the body out of town for a full autopsy in Richmond. It seemed that, for now, she'd just become the town forensic pathologist. "Of course," she said, eyeing the back door. "Just a sec. I'll just step out and see if I can find the rest of Mr. Bugg." There was no gentle way to put it.

"I'll come with you. Mavis is as fine as a wife can be in such a situation, but hopefully she'll stay on the couch. She's a Candy Crush addict. Started playing it when it first came out. She plays most often when she's nervous."

Together, Lu and Chief Ware stepped out onto the back porch. Lu scanned the yard. It took only a few seconds to find the rest of Marvin. His head lay in the yard not too far from the back porch steps.

Not only was it odd to see the man's severed head without the body, but there was something else Lu was sure she had never seen in all her years of police work. Mr. Bugg's head was torn in two. No, not torn, but split down the middle like an English walnut. And his brain was missing.

Lu had no clue what could have done that so precisely, but she was sure it wasn't human.

Lu and the Chief looked up as high screams and sobbing exploded inside the house. Apparently, Mavis hadn't stayed on the couch.

THOMAS

FLAPPING

*M*arch 17, Sunday

11:59 PM

Thomas was discharged from the hospital earlier that day. The process was uneventful with one exception. His fellow physicians didn't advise him leaving so early. Maria tried to talk him out of it when she dropped by.

"If you injure yourself, it won't be good. You do that, and it will take longer to get back on your feet," she cautioned.

She didn't bother to suppress the irritation in her voice. "While I am sorry you were hurt, we need you back in the ER, Thomas, as soon as you feel able and ready to work. The rain has flooded all of the rivers and creeks. The roadways are blocked by the overflow. People are coming to the hospital with associated flood injuries. Hypothermia. Cuts from broken glass. Nail punctures." She paused and looked him over. "Seriously, Thomas, take good care of yourself. Rest. Come back as soon as you can but do so safely."

He nodded, still determined not to stay one more day in a place where he could pick up a hospital nosocomial infection. He'd be safer recuperating away from sick people.

Of course, he no longer had a car and "home" was a room he rented from an older couple, Mr. and Mrs. Luck. They lived about ten miles east of town, right next to their landscaping business. He'd called to tell them about his accident and that he was okay. Even though he'd only been staying with them for a short time, he'd developed a fondness for them.

"You want us to come get you?" Lily Luck asked. "It's not a problem at all. We'll set you up in your room and you'll be right as rain in no time."

Thomas heard the mixture of relief and worry in her voice, and he knew the couple had a lot of work ahead trying to protect their plants from the continuing rain.

"No," he said, "Really. I'll be fine. I've got a room at the Horseshoe Inn. After a week or so, I'll get something to drive when the weather lets up. I'll be back soon. And don't worry about the rent, okay? I got it covered. Direct deposit like always."

"Oh, pish," Lily was never one to worry about a dime, unlike her husband, who counted every single cent. "That's not as important as you, dear. Please take care of yourself, you hear? And if you need anything, we expect you to call, alright?

He assured her he would, and a nurse rolled him out to the only taxi in town. It was a unique vehicle. The yellow VW van was decorated with painted designs that included hops vines, grapes, beer mugs and wine glasses clinking, as well as names of local businesses that provided food, drink and interesting tours of local haunted sites. The larger words on the side, in a pretty cursive font, proclaimed it Tati's Taxi.

Thomas recognized the woman when she came around to open the door for him. He hadn't remembered her name but only her diagnosis when she'd come into the ER. "The ruptured appendix." He knew her age, or ballpark. She had dark ebony skin, was in her twenties but dressed like a child of the 70's with a wide picked afro, large silver hoop earrings, bell bottom jeans and a worn jean jacket sporting 70's patches and peace pins all over it. The patch that caught Thomas' eye first had a black and white spotted cow embroidered on it with the phrase above the animal that read "Leave my tits alone."

"Well, hey, Doc!" She slid the side door open. "Guess I'm not takin' you to the River Rage, huh? Maybe later. Pain control?"

He smiled at that. *Pain control indeed. Maybe I can get a growler of the Green-Eyed Witch delivered to my room.*

Tati and the nurse helped him into the van, and he told Tati he was staying at the Horseshoe. When they got him checked in, she helped him to his room on the ground floor and he tipped her with some of the cash he had in his wallet.

Tati looked at him thoughtfully and said, "Doc, I know it ain't my business, but you look like a man who could use a few things while you're stayin' here. Most of the roads are blocked or washed out by rain. Out of the Closet has got some cheap threads if you trust me with your credit card. And the Dollar General will have your personal hygiene needs. Razor and all. Give me a budget, and I'll shop for ya."

A couple of hours later, she brought him some clothes, including a pair of faded jeans, thick hiking boots, a jacket, a few flannel shirts, and T-shirts with various rock band music designs on them. It wasn't his style, but he couldn't afford to be picky. He was grateful for the electric toothbrush he'd asked for, a fresh tube of toothpaste, and a clean package of socks.

"Here's the piece-de-resistance," she said and flashed him a bright smile as she produced a bag with Temper Tavern's logo on the side and another paper bag to go with it. "I know it wasn't on your list, but see'n as you've been dining on hospital food for a bit, I figure'd you could go for something with some flavor."

The smell of food automatically caused his belly to growl. He made her take the twenty in his wallet.

"This is great, Tati, thanks." He didn't bother to ask if what she'd ordered had meat in it. At this point, he'd feel fine with picking off the dead animal. He'd say a prayer for it, or them, and then maybe there'd be a stray cat he could feed, or perhaps the Morrow's had a dog who would eat it.

The Tavern bag held a container of hot butternut squash ravioli, potato wedges (packets of ketchup included), a large salad and a slice of carrot cake. It seemed as if Tati knew his diet. Not a dead animal in sight. He was as relieved as hungry.

The other bag held cans of the Green-Eyed Witch. Every bit of the food went right into his belly although the cast on his arm made it slower going. A can of the beer washed the food down, and the suds were cold, crisp and hoppy— just the way he liked it.

After his meal, he'd stayed in the scrubs he was discharged in, curled up in bed only vaguely aware of the patter of rain against his window. He drifted into darkness and slept harder than the dead.

When Thomas woke, he was briefly disoriented but then remembered where he was. The room was dark, and the necklace Hatton had given him was twisted around his neck. He unwound it, thinking he'd take it off, but then remembered her words, *"Never take it off. Promise me? Not for a while, anyway. It will protect you."*

Thomas ran his fingers over it, feeling the sculpted crow head and thought of Hatton. What had she meant, that it would *protect* him? Protect him from what? He grabbed the cord and slid it up his neck and over his head. It would be fine underneath the pillow for now.

A sound like the flapping of wings startled him.

A bird? Is there a bird in here?

He fumbled for the light switch on the lamp by the bed, finally found it near the lightbulb, and twisted it. The harsh light blinded him for a second, then his gaze swept the room and landed on something that caused him to emit a sound he didn't know could come out of his mouth—a gasp and a strangled yell combination that only scratched the surface of expressing the dread that sank into him.

A dark figure stood at the foot of his bed—the size of a man or larger—and a huge beak protruded from its face. There were sharp ridges of teeth lining the inside edges of the beak—top and bottom and the stench coming from its mouth was sour and fetid. The creature's icy blue eyes stared at him in such a way that he thought his heart would stop. And the overall smell of it—it was like the later stages of human putrefaction,

The black creature shook its body and appendages, which looked like long arms with feathers attached to them, and he heard that flapping sound again. With a strangled caw, it lunged toward him. Thomas backpedaled, pushing himself all the way up to the head of the bed as far as he could go.

I'm still asleep. Dreaming, he told himself. *I'm in a nightmare. I need to wake up!*

There was a yell, a scream, or something close to a scream rising in his throat, but it got stuck and would not burst out into the air. All he could do was pant in panic, undecided about what action to take next.

He felt something jab his heel. *The amulet!*

He reached down just as the creature moved around to the side of the bed and stretched out for him. Its fingers, if they could be called that, ended in sharp-looking talons that sliced the air as they snatched at him. He heard the snapping sound of its beak.

Thomas gripped the necklace's cord and placed it over his head. The creature cawed in anger and reared back. Thomas threw himself over the opposite side of the bed and hit the floor, groaning as he banged his arm and jostled his collarbone. At the same time, the bedside lamp on the far side smashed to the floor, and the room was plunged again into darkness. A whooshing sound flew over his head, and then there was silence.

Thomas didn't know how long he had been crouched on the floor, trembling, his arm and collarbone throbbing, but eventually, he reached up for the switch on the bedside lamp that wasn't broken and turned on the light.

The room was empty. He crept toward the closet and slid it open. It was empty as well, except for his clothes, a pair of boots, an iron, and an ironing board. Brandishing the iron, he checked the bathroom and the shower. The creature was nowhere to be seen.

He went over to the room door and checked the latch. It was locked, but it hadn't occurred to him that he should use the deadbolt. He slid it home now, still unsure if he'd been dreaming.

He turned on the television and all of the lights. When he crept back into bed, he took a couple more Percocet, sliding them down with another beer and draining the can. The bed covers, which at first felt warm and cozy, now acted as a protective barrier between him and the thought of whatever the thing was that invaded his room.

The medallion with the crow's head was warm against his skin, and he wrapped his fingers around it, staring at the design until his eyes grew heavy. He fell into a deep sleep once more— sleep peppered with icy blue eyes and black feathers and the feeling that he did indeed need to heal and fast. His survival, and the survival of others, might depend on it.

In his dreams, a distant voice, a woman's voice, called out a name. At first, he thought it could be his name, but gradually, the voice became louder and clearer. Then her words were unmistakable, though he didn't recognize the names.

Christopher. Christopher Miles, the voice said. *Find Reverend Christopher Miles. Find Chief Judith Ware.*

CHRISTOPHER

ANGER

*M*arch 18, *Monday*

8:00 AM

The rain pummeled against the slate roof. How many days in a row now? Six?

Christopher couldn't remember a time in his entire life that he'd seen so much water come down from the sky. The earth was so soaked, so slick that Job had gotten Persephone 3 stuck in the mud again—and it seemed she was down for the count for the foreseeable future. It wasn't too terrible since Job could dig a grave by hand and did on occasion, but it was inconvenient.

Christopher made a pot of coffee and drank it black. The bitter flavor seemed more appropriate for the day after Hellen had gone into the ground. He thought about all the things he needed to do, the people he needed to see, and the murder he needed to solve. Sure, he wasn't law enforcement, but there had to be something he could do. And doing something would bring him together again with Judith.

He finished his coffee and ate a scrambled egg while standing at the stove. Then, he put his dishes in the sink, vowing to wash them in the afternoon. He slipped on his jeans and a T-shirt, put on a jacket, and stepped out onto his front porch.

There was something very wrong in the cemetery. A lump of wet earth had risen from where they'd buried Marlie Moon.

He put on his rubber boots and strode toward the grave. There shouldn't be disruption of the mound, the way Job dug graves and anchored coffins. In general, Christopher did not make some of the usual requirements some cemetery owners made. Concrete vaults were not mandatory and so on, but still—there should be no problems here.

His eyes widened as he got closer. In the center of the mound was a deep hole right where Marlie's casket was buried.

He peered into the hole. It was hard to tell what shape the coffin was in because so much water had pooled at the bottom of the hole, but he could see that the lid had splintered outward, reminding him of Hellen's body—how it had looked like something had burst out of her belly.

He'd have to ring up her brother, Nick. He would want to know his sister's grave was disturbed. Maybe there was a grave robber with a penchant for stealing during rainstorms.

Or maybe it's something else, a little voice whispered inside his head.

God, he was going crazy. How he wished the rain would stop, and his world would finally start making some sense. As he stared down the hole, he had the weirdest feeling—almost as if someone or *something* was watching him. And as if there was something really bad about to happen.

9:15 AM

The clouds hung overhead like giant gray pillows, dripping steel tears on his shoulders as he walked back from the cemetery. How long had he just stared at that grave? Just stared at—nothing?

Halfway to his house, his cell phone played the first bars of "Enter Sandman." He thumbed the Accept button.

"Good morning, Marty. What can I do for you?"

"You know ol' Anger Thompson round-abouts Glen Way?" Marty asked.

"Yes, of course."

"Well, seems like he's missin' this mornin'. I heard his wife, Evalyn, called the emergency line, and she's scared to pieces. Overheard it at the Cup when Chief Ware was gettin' her coffee."

Good 'ol I.S. gossip news line. . .

"I see." Christopher glanced at the clock on his wall. It was nearly nine-thirty. Anger Thompson wouldn't have any outdoor work to do on his farm, given all the water coming down from the sky. His entire farm was agriculture. Corn and soybeans. Pumpkins.

"Wells, I thought you might be able to go over there? Calm her nerves? Chief Ware is at her house right now, taking her report."

"Thanks, Marty. I'll be there as soon as I can."

Christopher got his things together and jumped into his vehicle.

On the short drive to the Thompson home, he passed by fields and drainage ditches as sodden as Marlie's grave. The buds on the trees looked like they were about to burst open, though. Climate change seemed to bring spring earlier every year.

Judith opened the front door just as he was about to knock. She had dark circles under her eyes. Between the constant pounding of rain and threat of flooding, the recent town deaths, and the car crash she'd investigated when the ER doctor from James River General had taken a T-bone, he imagined she hadn't slept well the last twenty-four hours.

"How's Evalyn doing?" He jutted his chin toward the house.

"She's doing as well as a wife can after she wakes up to find her husband missing." Judith's words were steady and measured. "I'm worried about her, though. She's definitely distraught."

"She hadn't seen Anger at all since last night?"

"She said they went to bed together around ten. She was half awake, remembering she heard him get up to go to the bathroom. Heard him flush the toilet, then he went downstairs. Said he does that sometimes. Makes a midnight snack. Sandwich. Chips. She went back to sleep. When she woke, he wasn't in bed. She searched the house and the yard. Called his cell. It was still in the bedroom."

"He's never done anything like this in the past, has he?"

"No." Judith took a second to look at her cell. "Not that she can recall. He's always been there by her side, day in, day out, unless he's on the tractor working the fields."

"Okay." Christopher started for the front door. He held himself back from the reflex he usually had—that urge to hug someone in a time of tragedy. Judith wanted "professional," which he took to mean "distant." But God, how he wanted to hold her.

"I'll talk with her," he said. "Call you later?"

Judith nodded and headed for her vehicle, not even turning to look at him as she left.

His heart twisted. Would there ever be a time she'd let him past that razor wire she guarded her life with and be more than distant friends? He watched her drive off and then tapped on the door. It wasn't completely closed. He stuck his head through the opening.

"Mrs. Thompson? Is it alright if I come in?" The entranceway was empty, but he looked over to the right where their sitting room was. She sat on a dark red sofa, staring at the empty fireplace. She turned her head at the sound of his voice. Strands of her silver hair had escaped her sleeping cap, and her dark skin looked very dry. She wore a blue terry-cloth robe, pink pajama pants and white bunny slippers.

"Oh, yes," she said. "Yes. It's okay, Reverend. Please, come on in." She looked down at her hands. "I must look a mess, don't I? I'd offer you some coffee but I'm a-afraid I'm not much good for company right now."

Christopher sat on the sofa beside her chair and placed his hand on hers. Her hands were cold. Chapped.

"Evalyn," he started, thinking it was best to draw her thoughts away from hospitality. "I'm so sorry you are going through this. I imagine finding Anger missing this morning was very difficult. Judith and her team will find him."

He felt the hot tear on his hand before he saw it.

In times like this, when a person was distressed, it was important not to press ahead too quickly—to pause and just *be* with the person. To listen. He sat with her in silence.

Finally, she looked at him, her lips trembling. "I don't know what to do, Reverend. And I have a terrible, terrible feeling. Something evil has happened, I know it. The signs were there too—like—like the nest of spiders—the black widows I found in a nest under our bed. They ain't supposed to be there. Not inside and not in March. And then, those crows—all hanging out in my front tree yesterday. They bout drove me crazy."

He sidestepped the mention of signs and omens. That topic could only make things worse. "Anger didn't say anything to you? Not even before you heard him go downstairs?"

"Not a word. Lord Almighty, I'm praying that they find him. Hoping this is just some weird, strange occurrence. Maybe he went for a walk, got lost somehow. I just don't know." Her voice wavered.

Christopher patted her hand. "They'll find him, Evalyn," he said. "He can't have gone far."

"I hope you're right, I really do. I even made Cream of Wheat for him. It's gonna get cold."

More hot tears hit his hand. He usually carried a little pack of tissues for moments like this, but after finding Marlies's grave ruined, he forgot to put any in his pocket.

"It's just that I have this feeling making me all queasy inside," she said. "It's like a greasy rock right in the pit of my stomach." She looked up at him with dark gray eyes. "I'm so afraid I might not ever see him again." More tears slid down her cheeks.

"Would you like to pray?" Despite his personal doubts, he prayed with anyone who wanted to reach out to the universe in whatever way they felt was right.

Evalyn squeezed his hand. That meant yes. "But say some words," she said.

Christopher kept Evalyn company until her daughter, Mina, arrived around 10:30. After he'd left her house, he thumbed Judith's number. "I have something else for you, Judith. I forgot to say something this morning."

"What is it?" she asked, irritated. "I'm kind of busy trying to catch up on the reports."

"I know you've got a lot going on, but apparently, sometime late last night, someone dug into Marlie's grave."

Judith was silent on the other end.

"I mean, the casket's still there." He wasn't sure he should say the rest but then decided it was important enough that she needed the information. "I know this is going to sound crazy, but it looks like something broke out of it. Not like something got in. The wood protrudes outward. I've got it covered over with a waterproof tarp and a tent over that, but if you come—with the rain—I can't guarantee you'll be able to see anything."

More silence from Judith.

"Judith? Are you still there?" He pulled the phone away from his ear and checked the face of it, verifying they were still connected.

"I'm just thinking," she said. "I have no idea who would have done something like that or why. I'm guessing you didn't hear anything last night?"

"Just the rain." He paused. "Listen, can you think of anyone who could give me a hand moving the earth to help bring Marlie's remains back up? Making sure her resting place is set back in order? Job is coming later with something to hand-lift the casket out, but he can't use his backhoe. The cemetery is practically a bog now, and he's already got Persephone 3 stuck in there."

Judith sighed, and Christopher immediately felt bad piling this news on her. She was dealing with a lot of things right now, and the local flooding wasn't helping her in any way.

"Sure," she said. "I have a couple of guys in mind. I'll send them over in a few."

Christopher nodded, then felt stupid, realizing Judith couldn't see him. "Thanks, Jude. That would be great."

She sighed again.

"Something else the matter?" he said.

"You know Marvin and Mavis Bugg?"

"Yes." Somehow, he already knew what words she'd say next. And if he was right, there was soon going to be terror in this town that went far beyond a fear of a flood.

"Mavis found him dead in the kitchen last night," she said. "It wasn't pretty."

As Judith described the scene to him, Christopher made his way home through the water that covered most of the road. He started thinking about all the deaths that had occurred in a matter of days in Iron Shores and hoped, really hoped, that Anger Thompson wasn't going to be one of them.

12:00 PM

It was noon when Jansen and Morrey Pine knocked on his door. When he opened it, the brothers were both standing there soaked as the rain pummeled them, no umbrella. They were nearly identical. The only difference was that Jansen had fine, straight blond hair, and Morrey's crop was thick and curly. If he didn't know better, he'd swear the boys were twins, except that at age eleven, Jansen was born a year before Morrey and was a little taller than his brother.

"Chief Ware said you needed some help? Said you might pay us?" Jansen was always looking for a way to earn money around town.

"Sure," said Christopher. "Someone dug a hole right into Ms. Moon's grave last night. I need help digging the earth out so we can bring up her casket. It's a lot of mud and water right now, even though I covered it with a tent. Her brother wants to bury her proper again, so we are going to take her to Hatcher's."

"Sure thing." Jansen flashed a toothy grin.

Morrey said nothing. He just stood there, staring at something invisible in the distance.

After gathering shovels, a bucket, a rope, and a ladder, Christopher led them over to Marlie's spot in the graveyard under the tent he'd erected. The boys climbed down with shovels to slog the mud out. The three of them soon fell into a rhythm. Christopher lowered a bucket, and they filled it; he hauled it up, emptied it, and sent it back down. Despite trying to keep the area dry, muck kept running back into the grave.

Jansen suddenly yelled, "Oww!"

"What is it?" Christopher peered down and watched as the boy clutched his leg.

"My foot just punched through something!"

"It punched through?"

"I think," Jansen looked up at him as the rain kept pouring down, "my foot just sunk into the hole in her coffin."

"You hurt?"

"I don't think so."

Morrey hadn't stopped digging. He acted as if he hadn't even heard his brother.

Christopher said, "You're doing the best you can. Don't worry about that now. We just need to get her topside and take her back over to Hatcher's. Job will be over soon to help us lift it out."

Marlie's coffin hadn't been the most expensive in the mortuary, but it should've been strong enough to keep someone from breaking into it. Or out of it, as the case might be.

"Yes, sir." Jansen pulled his foot out of the coffin while Morrey stared. A shred of Marlie's dress was stuck to his shoe.

JUDITH

FOUND

*M*arch 18, *Monday*

1:30 PM

Unfortunately, the search party found Mr. Thompson's body that afternoon. Judith got the call from one of her squad, reporting him about 2 miles away from his house. Not reporting him so much as reporting his body.

It was out in the middle of a field. At least, they thought it was his body. There was a corpse of a sort. Mostly pieces. Ripped to shreds.

All of his internal organs except the intestines were missing. The bones of his appendages and his buttocks were stripped of all the flesh. Just like Marvin's.

Judith drove to the scene so she could see it for herself—conceptualize it. She'd called Lu to come out, take photos, walk the grid, and bag any evidence. She hated doing it, but Lu knew what she was doing, and they needed her expertise.

When Judith returned to the station, she called Christopher. He picked up almost before the first ring was complete.

"Hey . . . "

"Hey," he said.

She cleared her throat. "Members of my team found Anger. Where are you?" She drummed her fingers on her desk, index finger first—then reverse.

"Bia. Getting a coffee and a couple of hot chocs for some helpers of mine."

She heard some young male laughter nearby and wished she could smile.

"Soon as you can, come over this way. I need to tell you in person what I found. I think it's important—because you are going to be needed." Judith didn't wait for his answer. She just knew that after what she saw of Anger, she didn't have the heart nor the energy to describe it over the phone.

Christopher was there in less than ten minutes since Bia Cup was practically across the street. He looked extremely tired. Judith imagined she did as well.

Sleep had been a hot commodity these past few days. But she could smell that he'd freshly showered, and the scent of his mocha latte seemed stronger than usual. She allowed herself a smile.

"Three espressos today?"

Christopher arched an eyebrow. "How'd you guess that?"

Ignoring his question, she said, "Have a seat," and rolled a computer chair over to her desk.

Before he sat, he leaned over and slid a Cafe Americano onto her desk, his gaze lingering on her face. He knew she liked it black, no sugar.

And by the Universe, she needed that coffee, too. She hadn't even asked. She'd even said she needed nothing when he offered to get her something. He'd brought the coffee, anyway.

It was hard to ignore the way Christopher always looked at her. She knew what he wanted—but she wasn't ready. Didn't know if she'd ever be ready and she didn't know how to tell him that.

And what would he do when he found out about her family? Her *real* family? They were the reason she'd changed her last name to Ware. Her real family name. They were the reason she always had to be on guard, not only for herself, but for her daughters. She nodded thanks.

Judith chose her words carefully and started with a description of her encounter with Mrs. Bugg and her husband's horrible murder.

"Poor Mavis. Many of us chipped in so she could go stay at the Horseshoe until a group of volunteers from the fire department bagged Marvin and cleaned up the kitchen." She also described the medical examiner to him, Dr. Lu Crane.

"She's an amazing person. A real forensic pathologist, and although people make fun of her psychic abilities or ability to commune with the dead—I'm holding out on that one. We'll see. You and I have seen some things beyond believable in the I.S."

They shared a stare that only those in Iron Shores could ever share. From Mudrogs to Steel Narbs to so many other strange things that ordinary folk did not know existed here. And who knew? Maybe modern construction would eventually stamp it out. Her bet was that the modern world would only change it. These creatures would always adapt.

"Anyhow, she took photos of the crime scene and examined what she could of Marvin's body on site. And just now, she helped with Anger Thompson's case. Didn't bat an eye when I asked. She's a bit of a germaphobe—wears rubber gloves just about everywhere and she fanatically Purell's herself head to toe, but we all have our quirks."

Christopher thought it odd that a Forensic Pathologist was visiting their town during such god-awful weather and said as much.

"What do you think is going on?" said Christopher.

"I have no clue," Judith said, "but—"

It was then that she got a call. The number was from James River General.

"Ware here."

"This is Doctor Bedi." The man's voice was decidedly Indian, carrying that beautiful lilt characteristic of the accent. "I'm calling"—he cleared his throat—"I'm calling about Doctor Craig,

181

the young emergency room resident here at the hospital. He was a victim of the car accident just a few days ago?"

"Yes," she said, keeping her eyes on Christopher. "What about it?"

"Well, he was discharged from the hospital just yesterday. Now he is back in the ER babbling about something quite unsettling. He says he's had a vision he wants to see both you and Reverend Miles. He was very specific that it needed to be both Reverend Miles and you, Chief."

Judith sighed. The reports she had to write would have to wait a little longer. If this Doctor Craig had some type of lead, she needed to interview him.

She hung up and said, "We gotta go to the hospital."

Christopher raised his eyebrows.

"Something's up with the guy Marlie Moon T-boned," she said. "He was discharged from the hospital, but he's back now, and he's asking for me. And the weirdest thing is, he's asking for you as well. You okay to go?"

"Sure."

Christopher's shoulders drooped. He was taking the town deaths hard. She wanted to reach out, hug him, and tell him it would all be okay. It wouldn't have cost her anything except a moment of her time, but instead, she turned and said, "Meet me there in an hour. Call if you need me."

Christopher followed her as she left her office. Her heart felt ever so heavy as she crawled into her Interceptor and drove away, not even daring to look in her rearview mirror as she left him standing in the rain.

THOMAS

THREE MORE

*M*arch 18, *Monday*

2:30 PM

Dr. Bedi handed Thomas a cup of chai tea served in a lovely cobalt mug, and Thomas accepted it gratefully. The fragrance of cinnamon, cardamom, and other spices warmed him.

He stared at the creamy liquid then closed his eyes. The face of the monster from last night filled his brain and he shuddered.

"I appreciate this," said Thomas when he opened his eyes. He realized he should clarify. "Both for the chai and for you giving law enforcement and Reverend Miles a call."

He looked around the room. Dr. Bedi's office was neat and comfortable. One wall provided testimony of all his degrees, each one framed professionally in golden wood. Another wall held photos of family and friends. There were drawings from children tacked onto a cork board, as well as little handmade items probably fashioned by the same little hands.

Behind Dr. Bedi's desk was a window, the sill of it filled with plants. African violets in bloom, a Christmas cactus, and other greenery that Thomas recognized but didn't know the names for.

The sofa he sat on was plushily cushioned and decorated with classic Indian print. Burgundy with golden paisley designs.

"It is my pleasure, Dr. Craig." Dr. Bedi sat down in a chair next to the sofa, his hand cupped around his own chai. It sounds like you have been through a lot this past week. If you like, I can provide you with a referral to a therapist—just to talk with, I mean. It might help."

Thomas felt his nerves jangle.

"I know it all sounds crazy." Thomas tried to keep a sharp edge from creeping into his voice. He didn't succeed. "What I saw, what I experienced—it was *real*. Real as you sitting right next to me."

Dr. Bedi pressed his lips together and then took a sip of his chai.

A knock on the door startled them both, and Dr. Bedi opened it to reveal a woman in uniform with a tall man in a polo shirt and jeans standing beside her.

Saved by the wood, or the knock, Thomas thought. But not *really* saved. He was about to tell his story again to more people who probably wouldn't believe him.

The memory of the voice in his dream whispered in his head: *Find Reverend Christopher Miles. Find Chief Judith Ware.*

The tall man was likely Reverend Miles. The woman in uniform had to be Chief Judith Ware.

Thomas started to rise, but the woman in uniform strode over.

"Don't get up, really. Rest, Dr. Craig. From what I understand, you've been through a lot." She shook his hand, and the tall man came over to do the same while Dr. Bedi pulled over a couple of extra chairs. There was a bottle of Purell on the table, and each of them used it out of habit.

"Reverend Miles. Chief Ware. Thanks for coming," Thomas said.

There was an awkward moment of silence, and Thomas was only vaguely aware that Dr. Bedi was fixing more tea for the others. He had a pot of chai staying hot on a single burner plate on his desk.

"Please, call me Christopher," the Reverend said.

Chief Ware offered no such familiarity, and Dr. Bedi placed a cup of chai in both of their hands. They thanked him and Christopher took a sip while Judith set her cup on the coffee table in front of her.

Chief Ware, with an air of impatience, broke the ice.

"Dr. Craig—" she began.

"Please call me Thomas."

"Okay. Thomas." She gave a curt nod of her head and cleared her throat. "Dr. Bedi called to say you needed to speak with us. Something about . . . a creature?"

185

Thomas glanced at Dr. Bedi and then nodded. "It happened last night," he began. "I was discharged from the hospital yesterday. I was in a car crash with another woman who ran into me. She died." He paused. Saw the Reverend nod. He may have known her.

"Anyway, instead of going to my room—I'm renting a space from the Luck family—I went to the Horseshoe instead. It's closer to the hospital, and I didn't want to be trouble to them while I'm still recovering. I don't have a car now and can't drive yet anyway." Thomas sipped from his cup. "Anyway, I curled up on the bed for some sleep and woke up to something in my room. I don't know how it got there, but I know I was not asleep—it was no dream. This was very, very real." He searched their faces.

"Right," said Chief Ware

"The thing," Thomas continued, "it was a—a man-sized bird creature, the best way I can describe it. Talons for fingers, a huge beak on its head, sharp teeth. The only thing that saved me was this." He did not know if showing the talisman to anyone was a good idea, but Hatton hadn't said he couldn't. He pulled it out from his shirt.

Christopher stood up and moved over to the sofa where Thomas was sitting. "May I?" he asked, gesturing toward the medallion. Without waiting for an answer, Christopher touched it.

Thomas tolerated the touch but didn't remove the cord from his neck. He looked at the others. Willed them to understand. "I'm not taking this off now. Maybe never. Not after what I saw."

Christopher turned the medallion over and looked at the other side. "Where did you get this?"

"A woman I met not too long ago."

"What was her name?" The Reverend looked at him, a strange expression crossing his face.

"Hatton. Hatton Profitt."

Thomas noted the Reverend's face was calm. "Why did she give it to you?" His gaze flicked over to Chief Ware and then back to him.

"She said it would protect me. Or, no, I'm not sure exactly what she said except that I should never take it off." Thomas looked from the Reverend to the Chief. The Reverend believed him, he could tell. So did she, for the most part. Dr. Bedi's face was unreadable.

Chief Ware stood up. "Thank you for telling us." She nodded her head to him in thanks. "We'll—"

She was interrupted by a voice that came from Dr. Bedi's doorway.

"Take his words seriously!" A brown-skinned woman stood at the entrance to the office, her face a mixture of fear and anger. "If we want this town, everyone else in this town to live, we need to take his words very seriously. Our very lives are going to depend on it!"

Chief Ware seemed to go pale when she saw the woman and heard her words, then came to herself enough to say, "Christopher, you know Renny. Renny, come in. This is Dr. Craig—his first name is Thomas—and you know Dr. Bedi. Thomas, this is Ms. Renny Branham. She owns the Tattered Page and is the resident historian of the town. And sometimes, a local healer," she added.

Renny nodded to them, and then she addressed Chief Ware. "We need to find Hatton. If she's given this young man a talisman, she knows what's been started. I suspect . . ."

The Police Chief's phone buzzed. "Ware," she answered.

Thomas noted how the muscles in her jaw clenched. Chief Ware looked around and appeared to decide the group was one she could trust.

"Three more bodies. Three men," she said. "Christopher?"

He nodded. It seemed he was going with her.

An electrical zing went through him when her gaze swung to meet his eyes. He could see her struggling for a name. She'd already forgotten it. Given the amount of mental trauma she'd been through the past few hours—the number of deaths she had to investigate for such a small town and little outside support during a flood, he'd give her a pass.

Still, she asked him, "What about you, Doctor? Do you want to see the other side of the coin? I'm pretty sure my friend Renny thinks your talisman and these murders are connected."

Thomas didn't even realize he was nodding until he said, "Yes."

"Renny, you too, if it's okay." The Chief tilted her head. "You know I won't have you see anything you aren't ready for, but it seems you think I may need your help. I guess that's why you came?"

Renny's face seemed to drain of color, but she nodded as if it were exactly what she expected. "I'm ready."

Thomas and Renny rode with the Chief. Thomas caught Renny staring as he rubbed his talisman. He wondered who Renny *really* was. Obviously, something more than a bookstore owner if she was coming with them. He found himself wondering what macabre scene waited for them at the other end of their journey.

Meanwhile, the clouds rumbled, and rain kept pouring from the sky.

CHRISTOPHER

FLOOD ZONE

March 18, Monday

3:30 PM

Christopher followed Judith to the new death scene, not sure why she wanted him there. He wasn't normally squeamish, but the multiple deaths in this town over the past ten days were weighing heavy on him, not to mention the strange desecration of the graves that had occurred in the same timeframe. If he believed in God, he'd pray for this town and pray for the people, especially the men. It seemed as if they were the targets of this particular killer, and he couldn't see the connections.

It was clear now that Judith was headed toward the river. That wasn't good. Most people were evacuating the downtown area.

The town had gone to the second-stage flood control alert. The fire department put up the flood walls yesterday. The town's flood pumps were already going full force, having activated as soon as the river water level reached thirteen feet. He suspected it was well above that now.

Their group moved past the road signs blocking downtown roadways and keeping drivers out of areas where water was already crossing. They pulled up on the highest ground, right next to Foam and Rock Rafting, where an ambulance and the Volunteer Water Rescue vehicles were parked. A short, wide man in neon-yellow rescue gear stepped out onto the road and motioned them to come his way.

"Watch your footing," Chief Ware said to everyone. Christopher noted everyone had on waterproof boots except for the ER doc, Thomas.

He's gonna get soaked feet, Christopher thought and made a mental note to provide the man with some dry socks and some rain gear when they got back.

There were chairs outside Foam and Rock's entrance under an orange awning.

"Stay here," Chief Ware advised them all. "I'll go see what we've got and then call you over if it's safe." She'd put on her hip waders and waded out toward where rescue squads waited.

Christopher heard the sound of cawing crows and was surprised to see several of them circling in the sky. He rubbed his temples, feeling a headache coming on. If there were more bodies, depending on where the families wanted them buried, his pounding head would be the least of his problems.

JUDITH

DEATHWING

*M*arch 18, *Monday*

4:02 PM

It surprised Judith to see that Dr. Lu Crane already by the river, near a boat snapping photos around the scene. Dr. Crane glanced her way and raised a hand in greeting.

"I haven't touched anything," she called out. "The Water Rescue Team came in for coffee at Bia's and saw me. They told me where they were headed and asked for an assist and some photos, knowing you were on your way too." She didn't look apologetic, just transparent and explanatory.

Judith didn't know why she felt a sense of irritation at seeing the medical examiner at the scene already, another odd death scene at that, but the practical part of her welcomed the woman's assistance once more.

With the roads flooded, almost nothing was drivable in or out. She nodded, not trusting what words would come out of her mouth or how they would sound.

With a sigh, she noticed the rescue personnel were standing around a flat-bottomed aluminum fishing boat. Her mind whirled with questions and she wondered, *What kind of crazy asses would be out on the river during a flood?*

Nick Moon waved at her, and she lumbered over, thankful she'd worn her thick hip waders. What she had on was overkill, maybe, but if she needed to go into deeper water, she could. The muddy water was already a foot deep or more where everyone stood.

"It's bad, Chief. Not good at all. You'll see. Three heads. No bodies."

"Who found them?" The boat didn't look familiar, and she couldn't imagine anyone else out on the river except the rescue team.

"Someone was doing a helicopter fly-over, checking out the river conditions," Nick said. "Called it in as a drifting fishing boat just upriver from Shores. We spotted it and pulled it in. Sammi thinks they were fishing in an eddy. They caught a couple of smallmouth bass and a huge flathead before . . ." his voice trailed off.

"Might as well let me see." Judith said, and steeled herself with a couple of deep breaths.

Dr. Crane flanked her other side, ready with her camera.

Judith peered into the boat. Two smallmouth bass, a two-and-a-half-foot catfish, a flathead, and yep, three human heads. And each head was split wide open. Each was empty.

Just like Marvin Bugg's.

No bodies. All white males. No one she knew. The Richmond OCME would rely on dental records, DNA and missing persons reports to find their next of kin.

There were three black feathers in the boat as well. These were much larger than any crow's feathers. Larger than a buzzard's feathers, even.

Dr. Crane's camera clicked and flashed. The sound and light brought Judith back to the present.

"Okay. Everyone needs to wear gloves before touching anything, got it?" Judith sternly looked around, sincerely hoping she didn't need to remind her teams of this, but knowing she had to do it, anyway. They all nodded, and some of them were already wearing gloves. Others were just starting to put them on.

Judith turned her gaze to Dr. Crane. "Touch the boat as little as possible, okay? Finish up the photos and collect the heads for transport. I'll notify the state authorities and the ME's office. Maybe we can airlift their remains over to Richmond. The rest of you, there's a boat trailer by the building. Get the boat on the trailer after we're done processing. I'm sure Zed won't mind if we borrow it for now. I'll take it back to the station and secure it until the State can pick it up."

Judith glanced behind her. "Nick, go get the others. There's the Reverend, Renny, and an ER doc—he's a young-looking guy with an arm in a cast."

When they were all gathered, the rain had died down to a mild patter, and Judith stood to the side to gauge their reactions. Christopher was obviously shocked, and his hands were trembling. Dr. Craig seemed more curious than anything as he strained his head around at different angles to see. And Renny, she was still as a statue, her dark skin noticeably pale.

After Dr. Crane had completed her photographs, she began lifting the heads out of the boat and gently sliding each one into a partial remains bag, tagging each one. From the front, each head looked like empty faces—masks nearly split in two.

"Wait!" Renny called out. She edged closer to the boat. "There," she said, pointing at something round and silver dangling from the hair of one of the heads. "What is that?"

Dr. Crane picked it out and bagged it. "Good catch, Renny. Wouldn't want that accidentally dropping in the water." She sealed the baggie and handed it to Judith.

Judith examined the front and back of the coin through the plastic. On one side was a carving of a head. Half was a human skull, and half was a crow head or perhaps a raven. The other side of the coin had a strange marking on it. She handed the bag to Renny, wondering how in the hell Dr. Crane knew Renny.

Renny gripped the baggie by a corner, and peered at the mark on the back. "This is the seal, or sigil, of Raum, what some call the Deathwing Queen."

She gingerly handed it back, and Judith carefully placed it into the main evidence bag that Dr. Crane held out for her. Next, she collected the feathers and bagged them as well.

As they turned to leave, torrents of rain dumped down on them from a black, angry sky.

"Hurry! Get that boat on the trailer!" Judith yelled. "Everyone else, get back to your vehicles!" There was a tug on her sleeve.

"Got room for an extra?" asked Dr. Crane. "I rode with Nick. My car can't make it down here."

"Right. The red Alfa." Judith almost smiled, and pointed forward, ushering Dr. Crane ahead.

The group waded toward their transportation, and Judith followed behind, making sure everyone made it out okay. Her right hand tingled. She looked at it when she got into the Interceptor. There was a red spot on her palm where she'd held the strange item. Even though the thing was inside a plastic bag, something about it caused a skin reaction. She expected it would go away soon, given her health and her special condition. At least the full moon would be here soon.

6:34 PM

The police station had all the minor comforts of home: a coffee pot, a refrigerator that included an icemaker, cabinets with some food supplies, and a small stove with pots and pans hanging overhead. Judith started a pot of coffee and supplied bottles of water to the group. Some packs of cheese, peanut butter crackers, and some Oreos were even there.

There were enough chairs to go around, given that some of the chairs stacked against a wall were fold-out.

"Pull up your chairs into a circle," Judith directed. "Okay. Renny, educate us, please. What is a Raum, and what is this sigil?"

Renny rubbed her forehead, then clasped her hands. "Okay. As I tell you this, I'm going to ask you to please keep your minds open, okay? If you are from I.S., it's easier. If you aren't," Renny rested her gaze a moment on Thomas, but Judith felt her curiosity rise when it didn't go to Lu as well. "Well, it might be a tad harder."

With those words said, she took a long sip of hot coffee and dunked an Oreo in it, ate a bite, then continued.

"Raum is often called the Earl of Demons in Europe. She comes as a crow but can present in human form, female or male. I'll call her 'she' since I've only known of the demon in female form, but demons are really gender neutral. They present to us depending on what gender might influence us the most. Some books say that Raum must be asked to show herself as a human so that we can see her, but some books don't know squat. The natives also know Raum in this area. She is called by the Cherokee, what I can best translate as the Raven Mocker. Other tribes have called her the Deathwing Queen because she's reported to present in the form of a crow or a raven. She steals people's hearts, literally, if they let her inside their mind, and when people die, if she's there, she can harvest the time people would have had during the rest of their natural lifespan and give that extra life to others. Usually, she gives it to those who serve her. A sort of reward for their loyalty."

Judith noticed that both Dr. Craig and Dr. Crane looked shaken at what Renny had just said. She held up her hand. "Hang on a moment. Dr. Craig—

"Thomas," he replied. "Just call me Thomas, please."

199

"Okay, Thomas. Looks like Renny's words struck a nerve with you. You want to explain why?"

Thomas nodded slowly. "A few days ago, right before my accident, someone brought a man into the ER, unconscious. He had no respirations. No pulse. We did CPR. Nothing. When we did his chest X-ray, it showed he had *no heart*. I mean, literally, his heart was gone. And there were no external injuries to explain it."

He glanced around at Renny and the others and held up his palm and his cast. "I know that's impossible, even so, that's exactly what happened. I think his body is still in the hospital morgue. No one's claimed him yet for burial." His fingers on both of his hands were trembling.

"Dr. Crane?" said Judith. "You too. What is it?"

"I can confirm Dr. Craig's account," Lu nodded. "I suspect we saw the same man. He was brought into the Richmond Medical Examiner's office for autopsy. The lead forensic pathologist there is a friend of mine. He asked if I wanted to assist him with a couple of autopsies from Iron Shores."

So, Judith mused. *That's part of why she's here, at least. A case investigation. But I think there's something more to this. In this weather, none of us is leaving town soon, so time will tell.*

Renny continued with her information. "The sigil on the medallion we found in the boat is Raum's personal 'signature.' I guess that is the best way to describe it. It can be used as a phone number or a way to draw Raum to others. Books don't tell about that correctly, either. The sigil has lines and symbols that represent the connection to Raum and it can carry whatever Raum or her agent has put into it."

"Like what?" Judith asked, looking at her hand. The redness was suspiciously larger now.

"Blessings, curses, whatever the maker chooses," Renny said. "Those who summon Raum draw the sigil while chanting her mantra. And in her presence, they might imbue an item with whatever properties they need. For example, a knife can be used for cutting vegetables or stabbing. If its properties focus on stabbing, then the result of that particular is dedicated to Raum, like an offering." Renny's gaze focused on Judith, and she realized she was unconsciously rubbing her hand. "You let that thing touch you?" Renny asked anxiously.

"Only through the bag. But don't you worry. I'm fine, Renny." She put her hand down. Then, her phone rang. She looked at it. Her daughters. She thumbed it and answered.

"Okay, you guys, what are you up to? I'll be home soon." *The girls are bored,* she thought. Damn. She needed to be with them. They might be worried about the town flooding, too.

It was Lilith, and she was screaming, "Mom! Come home! Come home! There's a monster, Mom! Please!" The line went dead.

Judith frantically called back, but no one picked up. She grabbed up her keys and coat. "Please see yourselves out. I'll talk to you all soon. Be careful out there. I have an emergency at home!"

With a squeal of tires, she turned her lights on and raced to her house hoping that whatever was happening; she wasn't too late.

Judith's home was just up the hill, not more than a mile away, but safe from any flooding. She'd grown up in that house, but when she graduated from the police academy and then met her husband

201

while working on the county police force, she'd left it and its memories behind her.

When both her uncle and his wife died from the flu, the house became hers again, although technically it already was hers—left to her by her father. After her husband, David, died from a gunshot wound obtained when he was trying to arrest drug traffickers, she left the county police force. She moved back into the house when she accepted the position as Chief of Police in town.

It was convenient to live near work even when she was technically off duty. It also afforded the girls easy access to town and the river. Judith's Interceptor roared up the hill toward her house. It was just past seven p.m., and the daylight was rapidly fading into the oncoming night.

When she rounded the corner to her home, every light in the house was on. Generally, when she came home in the evening, the kitchen, living room and the girl's rooms were the only lights shining. Tonight, her home was blazing with lights everywhere. Even the front porch light was on although the timer would not bring it on automatically for another thirty minutes or so.

Her Interceptor skidded to a stop in front of the house. Judith exited the vehicle, stuffing the keys in her uniform jacket pocket, and dashed up the steps. She thew the oak front door open.

"Girls!" she called out. "Rachel? Lilith?" She listened. The TV was on in the living room. The padding of paws and clicks of nails greeted her ears on the hardwood floor.

Lola, the funny little creature, dashed up to her—tongue lolling over her bottom jaw. The dog didn't look distressed. Didn't behave as if anyone was in danger. If there were a problem, Lola would let her know.

Judith walked steadily toward the living room, where she heard sounds from the television. The girls were there, huddled on the sofa. Rachel turned her face toward her, and she gave a shrug. "Sorry, Mom."

"Pause the movie," Judith said. *I am not going to get upset if they called me for nothing. I am not . . .*

Rachel pressed the button on the controller. Now Lilith looked at her, too.

"What happened? Why did you call about a monster?" Judith's ire was rising. People were dying in and around town, and the girls—

Lilith hopped off the sofa and ran to her to give her a hug. "I'm sorry, Mama!" She turned and pointed to a figure that startled Judith, in part because she hadn't even smelled— hadn't noticed he was there. "Mason came over to check on us, and when we looked outside on the porch, he had a hood on, and it was black, and we were watching *The Ring*, and we thought it was Samara and that we were going to die!" Lilith's run-on sentence might have been comical if it weren't for the emergency call and a certain Mason Profitt occupying her recliner.

Judith's gaze shot over to Mason. His dark brown hair was damp, and the humidity in the air was probably what accentuated the soft shoulder-length curls around his head. "Hey-ya, Chief." He didn't get up but stayed sprawled across her Lazy-Boy as if he were the advertisement of the chair name. In her irritation, Judith didn't respond but looked back over to her oldest girl.

"Rachel, why is he here?" She regretted the sharp tone of her voice, but the emergency call—and now the unexpected Mason—had squeezed her patience down to the size of a peanut.

"We saw him in town today, Mom. Went to the Food Lion for some munchies after you didn't come home, and we ran into him." Rachel smiled her winning. *I'm the oldest, and I know what I'm doing,* smile. We talked for a bit, and I told him if he'd like to come over and watch some flicks that we were down."

"Uh huh," Judith eyed Mason again and then Lilith. "So . . . if you knew he was coming, why the emergency call?"

Lilith hung her head for a moment, obviously embarrassed at this line of questioning in front of Mason. "We didn't know he'd come tonight for sure. He doesn't have a cell phone, so he decided to drop by since he was in town. He looked like a monster at the door, Mama. He was in a black rain poncho—he looked like—like a giant crow!"

Lilith's words startled Judith. It was odd that Lilith used that description. "What did you guys hear when you were at the Food Lion? People talking?" she asked.

All of them were silent. So they'd heard about the murders.

Mason shifted his body and made as if to get up, "Chief, I'll go. I just—"

Judith saw the hurt look on his face and regretted the tone she'd used. "No, Mason, it's okay. Really. Stay. I was just surprised. Listen, guys," she said to all of them. "Yes, something is going on in town. Be on guard, but don't panic, alright? We've got a team put together, and we're figuring it out. Mason, where's your car? I didn't see one when I pulled in."

"Don't got one, Chief. My brother dropped me off in town today. Didn't say when he'd be back. I got tired of waiting for him, so I walked up here."

"You can use our phone to call him if you like." Judith and the girls all had their own cells, but Judith kept a hard line with an old-fashioned rotary phone for emergencies.

"He won't come," Mason replied. "It's night now. If you've been to our house, you know the road. No lights, slippery clay."

Pretty much the same reasons I don't want to drive up there tonight to take him home, Judith thought.

"Think your family will mind if you crash here for the night?" Judith hated asking the question, but she couldn't put Mason back out into the weather without a ride or somewhere to go. "We'll make up the sofa before we go to bed. The bathroom's just down the hall if you haven't found it already."

Mason visibly brightened. "No, Chief, not at all. That'd be great. I'm eighteen, ya know." He said it as if that explained everything, and Judith was too tired to ask any more questions. He'd be safe here for now, as opposed to in seven days when the moon was full.

She went to the linen closet and got some sheets, a blanket, and a guest pillow with a clean pillowcase, all the while with Lola sticking right between her ankles as she walked. The dog followed her everywhere whenever she got home.

The kids had resumed their movie, but Judith gave them one last assignment as she kissed them goodnight. "In bed by ten, guys, you got it? I'll know if you don't. Rachel, you, and Lilith help make up the sofa for Mason and turn out the lights. And don't forget, you have homework assignments. I know you need to finish them by tomorrow."

The girls murmured a half-aware, "Okay," and Mason thanked her once more before Judith headed toward her room to take a shower before she hit the sack.

Peeling off her dirty clothes, she was glad to turn on the hot water and climb under the pounding spray. Judith's right hand still tingled from touching that coin or medallion with the sigil.

But it was in a plastic bag, so why did it affect me? She rubbed the area with soap, wondering why the red spot was still there. Due to her body composition, something like that usually faded by now.

As she climbed into bed, planning to read another chapter from James Kaine's '*My Pet Werewolf*,' the sounds of crows cawing and wolves howling filled her mind. And even though she was determined to stay awake until the kids had gone to bed, her eyes grew so heavy—and then she was running through the woods, fast on four legs, chasing the shadows and snapping her teeth at feathered nightmares. She chased them away from her children and from Christopher, ready to kill . . .

Meanwhile, Lola slept at her feet, peering now and then through the cracked door—her ears perked and ready to respond to the least odd sound.

CYNTHIA

SILENCE

*M*arch 18, Monday

6:40 PM

Cynthia Pine stepped out of the shower and onto the bathroom scale. She knew it wasn't good to do at the end of the day, but she was in a battle for her life—that's what her doctor said, anyway. She was five feet tall, four inches, and weighed two hundred and fifty-two pounds.

It was two-sixty last week, so things were moving in the right direction, but damn—it was so hard with two young boys in the house and a husband that never seemed to gain an ounce no matter what he ate. They all had to have chips, candies, cookies—freaking Oreos—baked lasagna, and triple cheese pizza in the house.

Cynthia sighed and got off the scale. The way things were going, her weight would probably just creep right back up.

Once she was dressed, she sat down at her computer.

Today's game? Maybe I'll go back and play a little old Divinity, Original Sin.

She had mentored a couple of newbies last week on the game and taught them the ropes, and now was as good a time as any to drop in on them and see how their adventuring was going. Her husband, Paul, was out somewhere—he should have been back by now—and the boys were sleeping overnight at a friend's house.

Jansen had texted her and told her they were fine. She texted back and told them to be home by noon tomorrow, and just like that, all was good.

Cynthia pulled up her Steam account online. While waiting for her program to load, she thumbed through the mail she'd brought in earlier.

This is odd.

A circular ceramic thing slid out onto the desk from between two pieces of junk mail. She picked it up.

Weird.

On one side, it had etched a half-human skull and a half-bird face, and on the other side, strange red markings that almost looked like electrical schematics.

It could have been a game piece for something if it wasn't so big. It was kinda cool. She set it down on her desk and hit "Resume" on the game screen.

Her fingers tingled. They usually only did that when she was cold, and it was pretty toasty in the computer room right now. She tried to ignore the sensation while she changed around some of the equipment for the character she'd named Righteous, but the tingling got worse.

She suddenly got light-headed and didn't feel so good. Maybe she should go lie down for a while. With the boys gone, she'd be able to rest.

She hefted herself out of her chair and headed down the hall. She almost made it to her bedroom when she felt a crushing pain in her chest.

Fucking Christ!

Her doctor had warned her about this.

The sound of her blood pumping filled her ears.

My phone—where's my phone? She cast a glance toward her desk.

It was back at the computer. She'd never make it that far. And now she was stretching flat on the carpet, trying to make the pain go away. Her vision clouded, but she could hear something.

What was that? Something was tapping—tapping at the windows—tapping louder and louder, punctuated by a squawking of birds. The sounds were deafening in contrast to her heartbeat, which was fading—fading—fading into—silence.

MASON

HAIR OF THE DOG

*M*arch 18, Monday

10:30 PM

Rachel and Lilith made sure Mason had what he needed on the sofa. Lilith gave him a squishy beanie for a pillow. Rachel placed a glass of water on the coffee table beside him just in case he needed it and gave him a new toothbrush from a bag their mother kept for guests.

"If you need anything—since you don't have a cellphone—you can just knock on our door. Just watch out for Lola. She will bite if you try to come in."

Mason nodded. He wasn't planning on going into their bedroom if he didn't have to. He had specific goals.

The girls settled for bed, and then he went into the bathroom to brush his teeth. Studying the shelves, he saw exactly what he needed. Bam!

He took those few extra moments to pluck hair from two hairbrushes resting in two separate baskets conveniently labeled *Rachel* and *Lilith*.

This part was *so* much easier than he'd imagined. All he required was right here. He placed their hair separately into two plastic baggies and stuffed the bags in his pockets.

When he opened the bathroom door to return to the living room, Lola nearly scared the living shit out of him. She was planted right in front of the door. No growl. Just a steady stare. She followed him back to the couch and then went back to the Chief's room.

Curling under his blanket, he pulled out his cell phone from his front pants pocket, thumbed it, and texted:

I got them. No problem.

The Ware family had been so nice to him. They'd shown him nothing but kindness. And even the Chief of Police—the fucking Chief—hadn't treated him like he was a piece of shit.

Now, he felt a little guilty at what he'd done, but his Pa and Savral were counting on him. Really, he had no choice. For the sake of his family, and mostly for little Precious, he had to come through.

Mason turned his cell phone off and then settled down to sleep. Tomorrow, he'd bring what his pa and Savral needed so Precious would have a long, healthy life. They would all live long, happy lives together.

MASON

SECURITY

M*arch 19, Tuesday*

5:00 AM

Mason woke at his usual time—five in the morning—found a piece of paper and a pen next to an old rotary phone in the kitchen, and wrote:

Thanks for the sleep space. Didn't want to wake anyone. Called my brother. He'll be in town to pick me up soon. ~Mason

He plucked a red apple from a fruit basket on the counter, removed his rain poncho from the coat rack, and turned to exit the front door. That's when he heard the click of nails on the wooden floor and a low growl behind him. Lola was awake and obviously not liking the fact that he was slipping away.

Gotta keep that dog in mind when I come back, he thought. He considered whether or not he should try to turn around and pet her or keep going.

In the end, in his experience, he knew dogs all too well. To try to hush the dog or keep it from barking wouldn't matter—it might only make it worse. Lola didn't know him. She was an intelligent dog. He'd seen that yesterday.

So, he opted to move forward. He turned the knob, opened the door, twisted the lock to secure the house when he shut it, and then slipped out. And, thankfully, Lola didn't bark.

Secret Agent Man . . . he sang in his head.

Mason found himself wondering why Chief Ware's house wasn't more secure. And why hadn't the dog woke anyone when he left? Was it smart enough to figure out leaving versus leaving after having committed a crime?

It was a mystery to him why the town Police Chief didn't have a security system or alarm in her house, but of course, that was much better for him, Pa, and Savral as the right time drew near.

JUDITH

GUARDIAN

*M*arch 19, *Tuesday*

5:13 AM

Judith watched the boy, Mason, leave their house from her window.

She was certain he'd been up to something and that his visit wasn't just a friendly drop-in. His body language told her a lot. He skulked away instead of walking away easily like an innocent man.

Last night, she'd detected a pungent odor on him, something that reminded her of dark, damp places with hints of wood smoke. She was sure it was somewhere she'd never been. She wondered if Rachel smelled it too, though she hadn't let on that she'd smelled anything out of the ordinary.

Lilith was too young, yet her senses were still undeveloped. The change would happen for her any day now. Maybe even with the Crow Moon.

If so, given the continuous rainfall and these creatures Dr. Craig described—creatures that Renny had some knowledge of—it would be a dangerous time indeed.

It hurt that she couldn't protect her daughters like she wanted. But that was life, wasn't it? The Great Mother knew. The Great Father knew as well. Life and Death intertwined. Risk and Reward. Everything in between balanced on the knife's edge.

In the end, she could only guide her young ones and be at their sides as much as possible to help them grow.

And she'd give every bit of her life to do just that. Lola thumped her tail on the bed, reminding Judith that she could grab thirty more minutes of shuteye or make coffee early and get lunches ready to go now.

Judith looked at her friend. She'd hardly had any time for Lola the past few days.

"How about fifteen minutes of a curl-up and cuddle, and then we'll get things ready for the girls?

Lola panted and smiled.

Outside, thunder rumbled in the distance, and the wind started to howl.

THOMAS

COMFORT

*M*arch 19, Tuesday

9:00 AM

Thomas made his way down the corridor toward the Horseshoe Inn's dining room for breakfast. It wasn't difficult to find. It was just past the lobby, and he had only to follow his nose from there. When he entered, the room had several very cozy tables set with green

217

tablecloths inside it, and a woman standing just inside the door advised him he could sit anywhere he desired.

The Morrows' buffet table featured an excellent variety of homemade dried blueberry and crunchy nut granolas, banana and raspberry muffins, bacon and savory meats, eggs fixed any way you like, and biscuits. A drink table held juices, cow milk, almond milk, and coffee.

The warmth and cheer of the room did not reflect the outside horrors growing in the town. It was a true refuge—secure and snug. The damp didn't sink into the walls like other places when it rained too long.

He was ravenous once the warm odors of breakfast foods and coffee filled his nose. It was difficult not to grab everything at once. In the end, he settled for a pastry, a large scoop of scrambled eggs, a bunch of grapes, two biscuits—with butter and blueberry jam— and some vegan sausage.

A sign beside the tray of vegan sausages read: No Cholesterol! He'd tried all kinds of plant meats on his diet and figured he'd give this veggie meat a try. Sitting down, his first bite was of the sausages, and he was surprised at how much he liked them. Making a mental note to find out where to buy them, he sucked down his coffee and a glass of orange juice and then launched into his eggs.

Next, he pulled apart a biscuit, pleased to find it still steamed when he did it, and the aroma coming off it was to die for. He slathered some butter on half and watched the golden pat melt as he prepared to dollop what looked like homemade blueberry preserves right in the center.

Mrs. Morrow wandered near and stopped at his table. She smiled, very nearly meeting his eyes. "How you doing, there, Dr. Craig?" The woman was blind as a snail, but she moved around as well as a sighted person, maybe better. She caught him just as he'd taken a huge bite out of his biscuit.

Of course, she'd ask *now*.

Thomas settled for making yummy noises, hoping she'd realize his mouth was full.

She smiled and held out a pot of coffee. He pushed the edge of his cup against the spout, and she freshened his drink. Not spilling a drop. He was impressed.

Thomas swallowed, and finally, he could speak. "Please, Mrs. Morrow, just call me Thomas."

The old woman smiled again. "Thomas, it is, then, as long as you call me Faye."

He added almond milk creamer to his cup while he said, "You got a deal, Faye. And, if I might ask, how did you know it was me?"

"Ah," she was still smiling. "When the vision goes, other senses kick in a little stronger, you know. It's your walk and your smell. Everyone's different. With your arm in a sling, I noticed your gait is slightly off. Picked you out when you came in. And you wear a cologne with sandalwood in it, right? It's one I haven't smelled before."

Thomas took a sip of coffee. "The cologne is Dolce and Gabbana, called *The One*, I think. I can't take credit. It's something Tati picked up for me when I said I wanted something with an earthy scent. Not too strong."

"Ah, Tatianna. Kevin's sister. You've met Kevin?"

Thomas shook his head, then realized Mrs. Morrow couldn't see him doing that and said, "No, ma'am, never met him." He noticed how her rose flower embroidered cardigan, pink shirt, and lavender pants accentuated the rose tinge in her cheeks. "Don't worry. You will." She chuckled and drifted away to the next table.

As Thomas sipped his coffee and scooped eggs onto his fork, he thought about the three heads in the fishing boat. Who were those men, he wondered. How had they come by that strange medallion? He found it interesting how, after all these months, this injury had brought him closer to the community than any of his time working in the emergency room.

As he ate the last bite of his second biscuit, his cell phone buzzed. He picked it up and looked at the message. He didn't recognize the number, but the message seemed legit.

It's Christopher.

Meet me at Renny's at noon.

That's all it said. He guessed that "Renny's" was The Tattered Page since the Reverend didn't say.

Well, the rain was still pouring down, but the town's flood walls were holding, and Thomas had nothing else to do other than sit around and heal. He slugged down the rest of his orange juice and coffee, then headed to his room to get his things. He'd call Tati and see if she could give him a ride to the bookstore. If not, perhaps he'd walk. Brave the wild.

Might as well see what kind of strangeness he could experience today. He felt the round crow talisman rub against his chest with every step. That was some comfort, at least.

THOMAS

COMPLIATED

*M*arch 19, *Tuesday*

11:25 AM

Tati picked Thomas up at twenty minutes to noon. She was a dot of bright sunshine on this dreary day, and the drizzle of rain, normally inconvenient, was like a blessing because it wasn't part of a torrential downpour.

"Where to, Doc?" Tati asked.

"Tattered Page," he said, and he might have gone straight there if he hadn't seen Hatton Profitt walk into Bia Cup as they were passing by.

"Stop," he told Tati. "Can you stop right here, please?"

The driver arched one eyebrow at him and then looked over at the shop. Hatton was out of sight, but he guessed Tati had seen her go in. People didn't miss much in this small town.

"Ms. Morrow's coffee not good enough for you, huh?" She smiled knowingly. "Maybe the coffee here is just a little richer?"

Thomas felt warmth rise to his cheeks, paid the woman her fare and a generous tip on top. "See ya round, Tati."

The yellow van drove off, the sound of "Chevy Van" playing seductively through the speakers.

11:28 AM

Thomas stepped into the shop and looked around. There was a big hand-hewn wooden counter with wooden stools right in front of him, and a waitress taking orders. To the left and right were booths lining the sides near the windows and a back room to the left filled with books and some musical instruments where some people came, had coffee and did readings sometimes.

The odor of espresso filled the air, and local conversation buzzed as if it were its own symphony. It played in harmony alongside the sound of the espresso machine and the machine that made the foam, the blender and the other sounds of the Bia.

The wheat-colored walls sported art from local artists. This week's art came from Ensey Winter. She made shadow-box art with tiny little lights inside boxes that created a variety of shadows depending on which lights were turned on. The shadows interacted and played—and her work was truly inspiring and inventive. Some even said that certain shadow boxes came to life.

Thomas squinted down the counter, but Hatton wasn't anywhere to be seen. But he'd seen her come in, he knew he did. Disappointed, he ordered a caramel macchiato and was paying for it when a small touch to his right shoulder caused him to turn. And was Hatton.

"Whatcha doin' there, Doc?" Her smile was exhilarating. White teeth, laughing eyes. She smelled of vanilla and patchouli.

"Looking for you," he said.

She dipped her gaze down and then looked back up at him. "How's your arm?"

"Okay." He hated this small talk. The woman at the counter handed him his drink, and he tugged Hatton over to a table, motioning her to sit. "I'm not good at this sort of thing . . ."

Hatton opened her mouth to say something, but Thomas put his finger to her lips.

"Wait," he said. "I gotta get this out or I might not ever have the chance. I enjoy being with you. I'm attracted to you. As an ER resident and someone who's spent years making my studies a priority, I've never had time for relationships, and I don't want to waste time slowly trying to find out if you like me or want this go further . . . "

I'm babbling, he thought, *and bombing this big time.*

Hatton stared at him, then got out of her seat.

He looked down and shook his head. *Great, she's leaving. You idiot!* His brain was on hyperdrive. She hadn't even given him a chance—

Then he felt her warm hands on his cheeks, her soft lips on his. She kissed him right there in the coffee shop, in front of everyone she probably knew. And the kiss was sweet and tender, like apple pie with cinnamon.

She moved away slightly. "I gotta go. Want to come out with me?" Her smile was gentle, mischievous. Infectious.

"Yeah," he said, probably grinning, and slid out of his chair. They exited the shop with quite a few curious eyes glancing their way. And Thomas felt like a big dopey dog following their favorite human who had the best treats. The human he loved.

11:30 AM

"You off to somewhere?" Hatton asked him.

It took him a moment to realize she'd really asked him a question.

"Geez! I forgot. I'm meeting someone at the Tattered Page." His hands motioned in the direction, and he made Puss-n-Boots eyes at her. "Come with?"

She smiled a genuine smile. He could tell because her whole face seemed to light up. "Okay, just for a minute. I'll walk with you there, then I gotta go."

They talked about his residency while the rain sprinkled on their heads. He asked about her family. She was evasive, though she did brag on her youngest sister, Precious.

"She's got a knack for knowing things, sometimes before they happen," she said. "Weird, right? Like, one time, a couple years ago, I got my V.W. stuck in the mud and came home crying because I didn't want my pa to know what happened. He'd wale on my backside if he found out. Precious told me not to worry. That a couple of guys from town would pull it out, wash it off, and have it ready good as new. I just needed to go pick it up and thank them. Then all would be good. And you know what, that's exactly what happened!"

"No," said Thomas. "Really?"

"Yes, and she knows things like—" She halted and stopped talking.

They were at the front door of the Tattered Page. A brindled pit bull was sitting beside the entrance. He didn't wag his tail. Thomas glanced at his eyes and noticed he was staring at Hatton. It might have been his imagination, but he thought the hair on the back of the dog's neck was slightly raised. He wasn't growling, but the look he gave Hatton wasn't friendly.

"Wanna come in with me?" Thomas wasn't ready to lose her company. Not just yet.

"Well," she hesitated, her eyes narrowing as she looked over at the dog. "Who are you meeting?"

"Reverend Miles. You know him, right?"

Hatton took a deep breath. "Um, yeah. He helped bury my sister," she said.

227

Now Thomas felt the moment turning awkward.

"Well, we are working to solve a mystery," he said and opened the door. Chimes jingled. "These deaths . . ."

In the back of the shop, beyond shelves of old books and curiosities, he saw Christopher's face, then Renny's, and then a man he didn't recognize.

Apparently, Hatton *did* recognize him— just as well as, and maybe more than, the others.

"I'm so sorry." Her eyelashes flickered, and it seemed to Thomas that they were threatening to spill over into tears. "I've really—gotta go. Family thing."

There was no time or opportunity for another sweet kiss like they'd had earlier. She pecked him on the cheek, mumbled something about seeing him later, and then ran off faster than a hunted fox.

11:50 AM

Thomas looked over at the group then closed the door, jingling the chimes again, and came forward. All of them were sitting on the floor with a pile of books.

"Sup, guys?" He looked pointedly at Christopher.

Christopher showed his hand toward the woman he'd seen at the hospital and the river, Renny—and the dark-skinned man he hadn't met before. "Renny and Job here are Iron Shores' historians. They've been digging into what we saw yesterday and thinking about the story you had to tell. About that creature."

"Okay," Thomas said. "What about it?"

Renny leaned forward and took Thomas's hand. "Have you had any more encounters with that thing?"

"No," he replied. "It's crazy, but I think that this," he pulled out the medallion, "had something to do with it. I swear it saved my life. And Hatton," he gestured toward the door, "she's the one who gave it to me. I think I told you that, right?"

Renny's whole body was reacting like a giant nod as she rocked it back and forth. "Job, how long since you've been out to the Profitt place?"

"*Years,* Ren. Why?" Job was marking pages in the books with little lime-green stickies.

"Wait! Don't close that one." Renny reached over and picked up a book. "This is one of the town's history books. It includes myths and legends from the area." She showed Thomas a black-and-white lithograph. "Was this what you saw?"

Thomas stepped backward. His body felt cold, and the deep sense of dread that had come over him inside his room at the Horseshoe Inn when he'd turned on the light and seen that awful beaked face and icy eyes washed over him again. And now here it was, staring him down from a page in a book. He reflexively smacked the book away.

"I'll take that as a yes," said Renny. "Grab a chair from over there and have a sit." She turned the page as he dragged an antique chair over and set it beside the group sitting on the floor.

On the other side of the page with the lithograph, which should have been blank, was a hand-drawn map in pencil. The men edged closer. The river, the railroad tracks, and the town were sketched in

230

neatly, but Thomas was shocked to see the Raum sigil they'd seen on the medallion in the decapitated man's hair drawn onto an area that looked like hills near Iron Shores. Beside the sigil was a dark horseshoe arch and the word *Cave*.

"Pretty cool, Renny," Job said. "All my time around here, and you know I love my archeology, I've never seen or heard of any caves over that way. And the mark there? What do you think it means?"

Renny's eyes surveyed them all as if weighing each of their souls. "It means if we want to stop whatever this is, we'll have to go there."

"Go where?" A musical voice came from a corner of the room that wasn't as well lighted.

Renny sighed, answering all of their unspoken questions. "Gentlemen, meet my daughter Melody."

The girl stepped quietly out of the shadows. Thomas' sharp intake of breath had to be audible. He knew it was. And yet, he could not help himself.

Melody was, without a doubt, one of the most beautiful girls he'd ever seen. Her afro hair, coifed as if it were a halo of light around her head, had a red tinge to it, but he doubted it was colored. It had a sparkle, a sheen to it that was intriguing. Her skin was a perfect shade of mocha, like a mixture of coffee and sweet cream swirled together and her eyes glimmered with emerald, green irises that couldn't be real and yet somehow, he knew they were.

She was no taller than her mother, but built willowy, slender. The shirt she wore that clung to her like a dancer's leotard and her skinny jeans only accentuated her thin build.

Thomas glanced at Christopher, noting that he too was marveling at the girl and wondering why he was surprised. Hadn't he met Renny's daughter? Supposedly, he knew her well.

Christopher must have been reading his mind. He said, "Since when do you have a daughter, Renny?"

"Since last week," Renny said with a matter-of-fact statement that also held deep pride and sorrow in those words. Then she explained. "Melody was born sixteen years ago. Her father was very powerful, and I was naive at the time. Thought he loved me and that he'd love her. Things became—"

"Complicated," Melody interrupted. She came over and sat cross-legged on the floor next to her mother.

Renny's lips pressed together gently, not in anger but more as if to say, *Not now. Another time.*

"Mother," Melody looked at Renny with an expression Thomas didn't know how to read. "Where is it you need to go?"

Renny leveled her gaze at the men and said, "Into the belly of the beast, my dear. It will take all of us to fight this thing."

In the distance, a wail of a siren reached their ears.

Christopher pulled out his phone. "Damn. Four texts from Judith. Gotta go, guys. Somethings up." He raced to the door and was gone.

Everyone else pulled out their phones and checked messages. Everyone except Thomas. Who would message him? Not anyone right now. He was useless at the hospital for another couple of weeks at least, and aside from his work, he hadn't had any hobbies or other interests that he could do that would have kept him occupied.

"Oh no," Renny's voice sounded desolate and heartbroken. "They found him. They think so anyway. The Pine boy's father."

From the tone of her voice, Thomas guessed he wasn't found alive.

She provided more details. "It's a message from Nick Moon. He sent me a voice text. They believe someone dumped Paul's body in Hazard Creek. Rescue workers were helping evacuate some people since that area is flooding. They spied something strange in the water. Thought it might be someone stuck out there. One climbed into a tree to check it out with high-powered binoculars. They could see bones, mostly bones with some flesh, wedged into some rocks. The head was gone."

CHRISTOPHER

PUZZLE

*M*arch 19, Tuesday

11:40 AM

Christopher dug through some local history books while drinking coffee this morning. He was done with the first pot and finishing as he read about the canals that ran along the James River.

He mulled over the past few days. Marlie's grave desecrated, two deaths of local men in bizarre and horrific ways, and the deaths of three men from upriver somewhere—with their heads split open and no bodies to be found.

And there was the ER doctor's strange account of a bird creature, something Renny called a demon. Raum. Also called the Raven Mocker.

And the Deathwing Queen.

He thought about the man with no heart—Viktor—lying in some refrigerator drawer at the hospital morgue because no one claimed his body even after the OCME had shipped him back. Even after an anonymous call provided identification. Apparently, no one in town knew a man named Viktor Odol.

God, how Christopher wanted to get a good look at the guy. See if he looked anything like the child he'd played with all those years ago. The child in the supposed non-existent town of Passage.

It has to be the same person, doesn't it? What are the odds of the same strange name? But how could that be?

He'd half convinced himself that the entire experience was a dream, but when he'd told Job the story, the memories of those moments came back to him clear as day. Clearer than any nightmare he'd ever had. And that was saying something.

The automatic coffee maker beeped to let him know the second pot of coffee for the day was ready. He poured the black liquid into a red aluminum Thermos and added milk and maple syrup. He preferred the taste of maple syrup over conventional sugar.

He took a sip. The warm flavor gave him a sense of childhood comfort he never had. Growing up, he's heard from people about pancake and waffle mornings. Sunday laughter. Sometimes he was invited to Sunday breakfasts. He marveled at how differently other people lived. He'd never known such happiness.

After this morning's thunderstorm, the rain had slowed to a drizzle, but he grabbed his rain slicker anyway and pulled on his waterproof boots. The forecast for Iron Shores called for rain throughout the week.

He found himself wondering what would happen if the flood barriers broke and the whole town went under. The flood barriers were erected to stand between the river and the town when the water levels threatened to reach into the town's living spaces.

Depending on how high the water rose, his church, his home, and the graveyard might suffer some major damage. He shook the worry away since there was no sense in it. Worrying didn't help anything, particularly if he could do nothing about it. He worried more about other people. He tried to think about what he could do for them.

What he could do was learn more about this Deathwing that Renny spoke about yesterday. Maybe he, she, and Thomas could figure out what was going on when they met at the Tattered Page. Figure out how to stop what seemed like a series of grisly murders that, for some reason, focused on men.

The Tattered Page was just a few blocks from his house, and the rain eased to a drizzle. He decided to walk. He'd get some exercise and get a better view of how the flood situation looked in town.

The wind had picked up, and it was bone-cold, damp, and miserable out. When he was younger, he'd have gone climbing in this weather, loving the challenge, but now, at the age of thirty-four, he preferred sunny skies and warm weather if he wanted even to try tackling a rock face or boulder.

When he reached Renny's store, he was startled to see Grinch outside. The pit bull wasn't tethered, but sat firmly at attention on his haunches beside the door as if he were a vigilant doorman at a fancy hotel.

"Heya, buddy!" Christopher knelt and ruffled the dog's head. His face received an affectionate return greeting with a few wet sloppy licks of the beast's tongue. "What, no dogs allowed inside?"

Grinch gazed up at him with baleful eyes as if confirming that the dog thought he was the subject of unjust animalism.

"Ah, don't take it personally," Christopher reassured him. "I guess Renny has her reasons. She needs someone reliable to stand guard."

The Grinch's tail thumped the ground gently, but he remained sitting faithfully by the door.

After one final rub of the animal's brindled head, Christopher pushed open the door and stepped inside. Multiple chimes at the entrance jingled with a pleasant mix of high tinkling tones and deep Gregorian tenors.

When he gazed up, he spied at least four sets of chimes just inside the entrance to the shop. He studied the nearby windows, where even more chimes hung. They seemed like a pleasant alarm system, as if Renny wanted an alert in case uninvited visitors tried to come in.

"Back here!" Renny called out.

Christopher followed her voice past glass cabinets holding a variety of tarot cards, crystal balls and ornate wands. Himalayan salt lamps glowed on shelves in the back corner where observed Renny sitting on the floor with Job Graves. They were each surrounded by a number of old books. Many were open to display pages of occult drawings of dark-winged figures and sigils similar to the one on the medallion they'd found in the fishing boat.

"Looks like someone's doing homework." Christopher remained standing, not sure if he should sit and join them.

"Pull up a chair from over there," Renny directed. "Or grab a cushion. Either one is fine. We're finishing up here in a moment, but feel free to join us. We're just searching for more information to help explain what's going on."

The wooden chair she pointed at was on rollers and looked like an old accountant's piece. Polished arm rests, and wood veneer stained in golden oak at the top where a person's head might rest. It smelled of lemon oil.

"Job stopped in to lend a hand and share some things he knew," she went on. "Seeing as grave digging is on hold until the rain lets up."

Job raised his hand in greeting, but he didn't appear to be his usual jovial self. "You hear about First Baptist?" he asked.

Chills ran up Christopher's arms. "No. What now?"

"More plots in the cemetery opened up just like Marlie's. Recent deaths. All women. One of 'em was Sylvia Taylor. Died two weeks ago—complications from the flu or some such. She had a concrete vault for her casket, mind you. There was a hole right through it. And you know Cynthia Pine?"

"Sure, her boys were the ones who dug Marlie out. What about her?"

"She died yesterday evening. Heart attack. She was only forty years old. I found out when I went for a cup of Cat's Catawomba Latte at Bia's. The boys had a sleepover so they were gone, but

Cynthia's sister, Nellie, stopped by to see her. Door was unlocked and she found her dead in the hall. Cynthia's husband, Paul, is missing too," Job finished.

"Oh no. And the boys?" Christopher's heart twisted with sorrow for them. He hated to think what they were going through.

"They're at their Aunt Nellie's," Job reassured him.

"That's a shred of good news, at least." Christopher knew that Nellie and Harvey Luck lived a couple of miles away, up on Rachet's Hill. The boys would be safe until their father came home. *If he came home.* Christopher shook the negative thought from his mind and glanced down once more at the books spread across the floor.

"So," Renny said, "we've got holes in graveyards, but only over the graves of recently dead women. And we have men murdered in town, their flesh torn from their bones and internal organs missing. Not only that, but their skulls are cracked open and their brains are missing. And we've got a doc who's seen something he thinks is a giant bird monster."

Renny bit her bottom lip and pointed to two books on the floor. "These books are filled with local legends." She touched a thick green one. "This has stories about giant crows that eat little boys if they don't behave." Her hand moved to touch another book with a worn black cover. "This one describes how the Deathwing Queen kills adulterous human women and uses them to breed her Deathwing flock."

"That's ludicrous, and certainly doesn't apply here. Marlie wasn't married, and neither was Hellen." A vision of the crows pushed together, hopping on Hellen's body flashed in his mind. And then he remembered the one crawling out of her. Holy hell.

"Adultery only requires that one of the participants is married, Rev," said Job. "As a church man, you'd know—"

"They weren't adulterers!" Christopher snapped, and then regretted his tone. "Sorry. It's getting to me. Didn't mean to take it out on you."

Renny nodded her forgiveness, and leaned against the bookcase behind her, staring up at the ceiling. "All legends are based on some facet of fact. If we—"

"Hellen and Marlie were good people," Christopher emphasized, and then he wondered where his rising anger was coming from. Renny was only pointing out consistencies and musing about what she'd read.

"Not saying they weren't, Rev. But much of these tales rings true. We need to remember that as we put the pieces together and figure this out"

Just then, the chimes at the front door tinkled and thrummed, and Christopher guessed that Thomas had just come in. When he peered over, it was indeed Thomas, and next to him was someone he hadn't expected to see so soon.

Hatton Profitt.

RENNY

B<small>ELIEVE</small>

*M*arch 19, Tuesday

1:00 PM

Renny looked around at the faces left in her shop. Job, Thomas, and her sweetest Melody. She nodded her head, hating to have to wait but understanding that waiting was what had to happen for right now.

"We need Christopher and the Chief back here before we can make any solid plans," she said. "It's best to step back a bit and think about all that's been going on. Even if we know where to go to stop this, we don't know what to do to stop it." She closed the books.

Job stood up and cracked his spine. "Reckon I gotta go see about Cynthia and Paul's burial. Find out what the Price family wants."

Renny had seldom seen Job so somber. He generally took the good with the bad, and he considered death part of the circle of life, but death had been circling Iron Shores more than it should have lately.

She stood up as well. "You want some tea before you go? Or maybe in a cup to carry out? I've got a couple extra almond biscotti you can have with it if you like."

Job said that would be just fine and followed her to the store's mini kitchen.

Renny used a Japanese electric pot already filled with hot water to make Job's tea. "I'm guessing Earl Grey?" She knew what he wanted but spoke mostly to fill the silence.

"When are you gonna tell them everything, Ren?" Job's question was soft, almost whispered.

"Nothing I have to say will matter yet, Job. It won't make a difference until they truly understand and they all believe. We need believers to step into that cave. You know that more than anyone."

She squeezed lemon into his tea and put a top on the cup. Then she reached into a glass jar and pulled out a couple of iced almond biscotti, wrapped them in a paper towel, and handed them to him.

"I hope you know what you are doing, Ren," was all Job said.

She nodded. "Me too."

242

JUDITH

CHASE

*M*arch 19, *Tuesday*

3:00 PM

Judith stared at the remains of the body stuck in the rocks in the middle of the swollen creek waters.

One set of leg bones jutted out of the water like a bare flagpole. She used her thumb and index finger to rub and cool her eyes. She'd appreciate an end to this daily parade of headless bodies. She really would.

After watching the Mason boy slink away, she'd received a call from Reverend Price at First Baptist about the desecration of women's graves over at their cemetery, and now there was more of this.

Dead men. Death, fucking death everywhere.

And there was still the rain. It had fallen in torrents this morning but had backed off this afternoon. She mentally thanked the volunteer Iron Shores Water Rescue Team. In between helping people threatened by the rising waters evacuate their homes, they led groups of volunteers in filling sandbags and placing them wherever they were most needed to dam the excess water.

Judith suddenly felt a presence beside her—Dr. Lu Crane, her pockets stuffed with nitrile gloves and a token bottle of Purell. Apparently, she had been that way even before COVID-19.

Lu broke through her thoughts. "So, how are we getting out there?"

"Water Rescue Team is coming," Judith said. "They'll run some cables out, anchor them, and we'll get the body on a rescue basket."

"You want me to go over there? Get photos?"

"No point." Judith was fairly certain that the decedent wasn't killed here. "All photos would show is how the body washed up and got stuck in the rocks."

Harvey Luck called in. "Got a report from upriver," he said. "A young couple were walking over one of Hazard Park's bridges and found what looks to be Paul Pine's head. It's cracked wide open."

"I hate to ask," said Judith. "Brain tissue?"

"Gone," Harvey confirmed it. "Head is split in two. Never seen anything like this, Jude."

"I'm sending a photographer to walk the scene. Don't let anyone else go down there. The park's supposed to be closed anyway."

"Got it," he said, and hung up.

"I'm on it," Lu said, walking away.

Judith wondered how in the world the M.E. knew so much about Iron Shores, but there was no time to dig into that. She needed to get this body off the rocks and to the hospital morgue. Without the head, she'd need a Pine family member to identify it.

If there's anything left to identify, she thought. She could smell the body, of course, but she couldn't be sure it was Paul. Not yet. The rain made it difficult to catch and identify a scent and she hadn't known Paul all that well.

She heard the engines of Water Rescue team vehicles headed her way and prayed the rain wouldn't start coming down hard again. "Just let me get this body out of here," she muttered, then realized her hand was clenched tight and her fingernails, while clipped short, were still digging painfully into her palms.

Time was against her. It had been all week. No time to write up full reports, no time to spend with the girls. She felt helpless, like she was a dog chasing her own tail. But she didn't even have a tail.

And she thought of Mason. She doubted that the boy had come to their house without some outside direction even though the girls had invited him. And if he'd been encouraged to go there, then there was only one person who could be behind the boy's visit. His father, Jagger Profitt.

And what did he want? It had to be something to do with Hellen. None of this sat right with her. None of it at all.

Was it all related somehow? Hellen? The sigils? The deaths? The damn fucking rain?

Her officers were so busy in town, no one was getting bitten by Mudrogs, and there hadn't been a Dark Mists sighting with all the rain either. Still, she needed to solve this puzzle before the entire population of the town disappeared.

LU

HONESTY

*M*arch 19, Tuesday

4:00 PM

Lu was very familiar with Hazard Park. She'd often come here as a girl just to get away from the ghosts of her past. Both figurative and literal ones.

The bridge that Harvey Luck had called Judith from was straight ahead, right where a dense pine forest opened up into a clearing. She recognized him from the back, by his build and his red hair, although it had been a couple of years since she'd seen him last. He was engaged in conversation with a young man and woman, and the creek was swollen with water rushing under the bridge. He didn't look up as Lu parked behind his police cruiser.

She grabbed her camera and kit from the passenger seat, got out of her car, and called out to him, "Officer Luck!"

He waved at her and then turned back to the couple for a second, probably telling them to hold tight while he came to talk with her.

"Dr. Crane," he smiled and touched elbows with her. The line of his mouth straightened. "Guess the Chief sent you?"

She nodded. There was a sense of urgency here—ensure that the information stayed intact. What both of them wanted most was to get this job done. She followed him to a marked-off area where the head had been found.

She saw footprints in the mud. Large tennis shoes and a smaller set beside those. "Were those here when you arrived?" she asked.

Officer Luck glanced back at the couple. "Belongs to those two. Shane McCleod and Sephanie Cunningham. My trainee's getting their story now." He jutted his chin back toward the road. That explained the people standing around the police car.

Lu stepped under the yellow crime scene ribbon and readied her camera. If this had happened before the rain this morning, she expected not to find anything. Still, she had to look.

And maybe, just maybe, the man's spirit would show itself. It was confounding not to have the spirits at the scene of the crimes. Not one of them had shown themselves. Normally, they were always there providing information, showing her, telling her what happened.

She walked the entire grid, which was only about twenty feet in each direction, with the exception of where the head was found, right at the edge of the bridge. The rest in that direction was an overflowing creek.

She bent down to examine the head with her camera. The halves were face down in the mud, leaving the inside of the skull visible. It looked as if it had been ripped open, but she could not imagine the amount of force needed to do that. In the mud beside the head and the footprints was a clear imprint of something round.

After photographing the skull and the imprint, she put on nitrile gloves and turned the two sides of the skull over to reveal the face. She didn't know what Paul Pine was supposed to look like.

"Officer Luck? Harvey?" She motioned to him when he looked up from his phone. "Did you know Paul Pine?"

Harvey shook his head. "Not well, no. Not enough to identify him, if that's what you mean."

Lu nodded her head and then worked her way over to her collection kit. Plastic Ziplocks would have to do for now. No one had anything useful to store a skull in at the moment. She collected the two halves of the skull, facial tissue ragged and torn but still attached, and went back to her vehicle to label it. Harvey followed her, having removed the forensic crime scene ribbon.

He guffawed when he looked over at her red Alfa Romeo. She gave him a sharp glance that spread into a smile after a second. Under the circumstances, her choice of vehicle was funny, she realized.

As Harvey headed back to his truck, she said, "Let me talk to them before you go, will you?" She packed the evidence into another bag, labeled it, and then stepped out of her car to talk to the kids. She mentally called them kids, although they looked to be in their twenties.

"I'm Dr. Luanna Crane," she said, painfully aware that she was damp and that the rain, however light, had managed to plaster her hair to her head.

The young man's eyes lit up. "Whoa! We heard of you! *The* Dr. Crane? I'm Shane. This is Sephanie."

Shane was of medium height and build. He was nondescript except for a jagged scar on his cheek that looked like something he'd received as a kid. Maybe from a dog bite. He jabbed Sephanie with his elbow. She was a mousy thing with brown hair pulled into a thin ponytail. Gray eyes. She smiled shyly.

"Yes. So, you both found the head? What time?"

"Yeah, me and Seph," said Shane. "We got here maybe around eleven or so, not long after the rain let up. We were going stir-crazy in the house, you know, all this rain. Figured we'd see how high the creek was."

Lu nodded. "So, you stepped outside and came here? Then what happened?"

"Well, we walked over there, and that's when Seph saw it. I mean, she asked me, 'What's that?' We checked it out, and soon as we realized what it was, oh man, someone's freaking head—split open—crazy man—right? We called 911, you know? Waited until Officer Luck got here. That was it."

"Did you find anything next to the head?"

Shane hesitated. "N-no. Just saw the head, that's all."

"You sure? You guys didn't pick anything up? Like a coin or a medallion? Ceramic?"

"Nope. Sorry, Dr. Crane. Didn't find anything."

Sephanie remained quiet and motionless.

"Okay," Lu said, passing on the idea of having Harvey search them. This was going nowhere. Her only hope was that they hadn't picked up something off the ground and if they had—that it hadn't been one of those strange medallions.

Thomas had a medallion that protected him. The men in the fishing boat had one that obviously didn't protect them. And if the owner of the man's head had one in his possession, it obviously hadn't helped him either.

"Be careful going home," she said. "If you remember anything else, please give Officer Luck there a call, okay? It could be important. Anything."

The kids nodded, and Shane stuck out his hand.

Lu looked at it and then looked at him. He might decide to tell her or Officer Luck something else. A country handshake wasn't too much to ask. She slipped on a blue nitrile glove and gave his hand a hearty pump.

"Whoa," Shane said. "You really do the gloves thing."

Sephanie whispered into his ear, just loud enough that Lu could hear, "Paranormal stuff, remember? Energy."

"Oh, yeah." He grinned. "Thanks, Doc. Take care and—we'll see you on the other side!"

It was a catchphrase from her TV show.

Well, let's just hope I don't see you on "the other side" anytime soon, Mr. Shane.

Given the fact that she hadn't seen anyone from these recent deaths "on the other side" made her wonder if her gift was gone. She'd often wished she didn't have this strange power to see the sea, but the thought that it might be gone made her sad. Maybe something here at Iron Shores had caused her to lose it, or it had receded, dropped into a dormant phase for some reason.

There had to be a way to find out if her ability was still intact. Maybe a graveyard? But it worked best in cases of wrongful death. An angry spirit was much easier to see and communicate with.

Most bodies in graveyards had spirits at rest, meaning they had moved on. Sometimes, they left some residual energy—like looking at a photograph or hearing a recording—but for the most part, they were gone. Angry spirits, like those from wrongful death, didn't go anywhere. They stayed until they were avenged or pacified.

Lu said her goodbyes to Harvey, then got into her Alpha Romeo, wholly intending to return to the Horseshoe, but her subconscious mind had other plans instead.

SEPHANIE

SNAP

*M*arch 20, *Wednesday*

10:05 AM

Sephanie shifted, and her eyelids fluttered open. She was warm and cosy nestled in Shane's embrace, and even though neither of them worked yesterday and they were both off today, sleeping in was such a luxury. Perhaps they shouldn't have finished off a case of beer last night, but they'd had a blast doing it. They'd watched horror movies. Made sweet love. Fucked like banshees.

Yeah, they deserved to blow off some steam. She giggled to herself. A whole lot of steam, truth be told.

During a 24-hour shift at Beaver's Diner the day before yesterday, they'd worked their asses off. With all the flooding and emergency crews working through the night to evacuate townspeople who lived near creeks and small rivers, food service demands were higher than ever. The owner, old Mr. Gary Ginkman, was having a fit though, and he'd closed down for half a day. He didn't know how long he could keep the joint open since his supplies were running low and no one was making deliveries with the main river bridges closed.

Sephanie stretched and pushed the worries out of her mind. The blackout curtains she'd purchased at Target a month ago were the absolute best for their apartment. Only tiny darts of sunlight managed to get in, and with the cloudy skies this week, it stayed dark until they turned on the lights. They'd both managed to sleep sound as hibernating bears.

Reaching over to grab her phone, Sephanie touched the screen to bring up the time. It was just after ten in the morning. She stretched her body out again, trying not to wake up her hunk of a man. Jesus, she loved being with Shane. He was strong, funny, and smart. What he saw in her, she didn't know, but she was ever so glad he'd picked her, and by all the fucking hells, she meant to keep him.

If only he would ask her to marry him. They'd been together now for what? Six months? And they were deeply in love. Weren't they?

Shane moaned in his sleep, let go of her and rolled over, freeing Sephanie to get up quietly and go to the bathroom. On the way, she passed by his jacket, which was hanging on the back of his desk chair.

Wait. Shane had put that round ceramic thing in his jacket pocket yesterday, hadn't he? It bothered her a little that he hadn't told the famous star, Doctor Luanna Crane, the truth, that he'd found it. But that was his decision and she didn't bug him about it.

Still, since it was here, she wanted to see it. Sephanie reached her hand into the pocket and found the cool surface of the thing. She glanced back over her shoulder at Shane to make sure he was still asleep. His breath was heavy, punctuated with a slight snore when he inhaled. She smiled and pulled the round ceramic piece out of his jacket and padded to the bathroom.

She flipped on the light and sat on the toilet. While she emptied her bladder, she examined the curious piece. It fit neatly in her palm. It wasn't heavy even though it was maybe the size of a large dollar coin or bigger. She guessed the item was made of clay, definitely not valuable, but the designs were so cool.

On one side, a design was carved into it and painted red, decorated with some flecks of gold. It was a simple pattern—just a bunch of parallel and intersecting lines with little circles on the ends. But the other side had a sick picture of a head—half human and half crow—sculpted on it. She liked this side better. The piece made her think of the split human head they'd found yesterday. She wondered if there was any connection to this round thing.

She put the piece between her lips as she tore off a piece of toilet paper and wiped herself dry. A strange little tingle on her tongue surprised her when she did this, and she hurried took the item out of her mouth, dropped the toilet paper into the bowl and flushed. The tingle remained there, however, and when she washed her hands, she sucked some water into her mouth from her palms and swished it around. She wondered if something was on this thing. It was too early in the spring for poison ivy, but maybe there was something in the dirt?

When she spat out the water, blood gushed into the sink. And now she could taste it. It was pouring into her mouth, and she couldn't stop it. Dropping the ceramic piece on the floor, she dashed out of the bathroom to get Shane. She didn't care now if she had to wake him. She had to tell him, get him to help her, but when she entered the bedroom, she stopped short, blood bubbling on her lips. Her brain couldn't process the terror before her.

A huge black-winged creature stood over her lover, its massive beak that made up most of its head tearing into him, ripping his insides out. Its icy blue eyes turned on her then, and its mouth opened wide, revealing jagged teeth and a serpentine tongue. The creature seemed pleased—as if it found joy in her absolute fear. Just then a loud noise filled the air—the sound of birds flapping their wings, scratching and cawing outside her window.

Sephanie fell to her hands and knees in shock. Maybe from a loss of blood, too, although the blood bubbled and choked her, and it seemed to block her mouth and nose so completely that she couldn't breathe. As she frantically crawled backward, struggling to flee the horror before her, her eyesight faded, and she reached up with a palm and rubbed her eyes hard.

When she blinked, it cleared only for a moment—just in time for her to stare as the beast opened its beak wide once more and it snapped its toothy bill around Shane's neck, severing her man's head from his shoulders.

LU

AWAKENING

*M*arch 20, Wednesday

10:20 AM

Lu woke up in her car.

She was parked just inside a small parking lot on the side of the road, and she had no idea what she was doing there. Had she slept here all night?

A placard on a wrought iron fence in front of her let her know where she was. Iron Shores Confederate Soldiers Cemetery.

This place was far on the other side of town. Granted, it was away from the flooding, which was good, but this was a graveyard she tended to avoid. Yes, everyone deserved to be buried properly, but visiting a Confederate burial ground was not exactly on her bucket list.

And although there might be some spirits here who had suffered a wrongful death, likely most of these men here were killed in battle. A wrongful war didn't, by default, carry with it the angry stain of murder.

She got out of her car and leaned against the hood, staring at the cemetery. What *had* brought her here? There was a reason that her subconscious had taken over. Taken control.

Her brain tried to puzzle it out. What was the last thing she remembered? She dropped off evidence at the morgue at the hospital and then . . .

And then . . . she couldn't remember anything after that. Now, that frightened her. She thought back.

I didn't eat or drink any weird foods or substances, come into contact with any strange substances at the apartment, or touch the medallion.

She'd only been in the presence of that bird until they let it out. There might have been something in the air in that apartment that had an effect on her. She'd have to ask the officers on-site if they suffered any effects. And Lu also knew she worried about her abilities—not being able to see or hear the dead anymore. She hadn't seen the spirits of the two dead in the apartment. She should have.

Then, she saw them—not the two apartment spirits, not even the spirits of the Confederate soldiers.

No. These spirits all appeared African American. But why were they here?

It was raining harder now, but Lu kept walking forward, mesmerized by this mystery. Were these spirits of past slaves? If so, wrongful death could certainly apply here, but she wanted to understand. Maybe she could come back with Renny so they could do something together to free their souls.

As she drew closer, she realized there were far more spirits here than she'd anticipated: children, young men, healthy-looking pregnant women, mothers, elders, and the infirm. They all stood together, looking at her, and then pointed to a huge dent in the ground. It was basically a long, wide ditch.

Lu felt sick, and bile rose in her throat. She recognized what this was; she'd seen them before.

This was a mass grave. When the Union won the war, rather than part with their slaves and set them free, someone—likely certain Confederate soldiers—had murdered them all right here and buried them in a heap right on top of each other like garbage, while those who likely murdered them were buried next door with distinction and honors when they died.

Confederate soldiers were buried where their families could find their tombstones, visit their remains, and remember them. The slaves were buried in mass graves with unmarked remains. Unnamed. Lost to history.

The emotional agony of the spirits hit her all at once, and she vomited, heaving and retching until she was drained.

So. She could still see the dead. She could still hear the angry spirits who called for justice. Oh, she wanted to help these so badly, but they'd have to wait just a little bit longer. She needed to stop the strange murders happening now before whatever it was spread past the town and into somewhere else. The eyes of the spirits in front of her bored into her.

She heard their voices. *Help us. Free us! Don't go!*

Lu yelled out loud and used her mind. "I will return, I promise. I will get help, too—someone special to help!"

Her words didn't calm them. The spirits yelled in frustration, and she felt their sudden anger like hot needles piercing her brain. She had to leave. She'd be overcome by them, and then she'd be of no use to anyone.

Her body trembled violently as she stumbled to the car. She lunged into the driver's seat and drove off, spinning her tires so violently she swerved and nearly crashed into an oncoming truck. Gradually, the sickening feeling subsided, and she was not surprised to find she was sobbing.

All of those innocents trapped there together, victims of wrongful death and no way to escape. She would keep her promise as soon as possible. But right now, she had to help the living, and she suspected those who died from wrongful death at the hands of this demon— the Raven Mocker, the Deathwing Queen.

If she guessed right, when these victims died, their spirits were torn away, imprisoned in a place where she couldn't see them. Somehow, this Deathwing Queen—she stored souls. For what purpose, she didn't know.

Renny will know more, she thought. *I'll bet she has an idea or suspects what is happening. Maybe she's even guessed why I couldn't see their spirits.*

But if she had, Renny would have let Lu know, wouldn't she? Lu needed answers, and she needed them now. She heard another siren in the distance. She guessed the EMTs were on the road again, responding to another call, and something told Lu that their call wasn't for the living.

HATTON

POTION

March 20, Wednesday

12:00 PM

Hatton called the men to come eat lunch. Living in the country had pros and cons. Pros were privacy and fresh foods from the forest and fields.

Cons were, there was no pizza delivery when she didn't feel like cooking. It used to be that some days she could make a tuna casserole or soften some of her pa's deer jerky and put it in a pot of slow-cooked beans. Serve it with some fresh cornbread. She'd freeze the leftovers, and then they'd have enough cornbread for another meal.

That was then. It had seemed like years ago. But ever since Mason hit his teens, he had turned into a bottomless pit of hunger. She'd make extra stew, cornbread, or fresh loaves of bread, expecting the food to last at least two days. When she'd come home, everything would be gone.

She started buying in bulk and got twenty-five-pound sacks of rice and beans. She'd clean critters Pa brought home, fillet fish, dress ducks or turkeys, but she preferred pots without greasy meat. The flesh stank and spoiled faster than the meals made without it.

Vegetables, beans, and rice were so much cleaner and easier to cook. They smelled sweeter, too. She flavored them with herbs she grew on the side of the house in her own little garden: thyme, rosemary, oregano, and chives. She also used wild onions and tons of garlic she'd planted.

Still, she had to cook whatever the boys brought home—squirrel, rabbit, deer, or fish—it was her job to make the meals. The men hunted, and she kept the house as clean as she could with three men and her little sister living there.

And her other sister, Hellen, would never help her again. Hatton was a grown woman, but she knew her father would never let her go—not unless she ran away and never came back—something she dreamed about, but knew would never happen.

A sinister voice whispered in her ear. *And what about your mama?*

"No!" she yelled. That voice. It always spoke to her, taunted her when she contemplated leaving. It wickedly reminded her that her mama couldn't go, and if her mama couldn't leave, then why should she? How could she abandon her?

You'll take her place one day, the voice continued. *When the winged one has finished honoring her, then she will honor you!*

The back door to the house swung open, and Pa, Savral and Mason stomped in. Hatton had a pile of sandwiches ready, stacked on plates in the middle of the table. Fresh cold milk, squeezed out of the cow just yesterday, filled the pitcher, and there was egg salad made from the eggs she'd gathered this morning. None of the men said a word. They just pulled out their chairs, plopped down and started devouring the food. The chomping noises they made caused Hatton's stomach to churn.

She quickly grabbed a basket of food she'd set aside for herself and Precious, and snatched up a jug of water, and two plastic cups. They'd have to eat fast because if the boys finished quickly, they'd be looking for more, and neither she nor Precious could fight them off.

Precious was sitting at a small plastic picnic table in the middle of their bedroom, pretending to serve tea.

"Hey, sweets!" said Hatton as she placed their sandwiches on the table. "Grab it now before it goes away."

While some eight-year-olds could be picky, Precious never missed a meal and never failed to eat. And although Hatton did the shopping and sold some of her crafts at a consignment shop in town, they'd had times when neither pa nor she could put food on the table.

Hatton reckoned that Precious remembered those times. She quickly grabbed the sandwich and took a big bite, barely stopping to chew.

"Hey, hey, slow down, little girl," Hatton chided. Then she felt bad realizing she was doing the same thing. It was a simple truth that the Profitt house followed the laws of the jungle. Nature's laws. The strong survived, and the weak perished. The strong took the food, and the weak did not eat unless they were fast.

Despite the modern age, on the Profitt land there was no such thing as equal rights. Hatton stuffed the last bit of bread into her mouth and washed it down with cold well water. Her gaze roamed over Precious. The bruises on her body seemed to be everywhere now, and her nose was bleeding again. Hatton grabbed a tissue and blotted it dry. She had Precious put some pressure on her upper gum and hold the tissue steady. Precious did as Hatton directed, but she did not stop eating.

Pa's voice bellowed from the other room, "HATTON!"

"You stay here now, Pree, okay?" Hatton whispered. "Eat all your food. There's a chocolate chip cookie waiting for you at the bottom of the basket."

Pree's eyes widened, and she hurriedly reached in, pushed it to her nose, ignoring the blood, trying to breathe in that heavenly scent, then she crammed the whole thing into her mouth. Just in time too. Mason's head popped around the corner.

"Got anything left?" He walked over to her basket, noting her stuffed mouth. The basket was empty. "Damn," he said, and spun around. "Hatton, I'm still hungry!" But Hatton was busy standing in front of her pa.

Mason sauntered into the room asking Hatton for more food, and Jagger popped him in the mouth. "I'm talking, boy. Don't interrupt me, understand?"

Mason nodded, rubbing his lips. Savral just tilted his chair on its back legs and let out a loud, wet belch.

Hatton couldn't help it. Her thoughts drifted to the memory of that handsome doctor, Thomas. What would it be like to run away with him? Be his wife? If they were married, she could live in fancy places where they could go out to dinner and . . .

"Stop your daydreaming, girl," her pa said. "We got business to do—for little Precious, for our kin, for your ma, and for all y'all." His gaze swiveled to Mason.

"Boy, where's that hair?"

Mason scooted over to a cigar box. It was a place where he kept his few trinkets. He reached his fingers in and pulled out two plastic baggies. One was marked R on the outside and one was marked L. He handed them to his pa, and Hatton watched with terrified fascination.

"How did you . . . ?" Her question remained unanswered as her pa started giving orders.

"Sit!" he commanded. Everyone sat. As their pa spoke, he dropped the hair from the baggie that had an R on it into a black onyx mortar and grabbed up the pestle. Once, he'd said it was made of solid onyx. The bowl was his, for special purposes, and no one else used it. "Mason, your hair now, boy."

Grinning, Savral grabbed Mason's hair in his hand and yanked hard. Mason yowled as his brother pulled several strands free, and their pa glared at them both into silence. Savral handed the hair over.

Her pa lit a match and set the hair on fire, chanting sacred words she didn't know the meaning of except for *Raum*, a name she was told never to speak.

Once the hair burned to ashes, her pa mixed the ashes together with a pinch of salt then, swift as a snake, he reached out and grasped Mason's hand. "Savral," he yelled, and Savral flicked out the blade of his pocketknife. It was so fast, it must have already been in his hand—and lanced the end of Mason's finger. Her brother winced but did not cry out this time.

Hatton was impressed by how fast Savral moved. It was a neat little cut. Not messy, and not too big. Her pa held Mason's finger over the onyx mortar and counted the drops of blood out loud as they fell. Eleven drops. In their family, it was equal to eleven crows. *Secrets hidden or revealed.* Outside, a multitude of wings flapped around the cabin, and the raucous sounds of birds filled the air.

Her pa smiled to himself and poured a jigger of white lightning, his own homemade hooch, into the bowl and mixed it well. As he did, he chanted mysterious words Hatton didn't understand. When he was done, he used a plastic syringe that Hatton had stolen from the hospital back when she was visited Thomas and drew the liquid into it. He divided the liquid, squirting it into two red-topped blood tubes. Hatton had stolen those from the nurse's cart too. Her pa handed the tubes to Hatton. "Put an *R* on these. Label them with a black Sharpie."

Next, her pa went to the sink and rinsed out the bowl, then wiped it dry with a paper towel. He brought the bowl back and dropped the hair from the plastic baggie marked *L*. The ritual began once again.

Hatton's heart suddenly felt heavy. It was true she wasn't so keen on Chief Ware. The woman wasn't very friendly, and the way she'd talked to her pa when she came to tell them about her sister's death—she'd been downright mean. But the Chief's daughters—Rachel and Lilith—she really liked those girls. Sometimes she'd see them in town, or when she was shopping for groceries, and they always waved and smiled. Hatton hated to think of something bad happening to them.

Her pa turned his eyes on her as if he could read her mind. When he spoke, it was with his gentle voice—a voice he seldom ever used. It pulled on Hatton's heartstrings.

"The strong survive, Hatton. That's nature—the way it is. And I'm making sure that our family survives. We will all outlive, out-think, and survive far longer than anyone in these parts. And we won't just survive, but we'll all stay young and healthy for generations! And your ma, you know she's working in the cave for us too—working to serve the Darkwing Queen. So quiet your thoughts, daughter. Lend me your mind."

And Hatton did. She focused her energy on what her pa was doing and stretched out her hands as a beautiful light glowed from her fingertips. At times like this, she almost felt loved, and love welled up inside her too manifesting a power that brought a wave of energy into the room that her pa used to help him with his craft. When it was done, she wasn't sure how she felt about what he'd made with her love, or about how he planned to use his potion. She only knew that what he'd created tonight would bring Chief Ware's girls here and that, once they arrived, they would never leave.

JUDITH

DON'T TELL ME

March 20, Wednesday

2:00 PM

"This keeps going, and we're going to run out of room. I don't think Hatcher's can keep up, and there are only a few drawers here to keep people cold." Earl Brown's voice was low and deep, and it matched the juggernaut of a man he was as opposed to the too-small white lab coat he wore. His glasses were coke-bottle bottom thick, and Judith couldn't help but wonder how in the world that man saw anything under a microscope when he was working in the pathology department.

She nodded in agreement, though. They'd never had this many bodies to process and disposition, even during COVID. Add to that the rainy weather, and no one was getting buried, either. Not for a while, anyway.

Judith peeked through the window into the room next door, where Dr. Crane was performing autopsies. Since the roads were blocked and all the choppers were busy with other tasks, Lu had called the Richmond OCME and obtained permission to complete the postmortems in the town, on the hospital site.

Judith guess it was their best option, anyway. No one knew what was really going on here yet, and until they did, it was probably best not to transfer the forensic evidence they'd gathered, or the bodies, out of town.

Her cell phone rang. It was Harvey Luck. By the sound of his trembling voice, she guessed he'd found something bad.

"We got a call." He stopped. She heard him swallow. "We got a call . . ."

Judith sighed inwardly, recognizing the heavy emotion in his voice. "Officer Luck, tell me what you've got." She said the words firmly, with a matter-of-fact tone that she hoped grounded him and reminded him of his duties. She heard him sniff.

"Two." He took a deep breath. "Two deceased on site, Chief. At the Red Tail Apartments. We got a call thirty minutes ago. Someone heard a scream in the apartment above them on the second floor. We responded but got no answer when we knocked. Broke the door down, and they're dead. Both of em' dead. I just saw them yesterday on the bridge in the park, Chief. Me and the doctor, the one you sent. Dr. Crane."

They were the ones who found Paul Pine's head. Judith's heart went out to Harvey, but he, his partner and likely his trainee were there too. They all had serious tasks to complete.

"You taped off the place, right?"

"Yes, Chief."

Judith peered into the autopsy room again. Lu was stepping down from the stainless-steel table, removing her gloves. One of the assistants, a young blonde girl, was busy trying to get bare bones and remaining muscle tissue into a body bag.

"The doc you were with yesterday is right here. I'll send her over, okay?"

"Yes, Chief."

"You don't need to do anything except keep the site clear, alright Harvey? Just wait outside of the apartment and make sure no one goes in. Start filing your report on your tablet. You got that?"

"Yes, Chief." The poor guy sounded dazed. Numb. Well, he'd be okay. Then she remembered that he also had the Pine boys staying at their house. Those boys had lost both their mother and their father in a matter of days. She couldn't imagine what they and the Luck family were going through. Now was the time to make her words to him more personal.

"Harvey, hey, don't touch anything in there, okay? Same for your team. Keep your trainee and your partner out of there. It's important that we try to keep everyone safe, and I have faith in you."

She heard him rapidly tap his fingers against the phone.

"I know this whole week has been real hard, Harvey. And you and Nellie have your hands full taking care of Jansen and Morrey too. You both are good and kind people."

Harvey didn't say anything, but Judith heard the tapping slow. "Just sit tight, okay? Dr. Crane will be there soon."

His voice squeezed off a barely audible "Yes, Chief" before the call ended, and silence thundered in the air.

Dr. Crane came through the door, pumping Purell into her palms. "Thought you just washed your hands," Judith said.

Lu looked up, perhaps a bit embarrassed. "Yes, well . . ."

Judith appraised the medical examiner. Lu had been wonderful so far. Here she was, a television star, working death scenes, performing autopsies, and doing major scut work—she'd done anything Judith asked her to help with. The rest of her officers were neck-deep in assisting with flood emergencies and ensuring safe conditions around town.

Besides her, none of them had extensive death investigator training, though they all had decent forensic photography skills. Given what Harvey had just told her, she'd be sending Lu into a room where, just yesterday, she'd seen the very same people alive.

"So." Judith gave Lu a candid look, knowing that she'd have to provide frank words next.

Lu returned her gaze and seemed to read her face. "No, don't." She raked her top lip with her bottom teeth. "Okay," she inhaled and blew out a big breath. " Please, please tell me it's not the couple I saw yesterday. The ones who found Pine's head."

Judith said nothing. Figured she didn't have to now.

"Hell's freaking bells." Lu's lips trembled a little. She set the bottle of Purell down on a table and rubbed at a tear welling in her eye. Judith would have thought that, with as many deaths as she'd seen, as many spirits as she'd "talked to" on the other side, that she wouldn't be bothered by any of this, but she guessed, when it got down to the gritty hard truth, Lu was human—just like Judith. Just like most of the population. And it was clear she felt for these people. She wasn't a psychopath. That was good to know.

Lu exhaled another breath that puffed out her cheeks. "Okay. I need three things before I go."

"Whatever you need, Lu." Judith, who always observed her own actions as if she were critiquing her life, found it interesting that she'd dropped most of her formal persona with this woman.

Yes, Lu was Dr. Luanna Crane, a television personality on the Paranormal Murder show, but that wasn't how Judith saw her now. There was something more organic forming in the relationship between them. Given time, she felt like maybe they could be friends. And that was saying something. Judith had very few friends. Or better to say, very few *real* friends. She could count them on one hand. And two of them were her daughters. One of them owned the Tattered Page.

Lu held up three fingers and counted them down. "One, I need the address." Her middle finger folded into her fist. "Two, I have got to eat a granola bar or something or I'm gonna pass out." Her index finger folded down.

Judith waited for number three.

Lu's last finger, her thumb, tucked down. "Three, I really need a couple of Tylenol now and maybe two to go."

Judith went to her purse and produced a bottle of Excedrin. "Will this do? It's like headache relief, and a cup of coffee all rolled into one." Something in her couldn't help but add some humor to the situation. She held out the bottle as if she were a model showcasing an expensive item on *The Price Is Right*.

"It'll do. Thanks." Lu's face softened into a tired smile.

Judith snatched a bottle of water from a stack just inside the morgue's office room, shook a couple of tablets into Lu's hand, and gave her the water and the bottle of Excedrin. Lu popped the tablets in her mouth, then grabbed a Clorox wipe from the table and wiped the bottle down before she opened it and drank. She pocketed the meds and headed for the door.

"Stop," Judith called out. Lu turned around. "Granola bar." She lobbed it into Lu's hand, and Lu successfully made the catch. "And I'll text you the address," she said.

"Thanks, again," she nodded as she made her exit.

Judith watched the doc walk away and felt better knowing that Harvey and his team would be in excellent hands. She just hoped Lu didn't run into any trouble.

LU

PIECES

*M*arch 20, *Wednesday*

3:15 PM

If I keep doing things like this, I should get an all-wheel drive.

The Alpha was a car she'd fallen in love with a few years back, but it wasn't practical. It was something to drive that was in keeping with her celebrity status, but now she felt pretentious and self-conscious about it as well. She wished she had something else—another vehicle.

Twice, she had to drive through water-covered roads she wasn't sure her car would make it safely through. With waters like this, under flood conditions, there were apt to be boards with nails or something unseen that could easily puncture a tire. She made it to the other side both times without too much trouble. Only once did her car engine sputter, but aside from that, she was golden.

Siri got her to the apartment complex. It was just a few buildings on a plot of land no bigger than an acre. The cop car was easy to see.

She grabbed her camera bag and evidence kit. There was an elevator, but she took the stairs to the second floor instead. Officer Luck and a woman in uniform, whom she thought she recognized from a couple of years back, were standing near a door with a yellow crime scene ribbon strung across the entrance.

She hated seeing Harvey Luck under these circumstances. It had been so good to see him when she'd come back on the case that freed her mom. But this stuff—this was different.

Officer Luck introduced the female officer as Office Cat Rain, and the trainee was Officer Ren Coward. The last name was pronounced "Cohward" like "forward," the trainee said, but Lu couldn't help but think it was unfortunate for someone choosing law enforcement as a career.

He was a little guy. He probably barely made the height requirements, but judging by his look and build, Lu guessed part of his DNA ancestry came from somewhere in the Asian Pacific area. Regardless, she guessed from his muscle build he trained hard.

"Okay." Lu mentally put on her investigator cap. She slid a pair of blue nitrile gloves on and pulled another pair over those. "You guys stay here. I'm going in. Take note of date and time."

First, Lu examined the door, the lock, the hinges, and the door frame. Nothing looked disturbed, tampered with, or forced.

She sniffed the air. There was definitely a strange odor here. To be certain, there was the scent of early decomposition, but she smelled something more—something pungent and earthy.

Something about the scent seemed to stick in the back of her throat. She made a mental note to gargle when she got to her car. There was always a trusty bottle of mouthwash in her glove box next to the bottles of Purell and Clorox wipes.

Lu crept through the apartment, examining it slowly and methodically in a grid pattern, first up and back and then side to side in cross directions. She found nothing of interest in the living room or the kitchen.

She turned the lights out and used an alternate light source. Nothing. The windows were closed, and there was no sign of forced entry.

She entered the bedroom, where the odor was strongest. She wasn't quite prepared for this scene, even though she'd seen some of the other bodies the creature had ravaged. On the bed was an unclothed body, resting supine and sprawled across the mattress.

It was likely the young man from yesterday. She couldn't know for certain because his head was missing. The skin tissue of his neck was crisply severed at his trachea and esophagus, as if something had clipped his head off using very sharp edges. His skin and muscle tissue were missing from his arms, but the skin was still on his neck, shoulders, and hands.

His thoracic cavity was split open wide, and, as with the others, his internal organs were absent. Only the intestines remained, and they were strewn haphazardly over his belly and the bed. The man's genitalia were gone—snipped away from his body like Marvin's. His thighs were stripped of muscle tissue around the femur, as were his calves.

Lu took several photos, taking care not to disturb the body of the nude young woman—Stephanie—just a few feet away. It seemed she had just been returning from the bathroom.

"Where is his head?" Her dark sense of humor thought, *There's a line you don't use every day . . . and I've used it twice in less than a week.*

Then, she saw part of the young man's head beside the bed. She found the other half lodged partially under it. As with the others, it had been split in two and the brain removed. *Likely eaten.* After taking a few more photos, she slid the two halves of the skull out from under the bed and photographed the insides and then the two halves of the face. Once more she found the eyes uneaten.

It was a challenge to turn the body over while it was in bed, but with some effort, and given that he had very little muscle and no internal organs, she managed.

Her assumption was correct. The muscles of his buttocks had been stripped away as well.

Lu processed the rest of the room, photographing, dusting for prints, and gathering swab samples. She checked the bedroom window. It was the sliding type. No sign of forced entry here either, but it didn't seem as if the window had been locked.

Since the appartment was on the second floor and there was no balcony, the couple likely thought there was no need for a lock. Lu found two downy black feathers on the inner aspect of the windowsill. She bagged and tagged them and then started to photograph the girl.

Her skin was untouched, but copy-paper white. She swabbed the young woman's hands and fingers and swabbed her lips. When the team took her back to the hospital, she'd likely do the post on her as well and follow up with what she found here. Lu tried moving her body once her initial photos were done to see if anything was underneath her.

Rigor had already started to set in, but she could still flip her with some effort. Lu expected to see some form of livor mortis settling in her body, but there was none. That was curious.

After taking more photos, Lu returned the woman's body to its original position and then headed for the bathroom. There, in the doorway, she stopped in her tracks. Her mind returned to yesterday when she'd talked with the couple and asked them if they'd found anything shaped like a giant coin. Both had denied they had, but there in front of her, on the bathroom floor just in front of the sink, was a medallion covered in blood.

Oh, Shane . . . Sephanie, why the hell did you two lie to me, dammit? Fuck! Fuck you two! You'd be alive if you'd just—just . . . Lu closed her eyes for a moment and squeezed her gloved fists tight. She wanted to scream out her frustration.

Humans were such dumbass creatures! With everything she saw in the OCMEs and morgues ninety percent of the time, it was a fucking miracle that the human species wasn't extinct. She was sure the time was coming, and humans would be the reason for their own demise.

Lu photographed the medallion from the side and then from overhead. She placed four more layers of gloves on her hands and readied a round plastic container from her kit to hold the medallion safely. With care, touching the thing as little as possible, she flipped the medallion over and took a photo of the opposite side. Then, she carefully placed it into the round container.

She removed the first layer of her gloves, careful not to touch the outside of them, and dropped them into a separate plastic bag that she'd send to the incinerator as soon as possible. After placing this and some swab boxes into a large paper evidence bag, she returned and began processing the rest of the bathroom.

Lu was swabbing the sink when she heard an odd noise. Muffled. Grunting.

She turned and looked back into the bedroom and was shocked to see moving on the dead woman's body. She crept closer.

It was—no. It wasn't "on" her body—it was "in." Was that the head of a crow? It was protruding from between the labial folds of the woman's genital region.

"What the hell?" She said the words out loud, and when the bird heard her, it released a guttural croak and then cawed with a screech that reminded her of the worst chalkboard scratches one could ever imagine hearing. She stood transfixed, staring, as the crow pushed all the way out of the young woman, freeing itself from the woman's genitals. It flapped its wings and cawed again loudly.

Incredulous, but realizing she still had a camera in her hands, she popped off a photo, wishing she'd thought to do that earlier.

"Everything okay in there?" called Officer Luck.

"No. I need help, please!" Lu responded trying to sound firm but not overly excited.

Harvey dashed in and nearly stumbled when saw the bird. "How—"

"Stay calm. Open the sliding window," Lu barked. "It's not locked. Just open it." He did so, and the bird, who hadn't left the body the entire time, eyed her, then took wing and flew out the window and into the gray sky.

Lu and Luck gaped at each other. Then, without a word, Harvy turned and stumbled out of the room.

6:35 PM

Thirty minutes before she finished processing the apartment, she let Officer Luck know they could call a team to come pick up the bodies. By 18:35, she was done. She wrapped up a large paper bag, which contained all the evidence she'd collected, and on the evidence tape, she neatly wrote the date/time of collection and scribbled her initials across it.

She'd fill out a complete report on her investigation tomorrow after she slept. Right now, all she wanted to do was get back to the hospital, lock up the evidence and shower. The insides of her nose felt contaminated from whatever that stink was in the apartment. And after seeing that crow emerge from—well, she was just mentally and physically exhausted. Sleep would be her best medicine right now.

When she exited the apartment building, she was pleasantly surprised to find the rain had finally stopped. A few minutes later, she pulled into the hospital parking lot and called Judith to let her know she was dropping off the evidence. She'd do a post tomorrow on the couple and fill out more reports. The sky had cleared some, and the sun glimmered softly on the western horizon.

Clouds framed that precious bit of sunlight in purple, orange, and dark red. Red at sundown was supposed to be a good thing, so maybe tomorrow would defy the weather reports and be a day without rain. Maybe there'd even be some sunshine. If so, she'd have to step out and grab some of that light. She was taking Vitamin D supplements as it was. Her levels were historically low, and her chosen indoor profession didn't help things at all.

Grabbing the bags of evidence, she exited her Alpha and locked the doors. If she hadn't been so tired, her brain might have registered the harsh cawing of crows in the distance.

JUDITH

FOUNDER'S DAY 1

*M*arch 22, Friday

9:15 AM

It was the first day in over a week that water did not fall from the sky. Not only that, the clouds thinned, and the world was glorious. The grass was emerald, and daffodils abounded with their bright yellow heads. Crocus and iris flowers splashed yards and hillsides with lavender, amethyst, and plum colors, while several varieties of cherry trees had buds that burst into resplendent pink and soft rose-colored gems.

The local businesses and schools always observed today as a town holiday. It was Founder's Day, the day their town was officially founded in 1802.

Judith and the girls all slept late that morning, so when they awakened, it was to a changed world of sunshine and the intoxicating scents of spring. Judith opened her eyes, yawned, and caught the scent of her lily-of-the-valley bush in the backyard. It was opening to the beauty of golden light.

The buds had remained closed for what seemed like forever. Now, they were spreading wide and sharing their delicate scent. She wished desperately that she could just dash out into the wild, roll in the grass, and stretch her legs.

There'll be time enough for that later.

Her nose twitched. The lovely odor of freshly brewed coffee filled the air. And was that the scent of Cream of Wheat? Biscuits too?

Rising from her bed and putting on her robe, she padded quietly toward the kitchen, and her ears picked up the soft noise of ceramic bowls touching each other and then a clinking of silverware. Two young voices giggled.

Well, I'll be damned, Judith thought. The girls were cooking breakfast. When she entered the room, their heads turned her way, and they smiled.

Lilith ran toward her, wrapped her arms around her and said, "Surprise, Mom!" Rachel just beamed, poured a cup of coffee and set it down on the table for her mother. A genuine smile crept over

Judith's face, and she realized how nice it felt. How long had it been since she smiled? *Really* smiled and felt true gladness in her heart?

With the sun streaming in through the window and her two beautiful girls there in the kitchen working together, laughing, making breakfast, she told herself to imprint this moment, this absolutely normal and fantastic moment, into her brain. She'd be able to draw on this mental picture when she needed strength to get through challenging days in the future.

"What's up, my young cubs?" She hugged Lilith back and kissed the top of her head, noticing how much taller she seemed. Then she went to Rachel, gave her a squdge, and kissed her cheek. Lola raced around them all, happily yipping and rubbing against them.

"Sit, Mom! Eat! Before it all gets cold," Rachel encouraged as she squeezed and returned her kiss.

And so, she did just that. When she sipped her coffee, it was brewed to perfection—bold and black. The taste of it calmed her, and even though she knew it was a mental state—after a couple more sips—she felt energized.

Lilith was pulling biscuits out of the oven, and Judith noticed how perfectly done they were. The last time the poor girl had tried baking anything, the smoke detector had gone off. Maybe the girl's sense of smell was coming on, Judith mused. If so, this next moon might be her moment and that moment would change her life forever.

Rachel slid a bowl of Cream of Wheat her way, along with a stick of butter on a plate, some milk, and agave syrup. Lilith served her a biscuit, placed some raspberry jam on the table, and added a bowl of freshly washed grapes as a centerpiece.

The girls sat, and for at least an hour, they all ate, talked, and laughed, and Judith felt as if this were a dream—a beautiful dream that she never wanted to leave. Then, Rachel's phone pinged. She picked it up and looked at the screen.

"Got a text, Mom," Rachel said. "It's last minute, I know, but there's supposed to be some live music in town this afternoon at one. It's on the stage by Ascendancy Hall. Can we go?"

Judith considered the location. It was far enough away from the flooded area of town. It shouldn't be too messy. She was never much for public gatherings, but since the waterways still coverd the roads, and the bridges were closed going in and out of Iron Shores, the only people who might be there were local.

Maybe she'd take the girls over to the Unitarian church as well. Christopher usually had an eleven o'clock Community Gathering on Founder's Day. It brought people together—those who enjoyed helping others and sharing. A group of young people from the area often met there as well.

She mentioned it to the girls. They enthusiastically cheered, and that alone was testament to how the past few years had taken a toll on their social life. With COVID-19 and then the wet autumn, and cold winter, followed by the entire past week of rain, she knew they were going stir-crazy.

Sure, they had school, but most everyone went right home afterward. Social activities were few during the winter months when gatherings were only comfortable indoors. Most everyone still maintained a certain degree of caution even five years later, but it was getting better.

"Mom, you're the BEST!" Rachel's wheels were already in gear, Judith could tell. She was thinking about what to wear and who she could call to meet her at the church and then at the live music show.

Lilith, always more cautious and inhibited, seemed excited, but Judith had already sensed some of her anxiety starting to rise. Rachel sensed it, too. "Don't worry, Lil!" she said. "We'll get ready together, okay? I can do your hair if you want."

When Rachel was happy, her words were infectious. The opposite was also true. If Rachel was in a bad mood, the world around her not only knew it, but they also felt it like a solid kick in the pants.

Lilith bit her bottom lip but nodded her head, and both girls pushed their chairs from the table and ran to their rooms to get ready. Judith chuckled a little as she looked around the kitchen. Dirty dishes and cream of Wheat dribbled onto the counter. A messy kitchen was a little thing this morning after such a fantastic—and uninterrupted by work—breakfast with her girls.

Lola pawed at her, and she looked down. "Really, girl? You think you can manage it okay? It's been a while."

Lola spun in a circle twice, her white fur glorious and her brown and blue eyes sparkling.

Judith got on her knees and hugged the little dog to her. "Okay. Well, you know what to do. You want a ride?"

Lola shook her head.

Judith stood. "Be careful, girl. Do what you need to do, and I'll see you there."

She sobered a little with her next thought. *David would have loved this.* Despite her joy this morning, remembering him brought

290

the sting of tears in her eyes, and she gave herself a quick rebuke. She would *not* cry today, dammit. Today, she would be happy! Happy if it killed her.

She mentally asked her husband's forgiveness for pushing his memory away, took a deep breath, launched into a quick clean of the kitchen and a hot shower, and chose an outfit with layers that would let her cool herself or warm herself, depending on the outside temperature.

Thunder rumbled in the distance. Storm clouds gathered, and soon, they would engulf the town once more.

10:30 AM

Judith parked her Ford SUV in the church parking lot. It was a 2020 Escape, but since she hardly used it, it was fairly new. Rachel drove the vehicle more than she did, but that wasn't often, and when she did, the girl kept it clean, which was a blessing.

There were hardly any parking spaces available, which almost surprised her. She figured the townspeople and everyone in the vicinity would be out in droves, but seeing the people out and about in person was another thing.

The girls dashed inside the quaint white church. They probably already knew which of their friends were there. At least Rachel did. Judith hoped she'd be sure to keep her sister close. Make sure that Lilith got on okay with the others.

Geez, she was such a worry-wort. Judith decided right then to let go of all those worries for the moment. She sniffed the air. She knew the scent of every person inside. Although she almost never attended Christopher's Sunday services, she did admire them and marveled at how they seemed to bring the community together regardless of the townsfolk's primary faiths.

It was nice that he'd put something together on Founder's Day. Besides those who called themselves Unitarian, several denominations of Christians came, from Catholic to Southern Baptist. A couple of Buddhist and Hindu practitioners attended too.

There were also people who came who had no religious affiliation and just wanted a sense of community. Christopher accepted them all and treated each person as equally important.

After sitting in her vehicle and reflecting for a moment, Judith exited the vehicle. She only paused momentarily when she caught sight of a lovely blonde woman with snow-white hair striding along the sidewalk. She wore a pair of black jeans, a black scoop t-shirt and boots, and a zippered black jacket.

Lola carries that look really well, Judith thought as she ambled inside. *She looks better in my jeans than I do.*

As she entered, Judith noted the large boxes for canned goods donations stationed outside the congregation room, or what Christopher called the Room of Light. The stained-glass windows had been crafted by a local artist who chose artistic combinations of trees, flowers, hills, and lakes to adorn them. Everything inside was non-denominational. It was a room that anyone who wanted a quiet place to pray, meditate, or simply reflect on the meaning of life could go to.

She looked around and found a seat near the exit for a quick egress if needed. The spot also allowed her to watch everyone in the room. Judith heard laughter down the hallway. The youth group sounded as if they were in full swing.

At eleven on the dot, Christopher walked in. She caught his earthy scent even before he came into the room. He used a soap that was a mixture of sandalwood, and cedar. Combined with his own personal smell, it made her feel relaxed and comfortable. Christopher was a very nice-looking man. Not ruggedly handsome, but he was physically fit, tall and lean.

She knew he had been a climber at one time. And he walked. A lot. She imagined all of this rain had made it hard for him to get outside. The rain itself wasn't the problem, but the footpaths and terrain that turned solid ground to muddy bog could be a royal pain, especially in the areas where the red clay was so thick . . .

Don't get too relaxed, a voice inside her head whispered. *Stay alert.*

Most of the time, Judith was on edge, and that edge had saved her more than once. She wondered if she'd ever be able to really relax in her lifetime. The world had never felt solid beneath her feet. And when her uncle and aunt died, and she discovered the truth about her real family—something she still had a hard time accepting—she'd also fallen in love about the same time—only to have that love ripped away from her four years ago, leaving her with two young girls. It was no wonder she never had a moment of true relaxation.

Judith realized that everyone had stood up and was singing. She'd been lost in her own thoughts and was about to stand as well when everyone sat down. She looked for Christopher and found him, and their gazes locked onto each other. She felt his emotional warmth, his inner smile, and she was very glad she had come. It still didn't change anything between them, not right now, but she realized she was very happy at this moment.

The day had started beautifully, and now the sun was shining, the girls were socializing, and she was in this peaceful room Christopher had helped to create with people who, for the most part, had nothing but good intentions.

When it came time for the next song, a piece from the musical *Godspell,* she stood with the rest of the people there and whispered the words to the tune. Judith never sang. She had the voice of a buzzard—that was what her Grams used to say, and she was just telling the truth. There was only one time that she *could* sing, and in the company of others like her, their voices merged with an echoing sweetness in the night.

The service concluded and everyone exited to join in the community room for refreshments and socialization. Judith sat with her eyes closed as everyone left. Yes, this room was full of peace. Why didn't she come here more often? This place demanded no loyalty to a god she didn't believe in. It demanded nothing. It only offered its open space, its beauty, to those who needed such a place. She breathed in deep and let her breath out. Repeated the breaths and then caught Christopher's scent, stronger now.

She didn't open her eyes as he came near. His footfalls were barely audible to the normal human ear, but to hers, he might as well have been wearing tap shoes on a wood floor. He slid next to her on the bench, and she felt the warmth of his body. She was keenly aware of how much she wanted to nuzzle against him, to curl up next to him, to share at least one close, intimate moment—then a picture of David's face invaded her mind, and all of those thoughts and feelings raced away as if she'd been burned. She opened her eyes.

"You doing okay?" Christopher's voice was low, resonant like a slow wind breezing through a hardwood forest.

She nodded, feeling a little color rise to her cheeks, and she willed the sensation to go away. "Yes." She made herself smile. It wasn't difficult. All in all, she felt good today. It was just that Christopher was here, he smelled so good, his voice was kind and—and David was gone.

As if he sensed what was going on in her head and in her heart, he changed the subject. "Saw the girls earlier. They're beautiful,

Judith. And they looked so happy to get in there and meet with the other kids."

Judith's sense of pride in her girls took over. It covered her wounded heart, and she could finally look at Christopher without having to put up her mental barbed wire fence.

"They actually fixed me breakfast this morning," she said.

His eyebrows arched. "Wow, what was the occasion?"

"Probably sunlight," she chuckled. "It's been over a week since we've had a break from all of the rain."

Christopher sobered. "I'm guessing no calls last night?"

A heaviness started to settle on her again. Why hadn't he just left that topic alone? She didn't want to think any of the horror today. She wanted a perfect day with her girls. No death. No mysteries . . .

She stood. "No, no calls." She didn't have the energy to let him know about yesterday. Before she broke down and started crying, she left the beautiful room and the wonderful man in it, and steeled herself to face the world once again.

LU

FOUNDER'S DAY 2

*M*arch 22, *Friday*

10:45 AM

The hospital morgue was quiet today. Of course, it was normally quiet, but it was eerie without Chief Ware and an assistant.

Lu had felt the need to sleep in. She'd left the morgue last night only after ensuring that the ambulance team had brought the bodies in and placed them in the drawers she'd selected for them.

Technically, she didn't have to do the autopsies today, but she wanted to get them over with.

As she drove from the Horseshoe to James River General, the long overdue sunlight plucked at her need to get outside and enjoy the day. The sooner she got these two cases over, the sooner she could get out into the fresh air and grab some of that well-earned Vitamin D.

She pulled out the paperwork she needed to document her examination and set it on a counter nearby, along with a pen and some scratch paper. After donning protective gowns, face, eye, and foot coverings, and layering her hands with gloves, including autopsy gloves made from fine chain mail mesh that prevented examiners from accidentally cutting themselves, she turned and faced the row of stainless-steel body drawers. Luckily, this morgue was small.

There were two rows, top and bottom, with ten refrigerated drawers on each row. Every stainless steel door was numbered. Levered handles opened the doors, and the bodies were kept on long stainless-steel trays that rolled out so they could be retrieved for autopsy when one was needed.

Lu brought up a gurney. Odd-numbered bodies were on the top, and even-numbered ones on the bottom. She'd placed Shane McCleod in drawer seven.

The woman he came in with, Sephanie, was below him in drawer eight. She checked the tag on the zipper of the hospital body bag and confirmed this one was Shane.

Getting him to the gurney wasn't difficult. His drawer stood about chest high to her, so all she had to do was lock the gurney and pull the bag on to it. Since it had minimal body weight, the bag slid without much trouble and dropped onto the gurney's stainless-steel surface.

Once she'd weighed it, subtracting the standard weight of the gurney and body bag, she did her best to measure his height. She lined up the two halves of his severed head with his body and got the best measurement possible.

Next were digital X-rays, which were taken on the X-ray table in the next room. Positioning the skeletal remains proved challenging yet straightforward. With no organs or much muscle left intact and the skull in halves, her sole focus was achieving the proper bone alignment and articulation.

It was almost easier in a way without flesh obstructing her view and work. However, the interlinked nature of the bones created its own awkwardness. The remains resembled a disassembled bundle of Lincoln Logs, with some of the "logs" strung and knotted together as if linked by twisted wires, encrusted by desiccated scraps that used to be muscle connected by not-completely-dried tendons.

Once the X-rays were completed, she removed the body from the bag, slid the body onto the smooth surface of the gurney, and obtained more photos, including photos from above which she used a tall step ladder. After the photos came the fingerprints. Finally, she wheeled the body over to the autopsy table and slid it from the gurney to the table.

A voice startled her process.

"Hey, Dr. Crane! Yo! Need a hand?" The autopsy assistant was here? Lu thought her name was Hannah. The girl smiled and started her way. "Chief Ware called me. Said you might want some help. I'm free today."

Lu's brain clicked away. She still had the Paul Pine case to do yet and then the young woman Sephanie. The woman would take longer.

While Lu enjoyed the chance to really focus on cases all by her lonesome, she'd be here until after dark if she didn't accept Hannah's offer.

Lu nodded an *okay*. After working with this assistant yesterday, she felt confident of Hannah's skills, and it seemed the woman already knew what to expect from Lu. Straightforward directions. No chit-chat. Lu liked that.

"I need the X-ray table wiped down," Lu directed. "Then you can pull drawer six. Let me know when you're ready, and I can help you lift him. You know the rest."

Hannah was already gowning up. "They still got their eyes, right? You doing vitreous?"

Lu looked at the remains of Shane's head. She had wondered about the eyes. She'd completed a post yesterday, and it made little sense that all the man's organs were devoured except the intestines and the eyes. Sure, she had planned on gathering vitreous, but it occurred to her just now that whatever had done this had left the eyes.

Why?

Most predators and insects took the eyes first, either eating them or, in the case of flies, laying their eggs on them so their maggots could eat the tissue. In all of the other cases, hadn't the eyes been eaten? She tried to think.

Hannah was standing there, waiting for an answer, she realized.

"Yes. Vitreous." Lu turned back to the table, her subconscious taking note of water running as Hannah filled up a cleaning bucket, preparing to wipe down the X-Ray table.

Lu examined Shane's eyes. There were petechiae, probably from the pressure of whatever severed his head. Nothing else abnormal that she could see.

She filled a syringe with a bit of air, then pushed the needle into the side of the eye until she could see the needle's tip through the window of the iris. Then she drew the fluid out. She didn't know why she always liked this part. The eye collapsed slightly when the vitreous was withdrawn. She went to the next eye and repeated the process, then grabbed a test-tube labeled "V" from the rack she'd set up and put the contents of the syringe in there.

Next, she examined where the split skull. She couldn't understand how something could cut a skull into two halves with such precision. The bone wasn't even crushed. Where the two halves were separated, there were several very fine indentations, but no cutting marks like one might see from a saw or a specialty bone saw like they used during autopsy. She got her camera and clicked off a few macro shots of the edges of the separated bone. Maybe she'd discover how this unique separation happened later. It was quite a puzzle.

"Dr. Crane?"

Hannah must be ready.

Lu helped Hannah lift Paul Pine's body bag to the gurney.

"You okay doing the rest?" she asked, knowing that Hannah would be fine.

"Just a walk in the park, Kizanski," she quipped and wheeled the Pine body away.

Lu smiled knowing the girl couldn't see her. *She must be a* Top Gun *movie fan.*

After the examination of Shane's head, Lu worked her way down and examined where the muscles were torn away. Like what she'd examined yesterday, everything suggested that something sharp had cut across where muscle attached to tendon or bone and ripped the flesh away.

She thought about humans and how they ate chicken legs, breasts and wings. Their teeth were not particularly sharp, so biting flesh was more a blunt pressure to the muscle and then a pulling to remove the muscle from the bone. These lines looked almost surgical the way they were practically sliced then ripped.

She found very little blood in the body cavity even though the central artery and vena cava were shredded. The only organs that remained in the body were the intestines and the bladder. Behind and slightly beneath the bladder was where the prostate was supposed to be, but that was gone as well.

The bladder was intact, and Lu drew fluid from it and placed it in the test tube labeled "U" for urine. After that, she documented the man's missing genitals and then examined his legs and feet. Every bone in the corpse was intact, except where the head had been severed at the neck and the skull precisely halved.

Lu felt more than heard Hannah come up beside her.

"Ready for me to take him?"

Lu nodded. "I'll help you get him into the body bag and back in the drawer." Together, they made quick work of it.

"If you want to go document, I'll wipe the table down," Hannah told her.

Grateful that she didn't have to explain anything to the woman, and sensing that Hannah had everything in hand, Lu peeled off her protective gear, went over to the sink and thoroughly scrubbed her hands and arms.

When she went into the bathroom, she repeated her cleansing ritual with another strong facial and hand ablution. She'd have preferred to take a full hot shower and scrub her whole body, but that would have to wait. After drying her face and arms and using the paper towel to turn the doorknob, she exited the room only to hear a scream of horror slice the air.

When Lu dashed into the morgue, her mind barely processed the scene before her.

Hannah was just inside the doorway. Behind her, Sephanie's body was splayed on the tile floor, and gobs of shredded human tissue protruded from her abdomen as if something had detonated inside her.

By the far back wall of the room, a creature loomed at the end of the stainless-steel drawer section. It stood erect like a human, but long, black feathers covered its body and the figure seemed to grow larger before her eyes.

Strangely shaped arms coated with a rough orange skin tapered into talon-like claws, and those talons reached out toward the top drawer labeled with the number "1." The monster twisted the lever and opened the door.

Both Lu and Hannah stood transfixed as they watched this growing hulk of a creature pull the body bag from the drawer and lift it easily in its strange birdlike arms. Then it turned toward them, opening and snapping its huge beak, flashing its razor-like teeth.

It looked upon her with icy eyes that seemed to bore right through her, and her feet felt as if they were cemented to the floor. Every fiber of her being screamed at her to run, but despite how hard she struggled, her feet wouldn't move.

The creature cawed, its voice a shrieking, growling, and howling sound that shook the room. Then, it spread a pair of giant wings and knocked over the gurney with Paul Pine's body on it. Test tubes and instruments scattered across the floor.

The creature stepped toward them. Its feet were much like its arms but larger. Though Lu could see it coming closer, she still could not move. It took another step and then another. The giant maw on its head opened and snapped again, and if it were possible that a huge beak like that could grin, it was indeed grinning.

It seemed to thrive on their terror. Lu tried to remember the breath work she used for meditation, and she searched her brain for some way to break this horrible frozen moment.

Sarah's hand grabbed her wrist. "Doctor Crane," she whispered. It was not a whisper designed to be quiet; it was likely the only sound the girl could manage to utter.

"D-doctor Crane. We need to move. Now!" She tugged on Lu's arm, then pulled furiously.

Lu's brain was suddenly in gear. The bathroom door had a bolt on the inside. This creature was carrying a body.

It likely only wanted to leave this place. It didn't want them. And, if this thing was what had been killing men in the town, it was not interested in killing women.

Something killed Sephanie, she thought, *but whatever killed her is not here right now.*

"Bathroom!" she yelled.

They raced for the bathroom, slammed the door, and shoved the bolt home. If that thing decided it did eat women, then they were likely done for. They had no place else to go. Lu remembered her cell phone was in her pocket. She tried calling Judith, but she didn't pick up.

Lu left what was most certainly a harried message and then tried to think of who else she could call. She didn't want to put anyone in danger, but she needed to know if the coast was clear before they came out. Everything was silent on the other side of the door.

"Security?" Hannah suggested. She pressed her ear to the door, then shook her head. She couldn't hear anything.

Lu's phone still had service. She looked up the number for Security at the hospital, and someone answered. She asked if someone would come down and assist. They'd had an intruder and they thought he was gone but needed to be sure.

Moments later, they heard footsteps and doors opening and closing. There was a knock on the bathroom door.

"Doctor Crane? You in there?" The voice was female.

Lu sighed with relief. She opened the door to find a large woman with broad shoulders in security uniform.

For one of the many times in her life, Lu drew back in a long pause. It was hard to describe this woman. She looked like she was a melting pot of every ethnic group Lu had ever known.

Her eyes were almond-shaped like she had Asian ancestry, and she almost had a Samoan—thick, wide, and strong. Her eyes were green, and her hair was red—Lu would swear her hair was naturally red—and the texture was that tight African curl. The woman's skin was maple brown. When she spoke, her voice was nothing like how she looked. Her voice was calm, like the gentle wind. Lu couldn't help but think, though, that this woman could become a storm when she wanted.

"Thank you," said Lu, getting herself together. We were scared to death." Lu did a cursory scan of the woman's ID badge and her radio. The dates, her photo, and her equipment were appropriate. The woman's name was quite remarkable.

The nametag read: *Sunder Rage*

The woman in uniform introduced herself. "I'm Sunder. Or Ms. Rage if you prefer professional, but I prefer Sunder." She gestured toward the morgue. "Saw the mess in there. You guys okay?"

Lu and Hannah nodded.

"You see anything on your way down?" Lu asked.

"Nope. Heard a door shut at the exit near the stairwell, but when I opened it to check it out, there was nothing to see."

Lu bit her bottom lip.

"Either one of you hurt?" Sunder asked.

They both assured her that they were fine. No injuries. Sunder took some notes and said she'd check the security cameras near the loading dock to see if anything went by that way.

"I'll let you know if something turns up," she said. "You need any help in there?" She pointed to the morgue. It was clear she hoped the answer was no.

Lu obliged.

12:00 PM

Once Sunder was gone Lu and Hannah returned to the morgue. They had to get a mechanical lift to pick Sephanie's body off the floor.

Lu cleared her throat while they were raising her up to put her on the gurney.

"So, what happened, Hannah? What did you see?"

Hannah sighed. "I heard a noise coming from the drawer. It was something strange, like a croaking and then a tapping. I went over, and when I slid the drawer open—when I slid the woman's body out—that thing lunged at me. I fell back onto the floor. It surprised the crap out of me. The thing was already about the size of a large cat or a small dog—take your pick. When the creature lunged my way, it was like a part of it was still stuck inside the woman's body. The body slid off the drawer table along with it. I got up and ran to the door where you found me. I was scared shitless, and then, as I watched it, the thing started growing. I mean, it grew fast! Dr. Crane, I've never seen anything like it in my life. The creature shook the body away from it and then turned toward me. I meant to call for help, but I realize now that I was screaming. And you know the rest."

Silence hung over them for a minute, and then the sound of the clock on the wall, its secondhand tick-ticking, suddenly seemed thunderous.

"Well, we might as well do her now that she's out," Lu said.

"If you do Pine, then I can get Cunningham's weight, measurements, and X-rays." Hannah looked the body over. "I can get her photos too. She just won't look the same as when she came in."

They both looked at the gaping hole in Sephanie's abdomen.

"Okay." Lu really wanted to open Sephanie up right now and see what was inside her, or what wasn't there, but Hannah was right. It was best to stick to the process as much as possible. Hannah rolled Sephanie's body away on the gurney.

Lu put on a fresh set of protective gear and began her examination of Paul Pine's remains.

First, the severed head. Eyes were intact here, too. She went through the process, taking photographs and collecting fluids. She finished up Paul much more quickly. The findings were all similar to those of the other bodies.

Hannah assisted Lu with placing him into his drawer. Lu completed the documentation on the computer for both the Shane McCleod and Paul Pine cases and uploaded their photos. She had separate files and photos from the scenes for forensics later once the team could make it into town and get them.

Lu tried not to think about what would really happen. Was the Richmond ME going to do anything? What was he going to tell anyone? Would he even bother to tell the investigators about what happened? If he did, what would he say?

Hannah had finished wiping down the morgue and completed setting up for Sephanie's case when Lu returned. They placed Sephanie Cunningham's body on the autopsy table. Lu looked at the clock. It was almost three in the afternoon. She'd missed most of the beautiful day outside.

And what was with that creature coming out in the middle of the day? In scary films, creatures waited for the cover of night, yet that feathered thing that had burst out of Sephanie, and it had grown at an amazing rate right after. The creature must have left the hospital in broad sunlight and carrying a corpse with it no less.

Wait, that thing was carrying a corpse. The corpse from drawer number 1.

"Hannah, what body was in drawer number 1?"

"Hang on a sec." She went over to the drawer and read the tag next to the number. "Says it was "Viktor Odol.""

Lu felt like she'd been hit with a jolt of high-amp electricity.

She thought about the hospital's location. It was up on a hill, away from the flood zone, and backed up against a national forest. There was nothing behind it but forests and fields.

You're not finishing this job any faster thinking about it, Lu admonished herself.

But, she did have an idea of who she needed to talk with in person either tonight or tomorrow. Renny had to know something about what was going on, and she had to hear about this Viktor Odol. Lu hadn't had the opportunity to properly visit Renny since she'd been here but now it was time to make the time.

Hannah came over to the table so she could watch Lu open up Sephanie's body.

"I can get the vitreous," she said and completed the task while Lu made the Y-incision, freed the tissue from the chest, and then snapped the ribs with the rib shears.

Cutting the ribs made Lu think about the skulls of the men's bodies and how easily they seemed snapped into two halves.

She couldn't figure out how those bird creatures could do that so precisely. And none of the women had their skulls snapped open. Why?

Hannah joined her as she was removing the breastplate.

It was as she suspected. No heart. No lungs. No internal organs except for the intestines and the bladder. The woman's ovaries were gone. And there was absolutely no blood.

When Lu took the bone saw to the woman's head, the brain was still there, but again, there was no blood. The brain tissue and everything around it was whiter than a lab jacket.

She removed the brain, weighed it, sliced it into sections, and then took a sliver for pathology. Hannah handed her the pituitary, which was so pale it looked like a little white pearl.

Lu took more photographs and then went to document everything while Hannah sewed up the corpse. For more than one time that day—for practically the whole week—Lu wondered what they were going to do with all of this information.

They had the corpses right here, concrete proof that something bizarre had happened. But bizarre things happened at Iron Shores every day, and not a word of it ever made the news. And maybe that was just as well.

Still, the information was useful. Wasn't it?

Lu gowned up again to help Hannah put Sephanie's remains back in her drawer. Then, they both stripped out of their gear and went to wash up. Hannah would come back in just a few minutes, but she said she had a sandwich she wanted to eat.

While they were scrubbing their hands, Lu looked over at Hannah's wrist. There, etched in black, was a tattoo of a flying crow, its wings outstretched as if it were taking flight. A human skull poised as if looking upward was in the middle of its body.

"Strange tattoo," Lu remarked, suddenly feeling tension in the air.

"Yeah," Hannah replied. "It's a family thing."

MASON

FOUNDER'S DAY 3

*M*arch 22, Friday

12:15 PM

Pa is gonna be so proud of me.

Mason made his way along the backside of town on his pa's ATV. It was shorter that way. It followed the path of the power lines down the hills, and there were no fences blocking his way. He swerved off the path when he saw the back of the library. He could park there. It was Founder's Day. No one would care.

Maybe, if this potion did what it was supposed to, he'd not only get Rachel to the cave, but he'd get Lilith there too. If he did that, his pa would really love him. Maybe love him more than Savral. No way Savral could do what Mason was doing right now. His brother was too old.

The girls would never fall for him. But Mason was smart, read books, and stayed in shape, and girls liked him. That part made him a little sad. They liked him, and here he was, planning to take them to the cave.

On the bright side, they'd get to meet his mother. On the not bright side, the meeting wouldn't be long. Or worse, it would be forever.

Mason was happy to feel the sunshine on his face, and the day was as fine as could be. It was even better when he heard the music. The Iron Corn Pickers were playing, and their combination of banjo, bass cello, and mandolin always made him feel happy inside.

He'd heard Nanny Cakes was gonna play next and that some new girl was gonna sing. He breathed in deep and enjoyed the cool fresh air.

Things were gonna work out for him now, he knew it. He and his family were gonna live for hundreds of years, thanks to Mama, Pa, and the Deathwing Queen. He felt bad about Hellen. He'd wanted his sister to be with them too, but if Savral hadn't tried making that potion to see if it would work for him, she'd be alive now.

His pa said not to worry. That Raum, the Deathwing Queen, had her soul and that she was happy. She'd helped to birth a Harvester,

THE first Harvester in over a hundred years, and there was honor in that. That's what Pa said, and it must be true.

And, boy, Mason wanted to believe his pa, he really did, but he'd lied about things in the past. Like Precious and who her daddy really was. And if he would lie about that then how could he be sure his pa would always tell him the truth?

Mason didn't care much about any of that, though. He just wanted his pa to be proud of him, to like him more than Savral, and he—of course—wanted to live forever. He'd figure out what to do with eternity as soon as he had it. For now, he had to get the Ware girl to the cave. Maybe both of them. But first things first.

THOMAS

FOUNDER'S DAY 4

*M*arch 22, *Friday*

1:00 PM

At breakfast, Mrs. Morrow—*Faye*—had told Thomas that today was a special occasion, the occasion being Founder's Day and a break from the rainfall with some much-needed sunlight. The good weather brought on the quick decision of a local group of musicians to play outdoor music for anyone who wanted to listen. She said it might be odd to say it was the "talk of the town," but it really was.

"There'll be a couple of food trucks, I hear. There are two in the area that don't have to worry about the flooded roads. One serves Mexican food—that'd be Earl Brown's son, Sergio—everyone just calls him Serg. Earl's wife, Camila, is from somewhere in Mexico. I don't know what part. The other truck sells vegetarian fare. A guy who used to live near Yogaville runs it. Roger Waters is his name."

This caused Thomas to smile. "Don't tell me," he said, "the truck's name is *Dark Side of the Moon*."

"Heavens, no," Ms. Morrow wrinkled her forehead as if puzzled. That wouldn't make any sense at all now, would it? It's called *On the Light Side*." Then she chuckled and made her way around to the other guests.

Thomas had showered, careful to keep his cast dry, and put on the best clothes he could find in the stash Tati had brought him. Faded jeans, a Pink Floyd T-shirt (he just couldn't resist), and a flannel shirt he'd wear like a jacket—it all seemed to go fine together.

Luckily, the T-shirt and flannel shirt had armholes large enough to fit his cast through. He dressed and then put his arm back in the sling. He placed a chopstick in the sling along with his arm. The cast got so itchy, and the chopstick was perfect for slipping in there to scratch.

The sun was a sight for sore eyes. It was so bright that his eyes watered, and he had to keep wiping them as he walked. He'd decided not to call Tati and that the walk would do him good. It was amazing to see others out and about. Yes, the rain had stopped, but he wondered if any of them knew what was happening around town. Surely, they'd heard about the deaths.

And he couldn't imagine that he was the only one who'd seen the giant beaked, black-feathered creature. But as he walked, he noticed there was no semblance of fear or concern anywhere he looked. That was probably best. There was nothing any of them could do about it right now anyway. And soon, everything would be over. Still, he was glad he had a protective medallion around his neck, and if he hadn't seen it himself, he never would have believed how well it worked.

He headed toward the center of town, toward the old Ascendancy Hall, and was soon rewarded with the sound of banjos and laughter as well as the savory fragrance of food truck food. As he got closer, he was surprised to see so many people. The food truck lines were long, but he didn't care.

The golden day and cheerful voices made it not so bad to be in line. He even struck up a conversation with an older woman in front of him who ended up being a nurse on the pediatric floor. She asked about his arm. He said he was in an accident but didn't go into details.

He'd learned that everyone knew just about everyone in this town, and he could be speaking to Marlie Moon's aunt, cousin, or friend of a friend. It was safer to steer clear. She seemed delighted to learn that he had worked in the ER and that she looked forward to seeing him when he finally came back.

As Thomas looked around at the people gathered there, he saw a couple of faces he recognized. The Reverend Christopher Miles stood near the stage, watching the musicians, eating from a box of cheese-laden nachos. The Police Chief was in line up ahead with two young girls getting food from The Light Side. It looked like three sandwich wraps and some fried zucchini.

The woman from the Tattered page—what was her name? *Renny*—yes, Renny. She stood next to the music stage with her beautiful daughter, Melody. Nearby, Tati had her vehicle waiting in case anyone decided they needed a ride.

Funny that it took a car crash and a broken arm for me to really start to see and know the people here, Thomas thought. There were more faces he didn't know than ones he did, but still, he knew some, and part of him started to feel more comfortable at home. He'd hoped maybe Hatton had come from home to join the fun, but he didn't see her anywhere.

"Next!"

It was Thomas' turn to order, and he hadn't really looked at the menu.

"What's your favorite?" he asked the man inside.

"Well—Hey! Dude! We're twins!" Thomas looked. Sure enough, he was wearing the same Dark Side of the Moon t-shirt.

Thomas smiled at him. "And you must be Roger Waters," he said.

"Indeed, I am," Roger said with pride. "Let's see—let me hook you up."

He supplied Thomas with a fresh squeezed lemonade sweetened with Stevia, a Greek-style sandwich wrap stuffed with roasted, thinly sliced, vegan meat coated in a vegan-yogurt dill sauce, and his version of baklava using fresh pineapple and black walnuts.

Thomas thanked and paid the man and added a tip.

"Thank *you*," Roger said. "See you on the flip side!"

And then Thomas wandered off to find a place he could set his cup down and devour his sandwich. He had to admit, it smelled really good. He'd just unwrapped one end when he saw her.

Hatton!

Her dark chestnut hair fell beautifully around her face. She wore simple silver hooped earrings, and she was talking to a younger man who looked very much like her.

A brother maybe?

Thomas scanned the crowd checking to see if the older man, who may have been her angry father, was anywhere to be seen. That was a negative. He took two bites of his sandwich and wrapped it back up, preparing to head her way. He'd just grabbed up his lemonade and turned to try to catch her when he ran right smack into her.

Lemonade splashed all over the front of her blue blouse, and the liquid flew up and hit both their faces. The coveted sandwich he was going to save for later plopped to the ground, and immediately, a stocky, brindled dog scrabbled by and scarfed up the food, wrapping paper and all.

Wasn't that the dog from the Tattered Page?

Thomas gaped at Hatton in pure embarrassment. He was an utter klutz! "I'm so sorry, Hatton. I thought you were way over there, and I was—"

She interrupted him with laughter. "It's okay. Really. I'm fine."

"No, you're not. You're soaked." He walked up to the counter and asked Roger for some napkins. Roger had seen everything and winked at him when he handed him some paper towels.

"Get back in line and get another sandwich, and your lemonade's on me," Roger said and winked.

Thomas half grinned and returned a <*Yeah, I messed up, but maybe it will be okay*> look. He dashed back to Hatton with the napkins and wiped her arms and her neckline. He gave her some napkins so she could dry areas that only she should touch.

Thomas would have bought her the world to apologize if he could right then. He felt like such an ass.

"Hey," Hatton grabbed his chin with her thumb and index finger. "Slow. Down." She smiled at him, and something inside him melted. What the hell was wrong with him? He felt wonderful and klutzy all at the same time. He was like a school kid whenever he was around her.

Thomas looked into her eyes. "Okay." He collected the wet napkins and paper towels from her after she'd dried off as much as she could. "Hungry? My treat. It's the least I can do."

She laughed. "Sure. If it will make you feel better. Especially after Grinch scarfed down your sandwich."

Grinch? Thomas spied the brindle thief wagging his tail, standing right next to the man he'd met a couple of days ago.

"Who's the man next to that four-legged opportunist?" Thomas asked.

"Oh, that's Job. One of the smartest men you'll ever meet," she said.

"Really?" He was intrigued. Job didn't seem so high-brow at the Tattered Page the other day.

"He's brilliant," she said. "Ph.D. in anthropology, I think."

"Huh." The man didn't look like a Ph.D. "Where's he work?"

Hatton looked him right in his eyes when she told him. "He's a gravedigger."

"Grave. Digger." The work description didn't compute. Why would a man with a Ph.D. come back to a place like Iron Shores and dig graves?

"Yes. Among other things," she said. She sobered a bit and added, "Things are not always what they seem in Iron Shores. You've been here long enough to know that now."

He nodded. He had indeed, and yet something told him the things he'd seen were just the tip of the iceberg.

They finally got back up to the food truck counter, and Roger Waters made him two sandwiches. True to his word, he supplied not only one but two free lemonades.

While they were waiting to pay, the young man Hatton was talking to earlier came up to them. "Sis, can you pick up three hot chocolates for me?"

"I got it," Thomas volunteered. "I bathed your sister in lemonade earlier. I'm searching for penance."

"Sweet," the teen said. He looked at his sister, who didn't seem to be volunteering to introduce them. "I'm Mason."

Thomas tried to act cool but wasn't sure what 'cool' was to a teen around here. He couldn't shake hands but acknowledged him with a chin jut and said, "Thomas. Good to meet some of Hatton's family."

"Hey, yeah, good to meet a—friend—of my Sis. Thanks again!" And soon Mason was off with three hot chocolates.

Thomas mentally sent a prayer with him that he not run into any women and spill hot liquid on them. A few minutes later, as he and Hatton were chowing on their sandwiches, he saw the teen talking to Chief Ware's girls and handing them the cups of chocolate. Apparently, Hatton saw it too, but she looked away quickly and focused on her sandwich. She suddenly seemed uncomfortable. Why? Did he do something wrong?

She looked up, about to say something, when applause hit the air. The Iron Corn Pickers were finished, and a young girl was coming up on stage.

No. Not a young girl. It was the young woman, Melody.

Her mother, Renny, stood by at the bottom of the stage and just beamed as Melody pulled a ukulele to her chest and positioned her hands to play. Whereas everyone had talked and laughed during the banjo music, they all turned as Melody hummed a few notes and then began to sing.

"Over the Rainbow" came out of her mouth in the sweetest rendition of the song Thomas he had ever heard in his life. It was nothing short of—*magical*—yes, magical. Her voice soared, and the air was so still, the crowd so quiet, that as he watched and listened to her, everything else in the world melted away and disappeared. There was just her, the music, and her transformative voice taking him on a journey.

Melody strummed her final note in concert with her last musical word in the tune. Wind ruffled everyone's hair, and then there was thunderous applause. As thunderous as it could be at an outdoor stage next to a town parking lot. The beautiful young woman bowed and gracefully left the stage and went right into her mother's embrace.

Hatton looked at him, her mouth open in amazement. "Wow. I have never heard a voice that good in person," she said. "She might be better than Amy Lee."

"Might be," he agreed. "I've love to hear her sing 'Broken.'" It was his way of slipping in that he knew who Amy Lee was, the lead singer for Evanescence.

"Ah, you know the music?" It was clear she really enjoyed it and hoped he did, too.

"Of course!" He wanted her to know what his jams were too, though, and added, "But, I'm much more an Ozzy Osborne, Lita Ford, Metallica, Alice Cooper kinda guy. Old, REAL metal. Rock that rules."

She laughed, and she didn't seem to mind his taste in tunes.

He looked around and said, "Hey, how'd you get here? Your Beetle?"

She nodded. "It's just down the way. It was kinda hard getting it down the hill where I live. . ." Her voice trailed off, and it was clear she was remembering his accident. "I called 911 that day, you know," she said quietly. "My Pa, he—he wouldn't let me go out there to check on you." She bit her lip and added, "Said it was too dangerous. I used his cell phone."

"I don't even remember much about it," he admitted. "I remember him coming down the hill and you telling me to leave, then—nothing." He didn't tell her he remembered the sound of crows cawing in the air. And he didn't tell her about the thing, the creature he saw in his room the other night. Sure, she'd given him the medallion, but did she really know what it was for? Had she ever seen the things it was supposed to protect against?

"You wanna walk with me back to the Horseshoe? Hang out for a bit?" He desperately hoped she'd say yes. *Please say yes. Please say yes.*

"Yes."

His heart spun in circles. Maybe she'd come to his room. Watch a movie or just sit and talk. There were so many things he wanted to know, so many questions he wanted to ask. About her father, her brother, and the rest of her family.

And he wanted to find out what she knew about those creatures if she knew they were *real*. She had to on some level, right? Or else she wouldn't have gone to the trouble to give him the necklace.

3:30 PM

Thomas and Hatton strolled arm in arm together to the Horseshoe. He didn't see Faye Morrow when they walked in, but Mr. Morrow was busy trying to fix one of the doors inside. He didn't say a word when they passed by but watched them carefully until they were out of sight. Thomas couldn't shake the feeling that the old man wanted to tell him something.

There was a sense of alarm in the air, and it didn't go away until he brought Hatton into his room and shut the door. He was ready to suggest that maybe they relax and watch a movie or something when, quite suddenly, her lips were pressed against his, and she felt her fingers reach for his shirt to remove it.

She was warm. Intoxicating, and he felt that pleasant tingle in his groin.

How long has it been? So long he couldn't remember. And he didn't want to expect anything. He didn't want to scare her or go too fast, but now she was the one moving fast, bringing his t-shirt up and over his cast, unzipping his pants, and pushing him gently onto the bed. He lay there and watched her undress.

She removed that blue top, once soaked with lemonade, now dry, and revealed her black lace bra. She removed her jeans and crawled into the bed with him, her bra and underwear still on. She was breathtaking—yes, breathtaking.

"You are so beautiful," he said, really meaning it, hoping it didn't sound corny like it was a line any guy would just say.

He reached out with his one good hand and caressed her face, her arm, the curve of her breast, and she removed the bra. He bent his head to kiss the tops of her breasts and then she slipped off her underwear.

His eyes feasted on all of Hatton, and he was drunk with desire for this gorgeous woman who was so much more than her beauty. Strong but vulnerable. An enigma of the Virginia wild. Now, he reached for her and pressed his lips on hers. They breathed together, and they kissed again, deeply, hungrily, pressing against each other.

And then, there were no more words.

There was only the sweetness of the moment that ebbed and flowed and eventually crashed with the uncontrolled and wild abandon of a giant ocean wave.

MASON

FOUNDER'S DAY 5

*M*arch 22, *Friday*

3:45 PM

Throw the line out an reel 'em in.

Mason chuckled to himself, hopped on his ATV, and headed to the cave to finish what he'd started.

It had been so easy to achieve his goal. Mason had sipped on his hot chocolate, watching the girls in front of him drinking theirs.

They'd all laughed, joked, and shared some memes on their cell phones, but during that time, Mason was pleased to see that they'd pretty much emptied their cups.

"Hey, playground's on the other side," he'd said, "Wanna go see if it's dry enough to hang? Get out of the crowd?"

They did, and as they walked, Mason focused on turning on his best charm. It was his gift, his pa said. His sisters agreed. Savral was the only one who seemed to ignore him, not influenced by what he could do. It wasn't always easy.

Over the past couple of years, he'd had to work on it, practice, to make the effects of his charm last. When he was younger, it only lasted as long as he was directly in front of a person. But he got better. Now, he knew if he tried he could create a lasting positive impression that helped to influence anyone to like him and to go along with his suggestions for a long time.

Of course, much of the playground had pockets of water in the ground by places that would have been fun to play. The swings had puddles underneath them and such, but the back stairs to the building were dry and offered a private place to talk. He suggested they go over there, and they went, sat, and he said he had something to tell them, something they had to swear not to tell anyone else.

"We promise, don't we, Lilith?" Rachel had said.

The younger sister had looked dubious but had nodded in response.

That was when he turned on the charm, full power, and told them about this secret cave not far from where he lived. He described its cool features and said that almost no one knew about it. Just him and his family.

"You guys should come see it," he'd said. "On Friday night, it'll be a full moon. It's the best time to go there. There's natural lighting that makes the inside glow in places. And, there's paintings on the walls and a statue!"

He'd talked it up until he could see that glimmer in their eyes that let him know that he had them cold.

"If you can sneak out of the house, I can pick you up," he'd suggested, and both girls excitedly nodded their heads, obviously ready for a great adventure. "Just remember," he'd cautioned, "No one can know, not even your Ma. It's a secret place. Other people find out, and everyone will want to go up there. My pa would skin me, and the whole thing would pretty much be ruined."

"Don't worry," Rachel had told him. "We'll never say anything, right Lilith?"

Lilith nodded again, silent, but Mason had seen the special glow in her eyes too. The one that let him know that the girls were in his pocket. The potion he'd put into their hot chocolates was icing on top. They'd come to the cave alright, and the Deathwing Queen would have her vessels.

On the way back toward the music, he'd thought about that beautiful girl who sang on stage before they went to the playground. He'd have to find out who she was. Meet her. Maybe the Deathwing Queen, Raum, would want her for a vessel too.

On their way back, things hit a snag. They'd run into Rachel and Lilith's ma. He didn't know how she knew where to find them. Maybe she was a tracker or something. But he'd turned on his charm and said they were walking around and talking and the girls said the same. A few more sentences, and he saw her face change. She looked more kindly on him then.

Damn, I'm good, he gave himself a mental gold star like the teachers gave in school, as the ATV spun up the hill kicking mud. He'd reach the cave soon, and there he'd give the Queen the girl's scent.

KADISHA

FOUNDER'S DAY 6

*M*arch 22, Friday

9:30 PM

Kadisha was thankful she didn't have to visit her mother's grave in the rain this time. Her mother had died almost a year ago. After the funeral, Kadisha had made a promise to herself and the spirit of her mother that she'd visit where her mother rested every night and that they'd say bedtime prayers together just like they used to do when she was alive. The past few days of cold and rain made it miserable to come here, but she was determined to complete her year of prayers with her mother.

The moon was so bright tonight, and with the rain taking a break, she didn't even need her flashlight to get to the graveyard. Reverend Miles had been so kind to allow her evening visitations when the cemetery was normally closed to everyone else at sundown. He'd told her she was a special case, and Kadisha had been extremely thankful.

Now she stood before the white headstone where two angels were chiseled on either side of her mother's name. It was a lovely spot, right beside the church near the stained-glass windows. She spread her tarp on the ground next to the stone, but she could still see her mother's name and kneeled.

That's when she spied something odd.

Something glittered at the foot of the headstone, and she couldn't tell what it was. She reached out. It was something cold, hard, flat, and round. She picked it up in her hand and tried to get a good view of it, but even with the moon so bright, it looked just like a large ceramic medallion of some kind.

She put it beside her on the tarp, vowing to look at it later. What she couldn't figure out was what it was doing there in the first place. Who would have placed a large coin on her mother's grave, and why?

A breeze ruffled her hair, and she caught the scent of cedar trees and wet earth. It was so peaceful tonight. How she wished her mother were still alive, that they could enjoy this night together.

Kadisha shifted on her knees a bit, trying to get comfortable, and then bent her head.

She thought about how, as a child, her mother would come in and read a bedtime story or two and then they would sing the Unity Song. She sang it now, imagining her mother with her, remembering the smell of her clothes scented with Downy dryer sheets and Snuggle fabric softener. Remembering the cool touch of her hand on Kadisha's forehead, her mother's fingers stroking her head and her hair.

"You are the sun, you are the moon, you are the space inside this room—" she sang, "You are the Earth, and you are the sea. . . "

Kadisha paused for a moment, feeling a strange tingling in her fingers and then in her eyes. She held her hand to her chest. "*And I am you*," then she pointed to her mother's headstone, trying to ignore a sudden metallic flavor in her mouth, "—*and you are me . . . *" she placed her hand back to her chest as she finished the song.

Next was Puff the Magic Dragon. She wanted to start singing, but her lungs felt clogged, and then something dripped from her nose. She rubbed at it. It was probably allergies. Her hand came away with a blackish-looking liquid on it. She smelled it and was slightly alarmed, thinking perhaps it was blood.

But why would my nose be bleeding?

She tried again to open her mouth to sing, but it was suddenly full of fluid bubbling up from her throat and a sharp pain in her chest took her breath away. What was happening to her? She was only twenty-nine years old. She was too young for chest pains, for something like a heart attack.

I should—I should go rest . . .

But the thought disappeared as the world started to fade around her and she crumpled onto the tarp, grateful for the cool surface to spread out on. Then, she heard a flapping of wings and the sounds of birds.

It's too late for birds to be out . . .

It was night. Birds didn't fly at night. But they were most certainly birds. And now they were flying down, landing on her and plucking at her clothing.

She wanted to wave them away, but she didn't have the energy. Her arms were suddenly so heavy. More birds flew down and she felt them hopping all over her, cawing with hoarse voices, flapping their wings against her face, her arms, and her legs. Some of them were moving up her skirt!

Mother! Her mind called out for her mother, knowing the woman was long gone to heaven or wherever spirits go. And then she caught a glowing figure in the distance. The light drew closer.

Mother?

Had her mother come back for her in her time of need? Or was she, Kadisha, for some reason, dying, and her mother had come to greet her?

The figure reached its hand out toward her, and yes, it *was* her mother. She was here! Kadisha willed herself to reach out to the one woman who had always loved her no matter what, but then she was yanked away and pulled sharply by an unseen force. Something was dragging her away from her mother, separating her from her body and her freedom.

Now, she could see her body, lifeless, on the ground beside her mother's headstone, and the pain, the suffocation she'd felt, was gone. Black birds covered her body, and she wanted to scream at them, to tell them to get away from her! She tried to move, to will herself back —back to the place that was hers where she'd be—

Something gripped her mind hard and pulled her firmly away, and all she could do was scream into a black void—a silent, yawning scream—an endless cry—as this thing she was now—this spirit— was stuffed into a place where others like her screamed too.

CHRISTOPHER

FOUNDERS DAY 7

*M*arch 22, Friday

11:55 PM

Christopher breathed in the night air and filled his lungs with the sweet scent. Today had been glorious, and he'd enjoyed the music, the food, and his time talking with the people of the town. He'd listened to their worries and offered words of comfort. Often, after these events, he felt drained of energy, but this evening was different.

After closing up his church and community rooms, he'd gone on a long walk around the town, taking notice of some of the cherry trees starting to open their pink buds, the daffodils that had opened their yellow blossoms and the golden flowers of the forsythia bushes that had seemed to burst open with just a day of much-needed sunlight. The temperature had risen to nearly seventy degrees by four in the afternoon, and almost everyone had removed hats, coats, and scarves and basked in that beautiful warmth.

Parishioners and visitors alike breezed in and out of the Unitarian sanctuary. A group of local women had brought cupcakes, fruit, and vegetable and cheese snack trays to place on a community table. Townsfolk strolled in, passed by, and picked up tidbits here and there. It had seemed like forever since there had been such a sense of togetherness—of social camaraderie. Despite the tragedies, people still longed to come together—maybe even more so because of the recent terrible events.

And then, there was Judith. They'd had a special moment there in the church, and then, for some reason, it had all gone sour. He tried to think what he might have done to chase her away, but he couldn't think of what it might have been that caused her to get up and leave in such a moment of—bliss. All he'd done was mention the girls and then ask if she'd heard anything more . . .

That had to be it. Of course. He'd asked if she heard about any more deaths, and he'd ruined a tranquil moment. A moment when she was free, or trying to be free, of all of the horror and her responsibilities. He forgot sometimes that she needed those

339

moments, that they probably almost never came her way. And she had two daughters to raise on top of it all.

After he'd closed up the church, he'd stopped at Mama's for some pizza and wine, then walked over the River Rage for a couple of beers. There was a bonfire in the beer garden out back, and some young folks were playing guitars, all sitting in a circle and singing Wagon Wheel. He'd talked with the bartender there, Colin, who told him about his recent trip back to his homeland, Ireland.

And Christopher had listened with fascination as Colin's accent dropped into a deeper Irish brogue when he talked about his mother and his brothers and sisters all still there on the Emerald Isle. Before he knew it, the brewery was closing down, and he'd felt so good, so alive, that he just strolled around the streets and the local park, enjoying the cool breeze and the sorely missed stars overhead.

His phone beeped, and he looked down to discover that it was nearly midnight. He couldn't believe it. The day had sped by him—it had gone so fast!

There was a small trail that broke away from the main road in town and cut through the cemetery to his church. He chose that route instead of walking on the pavement. The ground was still soaked, but he enjoyed hearing the high pips of the frogs singing and feeling the earth beneath his shoes. He parted some branches of the bushes ahead of him when he heard a strange sound and paused.

He squinted, looking ahead. The lights to the church were still on—he'd forgotten to shut them off—but below one of the stained-glass windows, there was something moving, and he couldn't quite tell what it was.

Christopher always carried a small set of binoculars with him. He liked to bird watch from time to time when he was hiking, and sometimes, if he was very still and quiet, he could glimpse a deer, a coyote, and even a bobcat. He fished his binoculars out of his jacket and worked to focus them.

Aiming them toward the church and then beneath the stained-glass window where he'd seen movement, he had trouble figuring out exactly what he was seeing. He noted Ms. Kendra Clay's headstone and remembered that Kadisha, her daughter, went there every evening to pray with her mother. She wouldn't be out this late, would she?

He focused his binoculars on the stone, and then something moved in front of it. It was so hard to see. Whatever it was, it was partially covered in shadow.

Wait. That is Kadisha, isn't it?

However, her body was flat, and she appeared partially unclothed. Christopher started to put his binoculars away and to go quickly in case he needed to render assistance when Kadisha moved. Or, more like, her abdomen moved. He watched, transfixed, as her belly stretched up and tented almost by itself, and then he both saw and heard the woman's abdomen tear apart with a wet, sucking sound.

This is not happening. No . . .

Every fiber of his being told him he should run, run away—and another part of him told him to stay—to help the poor woman. He did neither. He was rooted to his spot, watching, waiting to see what would happen next. Something large and black pushed its way out of Kadisha's body, and then more of it emerged.

341

Is that a—bird?

No. This was not like what he'd seen with Hellen. Through his binoculars, he could only gape at this large protrusion that looked very much like a beak but was much larger. Kadisha's body rocked, and more of the strange oddity emerged.

Damn my soul—he refocused his lenses.

The *thing* that pushed out and emerged from Kadisha's body was no bird. It had a beak like a bird, but a very long beak. It was curved and pointed, with what looked like jagged teeth running along the inner ridges. Long black feathers ran the length of its spine and shoulder blades and along the back of its arms and legs. It leaped out of the corpse and shook itself.

Its form was most certainly human-like. The creature opened its large beak and let out a half-caw and half-nerve-jarring scream, which caused Christopher to stumble backward a step or two. Then, it seemed to grow larger right in front of Christopher's eyes.

He couldn't see clearly since the moon wasn't full—but the thing—framed by the light from the church window—was definitely getting bigger. It transformed from infant size to toddler, child, teen—then it planted its feet and rose up—dark downy feathers covering the front of its body.

How long Christopher stood there, mouth gaping open, observing this strange metamorphosis, he couldn't say—but when the creature's piercing crystalline blue eyes turned toward him, he knew if he didn't leave now, he'd never have another chance.

Perhaps the shrubs and some of the evergreen foliage hid him well enough. The creature's beak lifted, almost as if it were testing the air for scents around it.

How well can birds smell?

Christopher didn't want to find out. He catapulted himself through the bramble and past the trees, heedless of the cracking sticks and crunching leaves. He had to tell Judith what he'd just seen. It made little sense, but somehow, these creatures were growing out of dead human bodies—female bodies.

His mind flashed back to the image of Hellen covered by crows and then seeing one crow come out of her genital area. He remembered when Justin had shown him the hole in Hellen's lower abdomen. He hadn't considered it then, but now he wondered if the crows were somehow breeding these creatures inside women's bodies.

But that was impossible! His brain whirred as he finally reached the pavement of the main road. Ahead of him, the police station had welcoming lights in the windows that beacon'd him to safety. He paused for a moment as a purple Dodge Charger rumbled by, and Christopher caught the license plate—ATOMIC13. At least some things never changed.

Still, his brain buzzed. If that thing resulted from such a strange, necrophilic mating—if those twisted monsters were offspring—was that the creature killing the men in town? Eating the flesh off their bones and devouring their brains?

A mental picture of the hole in Marlie's grave invaded his head, and then he thought about what Job had said about other graveyards with holes tunneling down through the tops of coffins—all at the graves of recently interred females. What caused these creatures to form? The women's bodies were dead. How did these bird monsters

343

come to exist in this macabre cycle of death and rebirth? How did they relate to this Raum?

Christopher stopped in front of the police station, his hand on the doorknob. All he had to do was go in, and he'd be safe. He wasn't sure who was on the night shift tonight, but he knew that they'd let him hang out there for a while. Maybe even talk for a bit if he wanted.

But, Kadisha's body—and the creature.

He remembered Judith's face just hours before, how she'd looked so happy and relaxed until he'd asked if she'd had any more reports come in—he pushed the door open, his full intention to call Judith when he got inside. Instead, his fingers dialed Renny's cell. It rang only twice before she picked up.

"Christopher," she answered, with a combination of sleepiness, confusion, and concern in her voice all at once.

Before he knew it, she was there picking him up. They drove to the cemetery first, and after making sure all was clear, they placed a blanket over Kadisha's body.

"I'll call Justin first thing in the morning," she assured him. "He's an early riser. He'll bring her over to the funeral home—no fuss, no muss."

Kendra Clay's headstone was on the side of the church, facing away from the road. It was likely no one would notice it that early. Christopher nodded, too shaken to say anything.

"Now, don't you worry. I got a guest bedroom. We can tuck you in for the night. You'll be just fine."

When they arrived at the Tattered Page, Renny escorted him in— the jingle of chimes announcing their entrance—and there was

Renny's daughter, Melody, rushing to his side, helping him upstairs to the guest bedroom where he plopped onto the mattress and almost immediately fell into a deep but troubled slumber filled with the flutters of wings and darkness.

JUDITH

SMELL

*M*arch 23, *Saturday*

6:30 AM

Judith poured a cup of coffee into her mug. It was back to the regular routine, as much as it could be regular.

She thought about yesterday as she thumbed through the messages on her phone. It had been a near perfect day yesterday except with Christopher during those last awkward moments at the church.

Damn.

She shouldn't have left things like that, but that was the way it was. She could apologize later but—

Wait a minute. Judith had taken a day off yesterday and asked her crew not to call her unless it was really important. And they hadn't.

What caught her eye, though, was that she'd missed a call from Lu and her voicemail.

She opened it up to listen, figuring it was something about the autopsies on the Pine, McCleod, and Cunningham cases. She pressed play and listened. It was about those cases alright, but not at all what she expected. She knew it was early as hell for most people, but Lu hadn't called back again to say she was okay. Judith pressed the number.

When Lu answered, she breathed in deeply with thanks. Although she sounded groggy, at least she was okay.

"Hey, Lu. Sorry to bother you. I was out yesterday and didn't see . . . "

Lu interrupted. "Judith! I am so glad you called back. Sorry. I was exhausted after yesterday, but we need to talk. In person. Not over the phone. Do you have time this morning?"

"Soon as I get the girls set up for hanging out on a Saturday while I work. Safety proof the house. Find some fun things to do. You want to come to the station or—"

"No. Let's meet at the Tattered Page. Say at eight?"

"I'll be there." Judith ended the call. It wouldn't have done any good to ask Lu to explain, and Judith wasn't up for it yet. Caffeine first.

At least it was a Saturday, and the girls didn't have school. She'd at least make sure that they had their chores scheduled, a list of things they could do, and then check on them before she went out.

She opened the door to Rachel's room first. She sniffed the air. There was a peculiar but familiar odor in here. Quietly moving around the room, she tried to pinpoint where the scent was coming from. It was stronger by her daughter's bed. She sniffed close to her. It seemed to be coming from Rachel herself. She sniffed her daughter's face.

Yes, it's her.

Judith paused for a moment. She tried to think back to when or where she'd smelled something like this.

The Mason boy. It was a bit like that.

Mason had talked with the girls yesterday, and she'd looked for her girls when she couldn't find them, and they were walking back to the outdoor stage just about when she started tracking them down. She thought more about yesterday. He'd given the girls cups of hot chocolate, and he'd had one himself. She hadn't noticed anything out of the ordinary.

Something twinged in her brain. It was most certainly unrelated, but she thought about those heads in the fishing boat, the strange odor that had been there, and that medallion. She looked at her hand. The red spot had long disappeared, just as she suspected it would.

Not much affected her or Rachel, for that matter. Any disease, cold, or rash came and went quickly from them. It would also with Lilith when she hit her time for the change.

Lola panted and spun around in circles.

"I know you're hungry, girl. Just wait a minute."

Judith stood by Rachel's bed, trying to sort out the information running through her head. Rachel hadn't come anywhere near any of the bodies or any strange coins, not that she knew of. She thought about Mason.

He confused her. Whenever he was near, she liked him. But the thought of him made her neck hairs stand on end when she was not, like this morning. Placing a hand on Rachel's shoulder, she shook her gently.

Rachel sniffed the air, smiled, and then opened her eyes. "Mornin' Mom," she said and yawned.

"Mornin' sweets." Judith looked upon the face of her daughter and suddenly felt so protective. She was sixteen, but she was still her little one.

"Hey," Judith started, "Yesterday."

Rachel stretched and sat up. "Yeah? Great day, right?"

"Yes," Judith replied. "I just want to ask you something, okay?"

"Alright." There was no guile, no sense of hiding anything in Rachel's voice.

"You guys spent time with Mason yesterday."

Rachel's forehead furrowed. "Yeah, I guess we did. That's kinda weird because I'm not sure why. Guess yesterday it seemed like a good idea. He brought us hot chocolate. I thought that was sweet."

"Did he give you anything else yesterday?" Judith asked. "I'm just curious. You guys were over at the playground."

"Mom! No!" Rachel was starting to get defensive now. "He was just nice, that's all."

Lola growled. She was probably feeling tension in the air.

"I don't mean . . ." Judith sighed, not knowing how best to phrase what she wanted to say. "Okay, I don't mean to ask or think that he gave you drugs or alcohol or anything."

Rachel snorted. "You would know. You've got the nose of a bloodhound."

"So do you," Judith smiled.

Rachel sobered at bit. "Well, I've got you to thank for that, don't I?"

"Come with me for a minute, will you? To Lilith's room."

"Why?"

"Just, let's see what you think when you walk in there. Smell the air."

They went to Lilith's room and opened the door. The girl was nestled all the way under her covers. Judith entered first. Yes. The smell was stronger in here.

Rachel came in next and breathed in. "Ew," she said. "Is that what my room smells like?"

Judith answered softly, "Yes. But not as strong." She was definitely puzzled. She went to move the covers and wake up Lilith so she could ask some more questions and gasped.

Lilith was gone.

JUDITH

CLAWS

*M*arch 23, Saturday

8:15 AM

Judith hoped her team wasn't writing speeding tickets today because they'd have to cite her if they were. She blasted through town, knowing that the answers she needed had to be at Renny's.

Lu had seen something yesterday. And the girls had that strange encounter with Mason, and there were unexplainable murders happening all around town during one of the rainiest springs on record. The ER doc, Thomas, had described a strange creature in his room at the Horseshoe, and Christopher had reported the desecration of graves. And he was the one who found Hellen, too. She wondered if he'd told her everything.

Add to that the fact that the town was fighting a flood, more rain was coming and there were no answers to solve any of these problems. Nothing certain.

Rachel was sobbing quietly in the seat next to her. Judith knew she was blaming herself for Lilith missing, but there was nothing to blame. She suspected the Mason boy gave them something, probably in their hot chocolate.

And yesterday, everything seemed fine. She'd liked the boy. Trusted him. Today, both she and Rachel wondered why.

When she'd discovered that Lilith was missing, she'd searched around the house for her scent, thinking maybe she went for a walk or who knows? Her trail led right to the main road and then a few yards toward town—then it ended. She'd obviously gotten into a vehicle, and now Judith was crazy mad with fear and anger.

Someone had her daughter, and when she found out who it was, they would pay with their lives. *No mercy.* There would be no mercy for the person or persons who messed with her children.

She bared her teeth while she was driving. Hackles raised up on her neck. She wanted to find whoever it was and tear them into bloody little pieces. Unconsciously, she growled with white, hot anger.

Without thinking about it, she pulled up and braked hard in front of Renny's. Then she spied Lu's car. She would have chuckled if she hadn't been in such a fury. She'd have to talk to the good doctor and ask her to consider using a more practical and less conspicuous vehicle when she was here.

Judith opened the door to get out of her Interceptor when Rachel touched her hand firmly.

"Mom," Rachel warned, slowing her for a moment.

She looked down. Judith's fingernails had turned into long, sharp claws, and long fur had sprouted along her arm. She checked the rearview mirror. Her eyes and teeth had gone wolf as well. She took a deep breath and exhaled.

Right. It wouldn't do for anyone here to see that.

Judith tilted her head side to side, cracked her neck joints, and then checked that everything looked normal.

Rachel looked her over. "You're good to go now," she nodded, with a hint of envy in her voice. "I can't wait until I have that kind of control."

"You're doing better than me right now, baby." Judith leaned over and gave Rachel's face a nuzzle.

Then, they both got out of the vehicle and met Lu at the door. None of them said anything. Lu turned the doorknob and the chimes sang their tune when they all walked in.

RENNY

GATHERING

*M*arch 23, Saturday

8:30 AM

Inside the Tattered Page, Renny knew in just a couple of minutes, that two of her friends were going to walk through that door looking for more answers. Judith was coming, and Renny knew she was beyond frantic. And Lu had been through a major ordeal.

When the chimes tinkled and then hummed in low tones, she looked up from what she was reading—a book on Devils and Demonology—and was mildly surprised. Judith had brought Rachel with her. *Why just Rachel?*

Then, she knew. She hadn't seen or felt this. *Lilith is missing.*

That wasn't good. Not good at all. She knew Judith would totally understand her next action.

Renny did a 180, ran down the hall, up the stairs, and quickly checked inside Melody's room.

Her daughter was still sleeping in, her hands and feet visible. Her hair and sweet face were partly visible beneath a cover. She stirred. Renny quietly shut a door—but not too quietly. Melody should get up soon.

In seconds, she was back at her counter. "I had to do that. Melody's okay. Let's go to the study room," Renny said.

They all went in, and both Lu and Judith looked surprised to see Christopher sitting in one of the wing-backed chairs. There were five seats in all, arranged in a circle. Renny grabbed a fold-out chair from a closet, opened it, and added it to the circle.

"You're expecting someone else this early?" Lu clearly didn't have the whole picture yet. None of them did. Renny wasn't even sure she did.

"Thomas will be here shortly," Renny said. "He has a part in this too, though he doesn't know it yet."

On cue, the front door chimes tinkled and hummed. Renny stepped out of the room and waved Thomas in. Soon he was seated with the rest of them in a circle.

Renny looked around at them. "All of you are here because each of you has a part of this puzzle, we need to put together to fight an enemy that is not only threatening this town, but could threaten many others. Jude, when you were here the other day with Thomas, you shared your stories with me, and Job and we told you what we knew so far. We were interrupted by a horrible event that needed seeing to, but it's important we all get together now. I believe that you four—" she paused and considered Rachel and realized she did have a part to play in this, "five—can stop what's coming but you'll need to be strong. The forces that have come together here have been building slowly for a while. Judith, tell the group what you came to tell me."

Judith worked her jaw back and forth and Renny felt how hard this was for her and how desperate she was to find her youngest.

"You all know about a number of the deaths we've been investigating." Judith's eyes searched the circle and landed on Christopher. "I think all of this started the day Reverend Miles found the body of Hellen Profitt at the bottom of a cliff. He thought she was dead at first, but then discovered she wasn't. He called the EMTs and she was medevac'd to James River General because the UVA trauma center was full at the time. Dr. Craig," Judith's gaze went to him next, "he tried to save her life and he stabilized her as much as possible. She was transferred to the ICU but kept losing blood and no one could find out where the blood loss was coming from. She died while I was at Reverend Miles' house asking questions about how he found Hellen." Judith's gaze switched back to him. "I think, Christopher, that something happened before you

356

called the EMTs. I think you didn't want to tell me for some reason, but I think it's important now."

Christopher looked from Judith to Renny, who nodded for him to speak. "I didn't know what to think at the time," he said, "but what drew me to look over the cliff was the sound of crows. The ground was covered with them. That's when I saw Hellen. I tried to scare the crows away before I climbed down and they did fly away. All but one." His eyes looked up at the ceiling. It was obvious to Renny that this was a key piece of the puzzle they needed to know but it was hard for him. She saw him squeeze his fists together. "Okay. So, when the crows flew away, I saw she was naked. As I was looking at her, I saw something moving—moving at her—groin. I thought . . . ,"

"What, Christopher," Renny prodded. "Tell us what you saw."

"Um, I thought I saw a crow crawl out of her private space." He clarified. "Her, um, genitals." He glanced over at Rachel and was obviously uncomfortable mentioning this in front of the girl.

"What did the bird do?" said Renny. "It just crawled out of her, and what?"

"Nothing," Christopher shrugged. "It cawed, shook its feathers, and then flew away."

Renny looked at Thomas next. "Thomas, the day you saw Hellen, did anything else strange happen on your shift?"

"Yes," Thomas answered slowly. "We had an emergency case come in later that night. The EMTs brought him in—said he'd had a heart attack. They were doing CPR when they came through the door. We worked on him and did everything to try to get his heart started. I asked for a stat chest x-ray and labs. I called it—his time of death—twenty minutes later. When I got his digital films back . . . they showed that he had no heart." He looked around as if daring someone to challenge him or say that what he'd seen was a mistake. "The attending who was on shift with me saw it too."

Lu cut in. "I helped with the autopsy. The man had no heart, but there was not an incision on him anywhere. Also, it was the same with the woman that Reverend Miles found, except she had a hole in her abdomen like something had pushed or eaten its way out of her. To the best of my knowledge, she didn't come in that way. When we did her post, her body was essentially drained of blood. The main blood vessels in the center of the body were empty."

Christopher said, "The man, the one with no heart, I found out his name is Viktor. Viktor Odol. Supposedly, I mean, technically, it's impossible that it's him."

Renny and everyone else waited for him to explain why it was impossible.

"He lived a long time ago. He was from the town of Passage."

"The ghost town," Lu breathed, the surprise audible in her voice. "The one that's not supposed to exist."

"This is all well and good to sit and talk!" Judith fumed and shook her head. Her lips squeezed together with anger, and Renny could tell she was becoming more frustrated by the minute. "My daughter is missing. MISSING! Let's get on with this because if any of this has something to do with where she is, I need to know, and I need to know NOW!" She stood up and paced by the window.

Renny spoke to her. "Judith, the other day, when the Water Rescue Team pulled in the fishing boat. Remember the medallion stuck in the man's hair? I think it's connected. The deaths, the split skulls, the medallions or coins—whatever they are."

Judith stopped pacing and looked at her hand. "I sort of touched it that day. It was through the plastic baggie that we put it in, but I felt something." Her eyes turned from angry to thoughtful. She looked at her hand. "My hand got a red spot from it, but it went away. I didn't think much of it."

Lu broke in again. "With Paul Pine's head, the one reported on the bridge, I found an imprint in the dirt, a round print by the head. I asked the couple who found the head if they'd seen anything else or picked up anything. They said no, although I felt they weren't telling the truth. The next day, both were reported dead. That's the case at the Red Tail apartments, Judith. I haven't had the opportunity to tell you yet, but there was a medallion there, too. It's in an evidence bag. And the young woman, the same thing happened with her that Reverend Miles said happened to Hellen."

Renny's head was pounding. All this information—if she'd only known sooner—these events as they were set in motion. "So, you're saying you saw—"

"I saw a crow come out of her vaginal opening. I wouldn't have believed it if I hadn't seen it myself." She glanced at Christopher when she said this, then turned her attention to a pile of books on a table behind him. "Yesterday, I was doing the autopsies on Pine and the couple from Red Tail. I'd gone to the bathroom to wash up, and when I came out, my assistant was screaming. I ran into the morgue and saw—I saw this black feathered creature. It had a huge beak on it and eyes the color of ice. The woman I was going to autopsy later, her body was on the floor, and there was a hole in her abdomen, just

359

like in Hellen's body. I hate to say it, but I was petrified. I felt a terror that—well—the large crow-like creature, it didn't attack. It made its way to one of the drawers in the morgue and removed a body. Carried it like it was nothing. Then, it started to come toward us. We ran for the bathroom and locked ourselves in. Called security. They let us know when it was clear."

"That thing," Thomas piped up, ". . . the creature you described. That's what I saw at the Horseshoe. That's what tried to attack me." He pulled out the medallion from underneath his shirt. "This is what saved me."

"What is it?" Judith walked over to look at it. "Where did you get that?" She didn't touch it, but Thomas showed the markings on one side and the sculpture crow head on the other."

"It came from Hatton," he said. "Hatton Profitt."

JUDITH

CHANGE

*M*arch 23, Saturday

8:45 AM

Judith stared at Thomas, and suddenly, she understood a little more. Thomas and Hatton had a thing for each other. She'd noticed he smelled like sex when he came into the room. His scent and the other that she now knew was from Hatton had a familiarity to it.

People of the same family had similar scents probably because they shared similar DNA.

Hatton's scent was like Mason's. When she'd gone in to wake her girls this morning, that was part of the stink she'd picked up in the girl's rooms. But there was also something else, something she'd never smelled before. And it was probably from the hot chocolate the girls drank yesterday. Chocolate that Mason had given them. But why would he put something into their drinks? For what purpose?

She relayed her information and this morning's experience to the group. Then she noticed Rachel was crying.

Judith squatted by Rachel's seat. "What is it, Rach? Why the tears?"

Rachel sniffed. "Yesterday, when we were with Mason. I mean, he was so friendly, and I liked him so much, you know? He—I'm not supposed to say anything—but he told me that he wanted to show us something. He said there was a cave near his house, something really sick. We weren't supposed to tell anyone about it. We were going to sneak out next Sunday. I'm sorry, Mom, but he was going to pick us up and take us there. He said it was better to see at night because parts of the place glowed inside. We promised we'd go and that we wouldn't say anything. Mom, is that why Lilith is gone? I wanted to do it. I promised, and now . . ." Rachel broke down into tears, and Judith gaze up at her face.

"Thanks for telling me, Rach. This isn't your fault. You didn't do anything wrong. But I know who did!" She stood up, furious. "This is Mason Profitt's doing. I don't know how, I don't know why—"

"Hold on, hold on, Judith." Renny's voice cut through her anger, though Judith barely heard it. She was going to go up the hill to the Profitt place, find this cave, and get her daughter.

"We don't know if that's where she's really at right now," said Renny. "We don't know if Mason is the one to blame. You go up there with what you've got, and you might get killed. Make things worse. You've met Jagger."

Oh yes, she had met that son-of-a-bitch, Jagger. She hadn't seen his wife, Herra, in years either. He or Mason probably killed Hellen. Threw her off a cliff.

"I'm going to go get my daughter, Renny." She stormed toward the door.

"Jude, wait just a second, wait!"

"WHAT!" she half yelled, half growled back.

Everyone in the room gasped. And suddenly, Judith knew why.

She hadn't bothered to put her jacket on, and she was wearing short sleeves.

Her arms had sprouted long furry hair, and she ran her long tongue over her teeth. Her canines were prominent now—already transformed. She guessed at least some of her face had too. She could either stay here and explain to everyone, hear what Renny had to say, or she could go get her daughter. Then, she saw Rachel. Her eyes were so huge, and the sadness and shame sucked the anger right out of her.

The chimes at the front door tinkled and toned. Everyone stiffened.

Dammit to Mudrog hell. This was not a conversation that anyone else needed to hear.

Judith turned toward the main room of the Tattered Page as Job and Grinch ambled in. And there was another dog shyly creeping in alongside them.

Wait. Not a dog. A small wolf.

"Hey, hey!" said Job. "Someone here lose a pup? Fur family member?"

Judith could not believe it. This little wolf was beautiful. She breathed in the air, and all of her worry, anger, and sense of loss floated away.

Job came closer to the entrance of the study room, and the little wolf followed. Judith bent down, sniffed the wolf cub, and then scooped the creature up in her arms. She went to her chair and cradled her, petted her, hugged her, and cried. She was so overcome with relief, joy, and emotions that she couldn't begin to verbalize. The wolf whined timidly, then licked her face all over.

Christopher, Thomas, and Lu looked confused.

Rachel sighed in resignation. "Everyone, meet my sister, Lilith," she announced.

CHRISTOPHER

RETRACE

*M*arch 23, Saturday

9:01 AM

Christopher didn't understand at first. How could this dog, this little wolf, be Lilith? Then, the partial transformation they'd just seen Judith go through hit him. The hair on her arms, the sudden change of the teeth, and the elongation of her face—he'd thought maybe he was seeing things. But no, it was real.

All these years. How had he never seen it? How had he not known? By the understanding and caring emotions on Job and Renny's faces, this was no surprise to them. Was he the only one who didn't know?

No. Thomas and Lu seemed just as shocked as he felt. But why shouldn't they? They hadn't known her as long as he had. The emotions that surged through him were like a raging river. Why had she never told him? Why did Renny know, and he didn't? How did this happen to her, and how did it all work?

Renny, somehow sensing his anger, confusion, and bewilderment, touched his hand. "It'll be okay," she said. "You'll be fine. Look, her daughter is found and she's okay. That's the important thing."

Christopher watched Judith as she nuzzled against the little black wolf and held her close. Rachel giggled.

"Someone want to tell me what the hell is going on here?" Lu was obviously amazed and curious but not disbelieving or scared.

Judith buried her head in her daughter's fur, then looked up at everyone in the circle. "This wasn't supposed to happen right now. Usually, a person's first time is during the full moon. It's corny, I know, movies and all. But adolescence—hormones are influenced by the reflective light of the moon and its gravity. It usually triggers the change for us. Some other people change too, depending on who they are."

Lu smiled, shaking her head. "I get it now. Ware. Ware wolf. That's priceless."

Job came a little farther into the room. "We found her on the roadside. I'm guessing someone picked her up in human form, and then she started changing. The driver probably got scared. Dropped her right by the roadside again."

Christopher wondered who would have picked her up and why she would have been outside late at night anyway.

Renny clapped her hands to get everyone's attention. "Okay. Now that we have EVERYONE here let's finish this and figure out what we need to do. Judith, you and I know that very few things affect the Wares. Not illness, infections, or anything physical. Your biological makeup clears it from your system. You got a red spot on your hand that went away the same day. Others who touched medallions later died." She rubbed her forehead with her fingers as if fighting a headache.

"Job and I researched some information on this. I've mentioned a bit of it before to a couple of you, but the medallion—"

"Show them the book," Thomas interrupted. "The one you showed me and the Reverend."

"Got it right over there. Job? You mind? And the other one with it. The one that's got the sigils."

She showed the lithograph to Lu, and Lu's reaction was similar to Thomas's but not as violent.

"That's it." Lu nodded vigorously. "That's the thing."

Renny opened the book on demonology to a marked page. "This look familiar?"

"Yes. That marking was on a medallion at the McCleod and Cunningham murder scene. Same kind as at the fishing boat, too."

Renny showed the page in the book to Judith. She recognized it as well.

367

"So what does this all mean?" Christopher understood the strange deaths now appeared to be intentional murders. Still, he didn't understand how Viktor Odol was involved in all of this.

"The book with the picture of the creature that Thomas and Lu saw," Remy said, "describes a few different legends of the Deathwing Queen, what the Cherokee called the Raven Mocker. This legend says, 'The Deathwing Queen prolongs life to the man who offers an immortal heart. With this token, she can breed in the dead. She will feed on female blood while her brood devours men.' And further below are these verses in a poem. 'A vase of many souls she keeps as a cache of remaining years. She may bestow time on her servants and erase their dying fears.'"

She turned to another section in the book.

"Here it says, 'Beware the Crow Moon lest the Harvesters in number gather with the Deathwing Queen, then life and limb and soul are lost.' There's a chant here, too, that a person is supposed to say in order to draw the Deathwing Queen's attention to them. I won't say it out loud for obvious reasons, but the chant includes the demon name Raum."

Renny held up a dark red volume.

"I researched the demon name, and in this book, Raum is described as 'the great Earl of hell,'—as a male—but in other books," she held up a black text and another red book, "demons are described a being bi-gender, gender fluid, and non-gender, basically meaning they can choose whatever form, gender or non-gender they please. Mostly, it seems they appeal to the human ego in whatever form they think that group of people, or a person, might prefer."

"So," Thomas said, "it sounds like right now, a Crow Moon is not a good thing. And do you think those creatures we saw are Harvesters?"

Renny nodded. "I do. Think about what happens. By some weird mating ritual, a crow or something that seems like a crow, enters a dead woman's body. Somehow, it plants—whatever it is—inside the body, and it grows to be a Harvester. The creature breaks out of its corpse egg.' It's hungry; it eats and only eats men." She added, "Oh, and the Crow Moon? That happens early Monday morning, around 3 AM. We have to stop everything Monday before its completion— six hours later. Before 9 PM."

"Holy shit." Thomas pushed back in his chair.

Judith, finally content to have Lilith in her lap and now paying attention, said, "The rain is going to keep coming this week, too. We are effectively cut off from everyone in terms of going anywhere. Our folks can get to high ground, but unless there's an available airlift that can take people out of town, we're all trapped here. We aren't the only ones having flooding emergencies, either. There's been quite a few places having trouble, especially by the rivers, all over Virginia."

Christopher didn't really want to state the obvious. He didn't want to do what had to be done. But his lips were ahead of his brain. "So, how do we fight it? How do we destroy it? Stop this from happening?"

Lu spoke as if she were thinking out loud, "The coins or medallions have something to do with it, right Ren? Everyone who has touched one has had something bad happen. We could try to put out the word to people that if they see something like that, not to touch it. To report it right away."

"True," Renny agreed, "but it will take some door-knocking. Most folks are gonna stay inside because of the weather, and most of 'em don't watch local news. Maybe the weather channel. Our younger folks are watching Netflix or another movie channel."

Job cut in. "If you can get me a picture of that coin, Grinch and I can door knock." He rubbed the dog's huge head. "It's too wet everywhere for us to dig. Might as well be useful somehow."

"We gotta get a look at that cave." Everyone turned to look at Christopher. *Jesus, did I just say that out loud?*

Renny's eyes were like little balls of light. "That is exactly what we need to do." She held up the book with the lithograph and showed everyone the map in it. "I'll make a copy for you. Who you gonna take with you?" She got up and bustled out the door, yelling back, "Never mind, you can tell me in a minute!"

Why did I even suggest such a thing, Christopher thought. *And now, they are all looking at me like I'm the leader. I'm not a leader. I'm just a classic fucked up kid, grown, still trying to make sense of life.*

"I can go with you, Rev," Thomas piped up. "I might be winged, but I can do something."

Christopher looked at Thomas' arm in a sling. The man was a physician. He might be useful, but he didn't want to put anyone in danger. Also, this was Hatton's family they were talking about. At the very least it involved Jagger, Mason and probably Savral too—they could all be part of this, even Hatton.

370

"And I can go," said Judith. "If you don't mind four legs. I might be more useful that way."

Christopher was still getting used to the Ware-wolf thing. He'd never seen Judith transform. Even with Lilith sitting in her lap—if that was really Lilith—and he wasn't sure he believed it.

Renny came back and passed copies of the map to Christopher and the others.

Lu spoke up. "As much as everyone's talked this past hour, I guess there's something I need to let you all know. It might not help, but it might." She raked her top teeth across her bottom lip. "My show, Paranormal Murders. It's real. I mean, I truly can see tortured souls. Usually, souls that have suffered wrongful death. Sometimes, I can hear them, too. With the deaths in the town over the past week, with the Harvesters (she said the name like it was something she was still getting used to), I don't think they just eat the bodies of men. I think that somehow, like Renny's book said, they capture or collect the souls of men. And maybe that happens to women, too, in some other way. The women who died before the crow, or whatever it is, exits them. Something sucks their blood out of their bodies. I'm not so sure it's a Harvester that does that. There might be a way that the Deathwing Queen can do it on a paranormal level, and if so, then she collects the women's souls, too. I say this because I have not seen any of the souls or spirits from these deaths. Not one. I worried that maybe I lost the ability. To find out, I went somewhere the other day and discovered that it was not true. I can still see them, so something is taking these souls because they were definitely not freely given."

"So, you're saying . . ." Christopher said, not sure where Lu was going with this.

"I'm saying that if there's a place in that cave that is holding captured souls, I might be able to find it. And if I, or we, can release those souls, it might take some of the power from the Deathwing Queen."

"That might be useful," Christopher said. "But that doesn't tell us how to destroy her."

"You can't destroy a demon," Renny wagged her finger at him. "If the Deathwing Queen is a demon, and she likely is, the only thing you can do with demons is banish them, capture them, or return them to where they came from. Preferably after you've drained all of the power from them so they can't come back for a long, long time."

That's not good, thought Christopher. *But at least there is a way to hurt this demon.* "So, we have to destroy the Harvesters."

"Yes," Renny agreed. "Destroy the Harvesters. Free the souls. Interrupt the path of these coins or medallions people in town are finding. We'll be good if we can do that by the time the Crow Moon is officially complete at 9 PM Monday. It will at least give us a chance to figure out how to protect our town against them. Right now, I wish there was a way that I could protect all of you before you go into that cave, but I've never faced something like this. I can't think of anything that can protect you."

"I can," Thomas volunteered, rubbing his medallion. "I certainly can."

10:00 AM

Everyone stayed until ten or so, after all the plans were made. They each checked to be sure they had proper contacts on their phones and everyone knew what they needed to do next.

It wasn't long after that each of them filed out and went their own ways to prepare. If all went well, they'd cut the Profitt family connection to the demon and pull the rug out from under the Deathwing Queen. Hopefully Job would have some success door knocking and warning people about the medallions. The plus was, with all the rain, not many people would be likely to find one. Judith would be educating her officers not to touch them if they found them.

Christopher stayed behind after everyone left. He wanted to tell Renny more about Viktor.

"What's on your mind, Christopher?" she said. "I can see there's something you want to say." Renny could make a mute man talk about his troubles.

"The man at the morgue. The one the Harvester took. I met him a long time ago."

She raised her eyebrows but didn't say anything.

"I've actually been to the town of Passage. I went there by accident when I was a kid. I was running away from home at the time. I met a boy there—and his brother. The boy's name was Viktor Odol."

Renny gasped. "You don't think it could be a relative? Someone with the same name?"

Christopher shook his head. "I don't think so. When I was there, he and his brother had me to their house to visit. They didn't want their parents to know. I remember how the house smelled like there was very strange food cooking. They left me alone for a few minutes, and I remember looking around and seeing some very peculiar and old pieces of furniture in the house. There was also a painting on the wall; it looked ancient, and in that painting, the boys were just a little younger than they were when I met them."

Renny didn't say a word, but her eyes told him to go on.

"The part you read earlier about 'the man who offers an immortal heart,' I think that was about Viktor. I think he and his family are immortal in some way. Maybe because they continued to live in the town of Passage, and it's still there. But by Thomas' description, the man was grown. Young, but definitely not a kid."

"Have you ever tried to find the town again?" Renny's eyebrows arched high, and Christopher found her gesture a little funny. The question was funny, too.

"No. I guess I was always a little scared to try. I mean, I think those boys truly saved my life. I don't know who or what their parents were, or maybe still are, but I always thought that if I were able, if I went back, I'd never leave there again."

"You mentioned he had a brother."

Christopher nodded. "Amadeus."

"You think he might still be there?"

Christopher hadn't thought of that. "I would think so."

"Thomas told me earlier that the hospital had not been able to find any record of the man or the man's family," Renny said. "What if the brother is still there?"

"Or Viktor and Amadeus left Passage to visit the 'outside' world?" said Christopher. "If Amadeus knew something happened to Viktor, it could explain the anonymous call that Darla got at the 911 center. But then why wouldn't he come forward? It doesn't make sense. Are you thinking that maybe he could help us? It sounds like the Harvester at the hospital took Viktor's body somewhere—maybe to the cave. If Amadeus wanted his brother back and if the Deathwing Queen has his heart—whatever that means and however that happened, he might be willing to help us."

"The only way you'll know, Christopher, is if you go back. Do you think you'd know how? Do you think you could get there?"

"When I went there as a boy, I found it by following the river. When I left, the boys showed me a path that eventually put me out at Gallows Road. I can try to retrace my steps back from Gallows. It can't hurt to try."

It was then that Job rolled around the door entrance. Apparently, he'd been listening on the other side of the wall. "Well, you obviously can't go alone, Reverend," he said. Grinch padded into the doorway by Job's side.

Christopher sighed, wishing that Job hadn't heard their conversation. "I can't put you in danger doing this, Job. It's bad enough what we'll have to face in a couple of days."

"I think that's my decision, don't you?" Job looked down at Grinch. "What do you say boy? You ready to go where no Grinch has gone before?' The pit bull wagged his tail and lolled his tongue in a wide-open smile. "There, you see? It's settled then. Shall we say tomorrow at sun-up?"

Christopher looked at Job's face and took note of his jawline set with determination. He wasn't going to talk Job out of this one. And truth be told, he was relieved to have the company.

"It'll be wet and boggy, but let's do it. We can but try," Christopher said. "Come by my house at seven?"

He walked out of the Tattered page knowing that he had no earthly clue what he was doing. He just hoped he'd survive, and that he wasn't the reason for anyone else dying.

JUDITH

IMAGINE

*M*arch 23, *Saturday*

12:00 PM

After getting her daughters home, Judith set to the task of helping Lilith with her return transformation to human form.

"C'mon, Lilith! You can do it!" Rachel coaxed her sister while Lilith sat on the floor and looked at them with a baleful stare.

Meanwhile, Lola raced around all of them and pranced happily at the sight and smell of Lilith's new form.

Judith watched her daughters, partly feeling the humor of it all and partly worried about what had happened last night. As soon as they got Lilith to return to her human state, Judith wanted to know everything. Like who picked her up and why Job found her on the road. She wanted to kill that Mason boy. That was one truth. She imagined sinking her teeth into his flesh and how good it would feel to rip some chunks out of his body—then she shook her head. Full moon time certainly brought out the worst in her. She had no intention of doing such a thing, but right now, oh, how she wanted to.

She thought about how easily he'd manipulated the girls and even her in town yesterday. Sure, the sun and music made everyone lighthearted, but that was all. She distinctly remembered how much she liked him and the deep sense of trust she felt with him then, and it bothered her.

With Lu's confession about being able to see spirits who suffered from wrongful death, she was beginning to realize that she wasn't the only one with gifts or things to hide. She'd noticed yesterday how Melody's song had captured everyone and caused them to drop all actions and conversations during her performance. While her voice was certainly beautiful, there was something else to it as well. It was mesmerizing—maybe that was the best word for it.

Judith sat on the floor with her daughters. "It's okay, Lilith. Everyone has trouble changing back the first time. It's easier to change into wolf form than it is to change back to human, especially when the moon is full. Just a burst of uncontrolled emotion when your hormones hit their peak, and suddenly, you're on four legs."

Lilith's tail was tucked between her legs. She whined. Lola sat down beside her and cocked her head as if wondering why Lilith was so scared. She looked at Judith with her heterochromatic eyes as if to say, "What's the big deal?"

Judith put her hand out to pet Lilith's head. "It's alright, sweets. You'll be fine, okay? You hungry?" She'd put leftover pizza from Mama's in the oven earlier, and now it smelled ready. Lilith wagged her tail a little.

"Wait, I've got an idea." Judith went to turn the oven off, then came back and started removing her clothes.

"Mommm," and Rachel made the, 'Oh no, you gonna do this, now,' moan.

"Hey, you can join in if you want or not," Judith said. "But your sister needs to see that she's not alone."

She wasn't naked long. All Judith had to do was think about how much she'd like to sink her teeth into that hoodlum—Mason's—neck, and the transformation was almost instant. She shook her body, letting her fur and muscles ripple around her. She always did like the strength she felt when she was in wolf form.

Lilith was obviously ecstatic. Her tail untucked and started to wag. She'd never seen her mother like this, and Judith went up to her face, licked Lilith's cheek, and gave her a nuzzle. Judith could already feel Lilith's fear and anxiety ebbing away. Lola barked and ran around them like a dog that had just sniffed an ounce of cocaine.

"Okay, okay—" Rachel sighed like this was a chore, but Judith knew she wanted to join in, "but I'm changing in my room."

Moments later, a smaller version of Judith came trotting out. They all played and tumbled for a few minutes, and then Judith rose to all four feet and looked at her daughter.

Just use your mind, she said, projecting her thoughts at Lilith. Her daughter looked confused for a minute, and though she hadn't done the same, it was clear she understood. Judith closed her eyes and envisioned herself human again, and then she was on two legs, putting her clothes back on. Rachel looked from Judith to Lilith and seemed to make a decision. Judith heard her send the thought, "Look, I just imagine myself back the way I was and poof!" And Rachel was back and running for her room to get dressed again, giggling.

Judith turned around to get some plates from the cupboard. When she turned back, there was Lilith, in human form, covering herself with a quilt that usually sat on the back of the sofa.

"Well, brava, sweets! Well done!" Judith hated so much that Lilith's first change had happened without her, but what was done was done. At least she'd learned to change back. Each time got easier. "You can stay wrapped in the quilt and come to the table, or you can go get jammies on. Your choice."

"I'm *really* hungry," Lilith said as she came to the table. She looked at the pizza. "I think I'll need more than that. Can you put one of the frozen ones in too?"

Outside, the rain started to fall in sheets once more.

THOMAS

PLAN

*M*arch 23, Saturday

1:00 PM

It was after twelve and Thomas couldn't help agonizing over what he was about to do. He had feelings for Hatton, but he had to know if she had anything to do with the town deaths, with all that was going on. If so, then he had to do something about it.

He sent her a text just minutes after one in the afternoon.

Thomas: *You Free?*

Hatton: Yes. Why?

Thomas: *Join me for dinner?*

There was a pause, and Thomas stared at the screen. He wanted her to say yes for two reasons: one, so he could see her and two, he just wanted to be with her.

Two, he had to find out if there were any more of the same kind of medallions like the one he was wearing. If Hatton had more or if he could learn how they were made, then he could help Reverend Miles, Dr. Crane, and Chief Ware. Right now, he felt useless. Doing this would be his way of contributing to the community.

She'll hate you if she finds out you used her. God, how he hated that voice in his head. *You know she's going to find out. There's no way to avoid it.*

His phone dinged. He read the message and smiled.

Hatton: *What time?*

Thomas: *How about six? Unless you want to come here first.*

Hatton: *There would be nice. Let me see if I can get away.*

Thomas: *We can go to Mama's or Red Batteau. RB's specials are good tonight. And maybe some wine?*

Hatton: *I'll come to your room, and we can walk. RB sounds great! :)*

And now things were set. He had no idea what he was going to do until then.

5:37 PM

The alarm went off, letting him know he had about thirty minutes before Hatton showed up. Thomas wrapped his cast in a plastic bag and jumped into the shower for a quick scrub. It was tricky washing his hair with one hand, but he managed to squeeze the shampoo bottle under his arm and get the shampoo into his open hand. A good wash, rinse and dry and he jumped into a pair of jeans (which was more like a 'wiggle' into them), and then donned another t-shirt and flannel shirt to cover him. He was lucky that even though the Red Batteau was Iron Shores' most upscale restaurant, it wasn't so upscale that it had a dress code. He used some of the cologne that Tati had brought him, brushed his teeth, and was ready just as he got a knock on the door. "Please let this be a good night," he told himself in the mirror.

Thomas appraised his reflection once more to make sure he hadn't missed a spot shaving and nodded, feeling sure he looked okay. He opened the door, saying, "I hope you're hungry—"

A large fist hurtled toward his face, and Thomas stared at it in surprise as it landed squarely on his jaw. Thomas stumbled back. A man he'd never seen before, with brown hair and features similar to Hatton's, drew his arm back and punched him in the gut this time. Thomas fell and hit the floor. He felt more than saw the kick to his ribs and then another.

"YOU!" the man yelled. "You stay away from my sister. Got it? Don't you call her, don't you fucking see her ever again!" The man stormed out, not even bothering to shut the door, and Thomas just lay there, coughing blood and struggling to breathe. After what seemed like some very long minutes, he managed to crawl over to the bed and pull himself up. He heard running footsteps. Mr. Morrow rushed in.

"You okay, son?" He looked at Thomas' face and then went into the room to get a washcloth. He pressed it to Thomas' face. "Here. Hold that there. You got a gash on your jaw. I think the fella had a ring on."

"Thanks," said Thomas. "Did you see him? Who the hell was that?"

"That," Mr. Morrow answered, "was Hatton's brother Savral."

6:35 PM

Thomas let Mr. Morrow know he was okay, thanked the man, and said he'd be alright now. He'd look at the injury and if it looked like he needed stitches, he'd go over to James River General and get a friend of his to patch him up.

Mr. Morrow gave him a measured look and a slight nod. "Alright. Ain't my business," he added, "but the Profitt family is bad news, son, as you already seen. The Hatton girl, well, as I said. You call me if you need anything, okay? I'm right up front. Sorry, I didn't see Savral when he came in. I'd of stopped him if I had, know'n he didn't have a room here and all and after see'n you and Ms. Hatton yesterday." He clapped his hand gently on Thomas' shoulder. "You take care now. I'll see you later on." He left, closing Thomas' door.

Well, that was not the way I expected things to go tonight. Thomas checked his phone just in case maybe Hatton had sent him a message saying she couldn't make it or something. There was nothing from her. Nothing at all.

He kicked his shoes off and flopped on the bed, grabbing the remote, trying to find a way to get his mind off what happened, but his brain was changing channels on its own. He had so many questions.

Pushing the channel key, he just kept surfing from one show to the next.

Another knock came at the door. This time, he looked through the peephole. It was Hatton.

He opened the door. Her face was red, and her eyes looked swollen, probably from crying.

She came into his room apologizing as she came in.

"I am so sorry, Thomas'. My brother saw the messages on my phone, and he went ballistic. Told my pa. They both blew up. Pa stomped on my phone and told me he wasn't getting me another one, and Savral was out of the yard before I could stop him."

Thomas looked at her. Her plump lips, dark hair framing her face in ringlets, and soft, sorrowful eyes. He couldn't be mad at her. This wasn't her fault. If he thought about it, it was really a case of domestic violence. Obviously, Hatton was captive in many ways. She had no freedoms, no way to leave her home. She didn't have a way to work except to sell some things she made—isn't that what she said? She sold crafts or something. She was twenty-five years old. She didn't have to put up with her father and brother, but she did for some reason.

Hatton's face perked up, and she produced a large paper bag. Thomas hadn't even noticed in when she walked in. "I thought you'd probably still be hungry. It's not the R.B., but Mama's has the best garlic bread sticks, fried zucchini, and vegetarian lasagna in town."

Despite the beating he just got not too long ago, the food smelled great.

She pulled a bottle of wine out of the bag. "Also got Mama's Tiramisu. It's awesome. And I picked up a Pinot from the Food Lion. It's a screw cap. I hope that's okay."

Here he was, all beat up, and she was feeding him. She probably didn't have the money for all of this. "Hey, I was going to take YOU to dinner. Why don't you . . ."

She put a finger to his lips. "Hush. Food's gonna get cold. Let's eat, and don't you mention what you were gonna mention, or you'll hurt my feelings. This was the very least I could do, okay?" She went into the bathroom and got a couple of water glasses, opened the wine, and poured it.

After all of this, how in the world am I going to get her to give me some more medallions? He inhaled the scent of the lasagna and breadsticks. Perhaps the answer would come to him with a full belly. They unpacked the food bag, made a picnic on the bed and the answer came to him in the middle of devouring a breadstick. All he had to do was tell the truth.

March 24, Sunday

    8:00 AM

Thomas' alarm on his phone woke him promptly at eight o'clock, and he rolled over to see Hatton gazing at him with what could only be sheer love on her face. He loved how her dark hair cascaded around her cheeks in waves and how, even after a night of sleep, she looked just as beautiful as she had yesterday. She never wore make-up, that he could tell, and he was amazed at how much he really liked that about her.

"Mornin'," she said and smiled as she reached out to caress his face.

When he heard the alarm, he realized he'd fallen asleep so easily after their meal and their evening of sweet lovemaking. He half expected her to be gone in the morning, given her jealous brother and family circumstances, but she was still here.

He also remembered he hadn't had a good moment to talk to her about his medallion, and he realized now was probably the best time for her to look at him with so much affection.

His fingers clasped the cool, round metal piece, and he held it up between them.

"I never had the chance to tell you that this thing saved my life."

Hatton's expression changed to one of confusion and then horror.

"Thomas?" She propped herself up on her elbows. "What do you mean?"

Okay, here goes.

"It was like two days after you gave this to me. I'd just checked out of the hospital. I rented this room, and that very night, something attacked me." He watched her face and noticed the stricken expression that traveled over her face.

So, she didn't really think those things would attack me.

That knowledge made him feel a little safer continuing on.

"I'd laid down on the bed to rest a bit and fell asleep," he continued. "And then something woke me up. I heard the flapping of wings, turned the light on, and Hatton—there was this THING—a huge, black bird—a like—a terrifying thing."

Hatton moved to a sitting position now, cross-legged facing him, her eyes wide.

"I'd taken this off," he said, raising the medallion, "because it got all twisted around my neck, but I was able to get it back on again finally, and when I did, that creature disappeared. I don't know how it did it. I didn't see because I kinda broke a lamp when I was trying to get away from it."

Hatton just stared at him and then swallowed, looking as if that simple action was painful.

"Hatton," Thomas ventured. "What was that thing? Is it what's been killing people around town?" He had so many more questions he wanted to ask, and he also had to be careful what he told her. If her family were the cause of what was happening, letting her know that there was a team of them now who suspected what was going on, who were working to figure out how to battle these things—well, it could be a disaster.

Thomas sat up too, now, cross-legged as well, and leaned forward. "Hatton?"

She blew out a deep breath and seemed to make a decision. "We—meaning the people that know of them . . . "

Thomas noted that she was careful not to say who those people were.

". . . we call them Harvesters. They are born from—okay, this will sound crazy, I know, but it's true—you've seen them—they are born from bodies of the dead. In particular, the bodies of women. Once they are born, they survive off of humans, particularly men. I don't know why—maybe it's because of hormones or something, but as you found out, they are extremely dangerous."

It was Thomas' turn to be silent for a moment, and then he took another step toward his goal. "Hatton, I have got to thank you seriously. If it weren't for this—the medallion you told me to wear—I would be dead right now." He rubbed his chin with his thumb and forefinger, feeling the stubble on his face and reminding himself that he needed to shave later. "But I'm also really worried. I have friends in this town that I want to protect, too. I don't want one of those things finding them and killing them. Are there any more of these medallions that you could possibly give me? To protect my friends?"

She puffed out her cheeks a little, keeping her mouth closed, then said, "You'll have to come with me to get them. Once I go home today, I probably won't be able to leave for a while. I have my little sister and my Pa —my brothers . . ."

Her voice trailed off, and she didn't finish the rest of it. She didn't need to. He understood.

CHRISTOPHER

QUEST

M*arch 24, Sunday*

7:00 AM

Christopher had just put on his hat and rain slicker when the knock came at the door. He opened it, and there were Job and Grinch. Job was wearing his "Shadow" raincoat, minus a red scarf.

"Mornin' Rev! " Job's spirits seemed bright despite the strange task they were going to attempt today. Grinch looked happy too, panting and his entire body wagging.

"You sure you want to do this?" Christopher asked. "I got no problem going solo."

"Rev," Job made a mock sad face. "You gonna hurt my feelings now. When you told me about your experience as a kid I was jealous as hell. How am I gonna be crazy and not go with you now? If we manage it, it will be a tale to tell!"

"It would be a tale to tell, but you and I both know we can't tell it to anyone. Jumping into something like the town of Passage—it must be some kind of time travel or alternate dimension or something like that. There's always an exchange of energy. You can't change something or participate in something without something else getting changed. It's the butterfly effect, if you will. With two of us—" Christopher looked at Grinch— "Three of us, I can't say what will happen, but it's going to change something, somewhere."

"No worries, Rev. I got a feelin,' you know? It will all work itself out alright."

After closing the door behind him, Christopher stepped out into the rain with Job. He hoped he'd see this place again. Hoped he'd be able to tell Judith how he felt soon. He took a deep breath and prayed Job was right.

Job talked as they walked. "I studied the maps last night and looked at some of my books," he said. "Now, you said you lived over on Gallows Road, right?"

Christopher nodded. "Yes."

"So, Gallows Road is named for where it went, of course. It was the road that went to the top of a hill where outlaws, murderers, and such were hanged back in the day. Near, there is a national forest now. To the best of my knowledge, those trees by there ain't never been cut. And next to those woods is the river. The town is s'posed to be close to the river.

"It is," Christopher said. "I remember it, seeing it from a distance. If the town existed in the 1800's then it was there when the canals were in operation. Before the railroad."

"So, we just gotta go that way," Job said. "It's gotta be there somewhere."

"Maybe." Christopher was doubtful. People in town went walking, hiking all of the time. National forests were prime places to go hike, fish, whatever. Someone else in town would have discovered the place and found the opening between dimensions if that was the right way to describe it.

They came to a place where they had to wade through water that was almost knee-deep. If the water got any deeper, it would start running into his rain boots.

Grinch was nonplused. Most dogs weren't happy about rain or excess water, but Grinch was a champ. He was the happiest dog Christopher had ever known.

"There, Rev. Gallows hill." Job paused, standing still, gazing at it.

Christopher nodded, not knowing if Job could see him or not but guessing it didn't matter. They pressed on, and after cresting Gallows Hill, they turned into the forest. As they did, Job said,

"Now, think back to when you was a kid, runnin' away. What was you thinking, you remember?"

It wasn't hard to remember at all; the thing was, he didn't want to remember. He thought about how much he hated his home life, how much he wanted to get away, and how he never wanted to go back. He tried not to think of his mother and the things she did to him, but the more he tried not to think about it, the more the memories surged. If it weren't raining, Job would likely see the tears rolling down Christopher's face.

Grinch started barking.

"Easy, boy," Job said. "What is it? What you smell?" Job never used a leash for Grinch, the dog was so well behaved. When the dog took off dashing into the brush, Job couldn't stop him. Job called out to him. "Grinch, c'mon boy! C'mon back now!" Grinch didn't come.

Job pressed forward in the direction that Grinch had gone, and Christopher followed. The brush became dense, and because they were in the forest and it was still early morning, it was hard to see. It seemed even darker here.

And then, there was a sensation he hadn't remembered before, but he knew it instantly when it happened. The only way he could describe was that it was as if he'd passed through a wall of static electricity. Despite wearing a hat and rain gear, it felt as if the hair on his head was standing on end, and the fine hairs on his arms tingled. He took a few more steps, and the feeling was gone. So were the familiar surroundings.

Job stood in front of him, ruffling Grinch's head and grinning.

"Rev, never in my years did I think that Iron Shores would surprise me again. But she sure did!" He opened his arms. "Get a look at this! I mean, you saw this before when you was a kid, but—Lord Almighty!"

Christopher couldn't help but smile. They'd done it. Was it just the wanting to find Passage that had done it, or was it something else? He'd known others who wandered out here and never had such an experience. Of course, some never came back. And given some of the history, most people who knew about Passage never really wanted to find it.

It was still light outside here, and unlike where they'd come from, there was no rain. Just a bitter cold wind whipping past the 1800's buildings, throwing dust up from the dirt roads and whistling through the branches of trees that were only beginning to bud.

"Okay," he said to Job. "We can't dally. It's still pretty early in the morning but most folks will be milling about soon getting to work and whatever. I think the house I was at was this way."

They traveled along the backyards of houses, a general store and other wooden buildings until they came to a dirt road.

"I think we go left here," Christopher said. And after a few moments, he spied the tall two-story brick house down the road on the left. There was the arch of brick over the wooden door, just as he remembered, but he didn't realize how grand the house was now that he could see it in the daylight. It looked like a Federal-style home, though he couldn't imagine how such a home could have been built here in the middle of nowhere.

But then, this wasn't the middle of nowhere back in the day. The canals along the James River were busy thoroughfares of trade and commerce, and when the railroad came along, it allowed for all kinds of materials to be easily transported from one place to the next. With the development and increased improvement of automobiles and then paved roads, cities sprung up in a number of places that didn't have to rely on the river or the train.

Gradually, the train system stopped carrying passengers and became useful mainly for carting large equipment to certain areas and resources like coal from the mountains of West Virginia to cities like Richmond, which burned the coal for electricity. Towns like Passage disappeared as people moved to places with modern conveniences and better trade capability.

Christopher led the way to the front door, suddenly feeling very unsure about what he was about to face in the next few moments. It had been years since he'd come here as a child. Was it the same year, or had time passed here as well? How did time pass in this now non-existent town?

Job and Grinch hung back as Christopher knocked on the door. There was no answer. He knocked once more, and then the door slowly swung open.

Passage Time

The man who opened the door was not the little boy Christopher had played with when he was here so many years ago. And he was absolutely sure the man was not one of the parents. The young man before him had long white hair that flowed nearly to his waist. He wore an open red satin robe and a pair of red satin pants. His skin was alabaster, and his stomach muscles were tight.

Ripped, the thought passed through Christopher's mind, *the word is ripped.*

The man did not even act surprised when he saw Christopher standing there in modern-day clothing, covered by his rain gear. One of his eyebrows did hitch up a little when he gazed toward Job and Grinch.

Mere seconds passed, which seemed like an eternity, and then the man opened his arms and stepped forward to embrace Christopher.

"I thought you'd never come," he said. He pulled back and smiled, and there were those telltale canine teeth Christopher remembered so well.

"A-Amadeus?" Christopher choked out the name, barely believing that this was the small boy—the brother—whom he'd eaten sandwiches within an ordinary kitchen. Bread, cheese, and meat.

The man's smile widened.

Grinch growled and Christopher turned to see the dog's hair on his neck standing tall.

"Ah," said Amadeus. "Dogs don't take to me so well. Your—friend—is welcome to come in but the dog . . ."

Job's timing was perfect. "Don't you worry sir. He'll stay right over there by the hedges, out of sight, until we come out."

"Very well," Amadeus said, welcoming them in. He made no pretense at covering himself but brought them into the living room, the one Christopher remembered had a large grandfather clock. He motioned them to sit on royal purple sofas that were opulent and well-cushioned. He pulled up an ornately carved wingback chair so he could sit close to them.

Amadeus sat, crossed his legs, and leaned forward. "Have you seen him?"

His question hung in the air and Christopher didn't know how much this man knew about the state of his brother.

"No," he said, measuring his words. "I was only told what happened to him. When I learned his name—well—I don't know how much you know. You may know more than me."

Amadeus leaned back, his smiling face dissipating and turning cloudy. "I know I have not heard from my brother," he said. "Something has happened where he cannot return."

Christopher felt Amadeus knew much more than that but decided he would be open and completely honest with the man. There was no reason not to be. No reason he knew of. He started with a question.

"What do you know of the Raven Mocker? What some call Raum? And what others the Deathwing Queen?"

Amadeus sucked in air between his teeth.

Christopher nodded and went on. "In our time, our place, there is a medical center with doctors. Viktor was brought into that medical center, and he was lifeless. He had no heartbeat, no respirations—he wasn't breathing at all when they found him."

Amadeus seemed to smile a little at that, but Christopher pressed on. "If you haven't been to our time, then it's important to know that we can take pictures of the inside of the body. The medical people took those pictures, and the one thing they noticed was that your brother did not have a heart."

It was impossible not to notice Amadeus gripping the armrests of the chair now. Christopher went on. "Please understand that our people, in our time, thought he was—human." He felt Job tense up as if merely stating that they knew Amadeus and his brother were not human would invite an attack. It was all Christopher could do to keep his voice steady with the next part. "In our time, if someone dies and we don't know the reason why they died, our people do what is called an autopsy."

Amadeus stared at him with golden eyes that seemed to spark red. He was not moving now. Not saying anything.

"Do you . . . ?" Christopher started.

"Yes," he hissed. "I know what an autopsy is! You mean to say . . . ?"

Christopher nodded slowly. "Yes. They sent him somewhere to be examined. His heart was indeed missing. And it looked like it had been surgically removed, but there wasn't an opening on him. How it was removed is a mystery."

Before Amadeus could respond, Christopher blasted into the next part. "So, because he came from Iron Shores and because we are a different kind of community than the rest of—the rest of—well, the world probably—they returned him to the medical place, and he was stored in a cold —a refrigerated drawer just like others who have died are stored before burial.

The man across from him remained still as a statue. His skin turned even whiter, if possible than it was before.

"The hospital received an anonymous phone call suggesting that the man's name was Viktor Odol. We thought the call might have been from you."

Amadeus said nothing.

Christopher pressed on. "My friend here, Job, told me about this a couple of weeks ago—a fortnight, you might say. While the medical people were waiting for a positive identification on your brother's body, one of our doctors witnessed a huge creature—something that looked like a giant crow—pull Viktor out of the drawer and carry him away. They didn't see where this creature went. They were scared and ran to hide. When they came out, Viktor's body was gone."

This telling had been more painful than Christopher could have ever predicted. He felt clumsy in his telling of the event and had kept his eyes on Amadeus every second. Suddenly, the man was standing, pacing the room. Christopher hadn't even seen him get up.

"Amadeus," Christopher ventured. "What is happening? How do we get your brother back to you? Can you tell us what to do to help you and him? And how to help our people?"

Amadeus slowed his pace and stopped. He looked at Christopher and then at Job. His face was full of fury, but Christopher was fairly certain his anger was not directed at them. Amadeus let loose a huge bellow of pain and frustration that seemed to shake the house. Then, just as quickly as he loosed the cannon yell, he silenced it.

"I know of the Raven Mocker," he said. "This Deathwing Queen. And I will help you destroy her—Harvesters—I believe that's what you call them?"

Christopher nodded.

"But, in order for me to cross the barrier to your time, I must have blood."

Christopher's pulse raced. *Am I about to die? Or Job? Or both of us?*

Amadeus walked over to a cabinet and pulled out a bottle of what was, impossibly, Johnny Walker Blue. He unscrewed the cap and produced three glasses, which were suddenly filled with whiskey and on the table in front of them. He picked up a glass and raised it while gesturing to the bottle.

"You see, my brother has been back and forth visiting your time on different occasions."

Holding his glass out to them, he invited a clinking of drinks together. He and Job complied, and they all took a sip. Amadeus paced slowly with his drink, swirling it in his glass. "To do this, he has what you might call a mule to ferry him to the other side. It's done by binding a creature such as yourself to one such as me. This bond is done willingly through a consensual blood offering."

Job blurted out, "Wait, you want him to let you drink his blood?"

Nonplussed, Amadeus simply nodded. "Exactly." He grinned, his sharp canines flashing. "Oh, you won't die. Don't worry about that. If that were my intention, you'd be dead already. No. Rather, you would be *bound* to me. What I suffer, you suffer. When I need you, you must come. No matter the cost."

That was a lot to take in at one time. Christopher had not anticipated anything like this.

Job was unstoppable with the questions right now, though, and again he blurted, "But wouldn't that make him into a—wouldn't he become . . .?" He looked over at Christopher, his face pleading and then back at Amadeus as if waiting for an answer that he hoped was different than the one he expected.

Amadeus didn't seem angry anymore. Simply thoughtful. Christopher discovered he felt very uneasy at the way Amadeus was staring at his neck.

"It doesn't work that way. It's not that simple," Amadeus said. "And we are being premature. Let's just say that I need to cross the barrier to retrieve my brother, and you both need me to help stop the Deathwing Queen. It is important to know that what is being done in your town can only be done during the time of the Crow Moon. This, in part, is why it is called the Crow Moon. Conditions are, "he seemed to be searching for the right word, "optimal," he finished.

Christopher had to ask because he didn't understand. "So, what does the Deathwing Queen, I mean, why does she need your brother's heart? And why take his body?"

Amadeus sat down once more and took another sip from his whisky glass. Christopher followed suit. Job finished his in a swallow.

"A human heart comes with a human soul. That soul is finite. It only stays in your world for as long as it's meant to be there. It has a time limit and an expiration date, if you will before it moves on. Now, our kind, we are not such creatures. Our hearts are continuous because our souls have no time limit in this world. It is difficult to explain why. Maybe when we have more time. But I suspect this Raven Mocker or Deathwing Queen has figured out how to harness an infinite soul like my brother's so that she will have continuous power. She won't have need of other human souls. So, the time those souls would have had on Earth can serve those she favors by giving them extra years to their life. It's an incentive for humans to help her. She provides this as a reward, or payment, to those who serve her. It's genius, actually. Before, she needed as many souls as she could get and had to constantly gather them here and there so she could stay in your realm. Payment of extra years of life for her faithful was minimal. An extra 20 to 50 years here or there, which, after a while, you realize is nothing. With my brother's soul, she can stay in this realm on Earth as long as she possesses his heart."

"I thought," Christopher decided to use the word because it was what it was, "I thought *vampires* are essentially dead. What good are any of their body parts? They don't use them, do they? And how can they have souls?"

Amadeus smiled like a grown-up explaining something patiently to a child. "Hollywood, books—all of the authors who write or make films about us portray us based on hearsay or imagination. We are not dead by any means. Far from it. Our bodies function very similar to human ones but we are on a different level due to a mutation that occurs when we are made—when we change from what you are now to what you see before you. We are stronger, faster, smarter— virtually limitless in our capabilities."

Amadeus took a sip from his drink as if to emphasize a point. "Remember how we ate in the kitchen that night, Christopher? You were surprised that my brother and I ate food and did not drink your blood. The truth is, we are a more evolved type of human species. We have infinite life as long as we care for our bodies—as long as we nourish ourselves with various foods, including blood. As you've noted, however, we do have vulnerabilities. If the part of our body that houses our energy, or soul if you prefer, is removed, it puts us in a stasis much like hibernation, but we do not die."

Christopher's brain was reeling. But in the end, all he could think about was Judith and her girls and the townspeople who were trapped by the flood waters, how they were threatened by the horrible Harvesters, and the nightmarish copulations of demon crows on dead townswomen's bodies. He thought of how the

405

women's bodies were completely drained dry of blood and then wondered something else.

"Is this thing, this demon, related to you at all? Is it she, he, whatever—I mean, we know that somehow, she consumes the blood of women who are used to grow the Harvesters. And the Harvesters only eat our men."

"As I said," Amadeus was evasive now in his answer, "we don't have time for a long explanation coupled with a history lesson. Give me a moment. . . ." And in a flash, he was instantly dressed in a suit and tie and dress shoes—a style a little strange for Iron Shores, where jeans and flannel shirts were always in fashion— but still modern.

Christopher stood, resolute in his decision about what had to happen next. "Job, go get Grinch and lead him around to the back of the house."

Job stood slowly. "Chris—"

"It will be okay, Job. Really."

The expression on his face must have let Job know that there'd be no argument here. Christopher was determined to do what he could to save Judith and her family, as well as the rest of the town. His longtime friend hesitated only a moment more before striking toward the front door. "I'll see you two in just a few, then." And the front door was opened, then shut.

Amadeus moved toward Christopher so very carefully and slowly that the motion mesmerized him with a dreamlike quality. Christopher smelled something in the air, and he would have found it curious if he weren't so terrified right now. The air smelled like Absinthe.

Reaching out with his hand, Amadeus gently caressed Christopher's cheek, and then he held him close, cradling his head against his shoulder.

"Neither of us enter into this lightly," he said softly. "You must know that this is a bond that, once done, we can never break. Understand?"

"Yes," Christopher whispered, his heart pounding in his chest. Part of him wanted to run, wanted to say the hell with helping others—wanted just to live his own simple, peaceful life. He'd earned it, after all. After so many years of family abuse, after taking care of parishioners for many years . . . after waiting for love and never receiving it.

Amadeus whispered into his ear. "Do you, Christopher, give yourself willingly to me? Do you accept me as your Master, your Maker, your Life, and Your Death?"

Holy hell. Christopher's brain reeled at the words. They were powerful. His words sounded almost like wedding vows. But if so, they were one-way wedding vows. Unless . . . unless he made them conditional. Unless he took partial control and added something.

He thought about Judith and her girls. And of Job, Renny, and many others he cared for in the I.S. If he didn't do this, they could, probably all would die. Knowing that he had to ensure their safety.

"I do—," he said, and then quickly added with a rapid breath, "—if—" as he felt the man's cool lips on his neck, "—you, Amadeus, vow to help me save my friends, and the people of my town now and as long as you shall live. What say you?"

Amadeus paused, removing his lips only millimeters from Christopher's neck. Then he clutched Christopher's hair tightly, growled, and tilted his head better, exposing his jugular.

His bite and the words "I do," came at exactly the same time.

JUDITH

UNCOVERED

*M*arch 24, *Monday*

11:30 AM

Judith had just set her cup down, thinking she shouldn't have had that second cup of coffee when her phone chimed.

"Lu and Thomas will be late," Judith told Renny. "The Harvesters hit the Horseshoe. Twelve total. Lu found more of those medallions with the red sigil in their rooms. She said everything looked like it happened early that morning."

Her thoughts turned to the girls at the house. School had, indeed, been canceled today. More people were moving their personal belongings to higher ground and staying with family members or friends who lived outside of the flood zone.

Judith and Renny had decided the safest place for the girls was her house. It was just outside of town, up on a hill, with plenty to eat and games and movies to keep them occupied.

Talking helped Judith ease her mind. Not doing anything was driving her crazy. She'd taken some phone calls from Harvey, who decided to keep her updated on what was happening even though she'd called in sick. He advised her that the rivers and creeks were cresting higher, and so many places outside of town had flooding problems, too.

No one had the resources to help them. State police were handling other emergencies, and they were lucky to have at least one chopper fly over to the hospital and drop off some supplies. Otherwise, they were on their own.

When Harvey called again, it was about the Horseshoe deaths, and he sounded pretty shaken. She told him to have his partner take photos and if they found anything like a ceramic medallion in the rooms to NOT touch them. He could store them in a plastic Tupperware or something, but it was a matter of life and death not to touch the things.

Next, she told him to call the hospital morgue to have the bodies taken there and stored there for now. If they didn't have room in the drawers then at least it was cold down there. He could also call

Hatchers to see if they had any extra storage until official identification could be made and an autopsy completed. When he asked questions and filled her in with the final information on the Horseshoe, the tone in his voice was both confused and understanding.

He knows something is up, she thought. *He knows I can't be there for a reason and that it has something to do with these deaths.*

Renny's phone chimed. She looked up at Judith. "Job is running behind, too. He had to help someone at Bia's who was having chest pain. Larry Williams, I think. It was bad timing because of what happened at the Horseshoe, but the EMTs are there, and he'll be over soon as he can."

Why does everything seem to be falling apart? They were supposed to be coming together to fight this thing, but now, there were roadblocks that were keeping them apart. They didn't have much time!

Judith shared her thoughts with Renny while they waited for the others.

"I can't figure out exactly how it works, but I think that the women, when they touch the medallions with the red symbols, they become infected somehow, and they die. Something drains the blood from them—from inside their bodies, and somehow, it takes their heart. I think it happens before the crow enters her and places that thing, the seed for the Harvester or, however, they do it, inside the woman. The Harvester hatches, maybe it incubates in the uterus, gnaws at the tissue and then it gets strong enough to snip and burst its way out. Maybe they get big enough, fast enough to kill the male right afterward, but I don't think so. I think an adult Harvester comes for the male—like he must have to touch the medallion too—and it calls the creatures to their prey. Maybe the men die first, and then the women? Hell, I just don't know!" She stopped finally and took a breather, trying to gauge the look on Renny's face.

And God, how she hated this feeling. She should be out there helping calm the chaos and working the investigation with the team at the Horseshoe, yet she also knew that if they had any chance of stopping what was happening to their town, then she had to be here. She had to help stop whatever was going to happen tonight at the cave.

Renny spoke up, echoing a thought she was having while she poured over some of the texts they'd looked at the other day on Iron Shores history. They were sprawled across the kitchen table. Judith knew she hoped to find something that told her how to defeat this Raven Mocker, the Deathwing Queen.

"So, I keep wondering—where are these medallions coming from, Jude? It's not like Jagger Profitt is running around town handing them out. Maybe his kids?

"Okay," Judith said, "Hellen was the first, right? Jagger's own daughter. She was riding with her brothers, drinking, and partying. They said she ran off and they couldn't find her. Christopher found her on the ground, covered by crows, and called 911. She wasn't dead then. When she got to the hospital, she died not long after.

The hospital sent her to the Richmond morgue for autopsy, and Lu told me that she'd arrived without a hole in her lower belly, but when she was brought out for her postmortem, the hole was there. All of her organs were present except her heart. There was no medallion on the ground—not that Christopher mentioned.

And early the next morning, the guy from Passage, Viktor Odol, was brought in as an emergency. The ER doc, Thomas, said they did a digital X-ray and that the man had no heart. They sent him to Richmond's OCME, and Lu helped do his autopsy, too. She confirmed it. His heart was completely gone. That's part of why she came here in the first place."

Renny added, "And the guy, Viktor, he's supposed to be immortal." She used air quotes with her fingers when she said "immortal." "How did his heart get taken in the first place? I mean, you saw those guys—especially that one, Amadeus. He's strong and fast. What would be able to take over a creature like that?"

"That's a really good point, and we need to get back to that. Keep looking in your books, Renny. We killed a ton of those Harvesters last night, and Amadeus killed Savral, and he did it easily." Judith was thinking out loud, hoping Renny would add her own thoughts. "So, Harvester numbers are down, and now the urn of souls is empty along with the other vase that held Viktor's heart. Thomas was locked in the cave, and we don't know why. Hatton was supposedly watching her sister, Precious. Savral is dead . . ." She paused, looking at Renny. "We have Mason—maybe he planted more of those medallions? Who else? Can you think of any other family or close friends who might help him?"

Renny squeezed her top lip with her bottom teeth in thought. "Well, there *is* Hannah."

"Hannah?"

Renny nodded. "Hannah Profitt. Jagger's niece. Her parents are dead. No siblings. She lives in town and works at the hospital. Pathology assistant or something like that."

Pathology assistant? Judith thought back to when she was in the hospital morgue with Lu, and the call had come in about the deaths at the Red Tail Apartments. She'd seen a young blonde girl struggling to get a body back into its body bag.

"What's she look like?"

"Blonde. Maybe 22 or 23 years old. Why?"

Judith took out her phone and pressed the button to call Lu.

HATTON

BETRAYAL

*M*arch 24, Sunday

12:00 PM

Sweet Mother, I need to hurry.

Hatton had arranged for Thomas to meet Thomas at the family graveyard at noon. He said he'd get Tati to give him a ride. She knew her brothers and maybe even her pa would be back soon, and she needed to get this done before they came home.

And poor Precious. Everyone thought she was her sister. Thought her mother died after giving birth to her. That secret could never come out. Not if they wanted to save her life. She could be taken away or worse.

A deep, resonant voice, dark and mysterious, spoke in her head. *"You'll soon have all you need. Your family will have all they need to live a very long and healthy life."*

Another voice spoke to counter. It was light and airy like puffs of clouds. *"But maybe then she'd get the medical help she deserves. The right kind of help."*

"STOP!" She yelled out loud—beating her head with her palms. "STOP IT NOW!"

She remembered Thomas. He was with her now. She'd driven him to the cave. Walked him past the Harvesters. She'd seen his face as he shuddered—the utter revulsion as he stared in horror at them.

He'd stopped a few feet behind her now as they went deeper into the cave. She turned.

"Are you okay?" she asked. His brow was furrowed in genuine concern. She could see that.

No, he didn't think she was crazy. Not at all. The only thing she read there was care, love, and fear for her.

The deep voice again. *"You're fooling yourself. He's using you, Hatton, just like you are using him."*

The cloud voice answered back. *"He sees you're in pain. Let him help you. Tell him, Hatton, tell…"*

The voices did battle in her head, and she tried her best to ignore them. She knew what needed to be done. Her family had decided on it together. This was the best way. The only way. But another verbal outburst from her and Thomas was sure to label her a schizophrenic like they did her mama.

Poor, poor mama. Well. She fooled them all. Broke away. And now she serves Raum. She's a Queen!

The cloud voice broke in, *"She's a slave. A slave, a fuc . . . ."*

Hatton shook her head as she walked, so keenly aware of how Thomas was watching her. She thought about how much she needed some happiness in her life, and she could be everything he wanted in a woman. They could run away—(*That's never happening*)—and be together forever—(*In your dreams, drama Queen*).

"Here is where my pa and his people come to worship," she told Thomas. "It's mostly our family and other kin, but there's some in town who are protected and know what is about to happen tomorrow night, too."

She watched Thomas' face when she said this. He was a picture of calm. He projected acceptance, and despite how both of the voices in her head cried for her attention, she ignored them for now.

As they walked further into the cave, which smelled of earth, dark wet, and minerals, Hatton veered off, taking a tunnel to the left.

Her heart felt so heavy. How long since Precious had seen the doctor? Only a few months, but it seemed like yesterday. Her entire family knew that only the Deathwing Queen, the great Raum, would save her. She'd promised. And she'd held up her end of the bargain so far.

For every soul the Harvesters took, the rest of that person's life—the life they would have had if they hadn't been harvested—went to Precious for now. She'd grown strong—so much stronger the past couple of days. No more nose bleeds. She didn't cry from the pain in her lungs anymore. Despite the rain, she'd even wanted to go outside and play.

How many months since that had ever happened?

Hatton led Thomas to a little room carved into the side of the rock tunnel.

"Right over here," she said. "My pa keeps them here." She shone her light into the carved room. There was a wooden table with two small wicker baskets sitting on it. The baskets were filled with medallions.

Thomas rushed forward, his hands outstretched to grab some handfuls of medallions for his friends. But before he even touched them, he swung around, probably intending to ask her if she was sure these were the right ones. That was when she pushed the bar gate closed. There was a loud—CLANK!

Thomas stopped and stared. Disbelief washed over his face as Hatton stood there on the other side of a set of bars. Bars that were meant to keep things, or people, in. It was a makeshift prison cell of sorts.

"HATTON!" Thomas yelled. He grasped the bars, shaking them, and his eyes widened into large saucers of shock. His face contorted into a mask of pain as he realized what had happened. As he realized his friends would be defenseless.

As if on autopilot, Hatton's feet carried her back to the mouth of the cave. And Thomas' wailing voice was still yelling, screaming for her to come back—echoing down the tunnel as she exited.

For a second, she paused, and she almost—but then she was out in the rain as the storm clouds thundered and the lightning streaked across the sky.

She passed the tall, feathered figures which stood motionless as she ran by. One of them croaked, and she stopped, looked into its hard crystalline eyes, and caressed the beak.

"Not him," she emphasized. "Please, not him. He's *mine.*"

Thomas may never speak to me again after this, but he's mine. And maybe, in time, he'll forgive me.

The creature croaked, and then they were all croaking and cawing. Hatton climbed up the hill and jumped into her Beetle, knowing Thomas was safe for now and that Precious was growing healthy and strong.

THOMAS

VOICE

*M*arch 24 ,Sunday

7:00 PM

There has got to be a way out of here, there has to be!

When he'd pulled out his phone to see if he had any kind of service, his phone had no bars. He couldn't call anyone. He couldn't do anything except to keep trying to find a way out of this cell. At least he had the flashlight feature for a little while.

Thomas could not believe that Hatton had locked him in here and just left him. Why would she do that? Did her father have such a hold on her that she'd do anything for him? Do anything for her brothers? He'd been so certain that she was on his side. That she loved him.

She does, whispered a voice.

That voice had to be his imagination because he was sure no one else was here, and it hadn't come from inside his head.

He looked closely at the walls around him. They were solid rock, damp and cold. He examined around the baskets of medallions, careful not to touch any of them. Even if he got out, how could he be sure these were protective?

They are, a voice whispered again.

It took him a moment to realize that the sound was not his imagination. Something in this cave was speaking to him. And it was reading his mind because he hadn't spoken any of his words out loud.

Given the strange things he'd seen and experienced over the past two weeks, he couldn't rule out that something or someone was trying to communicate with him. Maybe even trying to help him.

"Hello?" he called out, "if you can help me at all, please help me get out of here."

Patience, the voice said. *In time* . . . and the voice trailed away. No matter how hard Thomas yelled and asked for help, the voice did not come back.

JUDITH

ROAD TRIP

*M*arch 24, *Sunday*

11:00 PM

Judith's phone buzzed. Renny. She thumbed the Accept button.

"Ren."

"Jude! You at home?"

Judith had put the girls down for bed at 10:00 PM, although she knew they often read, watched a show on their phone, or played on their Nintendo Switch for a while before drifting to sleep.

"Yes. Of course. What . . . "

A knock at her door startled her, and she nearly dropped her phone.

"It's just me," Renny said on the other line. "We need a rescue party."

Judith opened the door to find Renny standing there with Melody next to her. They were holding hands.

It's past 11:00 at night. Why is Melody . . . ?

"I'll explain in a second. Okay, if we come in?" Renny pushed past her with Melody in tow.

Judith followed her into her living room. Renny and Melody were already sitting on the couch.

"Renny, what is this all—"

Renny blurted out, "They captured Thomas!" Her eyes were filled with abject terror. "I've seen it all. Hatton locked Thomas in the cave, so there's no way for him to reach us. We have to go get him."

"Hatton locked him in the cave?" Judith echoed. She was used to Renny's uncanny abilities, but this—then she realized she needed just to stop and listen to her friend.

Of course, Renny knows what happened.

"I searched for you at the Rage and ran into Lu there," Renny said. "We discussed what we needed to do. Then, Tati came in and told us she was worried about Thomas. She was supposed to meet

424

him at the bottom of the hill below the cave, but he never showed. She's in the car too."

So, Renny, Lu, Tati and me. Against whatever was up there—near or in—that cave.

Like it or not, she knew she had to help, though she didn't relish the idea of leaving the girls alone late at night. She'd let Rachel know she was leaving, at least, and ask her to keep the phone nearby.

"Is it okay if I leave Melody here with your girls?" Renny asked.

"Mom," the corners of Melody's lips turned down. "I want to help."

"Not this time, baby. And you will actually be of some help to the girls here in case anything tries to get inside the house, okay? Use your medallion to help cast a protection net around them like I told you."

Clearly still not happy, Melody nodded.

Judith took her up to Rachel's room and touched her daughter on the shoulder. Rachel was instantly awake. The full moon affected them that way. They slept very lightly when the moon was near and at its peak.

"Melody's going to stay here with you, honey," Judith said, noting the confusion in her eyes. "I have to go out with her mom and some others to help someone, okay? Please don't leave the house and stay close to Melody."

Rachel, still groggy, nodded. "She can share. I'll scoot over."

Melody looked back at Judith, a little dubious about sharing a bed with someone she didn't know well.

"It will be okay," Judith assured her. "And they need you nearby just in case. Is that alright?"

425

Melody nodded, crawled into the bed, and curled around one of Rachel's pillows.

"Thank you, Melody." Judith left and kept the door cracked so the girls might hear Lilith if she stirred. Truth be told, she'd rather Lilith be here as well, but she didn't want to wake the poor girl after such a wild day experiencing her ability to change.

Lola would patrol and give them a heads-up if anything sounded, smelled, or even felt funny. A scent immediately confused Judith when it snaked its way up from the ground floor as she started down the stairs. She smelled Christopher. And Job. Grinch. And then— this scent—it was unfamiliar, and the back of her neck prickled with an unsettling chill.

When she got to the bottom floor, she understood why. The tall, pale man standing with her friends was a creature she'd only heard about and had never encountered before. He smoothly turned to gaze at her with his startling golden eyes, and they roved over her body as if assessing every minute detail of her form inside and out. Then, he gave her a dazzling smile and stepped forward as she neared, his hand outstretched.

Lola growled furiously, barked, and snarled. She bared her teeth, and the instant he stepped forward toward Judith, she lunged, darting behind him and sank her teeth into his Achilles tendon.

Backing away, Lola's hair stood up all along her neck and shoulders. Judith had never seen the dog so worked up. The dog growled again as if daring the man to move once more.

The man didn't cry out or wince in pain. He just stood very still, which Judith found quite unusual. Her friends were quiet as well, all observing the altercation. And she observed that Grinch seemed to

426

be okay with the new guy, although he wasn't his normal goofy self. While Judith was not sure about this strange visitor, she decided Lola had done her job well enough.

"Lola, leave it!" she commanded. With a low growl still in her throat, Lola turned and sat on the far side of the room, keeping a careful watch on the strange man and Judith.

"Thank you," the man said. Again, he stretched his hand to hers. She accepted it, noting how white and perfect his skin was.

"I am Amadeus," he said.

"Judith," she responded, taking note of the odd tickle that ran along the length of her body when they touched.

Christopher spoke up. "He's not from around here. He's Viktor Odul's brother, the man—"

"—who was taken from the hospital morgue," she interrupted. "Right. And he's here because?"

Amadeus spoke for himself. "I need to retrieve my brother's body—ALL of his body. And I have special skills that may help you tonight," he angled his head, and a slight smile twitched at the corner of his mouth. "Much like you, there is more to me than meets the eye."

How would he know? Did Christopher tell him?

She looked over at her long-time friend—friend in a way that professionals could be, of course—and raised an eyebrow.

Christopher shook his head and then chin-jutted toward the man as if reading her mind. So, Amadeus *was* special. He could help them. She'd have to know exactly how before they got to the cave. She didn't get naked for just anybody.

11:30 PM

It was a tight squeeze, but they all piled into Tati's VW van and headed toward the cave near the Profitt house. Grinch sat in the seat next to Job, panting and grinning.

"I can't make it up those mud roads now," Tati advised them. "All that wet clay, I'd just spin in one place as soon as I started. Thomas wanted me to meet him where the road crosses the path going up under the power lines. I guess the cave is near there. I've got no idea who might be in there or what. And much as I would like to be some sort of hero and go with you guys, I'm gonna just park on the side of the road and wait for ya'll."

That sounded fine to Judith. That way, there'd be someone to wait for them and someone to call for help if they needed it. Before they'd left, Judith had pulled out her own pair of 9mm Barettas and made sure the magazine clips were full, and she'd packed two more clips just in case. It would be bad form to use police-issued firearms, and she always kept her own guns ready, cleaned, and oiled just in case she needed them. She also brought along her Motorola. She hated bringing a work item with them, but the Motorola might just save their lives if they got into trouble. Now, she had to figure out who to give them to since she couldn't carry a thing in wolf form.

As they bumped along the road, Judith broke the silence. "Okay, I've got two 9mm Barettas fully loaded and a Motorola radio. You all know I won't be able to carry them, so who feels comfortable with what? Who here knows pistols?"

Everyone looked at each other for a moment, and it seemed that no one was going to step up.

"I have some experience," Job voiced. "I can carry one if someone else wants the other."

Judith handed him a pistol and an extra magazine.

"It's already loaded," she said. "Just locate and be careful of when the safety is on or off."

Job nodded.

She looked at Renny. The woman was tight-lipped, but Judith knew that Renny knew how to handle a firearm. Judith had worked with her a couple of years back just in case she needed to know how to fire one. Renny had purchased a gun not long after. A .38 pistol.

And she knew Renny went to the firing range from time to time to practice.

"Ren?"

Renny sighed. "What about Christopher? He's a man, right? Bet he can do it."

Christopher smiled a little, but the smile was a sad one. "I never learned. Never needed to and really never wanted to." He glanced over at Judith. "I do, however, know how to use the radio. I'll take the Motorola if that's okay, Jude."

She handed it to him, hating how she loved his kind and gentle demeanor. And yet, there was something about him that warned her off from getting too close to him. She'd thought about it, of course, getting closer to him, but every thought seemed like a betrayal to her dead husband.

Another thought broke in with a strong voice.

The operative word there, Jude, is 'dead.'

She chose not to argue with that voice right now and handed Christopher the Motorola.

"The channel is set. Don't move it," she said.

"Got it," Christopher replied.

Renny looked over to Amadeus next. "You?" she questioned.

He shook his head. "I don't need a gun, Renny."

Lu was next on her list, but Lu was shaking her head before she could even ask. "Not gonna do it," she said. "And you guys need me to look for the souls that we can free. I can't be bothered with the piece."

"Job," pleaded Renny, "You can have two and carry them Tomb Raider style."

Job shook his head. "I'll be good with just one. I wouldn't know what to do with two of them."

"Oh, *okay*," Renny said, giving in with a growl. "Damn. Everyone take note that I tried, several times—" she looked at Judith when she said this, "to give the responsibility away to someone else. Don't sue me if I accidentally shoot you in the dark."

Judith placed the firearm in Renny's hands along with the extra magazine clip.

"When we stop, I'll go over it with you one more time before I change, okay?"

Renny nodded, and Judith thought she saw tears brimming in her friend's eyes.

Tati pulled the van over on the shoulder and stopped where the path went upward under the power lines. The rain continued to fall, but they all had decent hiking boots—all except for Judith, Amadeus, and Tati, of course.

Judith took Renny aside and reviewed the Baretta with her—safety on and off, aiming at a target with safety on, how to remove an empty magazine, and how to put a new clip in.

"Are you okay?" she asked. "You were upset earlier. I didn't mean to make you uncomfortable."

Renny blew out a big breath, and her gaze went up the hill as far as she could see in the dark. "I don't even know if I can make it up there, Jude. I mean, I walk a lot, but not uphill like that."

"Do what you can, Ren," Judith said noticing that Renny hadn't answered her question, and then she handed Renny something else. It was small, long, and silver, and it was attached to a chain silver chain.

Renny held it up and looked at it curiously.

"Dog whistle," Judith chuckled. "You need me, just blow, okay? I will hear it for miles. I promise you that." She took the whistle back from her friend's hand and then slipped the chain over Renny's head. The woman seemed a lot more at ease now.

When the team started up the hill, Judith shed her clothes, leaving them with Tati in the passenger seat.

Tati, always brazen as hell, looked at her as she stood there shivering for a second. "Chief, you're a rock, girlfriend! Who knew what shredded meat that uniform covers up?"

Jude couldn't help it. Naked in front of God and Tati, she managed to grin. It was kind of nice knowing someone could see the work she put into her body. No one else knew except her daughters, who probably assumed that she naturally looked that way.

In an instant, she switched from human to wolf, shook her body, luxuriating in the power and freedom she felt now, and then followed the others up.

CHRISTOPHER

CLIMB

*M*arch 24, *Sunday*

11:40 PM

The climb to the cave was not too difficult. Harder with the wet ground and cloudy skies.

Renny spoke to all of them. "When we get close, hopefully, there'll be some kind of light or something to show us where we're going. It will be on the right side of the power lines."

Lu walked next to her friend, determined to stay with her, particularly if she dropped behind.

Christopher glanced over at Amadeus, noticing he seemed to float over the ground. He made no noise, didn't stumble, and didn't need a phone flashlight or any other lighting. He thought about how quickly Amadeus had moved in his house. They could use that speed tonight. Before he spoke to the man, he tugged Renny's sleeve so she'd pay attention.

"Amadeus, we definitely need you to protect us while we climb, but when we get near the cave, can you move like you did in your house? Really fast? Can you scout ahead and see if we've got any of those Harvesters in the way?"

"Yes," he replied. "I'll let you know before I go, but when I do, then you'll be on your own until I return. Be on guard. It is dark, and the Deathwings are hard for human eyes to see."

Judith pushed past them, her body rubbing between Amadeus and Christopher's thighs.

Christopher had never seen Judith in "ware" form, and he was taken aback by her enormous size.

Amadeus took little notice but threw his voice forward—perhaps so Judith could hear. "Remember that the Harvesters are fast and deadly. Their beaks are razor-sharp and powerful. If they manage to grip any part of you, they will slice you open with the precision of a surgeon. They can amputate your limbs, and they can crush your bones with their feet."

Judith kept padding forward as if she hadn't heard them, but Christopher hoped she had heard the man and paid attention. They

434

had to succeed tonight so they could come back tomorrow and take this Deathwing Queen down once and for all.

A rock tumbled down the hill on their right, and Judith growled. She crouched and moved toward the sound. Christopher was about to call her back when something attacked her from above. It landed on her back, and she yelped. Then, there was a sudden rending and tearing sound and a sick, wet splash. A screech hit the air, and feathers and flesh plopped around Judith's wolf form as Christopher found her with his light.

Christopher noted that Job had his gun raised, as did Renny when he looked around. But Amadeus stood there in the light, right in front of Judith, the blood and feathers of the Harvester clinging to his shirt. He stretched his hand out and petted Judith's head. She must have been in momentary shock because she didn't do anything but stand there dumbfounded.

"Be on guard better, Jude," Amadeus cautioned like he was a long-time mentor on a trip with his trainee. "One down, and many to go."

At that moment, Christopher knew that his bond with this vampire was worth its weight in gold. Yes, he would have to pay this man a lifetime with the bond he made, but Amadeus had just saved the life of the woman that he, Christopher, loved. And the overwhelming gratitude he felt right now far outweighed the twinge of jealousy that rose up in his heart when he saw Amadeus pet Judith's head.

"Many to go," echoed Christopher. Those words filled him with dread.

It took close to fifteen minutes of climbing up the hill before Amadeus said, "The cave is just up there, maybe ten minutes more at your pace. I'll go now and check the area and make sure it's clear."

Christopher was ready to give his okay when Amadeus left in a flash, and then he suddenly thought two things. One—He wondered who was really in charge here now. And two—Would any of them be able to fight off a Harvester without Amadeus?

Another screech came, but this one was up the hill near where Amadeus said the cave was. Then, there was a flap of wings, and Christopher watched Job topple. The Grinch barked and lunged at the thing and then winced when it brought its beak around, barely grazing him but still slicing his leg with an edge.

Judith snarled and leaped on the Harvester's shoulders. She closed her massive jaws around the back of its neck. The beast reeled, and then a shot rang out. Renny stepped up and put another shot dead center in the creature, sending it squawking and gurgling to the ground. They all waited a few moments to be sure it was dead. Job bound Grinch's leg with some medical wrap.

Judith pranced over to Renny and rubbed up against her as if to say, "Good job!"

When Amadeus returned in a couple of minutes, they'd dispatched three more. He didn't seem impressed but looked at them all as if he was glad they'd survived. If anything, he seemed satisfied that they weren't as helpless as he thought they were.

"The outside of the cave is clear for now. I took down six up there. I think these Harvesters are simply sentries. The others may be out feeding."

"Did you check inside yet?" said Christopher.

"No. The Deathwing Queen is sure to sense me as soon as I enter her sphere of perception."

They trudged a few more steps up the hill until Amadeus steered them to the left, where they crossed over a rocky stream. Right in front of them was the entrance to the cave. On either side were some large movable bushes that Jagger usually used to cover the area and keep it hidden. There were no such attempts now.

The large space was softly lit with a glowing light fixed to the inside of the cave wall. Christopher thought they were probably solar lights, charged from panels somewhere outside.

"Amadeus," Christopher said, "if Thomas is locked behind iron bars, we'll need your strength to break him out. Who do you want to go with you?"

Amadeus didn't hesitate. "Job and his dog—Grinch."

This surprised all of them, but no one asked why. The three of them wasted no time and veered off to the left of the cavern.

Christopher turned to Lu, but she was already walking toward a white marble shelf. A bird-like figure was perched on it, and two large crystal urns rested on the floor beneath it. As he got closer, he noticed the bird figure's eyes shimmered with an icy cold light. She stretched out her hand to touch it.

"No!" Christopher cried out, and then Renny was at Lu's side, pulling her hand down. Lu blinked her eyes rapidly.

"It was calling to me, and I had to—have to—" she turned toward it again.

Renny got in her face. "Lu! Snap out of it! Souls, remember? We are here to find where the souls are trapped and release them!"

A chuckle suddenly filled the air and bounced around the walls. "Well, that's not gonna work out well for everyone, now, is it?"

Christopher turned toward the voice and saw Savral. He was standing at the entrance, a wicked grin smeared across his face, blocking the path for any escape. And he was alone.

Or better to say, there was no other *human* with him. Harvesters, many Harvesters, crowded around him, blocking the way out.

Savral wore a medallion much like many of the others Christopher had seen—the protective ones like Thomas and Melody's. Like the one he'd given Sammi.

Savral had a gun tucked into his waistband, and he carried an aluminum baseball bat, which he swung in a circle like a propeller.

"I do appreciate you bringing my compadres a little midnight snack," he gestured to the Harvesters.

Christopher turned toward Renny and saw she'd already raised the Baretta.

"Aww," said Savral. "Ain't that cute?" He pulled out his own firearm and aimed it at Renny. It looked like a .357, though Christopher couldn't be sure. It would do some major damage if he hit anyone with it. But Savral didn't shoot. Instead, he clicked his tongue three times.

A Harvester lunged at Renny, and then the rest of the creatures followed suit, pushing past Savral to get to them. In his entire life, even during the harsh abuses of his childhood, while learning to drive, when scaling tall cliff faces and nearly falling—Christopher never once thought he'd die.

This time was definitely different.

JOB

FAST

*M*arch 24, Sunday

11:58 PM

What Job appreciated about this guy, Amadeus, was that he didn't waste no time.

The man might be a bloodsucker, and he had just made his best friend enter into a contract that he'd never be able to get out of, but the man was tenacious. He was also faster than a sinner runnin' from the threat of hell—whatever that hell may be.

In an inhale of air, Job knew Amadeus had already gone down the wide corridor and come back as quick.

Job said nothing—but one look, and Job could tell that Amadeus knew what he'd done. Felt it. And Grinch wagged his tail.

"He's just down here," Amadeus flicked his hand. "Not far at all. Keep walking and still be careful. There could be things I don't sense. Maybe I'll have him out by the time you get there. If you find a medallion, put it on."

Job picked up his pace, a sense of urgency—like something was going wrong already—driving him to hurry. Nothing happened, although Job swore he had heard whispers in the air. When he arrived at Thomas's cell, Amadeus was bending the bars back.

"The steel is very strong," Amadeus grunted. He sounded surprised that he had to put so much effort into it.

Job looked in at Thomas. He was sitting on the floor holding a pile of protective medallions.

"You okay, Doc?" Job couldn't think of what else to ask. Grinch pressed his face between the bars Amadeus wasn't trying to bend.

"Best as I can be," Thomas answered, meeting Job's gaze. "I sure am glad to see you guys. I, um—this guy, Amadeus, introduced himself to me. He's Viktor's brother. I—saw his brother like two weeks ago. In the ER."

Thomas's eyes widened when he glanced at Amadeus, and Job reckoned his did, too, because when he turned to look, he saw the vampire had finally bent the bars far enough that Thomas could squeeze through—and then some.

Thomas handed a bunch of medallions to Job and Amadeus, and then tied one around Grinch's neck as well.

"I just hope these are what I think they are," he said. "I got bored, said what the hell, and took mine off—put another one on, and so on. I cycled through a few of them. A Harvester didn't come to eat me. I didn't die. This one worked just as well as my other one."

That was good enough for Job. He slipped one around his neck, and so did Amadeus.

All three of them started jogging back to the main cavern. On their way, they caught the shrill sounds of squawks and screeches in the air. Amadeus plucked the medallions from Thomas's hands and disappeared.

Thomas looked at Job in surprise.

"Yeah," Job said. "He's pretty fast."

LU

REVIVAL

*M*arch 24, Sunday

11:59 PM

Despite the chaos breaking out around her, with Renny firing her pistol at those creatures and Judith leaping on their backs to snap their necks, Lu couldn't resist turning back toward the figure. Where she was mesmerized before, now she fixed her gaze on it and then down to the urns beneath it.

She looked around the room and noted that there were still no phantoms, no unrestful ghosts in the cavern anywhere. And the urns below looked to be some form of crystal stone. Quartz maybe?

Could these urns hold the souls collected for the Deathwing Queen? She bent down to grasp one of the urns and tried to pull the top off, but it wouldn't budge. Just then, Renny backed into her, still firing her pistol, and that sent Lu sprawling forward.

Lu tried to catch her balance but tripped and fell. The urn flew from her hands and hit the floor hard, knocking the top of it loose. Lu raced to it, noting the lid looked loosened. As soon as she picked up the urn and started to twist, the lid popped off. A sudden blast of wind around her then swept through the cavern, and the Harvesters screeched in high-pitched and terrible voices.

Something whisked past her, and then a medallion was swinging from her neck. She looked around and saw Renny and Christopher now wore them as well. Then Savral was screaming, firing his .357 at anything. Everything. Lu dropped, hitting the floor of the cave.

In a flash, Amadeus was behind him. His eyes went to Lu and then she saw him flick his gaze at Christopher and finally on Judith's wolf form. He reached out and grabbed Savral's head and twisted it so hard Lu thought he'd pull the man's head right off. Amadeus tossed Savral's body to the side, and then he dispatched as many harvesters as he could. Judith joined him. Renny and Job emptied both of their first clips and then their second. When they were finished, and all of the Harvesters were dead, they surveyed the aftermath.

Amadeus's face was still stone, unsatisfied.

Lu motioned him toward the other urn. "I think your brother's heart, or his soul, or both are in there."

The cave shook violently. Amadeus picked up the second urn and opened it without trouble. There was no whooshing of wind. Instead, Amadeus's hair fluttered, and he turned the urn upside down. A large, shriveled lump of flesh fell into his palm. It most certainly was his brother's heart.

Amadeus's eyes glistened, and Lu found that fascinating. All of the myths, the rumors, the Hollywood films, and books about vampires were all wrong. While she wasn't sure she trusted this man, he definitely had feelings, and he appeared very human. Minus the really white skin and invisible blood vessels.

Amadeus whispered to the heart and then held it close to him as if listening. He closed his eyes and swayed with the organ held against his chest, and then his eyes flew open, and Lu saw his rage.

"She has his body," he growled. "Somewhere in this underground network, she has him stored away. He doesn't know where." He clenched his jaw. "I could search the vast network of twists and turns in these underground caverns and never find him."

But then Lu noticed that the souls she'd released had not left. They were sprinkled in different places around the cavern. She breathed in deep, and then stepped over to a spot that was away from the others.

"If you can help us find this man's brother—his body has been taken by the one who wronged you. Help us find his brother's body, and you can be at peace. You will have had vengeance on this demon who has tortured you so."

A group of spirits coalesced into shimmering semblances of hands that drifted like fog and pointed into the dark.

"Yes, please show me," Lu asked as she moved forward and turned on her phone flashlight. She motioned for Amadeus to follow and when Amadeus moved, Judith padded alongside him.

Christopher looked over to Job, Grinch, and Renny. He said, "Go back to the van and get Thomas to safety. You aren't needed for this, okay? It's better you go back now, just in case—" He didn't want to add, "in case Jagger comes," because they might not go.

And if Jagger did come when he saw the broken body of his boy, the empty urns, and the dead Harvesters everywhere, there wouldn't be hell to pay. Oh no. He'd bring hell to them all and unleash it with all of the force of an erupting volcano.

Renny hesitated but then nodded, and Christopher waited until he knew that Job and Renny had Thomas in tow and that they were all making their way back to Tati. Then he turned toward the corridor they'd stepped into, hoping there'd still be some light for him to follow. It was distant, but he could only just make it out. He hoped they wouldn't turn—that the light wouldn't disappear—and he trotted quickly toward it.

The light did disappear, but as he turned on his phone flashlight to see where he was going, he passed another tunnel and saw light in that direction. He changed his heading and followed it. A brush of feathers—and something flew past him but didn't harm him. By the noxious odor in the air now, it had to be a Harvester, and he thanked the powers that be, whoever they were, for Thomas had found them all the medallions they needed.

445

The light was nearly gone again—it was so faint, but he trotted as fast as he dared to reach Amadeus. He was drawn to the man, perhaps by the nature of their bond, and found he didn't want to be separated from him. The light was brighter now, and he emerged from the tunnel into a small chamber.

There, on the floor, was Amadeus's brother. His body was in the center of a very large circle drawn on the floor with something like chalk and there were other symbols drawn around him that Christopher didn't recognize. Apparently, Amadeus knew them though. He bellowed in anger and Christopher didn't understand why he was angry. His brother was right there.

Amadeus swiveled his gaze over to Christopher almost as if he could hear his thoughts. "Go ahead," Amadeus said. "Remove him from the circle."

Christopher started forward.

"No!" Lu shouted. "You can't let him do that! You know what could happen!"

Amadeus gave her a baleful look and then told Christopher again, "Remove him from the circle."

Christopher put his toe over the line of the outer circle, and nothing happened.

"Don't do it, Christopher!" Lu called out. "You might not be able . . ." but now Amadeus had reached out and covered her mouth, silencing her. Judith whined a little and gazed up at the vampire.

"That will be enough, now," he ordered, his lips pressed firmly. Lu detected a note of something she couldn't understand—almost regret—but sadder and more respectful. Still, he remained firm. And she understood. This was his brother. She only ever had one person

446

like that in her life. She touched her necklace—the silver 'Broken' wing.

Christopher was aware of all that was going on around him, but he could not stop himself. Both of his feet fully entered the circle, and suddenly, he felt invisible things tearing at his clothing, pulling his hair, and biting and ripping his skin.

Still, he moved forward until he could kneel down and pick up the man on the floor. The body was limp and very heavy, but Christopher managed despite his now bleeding arms, neck, and face. When he reached the border of the outer circle, he found he could not exit it, and those invisible things attacked him even harder. He groaned but struggled against the circle's bounds.

"Hand him to me," Amadeus commanded, and Christopher did as he was told. He stretched his arms across the circle border and transferred Viktor to his brother. The moment he handed Viktor's body to Amadeus, the painful bites, scratches and other attacks stopped. It was clear to him now. Until this circle was somehow properly broken, there had to be one body within it at all times but no more.

Christopher stared at Amadeus, and then he had an idea. Could it be anybody? A dead one even? Technically, Viktor wasn't completely dead, but his body had been inert as long as his heart, and therefore, his soul was separated from it.

"Savral," Christopher whispered, and the vampire understood. First, he lay his brother's body on the floor and then pulled his brother's heart from inside his shirt where he'd stored it. He opened the chest cavity and placed the dry, shriveled organ inside. Then, with his fingernail, he opened up one of his veins and let his blood flow over his brother's heart and into the chest cavity.

They all watched as the body twitched a little at first, and then there were larger, seizure-like motions. The chest cavity closed, and all of the cuts made to the man's body disappeared. Amadeus knelt over him, bringing his face close to his brother's. In moments, Viktor opened his eyes.

"Brother." Viktor's voice was gravelly, as if he were suffering from a cold or a very dry throat. "You came."

"Of course, "Amadeus gave his brother a grin and reached down to hold his brother's head tenderly.

Christopher noticed there was no talk of love or loyalty, yet he saw it in the way the brothers looked at each other, in the way their bodies resonated together.

Lu cleared her throat. "I do understand," she started, but Amadeus was on his feet before she could finish.

"Just one moment."

In a flash, he was standing outside the circle with Savral's body. Christopher reached for him and took him in his arms, nearly crumpling under the weight, and then the invisible things were attacking him once more, biting his neck, his back, his legs.

They stripped some of his clothing to pieces, but once he laid Savral down, he found he could exit the circle. He gratefully stepped to the outside, and Lu ran toward him to help staunch the places where he was bleeding.

"Even though he's not alive," Amadeus said, "his soul is still attached to his body. Most souls remain for a few days, not realizing that their body is dead. That is why Savral's body worked."

Lu looked at Christopher. "If we have any chance of stopping Jagger Profitt, I suggest we get back to the main cavern as quickly as possible and clean up the best we can."

Christopher nodded and followed down the corridor. Judith hung back, apparently still not wanting to leave Amadeus. He smiled sadly at her, his expression including a strange look of affection.

"Go," he said. "Help them. I'll be there with my brother in just a few minutes."

By the time they'd found their way back to the main cavern, all thanks to Judith's wonderful sense of smell, Amadeus and Viktor were already there waiting. Amadeus had already cleared the Harvesters away.

There had to have been at least forty of them. Where the vampire had stashed them, Christopher had no clue, but the urns were back in place under the crow figure on the marble shelf and everything seemed as it was before.

They all left to climb down the hill, and Lu heard more flapping of wings as they descended but nothing attacked them. Tati waited outside her VW bus, looking surprised to see one extra passenger, but while Judith changed back to human form and put her clothes back on, Tati called Thomas up to sit next to her on the passenger side.

Tati stopped first at the Horseshoe Inn for Thomas, Lu, Amadeus and Viktor—the two brothers deciding on a room there for the next two nights—and then prepared to take Christopher home. Lu was sure he'd stumble into bed, dirty clothes and all, and sleep better than the dead.

Tati said, "I'll stop at Job's place and then drop off Judith and Renny at Judith's house."

Lu smiled at how Judith and Renny were sacked out, leaning against each other. Everyone was so tired, and tomorrow was going to be a crazy day.

Lu fished for her wallet and pulled out the cash she'd set aside for this, but Tati wouldn't take it.

"Consider it my part in saving the world," she gave a tilt of the head. "See you tomorrow night!"

The clouds parted a little, and looking across the Horseshoe Inn lawn, Lu noticed how bright the moon was in the sky. It was after midnight, and the Crow Moon would be at its peak the next day. She tried not to think of everything that had happened over the past few hours and what they would all face tomorrow.

When Jagger realized his oldest son was dead and his plans were ruined, what would he do?

She, Judith and Renny—hell, the whole team—would have to make sure they were protected. They'd have to make sure the young girls were triple protected because she was quite sure that Jagger would try to murder them all.

450

JAGGER

RETRIBUTION

*M*arch 25, Monday

7:15 AM

Jagger sat at his dining room table sucking down the cup of coffee Hatton had fixed him moments before and he stared at his arms. The wrinkled skin and age spots seemed to have appeared overnight. Something was wrong. His body hurt too, and Precious was still in bed barely able to move this morning.

Savral was on watch at the cave last night, but the boy hadn't come yet. His room was empty when Jagger stuck his head in to see if he was there. The boy should have been back almost an hour ago.

Hatton placed a plate of bacon and scrambled eggs in front of him along with two slices of toast and a jar of strawberry jam. He eyed the food with some dissatisfaction before launching into it anyway. He picked up his toast and something was missing.

Fucking whore of her mother can't do anything right.

"Where's the damn butter, Hatton?" he yelled and slapped the table.

It pleased him to see she was appropriately startled, and he liked how she rushed furiously to get the soft stick over to him so he could slather it on his toast. He shoveled a large heap of eggs into his mouth and washed them down with some water.

He glanced over at the empty chair beside him. Savral never missed a meal.

Mason, on the other hand, was late and Jagger half considered eating his son's food too just to show him that it was important to show up and fight for what he wanted, but his stomach was full by the time the boy opened his bedroom door and shuffled into the kitchen. Mason pulled out a chair and looked at the empty seat.

"Where's Savral?" he asked, one of his eyebrows hitching up under his brown mop of hair.

"Just what I want to know too," Jagger grumbled. "That boy better be in serious trouble or dead if I have to go find him."

He took note that Mason wasn't worried. The boy almost looked pleased that his brother was gone. This irked Jagger to no end and

452

so when Hatton set Mason's breakfast in front of him and the boy picked up his fork, Jagger swept the plate off the table.

Mason stared at him. The boy was smart alright. He knew not to say a word. But sweet Jesus in hellfire, he wanted to beat on someone right now. He pushed his chair back and stood, raising up his fist, but . . .

Damn, I'm so god-damned tired. Something is wrong. Really wrong.

Instead of planting his fist into Mason's face like he wish the boy deserved, they'd go to the cave. Tonight was the ceremony when the Deathwing Queen ascended, and in her power she would grant them all long and healthy lives. He had to make sure nothing fucked that up.

"You ain't got time for breakfast now," he barked at Mason. "Get your shoes on. We gotta find your brother."

He turned to Hatton and saw her picking some eggs out of the pan and putting them on a small plate. Hatton eyed him and before he could yell at her for stuffing her mouth— fat cow that she was— she said, "This is for Precious. She's feeling real poorly this morning, Pa. I think her sickness is back."

Now, *that* worried him. The Deathwing Queen had promised she'd take care of Precious. Heal her and give her a very long life. And now she was ill again.

Still, Jagger couldn't show his concern to Hatton. He couldn't let his kids see any weakness in him or they'd rebel and fight him for his spot as the family leader.

Jagger grunted and went to his room to get his shoes. He sat down on the bed, feeling pain travel up his spine. It took longer for him to get his boots on than usual. Bending over hurt just as much as sitting down did. On top of his dresser, a piece of old wooden furniture with the veneer pulled away in places, sat a photo of his wife, Herra. He found he couldn't remember the last time he saw her in person, in the flesh.

If only he hadn't had to sacrifice Hellen. Then Precious would have her mother at her side and the girl could see to his child better than Hatton. Oh yes, he knew it bothered Hatton—having to tell everyone that Precious was her sister—but it would be much worse if they found out the child was her niece instead.

Well, it wasn't like his wife minded. She belonged to the Deathwing Queen now and he'd needed someone to warm his bed. He wasn't about to go without his needs.

Now with Hellen gone, he'd thought about having Hatton at night but something in him knew that if he did, his boys would never forgive him. As a fact, they didn't know who Precious's father really was. They thought she'd been knocked up but some local guy. Hatton was the only one who knew he was Precious's father and he made sure the cunt kept her lips shut about that.

Mason was waiting by the door. Jagger pushed past the boy and walked out of the house. The entire hike to the cave, Mason never so much as made a sound and Jagger forced himself not to look at him. The boy had a power that let him win people's hearts and Jagger wasn't about to let that happen this morning.

As they neared the entrance of the cave, Jagger looked around. The ground cover was slightly disturbed. Not so much as a stranger to the area might notice, but Jagger could see where the leaves were upturned in areas where they shouldn't be, and in some places the ground was slightly uneven as if the rain had wiped away most of a footprint. He pulled back the brush to enter the cave and saw it was empty.

"Savral!" he called out. There was no answer.

"You go check on our prisoner," Jagger ordered. Still without a word, Mason headed down the left passageway.

Jagger approached the figure on the marble shelf, taking note that the urns below. They didn't look quite right. They were not in the exact spots as before. A feeling of dread started in his stomach and worked its way to his chest.

"Savral!" he yelled again, but once more there was no answer. There were no Harvester's guarding the cave outside or in, but there were supposed to be over fifty of them now.

I HAD over fifty, said a voice in his head. And then he felt a thunderous pressure in his brain and a crushing pain in his chest. He dropped to the floor in front of the figure, gasping.

*YOU did not protect me, t*he voice accused, *and now your family will die unless you make everything right before tonight.*

Sharp daggers of fire pierced through his arms and legs, and as much as he tried not to, he cried out, "No, no, stop!"

The pain abated.

Jagger looked around the room, hoping that Mason wasn't here to witness this.

Come, the voice said, *touch me and see.*

Jagger slowly pulled himself up. His legs shook and he barely had enough strength to stand. He placed his hand on the figure. Visions invaded his mind.

He saw the group of pissant townsfolk and outsiders—Hatton's ER doc, that woman on *Paranormal Murders*, the half-breed whore from the Tattered Page, the weak-assed Reverend, and the gravedigger and his dog. He also saw a very tall white man with white hair whom he didn't recognize, and beside him a wolf. A very large wolf. They were all killing his Harvesters, and the tall white man—Jagger watched with rising fury as the killer stood behind his son and snapped his neck.

Savral is dead.

Jagger didn't know if that was his own thought or if it was *her* voice telling him. His eyes filled with tears of anger and shame. Savral was on watch last night and he'd failed. How could the Deathwing Queen ever trust Jagger's family again?

They have taken everything from us. The immortal's heart and his body are gone. The captured souls are free and most of my Harvesters are dead. Without the souls I cannot live in human form. Without the immortal's heart I cannot save you or your family.

Jagger heard Mason's footsteps as he returned to the main cavern. He bent his head in front of the figure and said, "I will not fail you, Raum, my Queen. You shall rise tonight in glory!"

And then her voice was gone from his head. The pain in his body trickled away with the exception of the aches and pains of age that had crept back into him. Raum had stripped him of the extra years of life he'd been given to preserve her place in this world. She'd stripped the health from his daughter, Precious—when he needed the girl most. She had the sight—something that would only grow stronger as she got older.

Mason approached him with hesitant steps. "The doctor is gone," he said. "Something bent the bars and he slipped out. He took some of the medallions for tonight too. There won't be enough to protect everyone who comes."

Jagger glared at Mason and then reminded himself that Mason was his only son now. He would have to groom him—teach him how to lead—how to take charge.

"We will choose who goes without protection tonight if we don't get the others back. The Queen will need more souls anyway to replace what was lost. There were people here last night who broke the ER doc out of his cell. That Reverend, the bitch from the Tattered Page and others, they emptied the urns and killed most of the Harvesters."

He eyed Mason, daring the boy to question him. When he didn't, Jagger was satisfied. Let's go," he said. "We've got work to do."

Years of backhands and punches to his face had taught Mason not to ask questions, and of that Jagger was grateful. He pulled out his cell phone and thumbed to his Favorites. In seconds the phone rang and then there was an answer.

"Hey, Uncle, what's up?"

"You alone?" he asked.

"Sure. Hospital's quiet right now. Why?"

"You got more of those medallions?"

"No," the voice said. "I used them all, like you told me."

"We've got problems and I need you to put out more—a whole lot of them before tonight. Can you leave and come get them?"

"Sure," Hannah said. "I'll be there in 30."

Yes, they all had work to do. And the work today was going to be painful. And messy.

RACHEL

CROW MOON

*M*arch 25, *Monday*

7:30 AM

When Rachel woke, she rolled over and was startled at first to see Melody in bed with her. The girl was cuddled around her pillow breathing softly in a heavy-sleep rhythm. She was really very pretty, and Rachel admired her rich, dark skin.

A sudden memory caused her to sit up straight in bed and she looked over at her clock. She and her sister should be getting ready for school, but when she strained her ears to hear her mother making breakfast, she heard nothing. No footsteps. No clickity-click of Lola's toenails tap-dancing on the kitchen tiles. The air was absent of any scents of food. Usually her mother had eggs, waffles, pancakes, or Cream of Wheat cooking by now, but she smelled nothing.

Careful not to wake Melody, Rachel backed toward the foot of the bed and crawled over the footboard. Her door was usually cracked at night because even though Rachel was well past the age of believing in monsters, the soft hall lights outside of her room gave her some comfort.

She passed by her sister's room and stuck her nose in to be sure Lilith was still there. She smelled the girl's fresh new-wolf scent and heard her breathing. All was good.

It was always tricky going down the stairs without making them squeak, but Rachel had mastered the art of descending them quietly. She padded into the kitchen only to find it empty. She decided to go to her mom's room to see if she was up and heard her voice speaking very quietly.

"Yes, I'm not well today. I need the day to rest and recover. I'll have Harvey take the lead. He's on day shift and he'll do fine."

Whenever something came up that affected law enforcement in the town, her mom called to let the mayor know. So, she wasn't going in today. Did that mean they weren't going to school as well?

Renny opened the door just as Rachel stood up to go back to the kitchen. They both jumped. Then Renny smiled and looked back over her shoulder.

"You got a curious wolf cub here wondering why she's not getting ready for school." Renny touched Rachel's head lightly. "Go on in, baby, your mom will explain what's going on." With that, Renny made her way toward the bathroom and Rachel stepped into the room.

Her mom looked dog tired, rumpled and just not good. She beckoned Rachel over and patted a spot on the bed beside her. "Hey, sweets. You sleep okay?"

Rachel nodded, wondering what in the world was going on. Her mom sighed, like she was trying to decide something. The sound of the toilet flushing down the hallway signaled that Renny would soon be back.

Rachel wished her mom would just say whatever was on her mind. She hated when grown-ups felt like they had to keep information away from teenagers, or worse, when they tried to make a situation seem less important than it was.

Renny came back sat in the floral armchair in the corner. "You might as well tell her," she said. "Melody's gonna hear it all as soon as she's up."

As if Melody's name conjured the girl, her face popped in the doorway. "Hear what? What happened?"

Her mom rolled her eyes and Rachel found the whole situation weird and comical. And behind Melody, Lilith was there. And Lola was so excited to have so many more people in the house in the morning that she yipped and raced around the room before jumping on the bed, rolling over and asking Rachel for a belly-rub. Rachel reached out to rub the dog's stomach and decided that it was time for the adults to tell them everything.

"Mom," she started. "Tell us what's going on, please. We're tired of being treated like children and if there's something we can do to help with whatever is happening, then we want to help!"

Lilith and Melody nodded. Melody said, "We know about the creepy deaths, and I know that this—" she held out her medallion from her neck— "keeps me safe, but I don't know exactly what I need to be kept safe from. You guys talked about those crow things, the monsters—Harvesters, right? But the only attack men, or that's who they've hurt so far."

Rachel looked to her mom, and she was looking at the ceiling. She sighed once more. "Okay, first things first. You guys are not going to school today. It may even be cancelled with the flood waters so high, so I'll look on the computer and see and if it's cancelled then we're golden and if not then I'll call the school and tell them you're both not feeling well and can't make it today."

Well, that answers that question, thought Rachel. But the *why—* that was what she wanted to know most.

Her mom said, "You guys know that Renny and I have been working with some others in the town to figure out what is happening with these strange deaths, right?"

"Murders, Mom," Rachel said. "Might as well call it what it is. We all heard about Mr. Thompson and the fishermen in the boat and what happened at the apartments with that guy and girl there. What is doing this?"

"Okay, here's the thing, and it's going to sound weird—alright?" Her mom looked at Renny and Renny nodded as if to say, *It's okay. Tell them.* "There's a cave up on a hill near where the Profitt family—where Mason and his family live."

"Mason told us about the cave, Mom," said Rachel. "That day at the Founder's celebration, remember? He was gonna to sneak us out tonight. He said the cave was a secret—that at night when the moon was full it glowed inside, and he'd take us to see it." Rachel felt bad reminding her mom about this now because she realized they hadn't really talked about it.

Her mom's eyes seemed to flash with fire, and it took a moment for Rachel to realize she wasn't angry with her. She was angry at Mason.

"Girls," she said, clearly speaking just to her daughters now, "you know how you change and it's even easier when the moon is full? I think Mason has a gift as well. Call it a 'charisma' gift if you will. Whenever you're near him he seems really nice, and you enjoy being with him, listening to everything he has to say?"

Lilith was nodding but Rachel was still as a statue, thinking about Mason. Had she felt like that then? And how did she feel about him now? He was cute and, well, she wasn't sure how she felt.

Her mom placed her hand on Rachel's shoulder. "When I found you both with him that day, when I talked with him, I liked him too. I felt drawn to him. Later, I realized I'd felt the same way when he spent the night at our house. I watched him leave that morning, slipping out the front door, and discovered I didn't feel the same when I wasn't with him anymore.

"Anyway—the point is he asked you to the cave. Tonight is the full moon, what we call the Crow Moon. Even if the skies remain cloudy, you know the moon still affects you, right? Our change doesn't happen only under the light of the moon or only at night. It's not like T.V. It has to do with how the change in gravity affects our bodies and we can change any time, it's just easier when the moon is full."

Renny spoke up, probably because she was a little impatient at how her mom was jumping around and not really explaining anything.

"The cave near the Profitt house is the home of a demon," Renny said. "In ancient days in Rome they called the demon Raum. Among the Cherokee, it was known as the Raven Mocker. In Iron Shores, she is known as the Deathwing Queen. Her power allows her to remove the very heart of a man without leaving a mark, and she can cause people to fall ill and die before their time. When she does that, she can absorb the years they would have had left and give those years to the people who serve her. In this case, probably Mason's father and his family."

Rachel was finding all of this a bit overwhelming and had to ask, "How do you know this is true?"

Her mom said, "Because we were at the cave last night. The things that are killing the men in town are large crow-like beasts with beaks full of razor-sharp teeth. We killed some of them last night. That's where we went."

"Your mom got a cut on her leg from one of them," Renny added, and her mom stood and shimmied down her satin pajama pants a little so they could see the bandage covering her flank.

"I was in wolf form, and you guys know we heal pretty fast, so I'm fine now. Swear," her mom said.

She raked her top teeth over her bottom lip and said, "The Deathwing Queen uses her Harvesters help her collect souls, and those souls—the time the souls are allowed here on Earth—is what she uses to reward those who serve her. I checked the death records. Mason's great grandfather lived to be a over a hundred and fifty. He was a corporal in the Civil war, fighting for the Confederates. His grandfather died much earlier only because he was hit by a truck and killed when he was crossing a road near town. The years added on to his life didn't make him immortal. Apparently, they can keep people from getting sick from things like cancer and can help keep them young but if the body is fatally injured then they die."

The room was silent after that as the women and the girls all looked at each other trying to figure out what to say next.

Rachel launched the next question, which seemed obvious. "So, then, what happens tonight?"

THOMAS

APEIRON

*M*arch 25, Monday

10:00 AM

Thomas was grateful that the breakfast bar at the Horseshoe Inn stayed open until 11:00AM. If it weren't for the work he did as an ER doc, he'd never get up early. That was why he enjoyed the night shift and took it whenever he could. It was easier for him to stay awake at night rather than the day and on his days off he usually kept up that same schedule.

He wouldn't have met Hatton if he'd been on the day shift, but he tried not to think of her now. He couldn't believe she'd take him to the cave and then trap him like that. She had to be in trouble.

There had to be an explanation as to why she did that. Her father? Maybe. But she was a grown woman. She didn't have to take that crap from him or follow his orders. Or did she? He remembered his classes about abusers. They made the person they controlled dependent on them for everything.

Yes, Hatton had a car, but she lived with her father and her brothers. Or *brother* now that Savral was dead. She took care of her little sister Precious and maybe her father threatened to harm the girl if Hatton left. Her sister Hellen had recently died, and Hatton probably felt more than responsible to keep Precious safe.

And she had no job, no money except for some arts and crafts she sold from time to time. He decided when he saw he next he'd try to find out why she did what she did. She might not have had a choice.

When he entered the Horseshoe's dining room, he noted that he wasn't the only one eating breakfast late. Dr. Luanna Crane was sitting at a table with the two strangers from last night. Both of them had very white skin and snow-blond hair, and they seemed very fit. One was the man who had helped him escape. The other looked vaguely familiar but Thomas couldn't place him.

Thomas grabbed a couple of hard-boiled eggs, a yogurt, a biscuit and a handful of fruit, along with a spoonful of blueberry jam he plopped on the side of his plate. Then he made a beeline to their table. There was an empty chair, and without asking if he could join them, he set his plate down so he could use his good arm to pull the chair away from the table and take a seat.

"Morn'in," he said. "Hope you all don't mind if I join you? Looks like you just got started yourselves."

The men made no comment, but Lu simply said, "Of course. After last night, you are absolutely welcome here."

The men remained quiet and sipped their coffee.

Thomas ate a few bites while looking at everyone and then he couldn't stand it anymore.

"Okay, are we going to talk about what happened last night?" He turned to the guy who'd bent the steel bars to let him out. The other guy had to be his brother, they looked so similar, except his brother had short hair and Thomas still felt like he knew him but couldn't figure out how.

"My name's Thomas," he said. "I wanted to say thank you for breaking me out of that cell. What you did was phenomenal. I'd never guess in a million years you were that strong but I'm glad you are."

A smile played at the corner of the man's mouth. "You're welcome. Like I said last night, I'm Amadeus. That's my brother, Viktor, who you have unofficially met before. He was confined there as well, and your friends were very helpful breaking him out."

Viktor nodded but said nothing, while Thomas eyed Viktor wondering how that heart got put back inside him and how that all worked. He was dying to know. It was beyond believable.

Lu remained quiet as well, pretending to eat but she was just shifting food around her plate.

Amadeus looked around to be sure there was no one within listening distance. "Since we will likely see this problem to its end tonight," he said, "you must know that my brother and I are not exactly human."

"Since he came into my ER with no heart and I only discovered it after trying to save his life two weeks ago, I kind of figured that already," Thomas quipped, his patience practically gone.

"Oh, for Pete's sake," Lu chimed. "They're from a hidden town named Passage. It existed in the 1800s and now the only way to get there is to cross a time barrier. Amadeus and his brother are not human because they're, technically . . ." she coughed the next word and said with a muffle, "vampires, okay? And supposedly they're just visiting."

If Thomas hadn't seen a Harvester in real life and didn't know about the murders happening in town, he would have laughed and called her crazy.

Lu continued. "They're not your evil Bram Stoker, Vlad the Impaler types, or the sparkly Stephanie Meyers *Twilight* vamps either. They're much like us."

"Except stronger, faster, smarter and much better looking," added Viktor, raising an orange juice to himself before taking a sip.

Thomas grinned. "Amadeus, what did you mean by 'see this problem to its end tonight'?"

"Tonight is the Crow Moon," Lu said before Amadeus could answer. "It's when the Queen of those Harvesters, like the one you saw, will try to take over the town. It's supposed to be when she's the strongest. Since Iron Shores is sort of off the beaten path and

469

since it has its own quirks, it's the perfect place for her to get a foothold—that's how I see it anyway."

It was then that both Lu and Thomas's phone chimed, signaling an incoming text.

Amadeus leaned over and asked his brother, "Do you have one of those yet? We must definitely get one."

Lu informed them what Thomas already knew. "That was Judith. We need to meet at noon at the Tattered Page, about an hour and a half from now. The road is flooded, but the building is up on a hill. It's still high enough to keep it out of the water and less than a quarter mile walk. Best if we go separately so the townspeople don't notice us gathering there."

"My brother and I send our regrets," Amadeus said. He leaned toward Lu. "May I see that?" he asked gesturing to her phone.

She handed it to him. "You aren't coming? There were probably more deaths last night and you said you'd help us. We don't know how many more of those Harvester things are out there."

"Ah," Amadeus handed her phone back. "I said we'd see this problem to its end, and so we will. But we will assist in our own way. My brother is still missing some pieces of his body and we need to get them. We are very much at risk right now and if we had common sense we would return to Passage. The Deathwing Queen ripped my brother's heart from his body without leaving a mark. He doesn't remember how she did it and we must prevent that from ever happening again."

Thomas remembered that dark moment in the X-Ray room after they'd just pronounced a man dead and realized that he had no heart.

"You're him!" exclaimed Thomas and then he realized his outburst had drawn the attention of other late breakfasters. He lowered his voice. "I saw you—I mean our EMT's—emergency people—brought you in and I tried to save your life! Then, in the X-ray room—on the X-ray—I could see your heart was gone. We thought it had to be a mistake. And there was something else." He tried to remember but he couldn't. It seemed important but . . .

Both men were extremely interested in Thomas now.

"What did you see, Thomas? What was it?" Amadeus reached out to grab his hand.

Viktor grabbed Thomas's face and gazed into his eyes.

And, in that instant, Thomas's mind traveled back to that day. He could smell his scrubs and he was talking with Maria about the man with no heart and she suggested he use the man as a case study. Then she shut off the lights for a second and —he remembered darkness pressing in on him, and the old, bent figure, the drip-drip, the glowing stone that lit only the water and then the figure leaning into him once more with that death scent on its breath saying . . . saying a word he'd never heard before, one he didn't understand. "Apeiron."

It took a moment before he realized that all three of them had said the word together. When he looked at the brothers, their jaws were set and any laughter that once existed in their eyes was gone. Both of them stood, heedless of the curious onlookers.

"You've helped us very much and maybe helped your town more than you know," said Amadeus, and before their eyes both brothers were gone.

LU

Bloody Monday

*M*arch 25, *Monday*

11:20 AM

Lu noticed that Thomas had hardly touched what he'd brought to the table. She snapped her fingers at him. "You want help peeling those eggs?" She nodded to his arm in a sling.

"Sure."

She cracked then peeled the eggs and deposited them back on his plate. "There you go!"

He grinned and then stuffed a whole egg in his mouth and began chewing.

"That's disgusting," she said, and couldn't help but laugh at how his cheeks puffed out like a chipmunk.

He made her laugh even more when he tried to talk, "Iphs petty gud! Ooo wunt de oddur?"

The laughter only lasted seconds. Someone was screaming and then there were more screams. Lu got up and ran toward the sound barely aware that Thomas was following her.

Two house-keeping employees nearly knocked her over running out of the hotel. Another one stopped at the desk. "They're dead!" she yelled to Ms. Morrow. "All of them! Every room we opened—everyone is dead! Call the police, ma'am. Call someone! Oh my god, holy Jesus—I gotta go be with my kids!"

Faye Morrow stood at the counter in shock.

Lu prompted her. "Ms. Morrow. Faye!"

The woman looked toward the sound while more of her customers pushed out of the building.

"Ms. Morrow," said Lu, "call the police, okay? Dial them now. I'll go check it out. You understand?"

Ms. Morrow pushed the button on her phone and said, "911."

Lilith hoped the woman's husband would come soon to help her, though they both were going to be in shock after this.

Seeing Thomas standing behind her she asked him, "You up for this? You want to come with?" She felt him hesitate, but he nodded and finally swallowed his egg.

They ascended the stairs to the second floor and saw the housekeeping cart far on the end of the long hallway. Judith pulled out her phone. She'd use this to take photos if she needed. As she drew closer and saw the spatters of blood on the entranceway of the opened doors, it was clear that photos would be needed although they'd never be seen in a courtroom. In the two rooms with open doors Lu looked in one and then the other. There was a couple in each room. All of them dead. The women had holes in their abdomens and not a drop of blood surrounded them. The males had been eviscerated—all of their organs gone. Their heads were snipped from their bodies and snapped open like a walnut with each man's brain absent.

Lu heard retching behind her.

Guess Thomas lost his egg, she thought.

And she didn't blame him. Working at the ER was different then seeing things on scene. She snapped photos of each room, careful not to touch anything. In the second room she entered, she noticed a glint in the palm of the woman's hand. She used a towel to pry the woman's fingers open and there was medallion with red symbols on one side. Like the other victims.

She photographed it then wrapped it carefully in a heavy towel and put the towel in the classic laundry bags hotel rooms usually had. She compared that medallion to the one she now wore which had a sigil of light blue markings on one side and a crow or raven's head on the other.

Then, she took note that the windows to each room were open. Returning to the first room, she checked as thoroughly as possible

474

for a medallion there and didn't find it until she decided to pull the woman's arm and roll her over. There it was on the floor.

"I'm going to the third floor," she told Thomas. "I understand if you don't want to come."

Thomas straightened. "Yeah, sorry about that. I'll come. I just wasn't ready for . . ." He didn't finish the sentence and Lu opened the stairwell door and climbed to the next floor where it was clear the Deathwings had been very busy.

All in all, there were twelve people dead. Housekeeping hadn't opened three of the rooms, but it was past check out time and Ms. Morrow asked if Lu would check those rooms too.

All the bodies were male and female pairs. No one with children. No one with pets.

LILITH

BEWARE

*M*arch 25, Monday

3:00 PM

"Yes, Mom, we're fine, really!" Lilith looked over at Rachel and Melody and rolled her eyes as if to say, *Mom's right?*

They smiled. "Nope. No strange people hanging around. No unordered pizzas. Just me, Rachel and Melody chillin' and watching T.V."

She rolled her eyes. "Yes, we're wearing them." She pulled out her medallion from her shirt and swung it side to side like a pendulum.

Lola yipped.

"Oh, and Lola," Lilith added.

"Just keep me posted if anything weird happens, okay?" Her mom sounded worried but after all that had happened, Lilith guessed their house was one of the safest in the area.

"Sure, Mom. Gotta go now! We're binging on *Sabrina*!"

"That's like, what, three times she's called this morning?" giggled Melody.

"Yeah." Lilith's stomach grumbled. "Hey, you guys wanna fix food first? A bingeing picnic?" She was surprising herself by feeling a little more outgoing today. Maybe it was *the change* that helped this happen, like for the first time in her life she was in control of her own world.

"Sure, I'm starving," Melody nodded.

They went into the kitchen. Lilith got out three trays for them to fill with food to take into the living room. They opened the refrigerator and the cupboards and came away with a bag of peanut M&Ms, baby carrots, a container of red-pepper hummus, Ruffles, onion dip, some provolone cheese and turkey slices.

"Soda?" Lilith called out. "Root beer, cream, grape or regular cola?"

"Root beer for me!" Melody answered.

"I'll take grape!" Rachel always loved the grape.

Lilith set the drinks down. "It's Zevia," she said. "Mom likes it cause there's no sugar and no aspartame—a sweetener she says is really bad for you."

They'd just settled down again in front of the T.V. when Lola started barking. There was a knock at the door.

Rachel paused the show and said, "I'll go check on it."

"Mom said not to open the door!" Lilith said this quietly but forcefully.

"There's no harm in looking though, right?" Rachel went toward the door.

Lilith and Melody stared at each other and then they both got up and decided to go too.

"It's Mason!" Rachel's voice sounded excited.

"Rachel, no!" Lilith put her hand on her sister's shoulder. "Don't let him in!"

Rachel puffed a breath of air from her lips. "It's just Mason, guys. He's cool."

Lilith whispered, "Don't you remember what Mom said this morning? He's in on this thing with his dad. We . . . "

But Rachel had already turned the knob and was opening the door.

MASON

CHARISMA

*M*arch 25, *Monday*

4:45 PM

Nothing could have been more perfect than the way Mason had made his play today. As soon as Rachel saw him and opened her front door, the effects of that potion he'd given her and her sister kicked in.

Add his charms to the mix and before they all knew it, they were piled into Hatton's VW and headed up to go look at the cave. Hell, he might not have even needed the potion. Even the pretty girl Melody came with him.

The little dog was more trouble than anything. The small rat had tried to nip him in the calf and bite his foot. A few special little treats for her, ones he'd made himself, calmed her right down though. She fell asleep in the hallway while the girls were putting on their coats.

"How far is it, Mason?" Lilith asked as they were pulling out of the driveway. "We really aren't supposed to be out and our mom will call soon to check on us."

"Thirty minutes, tops." He grinned and she smiled back at him with not a worry in the world.

She seemed to have forgotten that he'd convinced all the girls to leave their cell phones at home, telling them it would be really bad to lose them in the caves. Their phones were on the large coffee table in the living room.

If Chief Ware tried to track them, she'd see their phones were right at home and assume the girls hadn't gone anywhere. Even if she or Melody's ma drove over to check on them, by the time either of them discovered the girls weren't there, he'd be nesting them nicely in the cave for the ceremony tonight.

Damn, Pa's gonna love me!

And while he knew he should be sad that he lost a brother, he was glad that Savral was gone. More food for him, more attention from Pa. Everything was coming up "Mason."

Going through town was the most challenging part. He had to pass by the Horseshoe Inn and the River Rage then take the side roads since the town's main road was closed from flooding. What made him feel more secure was that everyone in town knew that the green VW was Hatton's.

They'd likely just assume it was hers and continue on doing whatever townspeople do. And, it was pounding rain outside again. Add in the commotion at the Horseshoe where Hannah had completed her job, and no one was gonna pay attention to a little green bug.

"Let's play some tunes!" he called out and the girls cheered. He knew music was a teen drug—hell, he loved it too. And getting pumped with some sweet plays would keep their minds from wandering back to what they should and shouldn't be doing.

"How bout we start with an oldie? 'Panic! at the Disco,' anyone?" He hit a playlist on his phone and the music started.

The girls cheered. Mason cranked the music up, and they drove through town rocking the bug yelling "Amen!" Mason kept his eye out for anyone who might spot him, but when he turned to take the detour around Main Street, he didn't see Job and Grinch coming out of Bia Cup.

JOB

GONE

*M*arch 25, Monday

5:02 PM

Not good, Job thought as he dialed. *Why in the world would the girls take a ride in Hatton's bug with Mason driving?* And it didn't take rocket science to figure out where they were headed.

Now he wished he'd showed up on time at the Tattered Page. But Larry Williams had chest pain and it wasn't the first time he'd forgotten his nitro.

"Judith," said Job. "We got a problem." and he hated to do it, but he told her what he'd seen. He hated telling her because he knew she'd want to launch right out there and get her girls.

And he didn't blame her, but they all needed to come together, to make a plan and figure out how to stop this thing. If she left, they'd all be winging it tonight and who knows how many more people would die?

Grinch growled as he stared at the road where the VW had turned. "I'll be there in five, okay? Don't, Chief, don't race after them, you hear? Wait for me. Ceremony isn't till tonight and we gotta be sure to take them all down—stop this thing once and for all. Chief? Judith?"

The phone beeped and ended the connection. Job, who rarely cursed, let a stream of words fly as he dropped his coffee and ran.

He made it to the Tattered Page in less than five minutes, but when he opened the door and checked the rooms, both the Chief and Renny were gone.

CHRISTOPHER

SOLO

*M*arch 25, Monday

6:30 PM

When his phone rang, Christopher looked at the number.

"It's Job," he told Judith.

Judith nodded and Christopher took the call.

"Reverend," Job started, "The Chief—"

"I'm with them now," Christopher interrupted. "Caught them running out of Renny's and made them take me."

"It's a bad idea—"

'I know, Job. But he's got Judith's kids and Renny's daughter. We might be able to catch up to them before . . ."

Christopher stopped. A logging truck blocked the road. It was turned on its side and two other cars had stopped to help the driver until the EMTs could get there.

"FUCK!" Judith hit her steering wheel.

"What is it?" Job asked.

"Wrecked logging truck. The shoulder's too narrow to get past it."

"Put me on speaker," Job said. "Chief. Renny. You ain't gonna get past that right now and it will be at least a couple of hours before Wilber's Towing can come move it to the side. Please, come back. We can figure it out when you get here."

"That son of a bitch has our daughters!" Judith screamed. "I'll walk, Job. I'll get there—"

"It's ten or twelve miles," said Christopher.

"There's no way," Job said.

Judith was already taking off her clothes.

"Oh, there's a way all right," Judith growled. "Four feet are faster than two! You drive back, Renny. Christopher, keep her safe. You all make a plan with Job and Lu and I'll find you when you get there."

Judith threw open the driver door and slipped off the rest of her clothes. Luckily, no one was behind her yet. She shifted form and disappeared into the trees.

Three things went through Christopher's mind as he watched her. The first was that the woman he loved had major stones, doing what she was doing now. The second was that he had no idea she was in such good shape. She reminded him of some of the female climbers he'd learned from when he was just starting to climb.

Finally, it didn't escape him that for the first time in years she actually called him Christopher. He was a bit overwhelmed hearing it.

"Chief? You there, Chief?" Job's voice was tense. Anxious.

"I believe she's decided to go on a solo run, Job," Christopher answered. "She's gone wolf. Renny and I are coming back to you and let's hope this wreck is cleared by the time we need to get to that cave."

"I'm driving," Renny said, and with the tone of her voice, Christopher wasn't going to argue with her. The paramedics passed by them on the way to the crash site and Christopher made out both Nick and Sammi in the front seat. He couldn't imagine the pace they and the other two paramedics had worked over the past two weeks. He both admired and was grateful for their stamina.

When they arrived back in town, Renny had to drive up on the road behind the Tattered Page since all of Main Street was under water and everyone was being rerouted. They entered through her back door and when they walked into the kitchen both of them were surprised.

Job was not alone. Lu and Thomas were there, and sitting at the dining table like they belonged there were Amadeus and Viktor. And beside them, trussed up tighter than turkey legs at Thanksgiving, sat Hannah Profitt.

RENNY

TRAITOR

*M*arch 25, *Monday*

6:50 PM

It annoyed Renny to see the Double White Vamp Duo in her kitchen making themselves at home, but then she realized that they were probably the reason Hannah was here. And having her here, right now, was very, very good. It was one less person for Jagger to rely on, if she indeed had been the one placing the medallions that helped to kill so many people in and around town.

The brothers had pulled out one of her bottles of wine, a 2019 Josh Cellars merlot. It wasn't fancy, but it was a Food Lion special. She had been planning to share that with Lu and Judith when they were done with this mess. Never mind that she had eleven more bottles in her pantry.

Renny hung Judith's keys on a hook by the door so she wouldn't lose them.

"Wel. Y'all just help yourselves, please," she huffed, almost regretting the sarcasm in her voice. "Make yourselves at home."

These guys had managed to get Hannah, so why didn't they go get her daughter instead? And Judith's girls? Why were they here? Weren't they like "super-people"? There was nothing Renny or the others could do for them that they couldn't do for themselves.

"Oh," said Amadeus, a sly smile creeping over one side of his mouth, "you probably would not want us to make ourselves at home." A twinkle flashed in his eye, and Renny found it odd that she was caught between feeling amused and slightly uncomfortable.

She was acutely aware of his stare at her neck and figured she'd launch right into the play then.

"I'd offer you something to drink, but it looks like you've got what you need." She looked around and found it odd that Christopher had pulled up a chair and now sat behind Amadeus. A long pause hung in the air and no one seemed inclined to take the bull by the horns so Renny grabbed the lead.

First, she covered Hannah's eyes and put earplugs in her ears and put headphones over those. The girl glared at her before she did it, but Renny had no patience for this traitor and what she'd done. If Renny didn't believe in karma, she'd have helped the girl meet her maker.

Next, Renny reviewed everything that had happened in the past twenty-four hours and then asked for updates from everyone. After that they all turned to look at Amadeus and Viktor.

"So, we went to the Richmond Medical Examiner's Office to get the rest of my brother's body," Amadeus said. "Apparently, in autopsy, they take the brain and store it along with pieces of his organs. He is good now we think, except the formaldehyde might affect him a little for a while. We aren't sure."

Viktor smacked him.

Thomas asked, "What about our conversation at breakfast? That blue stone and the word . . ."

"Apeiron," Amadeus said. "Yes. The word itself means infinite or eternal. It is also the name of the blue stone in your vision."

Viktor broke in. "It has many names. The *stone of creation*, the *chaos stone* and the *stone of unmaking*. A few years ago, I discovered that this stone was here in your realm, in your time, and I was curious. I went to look for it, but I used my mind to search for it you see. It is faster that way. There are many caves in this area along the Blue Ridge mountains. I could not remember at first but once we found my brain and reinserted it, I realized how this Deathwing Queen"—he made a disgusted and sour face—"was able to take my heart. You see, I have a house next to a lovely winery—"

Amadeus touched his hand. "Do not get off track, brother."

"Yes, thank you." Viktor continued. "I was in a meditation, searching everywhere, and found the cave, you see, the one we battled in last night. My mind travelled down into its depths. There I found the stone. Unfortunately, the demon was there as well. She trapped my mind and followed its thread back to my body. With no mind to defend itself, my body was vulnerable, and she simply plucked my heart from inside."

Amadeus took over. "The good news is that she cannot do this again. Not as long as we keep our minds with our bodies when we fight. The bad news is that it will limit us since using our minds would help us find your children."

Renny had been looking at some of her books and thinking as she flipped pages filled with sigils and spell patterns. She glanced around the room. "Everyone still has their medallion from last night, right?"

Each of them pulled their medallion out from under their shirts. Even Amadeus and Viktor had one.

Amadeus shrugged and smiled. "I did not see the harm since they are protective."

Her gaze returned to the symbols. "I think I know what we need to do, and we don't have much time. Everyone has always assumed that Jagger Profitt's wife, Herra, is dead. But what if she's not?"

Renny walked over to Hannah and removed her blindfold and earplugs.

"I won't tell you anything," Hannah snapped.

"Oh, I think you will," Renny replied. "Amadeus? Viktor? Which of you is best at this?"

Viktor was fast. Suddenly, Hannah's face was in his hands, and he forced her to stare into his eyes.

"You are correct, Renny," Viktor said. "The wife is alive. In a way. If we take her heart, then we close the door to Raum, and she will have nothing."

"Where is her body?" Renny hoped she didn't know the answer, but Viktor confirmed her fear.

"She is hidden inside the stone."

THOMAS

BONUS

*M*arch 25, *Monday*

7:00 PM

Sitting in Renny's kitchen listening to their plans for stopping the ceremony tonight, Thomas felt bad because he couldn't fight, couldn't do much of anything, but he could still be of some use. His fingers scrolled over the list of contacts on his phone, and he tapped the Iron Shores Police Department. The phone rang several times but finally someone answered. The voice sounded like a young girl's and for a second he wondered if he had the right number.

"I.S. Police Department. What can I do for you?"

"This is the Iron Shores Police Department, right?" Thomas had to be sure.

"Yes, Sir."

"And who am I speaking with?"

"This is Sarah Colman. I'm a volunteer on the call line today."

That explained some of it although the girl sounded like a twelve-year-old. And her name sounded familiar. Wasn't she the girl who found two bodies by the river?

"Sarah, there was an overturned logging truck going out of town toward Ked's. Can you check to see if they've moved it yet?"

"Stand by," the girl replied. It took a couple of minutes but she got back to him. "Yes, sir. The vehicle has been pushed over to allow for through-traffic using only one lane at this time."

"Great, thanks Sarah." Thomas ended the call and guessed that because of the flooding the kids were out of school and the town police needed the help after the Horseshoe this morning and then the deaths at the Red Tail.

"Good news," Thomas announced to the group. "Road's open now. Just one lane, but we can get through."

"Thank you, Thomas," Renny said. Then she gazed at him thoughtfully, like it just dawned on her how he must be feeling. Hatton had betrayed him and locked him in the cave. The group had to rescue him yesterday and he wasn't able to fight even though he wore a medallion that kept the Harvesters from attacking. Sure, he'd gathered the protective medallions they now wore, but they were planning an attack that didn't include him. "Thomas, can you get a medic bag of sorts together? We many need some emergency triage."

Thomas was grateful. That was something he *could* do. "How soon before we leave?" he asked.

Renny looked at her clock. It was one she'd made herself with various crystals like amethyst, citrine, and rose quartz pieces framing it. "Forty-five minutes, I need you back," she said. "I have some design work to do on everyone." She brandished a handful of Sharpies. "And when you get back, you'll be next."

"Got it." With that, he was out the door. He hoped he could get in and out of the ER without anyone noticing and if he ran into some of his ER crew—well, he'd think of something.

Getting a to-go bag ended up being much simpler than Thomas would have thought. The ER was crazy busy, but the supply room had a key code that hadn't been changed in months and no one was in there when he arrived. He dumped bandages, suture kits, alcohol wipes and gloves into a plastic bag. He was dashing out of the door when he ran into Nick Moon and Sammi Ware.

"Yo, Doc!" Nick looked as startled as Thomas felt. "Scared me, man. What are you doing here? You're still healin?," He looked pointedly at Thomas's cast.

"Good to see you guys," Thomas ignored the healing comment, but when he looked at Sammi he suddenly had a flash of insight. He keyed the supply room once again, dragged them in and shut the door.

Thomas held up his hand when he returned and Renny looked at the bright blue medic bag. "Looks like you ran into a couple of EMTs," she said with a smile.

"The bag was just a bonus," he said. "I ran into Nick and Sammi and they gave me an extra carry case. They're off in two hours and want to help."

Renny's eyes sparked with flash of anger. "Why did you tell those boys what's going on? What were you thinking?"

Thomas held his free palm out. "Whoa, Renny. Think about it. There's an old ambulance in the back hospital parking lot that's only used as a backup. It's got supplies. I don't know if Nick's got any special talents other than EMT skills, but Sammi's last name is Ware. I took a risk. I asked him if he's like Judith. He looked at me like I was nuts and then said, 'Yeah, dude, I'm a Ware."

Dude didn't hesitate to tell me he was planning on doing his own wolf thing with the full moon tonight since it finally stopped raining. Those kids are his family. He wants to help. Nick, too. He said he could monitor the airwaves and work with me if anyone gets hurt."

The fire in Renny's eyes died down. "Nick has his talents too," she said, but didn't provide what they were. "Do they know how to find the cave?"

Thomas nodded. "They'll be at the power lines when we get there."

"Well, then," Renny said. Let's get your designs on, shall we?" She brandished some Sharpies and turned to Lu. "Can you please check our guest Hannah and see if she's wearing one of those lovely medallions? If Judith's cousin is going into battle, he's gonna need some armor."

Renny had Thomas take his shirt off and she set to marking his body with protective symbols and magical signs.

"Hey," Thomas said to Viktor, "Where'd your brother go?"

"He's exercising," the vampire smiled in such a way that Thomas knew Amadeus wasn't exercising. Not in the traditional sense.

Thomas guessed he'd probably left to go help Judith. What Thomas didn't know was why Viktor didn't go too.

"Viktor, how's your sleep hypnosis skill?" Renny asked as she was finishing up the last of the designs on Thomas's back.

"Mmm…let's see." Viktor grasped Hannah's face in his hands once more and said, "Sleep." The girl was out like a light.

Renny's jaw dropped. "Man. If we could bottle that and sell it, parents with young kids would pay us a fortune," Renny's phone chimed. She glanced at it and said, "Put your shirt back on now, Thomas. Tati's just arrived. It's time to get my daughter back and save our town."

JUDITH

RACE

*M*arch 25, *Monday*

7:00 PM

There was no way for Judith to gauge how fast she was running, but if the cave was anywhere between eleven to fifteen miles away, she knew she'd be there in less than an hour. Every fiber in her body pushed forward with intensity and yet she found exquisite joy in her perceptions. The cedar and juniper trees were bursting with scent after all the rain.

The scents of raccoon, fox, deer and rabbit made her hungry. She stopped at a creek where a fresh spring bubbled up and the cold, crisp water revived her. And the maternal anger she felt at someone taking her cubs bloomed into a raging fire that drove her on.

She imagined tearing Jagger and Mason to pieces, shredding their bodies and wearing their blood. If they hurt her girls, or Renny's child, they would not die quick deaths.

The boy, Mason, is only trying to win his father's love.

Judith shook her head. That was not her own voice speaking to her. She'd experienced this before and realized now that there was another voice from the outside invading her mind.

Hatton is only trying to protect her sister. Precious is dying. Leukemia. The Deathwing Queen gave her longer life until the urn of souls was emptied.

Judith growled. *Stop your tricks!*

Don't hurt my children, the voice said softly, *and I won't hurt yours.*

The power lines going up the hill were dead ahead. She was close!

What did the voice mean, *Don't hurt my children?* Mason? Hatton and Precious? But that would mean Jagger's wife never died.

I'm a prisoner, Judith. To save us all, you must set me free.

A picture presented itself inside her mind. A glowing blue stone, very tall, sitting in the center of an underground pool.

Set me free.

Snarling, Judith pushed the voice away. The girls were what was important.

At least it had stopped raining in time for the Crow Moon. She shivered.

HATTON

DOGGIES

*M*arch 25, Monday

7:15 PM

It was a long walk down to the bottom of the cave network where the Blue Stone waited, and it felt even longer dragging the girls in carts their pa had fashioned for just this purpose. Thankfully, this part of the cave floor was fairly smooth. The large wheels went over the surface easily and since the trip was downhill, the most challenging part was keeping the carts from crashing into walls and keeping the light ahead steady so they could all see.

Precious rode in the cart that Hatton pushed—the one that held the smallest girl, Lilith. Precious held a high-powered flashlight to help them see their way down to where their mama waited. Both Hatton and Mason knew the path well since they frequently walked down to be with their mother.

Precious was humming. She turned toward Hatton.

"The Queen's gonna get angry, you know."

"What makes you say that?"

"Cause she don't like doggies!" Precious exclaimed.

Hatton laughed a little. "Well, luckily we aren't bringing her any doggies then." Around them, wings flapped, and crystalline blue eyes passed by.

Why did Precious mention dogs? Her father said that Raum showed him a vision of what happened last night. He saw Savral's death. That was something she wasn't too upset about, but he'd said that Raum showed him a wolf fighting alongside the man who'd killed her brother. Is that what Precious meant? The wolf was coming back?

"Mason, when we come back up, let's put more Harvesters at the cave entrance, okay? Precious thinks that the wolf will try to get in here again."

Mason grunted. "Did you have to give the girls most of our blankets? It's still cold in the house at night, you know."

Hatton rolled her eyes. Mason wasn't as bad as Savral, but he could be *so* self-centered. "We've got to keep them warm until Raum lets mama out of the stone and we put the girls in, okay? We have to wait until exactly midnight, and then you can have your blankets back, and we'll have Mama back, too." She added, "And she's probably gonna be cold, so we'll need something to wrap her in."

Up front, Precious sang, "Doggies, doggies, doggies, doggies, doggies!" to herself.

MELODY

FALLING

*M*arch 25, Monday

7:30 PM

There was so much about this that Melody found fun. Her mother was going to wring her neck for sure, but she was out with friends! First riding in the VW and listening to music, then singing while everyone listened to her and admired her voice.

And then there was Mason. He was so, so, so cute! How long had it been since she liked a boy? Her mother never let her get near them, saying there'd be time enough for that in the future, but she didn't want the future. She wanted *now*.

And soon, they were climbing on the path under the power lines headed for the cave where her mother said she should never go. But she didn't care. And the rain had stopped, and the sky was clearing. None of this could be bad. Not at all.

Mason motioned them over to the left, and they crossed a creek. It gurgled its own music, and Melody stopped to listen while Lilith and Rachel went through the bushes, and Mason disappeared with them. She looked up at the sky and felt a breeze on her cheek, and then—

Why am I here? I must be crazy. We all did the one thing our mothers told us not to do! I've got to leave. Run for help! She started to head back across the creek, when Mason called her name.

"Hey, Melody! C'mon! You gotta see this!"

His voice was intoxicating, but she turned to tell him she needed to go, and there he was—long brown hair and hazel eyes that changed from a gold oak to green. Then he was holding her hand, and she felt so very happy and willingly followed him into the cave.

Mason was right. This place was incredible. The main chamber was huge and little lights on the cave walls made it soft and inviting. They laughed as they called out each other's names and heard their echoes bounce against the walls.

Finally, he brought them to a white marble shelf where a black winged statue sat. They marveled at its eyes, how they glowed, and gushed over its beauty.

"Can we touch it?" Lilith asked as she reached out her hand.

Mason stopped her. "Not a good idea," he said. "It's been here as long as I can remember. My grandfather found this place. Did you know?"

The girls all shook their heads.

"We're having a celebration tonight. That's part of why I wanted you to come, so you could see this place. I've never brought anyone here before."

Melody spied a table over to the side of the marble shelf. There were bottles of water in a tub and some punch in a crystal bowl. She realized she was incredibly thirsty.

"Is it okay if we grab a bottle of water?" She felt guilty for asking, but she figured it couldn't hurt. Maybe they had extra.

"Sure," said Mason. "Everyone else want a bottle too? Or maybe some punch?"

"Punch for me!" Lilith looked so happy, and Melody could not understand why their mothers were so worried about Mason. About this place.

He gave Melody a water and a bottle to Rachel. Lilith got a cup of punch, drank it, and asked for another.

"Hey, guys!" A pretty woman with very dark hair was coming toward them. She was pushing a little girl in a small wheelchair. "I'm Hatton," she said, "And this is Precious."

"She's so cute!" Rachel made over her like she'd never seen a little kid before and then something started bothering Melody again.

Rachel sipped her water, reminding Melody she wanted a drink. She unscrewed the cap and chugged some of it down.

Why am I here?

Panic started to rise in her chest, and she felt the need to run, run away now! But the room swayed, and she felt incredibly dizzy.

The woman with the little girl came over and asked if she was okay. Melody started to nod and then saw both Lilith and Rachel passed out on the ground.

She reached out her hand to grab something, to keep from falling, and then darkness cradled her.

JUDITH

WHITE WOLF

*M*arch 25, *Monday*

7:38 PM

When she trotted toward the cave entrance, Judith was surprised to find very little there in terms of sentries. She knew they'd decimated a number of the Harvesters last night and that Jagger had tried to make up for the huge loss of souls by the horrific killings this morning. Still, she expected a larger group of black-feathered monstrosities guarding the cave. There were only two guarding the cave right now.

She started to approach and then caught a flash of white fur on the hill above the cave. In an instant, the animal stood in front of her—a magnificent creature—the first of her kind that she'd ever seen other than her relatives and the first white one. He stood in front of her, his fur rippling in the wind. She was instantly drawn to him but then realized—she knew those eyes! Around his neck was a medallion.

She'd never tried this before with anyone other than her girls, but she reached out with her thoughts to see if the other wolf could hear them, too.

<Amadeus?>

<I wasn't about to let you go to the party alone, Cherie.>

Judith was taken aback and had a hard time interpreting her reaction to this man, vampire, white wolf. *What was he really?*

She was embarrassed because she knew her thoughts were blasting out loud.

Amadeus didn't seem to mind. He nuzzled her cheek, and she felt a thrill she hadn't felt in a very long time. She licked his mouth, and his eyes shone with—with what? She didn't know, but she found this new sensation highly attractive despite the danger.

Last night, she'd fought beside him while he was in human form and never felt more grounded, surer of her skills. She was quite sure she'd fight by his side with him now in his glorious wolf form until death took her.

Then, her brain slapped the doe-eyed sentiment from her heart. *Your daughters are there somewhere inside the cave. Go get them!*

Judith thought she'd have to push the man aside, but he stepped away and then fell in beside her as they approached the cave. The Harvesters did nothing.

Inside the cave, Judith sniffed the air and made a quick assessment. There were bottles of water, which looked harmless, but there was a glass bowl of punch that stank of chemicals. She could guess their purpose.

Amadeus waited at a tunnel ahead. He already knew where they'd gone.

There was enough room for them to travel side by side. Judith was keenly aware of his scent, the moments he rubbed up against her in places where the tunnel narrowed. His scent suggested that his presence was not an illusion or some kind of glamour spell. He'd actually managed to transform into a wolf. Did he possess some form of Ware blood?

I am many things, his thoughts responded.

And I need to find a way to keep my thoughts to myself, her mind whispered to his. She felt his smile and his overall pleasure. He didn't hide that he found her attractive, and she couldn't fathom it. Why would someone like him be attracted to her?

And what about Christopher? Another part of her brain chimed. *And Daniel?*

It was a fact that she didn't feel the pangs of overwhelming guilt in animal form. She acted on instinct and how she felt.

We have time, Amadeus sent his thoughts to her. *First things first. Let us get your girls and then kick some backsides.*

Indeed, Judith thought and then slowed to a halt. She sniffed. Something was coming their way.

Both of them padded back to the last tunnel that branched off the main corridor and waited. Judith immediately recognized Mason's stink but couldn't place the other two.

His sister, Hatton, Amadeus, responded. *And her niece. The one called Precious.*

But Precious is Hatton's sister, she thought.

No, Amadeus responded. *She is Hellen's child and the child of her father, Jagger Profitt.*

Judith didn't want to accept it, but when she heard his words, she knew they were true. Their scent—it made sense.

And now the timeline made more sense. The family had said Herra died giving birth to Precious, but her quilting bee group had reported her missing two months earlier. When her officers went to investigate, Jagger said his wife had gone to visit family before birthing their next child, and it was over a year before anyone ever saw Hellen again.

If Judith hadn't hated Jagger enough before then she had truckloads of hatred toward him now. And the child, Precious, was sick. Leukemia, she'd heard. And they all had helped ruin any cure for Precious last night when they'd destroyed so many Harvesters, and Lu had emptied the urns.

They hid in the shadows, although the tunnels were lit with soft side lights. As soon as the Profitt kids passed by, Judith and Amadeus continued down the main tunnel, hoping they'd find all the girls alive. They moved quietly. Soundlessly.

The tunnel narrowed, widened, and ended, opening into a cavernous room filled with stalactites and stalagmites. One area looked almost like a beach, the way the floor of it was smooth and sloped down to the lake. Side lighting along the walls and some lighting overhead allowed everyone to see. In the center of the room stood a large blue stone that glowed and pulsed with energy. Near it, some sort of altar was erected with a black bird statue on it.

Judith searched for the girls, trying to home in on their scent. Then, she caught the strength of other scents. How could she have missed them? A pain slammed into her shoulder. Had she been shot?

She whirled, trying to get a bead on who had shot her. But then, Amadeus bent near her in his white elegance. The concern in his eyes was palpable as she tried to continue standing but then crumpled to the ground.

Judith growled as she caught sight of what was behind him. There was Jagger Profitt with a silver and black stick. He punched it into Amadeus. Amadeus yelped, whirled, and fell into a spasm.

"Here, Vamp! Thirty-thousand volts. Yeah, hurts? I know. But my little Precious told me you was comin and I need you. Now, kindly stay down on the fucking floor, if you will." Jagger pulled a large knife out of his boot knife. "I got work to do for my Queen. Mason! Pump a round or two in him!"

Judith groggily watched as Mason moved forward from the shadows. He lifted a gun and squeezed off a tranquilizer dart into Amadeus with a rifle he had slung around his shoulder. He loaded one more and did it again. Amadeus started changing back to his human-like form.

That's what hit me, Judith realized.

Jagger talked out loud as if explaining to Mason, "Ribs are easier to cut than you think. And then, the heart is right here . . . " He wiped his knife on his pants and slid it back into the spot on his boot. Then he reached into Amadeus's chest.

When Jagger withdrew his hands, they were drenched, and Amadeus's heart was still beating—the steam still rising from the muscle tissue. Jagger turned toward the lake—toward the statue and the urns.

Judith never thought of vampires having so much blood to lose. Did they die when they lost it all? The deep iron stench of it filled her nose.

Judith tried to hang on. She wanted, she needed . . . Oh, Amadeus! And then she was gone.

RACHEL

ALTERNATE

*M*arch 25, *Monday*

7:55 PM

All three girls sat on a blanket in the cold underground room with hands and feet securely bound. Although it probably hadn't been so long, Rachel felt like it had been forever. Her hands and her feet were going numb.

"I feel so stupid," she said. "I don't know what happened. I knew I shouldn't open the door, but . . . "

"I felt it too," Melody said. "It's like, when you're with him, you really like him. And when he's gone you wonder what you saw in him."

"Our mom said it's like he has a charisma power, or something," Lilith said. "I think she's right."

Rachel squirmed, pulling at her bonds, but they didn't get any loser. "I've had enough of this shit," she said.

"Rachel, Mom doesn't like it when we . . . "

"Really, Lilith? We're tied up in a cave somewhere, and Mom's just been shot. I think it was a tranquilizer gun, though. They talked about feeding her soul to the Deathwing Queen. We don't know where she is because they dragged her away . . . " Rachel could have kept going but realized there wasn't any point.

"Okay, Rachel," Melody said. "What are you gonna do about it?"

At least she gets it. Rachel thought it was nice to have someone her own age that she got along with. She felt like Melody understood her.

"I'm gonna change," she said. "See if wolf form can help me out of the ropes. I may need you guys to back up against me and pull the ropes off, and I'm not sure what changing will do when I'm in my clothes. I've never had to change while wearing clothes before."

Rachel closed her eyes and envisioned her body changing and then she was lying on the floor on her side, tangled up in her t-shirt and jeans.

"I got you," Melody said and scooted around so she could reach Rachel's paws. Slipping the ropes of her paws was easy. It was harder to get the back paws free at first until she realized Rachel's feet were up high in the pants legs and all she had to do was tug the fabric away from the rope.

Soon, Rachel stood up on all fours and shook her body.

"You want to try now, Lilith?" Melody arched an eyebrow.

"I—why can't Rachel just shift back and undo us?" Lilith seemed anxious about wolf transformation again since she had such a hard time shifting back last time and she hadn't practiced.

Rachel had already anticipated her sister's apprehension and shifted back to put her clothes and shoes back on. In moments, she had them free. Luckily neither Hatton nor Mason knew how to tie really strong knots. Their biggest challenge now was finding a way out. The tall blue stone sat in the middle of crystal water, but it didn't light the room much. But there was side lighting along the cave.

They all moved cautiously toward the main corridor, but shadows of others moving toward them came into view. They shrank back, but Mason came into the light and caught sight of Rachel.

"Pa, looks like the girls' got loose!"

Anxiety welled up through Rachel's bones. The men were headed toward them at a fast pace now. All Rachel could think to do was to yell, "Run, Lilith! Melody, run! Lilith, change!"

Rachel ripped her clothes off as she ran, and Lilith was beside her. She heard a gunshot. She glanced behind her and was sickened to see Melody on the ground.

"We can't help any of them if we get caught," Rachel called over to Lilith. "If you change, you'll run faster. You'll be a harder target."

Lilith nodded and pulled off her shirt. The one part that slowed them both for a second was their pants. Another shot rang out just as the girls leaped from their final piece of clothing and headed around the other side of the lake—opposite the glowing blue stone.

Rachel sent a thought to Lilith. *There has to be another exit here somewhere.* She lifted her nose.

There was a breeze dead ahead, and she could actually see better right now in wolf form. She felt Lilith at her heels as they turned down a tunnel. Rachel took another turn, and it seemed as if they were traveling farther down into the ground.

The men's voices faded, and the girls slowed to a brisk walk. A puff of cold air hit Rachel's nose, and she mind-screamed *STOP!* to her sister. She looked down.

Rachel's eyes met a deep, dark abyss. They had just avoided running off the edge of a cliff. They backed away and sat next to each other.

I'm scared, Lilith said.

Lilith nuzzled against her, and Rachel was amazed at how changing form could alter their behavior. Lilith barely touched her in human form, and a hug was rare. In wolf form, she didn't hesitate to get close.

Let's see if we can find a way out of here. Rachel stood, sniffing for a scent that would take them up and out.

CHRISTOPHER

LIFE

*M*arch 25, *Monday*

8:10 PM

The old ambulance was already parked by the hill leading toward the cave when Tati pulled her van up near the power lines, her large gold hoop earrings flashing even though there was no sun.

Nick and Sammi jumped out and met them all at the front bumper of the van.

"Wat up! Let's do this. Kick some evil ass . . . "

Tati leaned against the van's outside driver door, showed them her palm, unimpressed, and rolled her eyes. "Just get over there and help them, right?"

And they both scuttled over—in long-sleeved black tees and sweatpants—to help Christopher get Renny out of the van. She'd worn warm black pants, a black pullover sweater, and a black jacket, but despite that, Renny's body was shaking, and her eyes were unfocused.

"What happened?" Nick asked.

Christopher explained that because of the way that they were all bonded, Viktor and Christopher in their own ways to Amadeus, Christopher with his bond to Judith through Amadeus, and Renny with her bond to Melody—they all experienced what their loved ones were going through emotionally, as well as whatever pain they were going through.

"Renny's never had to see or feel Melody go through something like this before. She's angry. Terrified for her daughter. You can only imagine," Christopher said. "Then, just a few minutes ago—everything went dead. We all stopped feeling anything. No emotion. No pain. Nothing."

Everyone was very quiet. Only the wind swept through the branches of the trees, and the patter of the rain started again, filling the air.

Renny blinked and pushed back a few tendrils of chocolate hair to secure them under an elastic black bandana. Shook her head. "I'm sorry, everyone." She ran her fingers through her hair, a few bangles on her wrists making a jingling sound. "Gather in—c'mon. Okay.

Everyone knows what they have to do, right? Remember, Sammi has wolf skills. He's a Ware. And Nick. . . " Renny stepped back and let Nick step forward.

"Show the group what you can do, Nick," Renny said, and in an instant, Nick disappeared. But no. He wasn't 'gone.' Christopher caught movement where he'd just stood, and for everyone's benefit, Nick moved even more. He shifted back into focus.

"It's not real invisibility," Nick explained. "It's more like reflecting what's behind me in front of me, so you don't really know I'm there. Sort of like a chameleon, except I don't have to be touching the surface of everything. My body just covers me with the background when I want it to. It does it whether I have clothes on or not, which I think is more convenient than wolf-mode." He elbowed Sammi, and Sammi grimaced.

Renny explained, "So if Jagger has Melody, Judith, and/or Amadeus—he's going to try to threaten us by making us give ourselves up—by threatening to hurt them. We all know he's going to do that anyway—whether or not we give ourselves up. If we can get Nick into the cave and he can find them," she said, "maybe he can set them free. He's got a knife and wire snippers. Whatever they're bound with, he should be able to handle that. He's just missing one thing."

Everyone looked at Renny then with undivided attention.

"Neither Sammi nor Nick have a medallion," she continued." I'm going to give Nick mine since I know I'll be a hindrance up there. I could barely make it up there last time, and I'm slow. But the rest of you, aside from Tati, need to be there with whatever skills you have.

Excepting Nick and Sammi, you all are protected as much as possible by the designs I drew on your bodies."

Man up, thought Christopher. "Sammi can have mine," he offered. "He's going to get there before me. I'm bound to Amadeus. The vampires are bound to protect me. Viktor will cover me, then he'll get Amadeus as fast as he can, and they'll both be there." It wasn't the exact full truth, but it wasn't exactly a lie, either.

Life was like that. Life was a coloring book. We all used our own colors. Created our own rules for those colors. And every now and then, not only did we color outside the lines, but we drew outside the lines, too. Created what we wanted there—not what someone preordained should exist.

When everyone looked to Viktor, he gave a slight nod of agreement, his eyes resting on Christopher for a moment as if to say, *'I got you—as much as I can on the way to save my brother.'* And Christopher gave a gentle tilt of the head in response as if to say, *'I totally get it.'*

"Well done, then," Renny accepted Christopher's offer, and her face beamed with appreciation—so much that she almost made him feel good about what he was going to do. He took the medallion off and placed it over Sammi's head.

"Thank you, Reverend." Sammi tightened the cord around his neck.

"Just don't let it fall off when you shift," Christopher said, "or else do your shifting here before you go so we can make sure it's secure. The Harvesters only seem to eat male humans, but who knows how they'll treat a man in wolf form."

Christopher took a good look at everyone around him. Tati and Renny were staying with the vehicles, likely in the ambulance since it had a radio. Lu had her black outdoor gear on with a hat and gloves, and she carried two hammers on a light utility belt. Thomas's arm was in a sling, but he was ready to go as long as Christopher could carry the medic bag and use his extra set of hands for medical emergencies. Christopher also had four canisters of bear spray in his pockets, which might come in handy.

Job had knives, and Grinch had teeth. Nick was ready to turn his camouflage on when he needed it, and Sammi was already in wolf mode. Viktor was likely their ace in the hole, but he had to avoid whatever had captured Amadeus.

Their main goal was to take down as many Harvesters as they could, make it inside the cave, take down Jagger Profitt and the Deathwing Queen, and save their family and friends.

Let's hope all of us come back. Christopher didn't think of his next thought as a prayer, but he did send his mind out to the Universe and ask whatever powers that be to help them and keep them safe.

In his head, he heard a voice say, *<Be strong. You have more power in your good deeds than you will ever know.>*

He doubted that was the Universe answering, but that was a nice sentiment—wherever it came from.

Christopher and the rest of the team checked their gear one more time, then turned toward the direction of the cave. As they ascended the hill, he knew that Jagger Profitt was aware they were coming, but so far, no Harvesters had attacked them on the way.

He's saving them for when we go into the cave, Christopher thought. *He'll try to find a way to either break or remove the medallions.* As heroic as he wanted to look in front of the group by giving up his medallion for Sammi, deep down, he really wished he had it now.

JUDITH

Electric

*M*arch 25, *Monday*

8:16 PM

Judith ran on all fours in the sun and the day was glorious. She felt free, wild, and beautiful, and the white wolf Amadeus ran alongside her. It had been a long time since she'd felt this happy, this carefree. She raced Amadeus toward an oak tree but then the tree shrank and Daniel stood there and Amadeus disappeared in a puff of dark mist.

"I love you, my Wild Rose," Daniel said. "I'll love you forever." Now, she was in human form again, and Christopher stood there with love in his eyes. He said nothing but only offered his hand. She hesitated and was suddenly falling, falling, falling . . .

Mom, wake up!

She knew that voice. Rachel in wolf mind-speak. She opened her eyes to a blur.

Mom, Lilith, and I are okay. It was Mason's dad. He captured you. Used a tranquilizer dart on you, we think.

Judith worked to send a thought back. *Go home, girls. Please, get away. I can't let anything . . .*

Lilith's voice was now stronger and more determined than she'd ever sounded. *No, Mom. We're not going back. Nick found us as we were coming out of another exit of the cave. We found another tunnel. We're back near the main entrance now, and Nick is on his way to you with the others! Sammi's gonna come back as soon as he gets us safe.*

Judith thought she hadn't heard right. *Sammi?*

Another voice. *We're comin' to get you, Auntie. I've got Rachel and Lilith. They still have Melody.*

When Judith tried to get up, she found that her feet were bound and that her neck was in a tight collar on a chain fixed to the cave wall.

She turned her head, wondering what had happened to Amadeus. The walls were lined with Harvesters. She shuddered, not wanting to think what had to happen to create so many more. Then anger burned through her—anger at herself. Her head pounded. Everything was foggy. She couldn't remember what happened.

Her girls, Sammi, and others were outside. She had to help them as soon as she could, but first, she had to get Melody and Amadeus. She had to assume that Jagger had no clue that the Wares could all talk together via wolf mind-speak. If this were true, then that would give her family and friends an advantage.

The cavern is dimly lit where I am right now, with Harvesters along the walls. Fifty or sixty, maybe more. I'm chained to the wall on the far side of the floor. I don't know where Amadeus or Melody are.

A voice reached out to her. *Blue Stone.*

Judith wasn't sure who the voice came from. *Amadeus?*

Nothing. She reached out to her family once more. *Another voice spoke to me. Did you all hear it?*

They all responded, *Blue Stone.*

A gust of wind ruffled her hair, and then Viktor was kneeling by her, working to undo her bonds. *You're in the main cavern, Judith. Don't worry. I'll get you free.*

"Awww, isn't that cute?" There was Mason, walking toward them with something in his hand.

The girls cried out, *Don't let him attack! His dad had some kind of taser. It knocked the white wolf out!*

Judith was starting to remember. She tried to reach out with mind-speak, hoping Viktor might hear her. *Don't go near him! He has a charisma power and he's got a taser or some kind of electric thing. It's what they used on Amadeus!*

Judith felt fingers loosening the bonds at her ankles, but she couldn't see what was happening. Luckily, sight wasn't her only sense.

"Good to smell you, Nick. Glad you're here," she whispered.

"Don't you worry, Chief," Nick said under his camouflage skin, I got you. Viktor and I got you covered."

Viktor was at her neck, using his canines to break off her collar, but he was running out of time, and the collar was tough. Mason was two arm's lengths away now.

"Hey, there. I'm Mason. You're Viktor, right?" Mason stuck out his hand, and Viktor's hands left her collar.

Shit. He was responding to Mason. Judith tried to stand, to stop him, to get between them. Maybe she could bite Mason's hand before he used the—

An electric crackle filled the air. And then Mason dropped to the floor.

I hope that really hurt him, Viktor's mind spoke to her easily. *It was probably more voltage than your standard Taser. I've never officially measured it.*

When he turned, Judith caught the electrical arcs coming off his fingertips before they dissipated.

You could have told me, Judith started—

And ruin the fun? Absolutely not! But yes, electricity is a thing for me. A gift. It's part of why I can easily pass through the time barrier. She was free when he broke her collar off with two more bites. *I will kill a few of those disgusting creatures here, and then I must find my brother.* And with that thought, Viktor dashed away.

She pushed herself to her canine four feet and heard a screech. There was a thud to her left, and then there were more sounds and thuds all around the cavern. She looked down and noticed Viktor had left Mason's stun gun on the floor. She wondered if it worked on Harvesters, and then she wondered what else the group had brought with them to fight.

Her Barettas were at her house—particularly handy for Lola in case she had to use them. But she bet no one else brought a firearm. She picked up the stun gun in her teeth and ran toward the cave entrance.

Her girls were just outside the cave, and they rubbed noses and jumped and licked her excitedly.

Calm down now, she sent her thoughts. *Where are the rest of the group?*

Crossing the stream now. Sammi mind-spoke to her walked forward. His fur was golden and his eyes were still like pristine ice.

Judith was impressed at his size. *You eat Wolf-Wheeties or something?*

Then Lu, Thomas, Christopher, Job, and the Grinch came into view. Christopher wasn't wearing a medallion.

Christopher gave me his medallion, Sammi mind-spoke.

Judith trotted over to Christopher and held the stun gun out to him. He took it. She wished she could shift back to human form for just a few minutes—tell him how to use it, but the drug still affected her so much she couldn't do it.

Judith's thoughts raced. *I want to tell him Mason is just inside and knocked out still. He has a medallion. He could take Mason's. Or maybe I should go get it.*

But inside, the Harvesters already sensed Christopher, and there was a flapping of wings and a chorus of ghastly caws.

LU

TRANSFER

*M*arch 25, Monday

8:30 PM

The cavern entrance was just up ahead, and rain smacked Lu in the face as the sky. It was just after sunset, and her small flashlight didn't do squat for visibility. The scent of dead leaves, disturbed in the earthy wetness, met her nose as she and Christopher advanced with the others behind her.

And dear, sweet Mother of the Universes—Lu was so sick of the rain. It was wet and cold, and every bit of it hindered their rescue efforts. The forest floor was slippery all the way to the cave.

With the large number of Harvesters and the fact that she was armed only with two hammers, Lu knew she would only hinder this fight and die if she didn't reduce the Raven Mocker's strength. Her part was to be sure the remaining souls were released and to help destroy the Deathwing's perch in this place.

She ran toward the cavern as best she could. Harvesters swarmed outside, sensing an intruder. She waited as many of them darted away in response to calls inside or somewhere else.

Their cries were terrifying, and with so many of them together, their stench made her gag. If she got out of this alive, she'd probably spend a month scrubbing herself raw to be sure every molecule of stink from them was off her body.

Her timing had to be perfect because two hammers were not going to do squat until she had other people to help her take them down. They all needed to come together—-they needed their strength in numbers. But first, she'd help reduce their strength by destroying the Raven Mocker's—the Deathwing Queen's—strength.

When Lu made it to the inside of the cavern, she made a beeline for the white marble shelf and the urns. As she drew closer, she whirled. She was sure this was the place, but they were no longer here. There was a body lying on the floor on the other side of the cavern near a chain anchored to the wall.

Lu guessed this was someone Judith had escaped from or that Viktor had taken out. She crept over and noticed he was just a young man—maybe seventeen or eighteen.

"Don't touch him!" It was a young girl's voice.

Lu looked up. Rachel bravely and boldly stood naked in front of her with a little wolf beside her. The same little wolf from the Tattered Page.

"That's Mason Profitt," Rachel continued. "Jagger's son. He has charisma powers. When he wakes up, he'll make you like him right away, and you'll do *anything* for him. Sammi said Christopher doesn't have a medallion. Maybe he can use Mason's. If we get that to him, then we'll show you the Blue Stone room below. We think that's where they have Melody and the white wolf guy."

Outside, there were horrific sounds of cawing, screeching, and yelling.

Lu stepped over to Mason. The boy was flat on his stomach, moaning. She checked around his neck, and there was a satin cord. His medallion was likely attached to it.

The boy rolled over and opened his eyes. The kid didn't miss a beat recognizing his predicament and started to talk to Lu.

"Hey, hey there." he moaned. "I'm Mason. I need your help, p-please." He started to get up.

Lu looked at him and then at his medallion. It was broken, and only a small piece was attached to the cord. She couldn't use this for anyone.

Mason's eyes widened. "Give me yours," he told her as he pointed to her medallion. "Give it to me! They only eat the males anyway. You'll be fine. I'll die! You don't want me to die, do you?"

The poor kid, Lu thought. *He's right. I'd be guilty of killing him if I left him to die.* She started to remove the cord around her neck. *He seems so nice. I'll just give him my . . .*

The little wolf struck Mason on the side, flattening him back to the ground.

Lilith!

With Mason no longer looking directly at her, Lu realized she'd been taken in by his charm in a matter of seconds. But Mason was right about one thing if the pattern remained true. The Harvesters only attacked and ate the males.

They had no need for females. She held up a finger to both Lilith and Rachel, who were ready to run down the tunnel to the Blue Stone room, signaling them to wait. In front of them, three Harvesters were approaching.

She was vaguely aware of the retreating footsteps of a terrified Mason.

Lu returned to the cavern entrance.

Job and Grinch were fighting on one side of Christopher, trying to protect him. Thomas was on another side, holding a branch in his hand, trying to keep a Harvester away. Judith was jumping on the Harvesters to hold them down while Sammi sliced through their necks with his jaws.

Lu took off her medallion and worked her way toward Christopher.

"Put this on!" she yelled, "It will stop them from attacking you!"

Christopher tried to grab it, but it slipped through his fingers. A huge Harvester lunged for him. He applied the stun gun to its beak, and it dropped to the ground.

Lu picked up the medallion and tried again. "Take it!"

He was able to grab the cord this time, and he looped it over his head just as a Harvester stood high, poised above him, its claws ready to grab and rend—its razor mouth open wide.

The monster immediately stopped its attack. Then the Harvesters all turned and pressed into the cavern together. Within moments, there was a horrifying scream inside.

JAGGAR

REPLACEABLE

*M*arch 25, *Monday*

8:38 PM

This young girl was going to be perfect to take Herra's place. She wasn't no changing dog. The Deathwing Queen had not been happy about the other two.

Jagger felt quite pleased with himself for catching the healer's beautiful girl. Yes, Mason played his part, but the success was

Jagger's. It was Jagger who made the plans, and he was the reason the Deathwing Queen would rise and walk among them. And he, Jagger, would be her favorite.

He did not spare a glance for Hatton or Precious. Unfortunately, he still needed them both. They would help to carry on his legacy in time. He hoped they wouldn't be too disappointed that their mother would die as soon as she stepped out of the stone. He hadn't told them yet. If he had, they might not have worked so hard to help.

The stone preserved her, but through it, the Deathwing Queen fed on her soul. Herra had been more like a well-preserved package in a spider web that the spider came by now and then to sip nourishment from. It was an honor for their family, of course, but he doubted the girls or Mason would see it that way.

Mason should be here by now.

Jagger had lined everything up perfectly for him. The bitch wolf was tied tightly in the chamber upstairs as bait, and there were multiple Harvesters guarding the chamber. He'd even given the boy his own stun gun. With all of that and his ability to charm, he should have taken care of the Reverend, the ER doc, the gravedigger and the sappy *Paranormal Murders* chick. She was a hoot—like she even knew what a spirit looked like.

She found the urn of souls and emptied it yesterday.

This was one thing he absolutely would not miss. His fucking wife's voice in his head trying to share little wisdoms and to get him to "do the right thing." She had no inkling of the honor Raum bestowed on her, and she totally deserved to die when her body was finally released.

He hoped the Tattered Page bitch's little whelp did a better job. At least she was young. Raum could feed off her for a long, long time.

He checked over the girl. She was bound well and properly positioned on the edge of the water. In a few moments, he would walk her into the crystal water and up the steps of the Blue Stone. The Blue Stone would open as the others chanted Raum's mantra, and Herra would come out. He'd place the young girl in. He'd bring Herra to the shore, where his daughters could see her when she died.

You are a heartless man.

"Yes, I am," Jagger said out loud as he walked to the edge of the water. "And I will live a very long time because of it."

JUDITH

RED

*M*arch 25, *Monday*

8:40 PM

Judith gathered speed with Sammi behind her. Lu and her girls were up ahead. Damn it to hell. Her kids were not supposed to go charging in. Who did they think they were?

Members of a pack.

Get the fuck out of my head. And she just realized she mind-spoke that to everyone and chose not to address it.

Judith followed they girl's scents easily, but she'd traveled this route earlier and had a general sense of where the Blue Stone room was. As she got closer, she heard the chanting. A group of local people had come for this. They were part of this. Farmers, some in nice clothing suggesting office positions. Judith recognized a few.

Furca na alle laris Ra—um

Drumbeats bounced off the walls of the cavern, sounding like a heart beating at twice normal speed.

The scent of the girls was stronger, and Judith burst through a number of tightly packed people in time to see Jagger gripping Melody's arm at the water's edge. The Blue Stone's shape was changing, and a rectangle appeared on the side of it and light poured out. A figure wobbled from inside the stone, and Jagger reached out to steady her. He motioned for someone to take the woman to shore as he gripped Melody's arm and ushered her forward.

This cannot—must not—happen.

Judith felt—no—*knew*— that if Jagger got Melody to the door of that stone and pushed her through, Renny would never see her daughter again. She used all of her strength to bound toward the water, feeling Sammi behind her, close on her heels. Her girls were at the water's edge, preparing to pounce.

Judith sent out her thoughts. <*Rachel! Lilith! Get Melody! Sammi, on me! We're taking Jagger down!* >

With a powerful leap, she knocked Jagger away from Melody, who almost fell right into the rectangular doorway of the Blue Stone anyway, but Rachel and Lilith grabbed her clothing with their teeth and dragged her back and to shore. Women in the crowd screamed in outrage, and men shouted in anger.

Then, the cavern shook, and rocks fell as onlookers continued to yell, but now more in panic. They raced toward the tunnel's main chamber. The waters of the cavern lake swirled, and the glowing Blue Stone began to sink.

"NO! You don't know what you've *done*!" Jagger flicked open a large knife. "You bitches will pay—pay with your fucking whore lives!"

Judith launched herself into Jagger, snarling as she snapped for fabric— intent on holding him under the water until he no longer needed air. She gripped his shirt around his neck with her teeth, twisted, and arced them both into the lake. As she did, Jagger reared back and plunged his knife into Judith's chest. Sinking into the churning depths, the water turned red.

CHRISTOPHER

LOVE

*M*arch 25, *Monday*

8:50 PM

Once Lu had slipped the medallion over Christopher's head, the Harvesters showed little interest in fighting at all. It seemed their main function was to protect against any unknown males entering the cave, and those males would, presumably, not have a medallion.

Thomas was seeing to Job and Grinch's wounds and Judith bounded ahead to find the girls.

Christopher felt his pull toward Amadeus and Judith—his family—his true loves. As he propelled himself forward, he thought hard about the words, "family" and "love." He thought about what he'd been so foolish to deny himself for so many years—feeling he wasn't worthy of love—feeling shame for a past he didn't create.

Judith and the girls were gifts of the Universe, and no matter the relationship, he'd had a wonderful part of it. He was grateful for every moment and his friendship with Job. Christopher smiled despite the pain of his wounds as he entered the cavern and made his way down a corridor.

Job, and Grinch. Yeah. Tears welled in his eyes. He'd had a crappy childhood, but his adult life wasn't half bad. He'd had blessings. Who knew what the future would bring?

He didn't need a super sense of smell to follow where he needed to go. He had only to think of Amadeus's soul calling to his own. A left turn, another left turn, a right turn, and there was the circle he'd entered when he retrieved Viktor's body. Now Viktor stood helpless outside the same circle, unable to enter.

Somehow, Jagger had captured Amadeus. He'd ripped his heart out and placed his body inside the circle—making him take his brother's place. Christopher stopped, dumbfounded.

All around them, the tunnels and caverns started to shake violently. An enormous boulder crashed from overhead onto the ground and dirt flew up, obscuring part of his vision. Still, it was clear, if this quake continued, they'd all be buried.

Without hesitation, Christopher stepped into the circle. Still, he did not hurry despite the demonic teeth that slashed at him. Viktor turned to regard him with wide eyes as he picked up Amadeus's limp body and brought him to the circle's edge. Unseen forces ripped his skin. Blood pooled on the floor. He grunted but did not cry out.

"Take him," Christopher growled, reaching his arms over the boundaries of the circle. He transferred the vampire, his short-time Master, into the arms of his friend—into Viktor's arms. Christopher said, "Your brother and I are bonded."

"I know," Viktor's words cracked. Christopher thought he saw a tear fall down his cheek.

Their kind truly hold love in their hearts.

There was no doubt. That thought made this easier. Knowing Judith and the girls would be in good hands made it all much easier. Now that he'd released Amadeus to Viktor, Christopher spoke across the circle as Viktor regarded him.

"Viktor, you—my first friend in Passage— I will use you to remind your brother of our unbreakable bond."

Christopher reached out again to the body of the beautiful man, Amadeus, and cupped his cheek. He also fondly thought of Judith and her beautiful girls. God, he loved her. He loved them. He wished he'd be there to watch them grow, but this—well—this was the best he could do.

He turned his gaze to Viktor as the unseen forces once again tore chunks of flesh from his bones.

"My Master," Christopher said, "my Maker, my Life, and my Death, I ask you one last thing: Preserve our bond. Amadeus," he spoke forcefully as he gripped his head and spoke into his ear because the entities inside the circle were more vicious now, "remember, you vowed to help me save my love, my friends and the people of my town now and as long as you shall live. Now, I return you to your brother to fulfill that vow."

With those last words, Christopher kissed Amadeus's neck and then released him fully into his brother's arms. Viktor stared at his brother's body and then over at Christopher, who had so freely offered his life once more.

Christopher could have broken his bond with his brother in the circle. He didn't have to go in to get him. And yet, he did.

The earth shook harder, and more dirt, rocks, and debris fell from above. "Get out of here!" Christopher yelled.

Viktor's dark gaze sparkled. "I shall never forget you. Never forget this. And your family will always be under my protection as well. This, I swear." And he was gone.

And Christopher understood that with the Harvesters here, there likely wasn't a dead body around with a remaining soul to take his place. This was his watch. This was where he would die. This was what his future would bring.

It was all for love, all to help others. He sat down on the freezing cave floor as the lights went out around him.

He closed his eyes and smiled. He couldn't say it in person to everyone, but he'd tell them anyway.

"I love you, Judith. I love you, Rachel and Lilith. I love you, Job and Grinch. I love you, Viktor and Amadeus. I love y . . ."

THOMAS

No More

*M*arch 25, Monday

8:55 PM

Although Thomas had sent Job and Grinch back to the van and told them they were done, they hadn't listened. They'd at least taken it upon themselves to make sure that they got as many people out of the cave as possible before it completely collapsed. He hoped it didn't fall in on them.

Of course, that didn't say much for himself. He was still here. He couldn't in good conscience leave without Hatton. And she was probably taking care of her sister—(her niece)—Precious.

He didn't think she'd still be at the crystal lake, but he thought he'd have to try one more time if he didn't see . . .

Then, a hand grasped his. A warm hand.

"Hey. . . " a voice yelled in his ear. Through the roiling dirt, he saw Hatton and holding her older hand, Precious. "Let's get out of here!" she yelled.

Thomas scooped Precious up, pointed toward the exit, and they started running. As they ran, he could have sworn something busted some rocks along the way for them and made their path clearer.

Did he catch a glimpse of snow-white hair? If so, then the Vamps were pretty cool. Not just out for themselves. That was awesome.

He made it out of the cave with Hatton and Precious in one piece.

"You okay?" he asked.

She nodded, looking around. It was as if she couldn't believe what happened.

They both turned to look at the cave. Inside, it still rumbled. It was still lit, and now and then, someone came out. No one they recognized.

If it weren't for Hatton and Precious, and the fact he'd be no good with a crap arm, Thomas would go back inside and see what he could do to help. But looking at Hatton now, he thought he'd be better here making sure that they got down okay. Making sure they got home—if that's where they wanted to go—without complications.

"I think my Pa and my brothers are all dead." She stared at him, started laughing, and then broke down sobbing. She clung to him, and they all sank to the grass and the leaves in the dark. Thomas just let her release her emotions.

He couldn't imagine how she felt. Her family was dead in a matter of weeks. It was just her and Precious, as far as he knew. He'd be there for her. He knew that much.

"Let's head down. There's a van. We'll wait inside. Call a ride." There wasn't going to be room for all of them, but Thomas bet he could be one of the guys from the hospital to come pick them up if they needed. And he bet Tati had friends.

He shifted Precious in his arms. "You okay there?"

He could see her nod in the few outside lights that were meant to guide the Deathwing Queen worshipers in for the Blue Stone rite. Thomas pulled a small flashlight from his belt and started to lead the way, although Hatton probably knew the path blindfolded.

"It just occurred to me," Hatton said as they picked their way down the hill, "Pa's got no debt. I'll get Pa's land and the house. It'll be mine and for Precious, too. Pa didn't have no will. He planned to live forever."

"Guess that didn't work out so well."

They were quiet the rest of the way down, the headlights of the parked van helping to guide them.

Overhead, something flapped its wings, and Thomas thought, *Nothing should be flapping its wings at night anymore except owls and bats, maybe. That was too big for a bat. I hope it was an owl.*

LU

RESCUE

*M*arch 25, *Monday*

9:00 PM

Lu's part of the mission would not be complete until she found the urns. When she spied the Blue Stone sinking into the pool of light, she grabbed two flashlights left behind by the fleeing onlookers and turned them on.

By the water's edge, on top of a perfect wooden cube, perched the black statue of the crow with crystalline eyes. On a scarlet rug in front of the cube sat the crystal urns. She picked up one urn and listened.

<Yes.> a voice spoke to her. *<Release them. Release us.>*

The figure of a lovely golden-haired woman in jeans and a T-shirt appeared before her and then faded. Lu went with it—feeling it was right—and smashed it to the ground. She used her hammers to shatter the lid for good measure.

When the souls inside generated their wind—it was so strong that it swept dust into her eyes even though she'd kept them closed. After a few moments, she blinked furiously to clear her vision and kept moving.

She grabbed the other urn and smashed its lid as well. She wished she'd smashed these urns in the first place.

<Do not smash this urn—not yet. Turn it upside down.>

Lu wondered where the voice was coming from if she'd supposedly set it free. When she turned the urn upside-down, she was rewarded with the large, soft muscle of a vampire's heart. Then, she understood.

Herra Profitt. She'd never truly be free until the vampire was free. Not until his soul was taken from the Raven Mocker—ripped away from the Deathwing Queen—so she didn't have her life power anymore.

Lu had the first key—the heart. She sure hoped Christopher and Viktor were having success finding Amadeus's body. The two had to be joined, or Amadeus's soul would be under the control of the Raven Mocker until then.

More boulders and debris crashed on the floor from the ceiling behind her, and the two young wolves howled. Then, Lu spied their mother crawling to the shore near her and saw that she was bleeding profusely from her chest.

Still, one last thing that had to be done—and it was so important. This thing could not be allowed to function again.

Lu raised her hammer and brought it down on the black statue. It was hard, and it didn't fracture easily. She raised her hand again and again, using all of her body weight with the tool. Finally, the stone started to crack at the neck.

She broke the head, feet, and wings and threw the pieces into the water as the light faded from the pool.

Lu aimed her flashlight at Judith and the girls. Judith's wound was bad. The slash looked like a stab. It seemed very deep and may have punctured one of her lungs. Judith was panting. Lu guessed Jagger had stabbed her and just prayed he hadn't hit a vein or nicked her heart. She hoped he wasn't anywhere near.

Rachel yipped, and Lu shone her light around. There was a cart nearby that just might hold Judith so they could take her to the surface. Lu struggled to lift her and was working on propping up her flashlight with a rock so she could work out how to get her into the cart when a strong pair of arms reached out and took Judith's furry body and gently placed her into the cart.

If she hadn't seen the man before he turned —she might not have recognized him— but she was truly grateful for the muscular strength of Sammi Ware. She gave him a smile and nod of thanks.

She flicked the flashlight around but saw no sign of Jagger Profitt. She hoped he sank and drowned. Sank down into the depths with the Blue Stone. Let it and death have him.

"Girls!" Lu turned and yelled. "Run for the exit! Sammi and I will get your mom to safety! This place is coming down!"

The young wolves whined, paced, and yelped until Sammi growled at them. Even in human form, he was intimidating, which was surprising. Sammi didn't seem like he could ever go Alpha. He was normally so chill.

The girls spun around and raced ahead as Lu turned to help Sammi with the cart. Sammi said Judith was so big in wolf form that he'd have a hard time carrying her without losing a lot more blood. It would be easier to clear debris out of the way.

It was painfully slow going with the cart, with the earth shaking and boulders crashing around them, but finally, they reached the main cavern. The air was filled with the rumble of the tunnels collapsing all around them.

As they neared the exit, there was a far-off sound, almost like the sound of dominoes falling. Sammi grabbed Judith's wolf form out of the cart and yelled at Lu, "*Get out of here!*"

Sammi was right on her heels, clutching Judith in his arms as the cavern exploded behind them in a torrent of rock and dust.

JUDITH

BEGIN

*M*arch 26, *Tuesday*

9:30 AM

When Judith woke, she was surprised that she was still in wolf form. Little Lola was curled up against her belly.

Judith coughed, and she winced. Her chest ached. She desperately had to pee and painfully shifted back into her human form.

Gingerly, she moved away from Lola, careful not to disturb her, but Lola woke anyway and whined as Judith headed to the bathroom. It took some effort to get up off the toilet and crawl back into bed, but then Rachel and Lilith ran in to hug her and love on her gently. Judith was very happy to be alive, and even though it was a Tuesday, it was clear the girls were skipping out on school. She guessed they had a good reason today.

Judith decided on a day of rest. A rare thing for her, but her wound was deep. Renny had come an hour after she'd awakened, bringing Thomas in tow. They both looked her over and agreed. Thomas knew nothing about "ware" wolf physiology but was amazed at how quickly she was healing—although it wasn't instant, like in the movies. Renny gave her some healing salve specifically for her "kind of people."

Around noon, Lu arrived at the house at the same time as Amadeus and Viktor. Amadeus and Viktor told her about Christopher and how he'd died. Judith found the tears that welled in their eyes remarkable. First, she was surprised they truly shed tears. Second, their tears seemed primarily made of blood.

"There were no bodies to exchange in the circle for my brother's body like last time," Viktor told her. "None with souls. A vampire's body works because the soul is tethered to the heart in the urn. The two must be joined by an invisible energy thread. But without an immortal, there must be a body with a soul inside that circle. Strangely, it does not matter if the body is living or dead—only that the soul and the body are present. However, the soul energy is eventually used up. Then, the Raven Mocker—Raum—the

Deathwing Queen—however she is known—she must wait for another."

"Christopher gave his life for us. He was true to his bond," said Amadeus. "There is a certain compulsion once the bond is made, but a person can choose to break it if it is their greatest desire. He chose to keep his word, and I will keep mine through him, Judith. I am not returning to my time. Passage can do very well without me, and I am bound—through him— to protect you, your girls, and this town."

He approached her and said, "If I may," holding out his hand, clearly asking for hers in return.

Judith felt no apprehension and offered her left hand. Amadeus produced a black ring with a scarlet red thread of something shiny curling through its center line. He placed it on her index finger.

"This ring helps to tether you to me and my brother, should you ever need us. We are already bonded by promise, but this ring strengthens it. It is made of steel meteorite combined with our blood. You need only think or say my name or Viktor's, and we will come."

The ring seemed to glitter with power on her finger, and for a split second, she wasn't sure she was ready for such a bond—to be able to accept help like that when it was offered. But then, she thought about what Christopher sacrificed for her and the girls to be safe. He knew she was strong, and he knew the girls were, too. But this was his gift—something he felt he could offer in his final moments.

She closed her hand and nodded her head to him. "Thank you, Amadeus. And thank you, Viktor."

After the brothers left her room, Lu helped Judith shower, brushed her hair, and helped her do everything that makes a human woman feel like a human woman once more.

Several times, Judith broke down and cried but the alone time she spent with Lu did her a world of good.

"I could have been better to Christopher, Lu. He wanted more, but I wasn't ready. I couldn't give what he wanted. Every time I thought about it, I saw Daniel in my mind."

Lu consoled her and let her know that she didn't see Christopher's spirit anywhere. "Really, Jude—in the grand scheme of things, Christopher had an opportunity that many people don't get. He chose the date and time of his death." Lu looked deep into Judith's eyes to impress this on her. "He chose to make the end of his life one with purpose and meaning. That's really hard—but damn, it's beautiful."

Together, they cried some more, and then the girls, and Lu, Renny, and Judith—they all curled up on the sofas and La-Z-boy, along with Lola, and watched tearjerkers like 'A Dog's Purpose' and 'A Dog's Journey.' Next, they turned to comedies like 'Turner and Hooch' and 'The Proposal—because everyone loved the Bettie White/ Sandra Bullock dancing around the flames scene. They ate pizza and sliced fresh vegetables to have with cheese dip. Renny skewered some scallops and quick-broiled them before one of the movies.

The next day, Lu prepared to go back to Richmond and return to her work.

"I'll miss you," Judith said.

"Me too," said Lu. I guarantee, though, that I'll be back. Iron Shores has a way of throwing out a line and reeling you in when she needs you. But I do have a pit stop to make on the way out of town—an important place next to a Confederate cemetery where I promised I'd help."

Judith's heart hurt when she peeked through the curtains at Lu's red Alfa Romeo spinning away. Suddenly, Amadeus was at her side, asking if she needed anything. She hadn't even heard him come in. Her girls stampeded in to share some morning time, and he left, saying he'd cook up some breakfast.

Judith was still weak, but she was determined to visit Daniel's grave that afternoon. She felt a sense of peace and resolution as she approached his headstone. She placed simple flowers on his grave— flowers they used to joke about—thistles. Thistles were beautiful but prickly.

Daniel would call her "Thistle" when she was angry, which often made her madder than hell. Later, they'd laugh about it.

The wind blew softly in her hair as she bent at his tombstone.

"Ah, Daniel. If you could see the girls. They are beautiful. So grown. Lilith—she really looks a lot like you. But hey. I came to let you know— I'm not going to carry you around with me every day like a constant pain in my heart, okay? I love you. I always will, but I'm going to start living—really living my own life without you now. I'm letting you go, my love."

She fished something out of her pocket. At the bottom of his headstone, she tucked her wedding band into the ground deep. Then, she bid him farewell and turned to start a brand-new day—a brand-new chapter of her life.

A soft wind caressed her cheek.

EPILOGUE

WHEEL

*M*arch 1, 2025

11:30 AM

Fifty miles upriver, Dr. Beth Trestle decided to explore a brand-new cave. She'd discovered one on her many hikes across old man Dresden's Forest.

Over 4,400 caves were mapped in Virginia, and many of them were scattered along the mountains in her area. On this land, a good hundred acres or more, was a vast network of hills set against the southwestern end of Afton Mountain. She'd discovered two other caves on this land before, but neither went very far and both were too narrow to crawl through easily.

But this cave—this one—it was the motherlode of epic openings into the earth.

Sure, she should have brought someone with her. And yes, it was stupid to tackle an unknown descent on her own, but upon entering the cavern she saw signs that someone had been here before. There was a large wooden block in the center of the cavern. A perfect four-foot cube.

On top, in the center of the cube, sat a lovely statue of a crow. Its eyes glinted a bright icy blue, and she marveled at how the orbs shifted their shades of color. Beth thought perhaps it was carved from black onyx.

She reached out and ran her fingers over the smooth face of the figure. Its eyes glittered like wild hot blue fire, and suddenly the earth hummed.

ABOUT THE AUTHOR

Querus Abuttu, or Dr. Q., hunts ghosts and unnatural creatures in the backcountry by the James River but has yet to catch one. On stormy nights when the train rolls by and the river roars on Iron Shores, she crafts dark tales. And sometimes, those tales follow her into her dreams.

PLEASE REVIEW THIS BOOK

QUERUS ABUTTU (DR. Q.)

Fantastic! That's how I feel whenever I know a person has picked up a tale of mine, read it and enjoyed it.

If you enjoyed this book, and especially if you'd like to read more about the Iron Shores world (because there's a lot more), then please leave a review at your fave spot.

Amazon, Goodreads, or wherever you like. You can follow my work at https://www.querusabuttuauthor.com. Until next time, stay chill on the night side.

www.ingramcontent.com/pod-product-compliance
Lightning Source LLC
Chambersburg PA
CBHW072008020726
47501CB00006B/1730